W9-CBA-604

If These Walls Could Talk

Appomattox Regional Library System
Hopewell, Virginia 23860
07/07

If These Walls Could Talk

Bettye Griffin

KENSINGTON PUBLISHING CORP.
http://www.kensingtonbooks.com

DAFINA BOOKS are published by

Kensington Publishing Corp.
850 Third Avenue
New York, NY 10022

Copyright © 2007 by Bettye-Lynn Griffin

All rights reserved. No part of this book may be reproduced in any form or by any means without the prior written consent of the Publisher, excepting brief quotes used in reviews.

All Kensington titles, imprints and distributed lines are available at special quantity discounts for bulk purchases for sales promotion, premiums, fund-raising, educational or institutional use.

Special book excerpts or customized printings can also be created to fit specific needs. For details, write or phone the office of the Kensington Special Sales Manager: Kensington Publishing Corp., 850 Third Avenue, New York, NY 10022. Attn. Special Sales Department. Phone: 1-800-221-2647.

Dafina Books and the Dafina logo Reg. U.S. Pat. & TM Off.

ISBN-13: 978-0-7582-1670-0
ISBN-10: 0-7582-1670-X

First Kensington Trade Paperback Printing: June 2007
10 9 8 7 6 5 4 3 2 1

Printed in the United States of America

For Glenda, wherever you are

Acknowledgments

The author would like to acknowledge the assistance and support of the following people: Bernard Underwood, Mrs. Eva Mae Griffin, Elaine English, and Monica Harris, a superb editor.

Also, Kimberly Rowe-Van Allen, Lillian Morton Walton, Alisha Griffin Baez, Sharon McDaniel Hollis, Veronica and Tommy Johnson, Craig and Tonya Burns, Barbara Qualls, Lillian Tyee, Jacqueline McGuggins, Dorothy Hicks-Terry, Sheila Tyler, Karleen Burke, Theresa and Lauren Clements, Beverly Brown, Jackie Moore, Cheryl Warren, Dorothy Clowers Lites, Cynthia Abraham, Cynthia Williams.

A special shout-out to the Morris family of Westhampton Beach, New York, the Morton family of Yonkers, New York, the Williams family of Gary, Indiana, and the Jones family of Tampa, Florida.

Chapter 1

Dawn unlocked her mailbox and tossed the contents into her tote bag without even looking at it. She just wanted to get upstairs to her apartment, take off her shoes, and sit for a few minutes before starting dinner. Funny, but lately she'd been thinking about how nice it would be to retire, a notion rather premature for a thirty-seven-year-old who'd likely be working at least another twenty-five years.

By now she had a pretty good sense that those twenty-five years of middle age would hold nothing extraordinary for her—nothing other than an average life of subway rides, working five days a week, paying bills, and taking an annual vacation. After that she and Milo would probably retire to Delaware or the Carolinas for more of the same, with their lives brightened by visits of their grandchildren.

Lord, that sounds boring. But even as Dawn formed the thought she also knew that she, Milo, and their son, Zachary, ranked among the fortunate. She couldn't really complain, at least not with any honesty, that they never did anything or went anywhere. They ate out most Saturdays, ordered takeout at least once during the week, usually on Fridays, and barely three months ago they enjoyed a week-long cruise to Bermuda, the latest in a string of annual vacations.

She knew that the terrorist attacks last month were behind her restlessness. They made her more acutely aware of all the things she wanted to do and places she wanted to see in her lifetime, and now she feared there wouldn't be enough time. The people behind bringing down the Twin Towers might be poised to do something equally evil, like blowing up subway tunnels all over the city during rush hour. She could practically see the sand running through the hourglass of her life, and it was already almost halfway through—maybe more, she happen to be in the wrong place at the wrong time, like the thousands who perished that fateful Tuesday morning.

But how did that saying go? Something about life being short for everyone, but that its sweetness depended on each individual. If she'd fallen into a rut, she'd allowed it to happen. Maybe she'd do something different tonight after she finished the dishes, like mix a cocktail for her and Milo. Something different from the typical Rum and Coke or Vodka and Orange Juice, something a little exotic. They had some liquor in the cabinet that they rarely drank.

Dawn smiled faintly at that idea. Then, as she left the large mailbox vestibule, she noticed a large group of residents crowding around the two elevators. "What's going on?" she asked no one in particular.

"The elevators," someone answered. "Both of them are out of service."

"Both of them!" Dawn shook her head in disbelief. "For crying out loud! And at this hour, with people just getting in from work. Do they say when they expect to have at least one of them running?"

She recognized the heavy, almost masculine voice of Gloria Hudson from the fifth floor. "They're saying they don't know. Can you imagine? And all that rent I pay every month."

"I guess that means they're both empty. They wouldn't be so vague if somebody was stuck inside; they'd be trying to get them out," Dawn said thoughtfully.

She found Gloria's comment amusing, in spite of her annoyance at the situation. Gloria and her husband had lived in this building for over thirty years. They'd raised six children in a three-bedroom apartment and then downsized to a one-bedroom when the last of their offspring left home. This eighteen-story building and its twin next door had been constructed in the early sixties by Mitchell-Lama, a major player in building affordable middle-income housing in New York, and for that reason the tenants paid rents substantially lower than market rates. Dawn and Milo paid only $720 for a two-bedroom apartment with a terrace on the twelfth floor with fabulous views of the Manhattan skyline. She felt fairly certain that the Hudsons, with all their years of residence, paid less than five hundred for their one-bedroom. Gloria complained as if they paid three times that much. But Dawn did feel bad for Gloria who had to be near seventy, though her skin, like that of most black women, didn't tell on her. She shouldn't be forced to walk up five flights of stairs at her age.

Fortunately, Dawn noticed no other senior citizens among the group waiting in the lobby. Most of them did their errands and laundry in the morning and were back in their apartments by noon.

"My daughter told me they were out when she got home from school," another woman said.

Dawn immediately thought of nine-year-old Zach. He'd called her this afternoon, as he did every day, to report he'd gotten home safely from school, and he didn't mention anything about having to walk up twelve flights. Thank God he hadn't been in one of the elevators when it stopped. She'd had that experience once when she was seven years old in the East New York housing project where she lived with her family, and the experience still traumatized her.

She had been trapped in that small, windowless box that smelled like pee and, to make it worse, the elevator light kept flickering off and on, sometimes leaving her in total darkness. She'd pressed and held the ALARM button, which drowned out the sound of her terrified screams. It had taken a very long hour for the maintenance staff to get her out, crying and shaken. For years afterward she never entered an elevator alone, and if the person with her got off below her family's eighth-floor apartment she, too, would step out and take the stairs the rest of the way.

She sighed. She'd long since gotten over that childhood trauma, riding the building's elevator alone again, albeit uneasily, from the time she became a teenager. Even then she'd realized she had no choice but to conquer her fear. People who lived in New York City had to deal with elevators, just as they couldn't avoid going underground to ride the subway. There was no way around it, even if one had money.

No, that wasn't right, she thought. Rich folks didn't *have* to ride the subway, and they could avoid living in high-rises in favor of townhomes or brownstones, but chances were that wherever they had to go to earn those big paychecks was located many stories above street level.

The concept of wealth didn't apply to her and Milo, anyway. They belonged to the great mass of middle-income citizens. Even if they lived in Westchester or Jersey and worked in one of those sprawling suburban complexes where people drove to work, their home life would almost certainly involve an elevator. Apartment living was a way of life for people like them who didn't have thirty thousand dollars for a ten percent down payment on a house, plus thousands to put out for a monthly mortgage. Even those nice garden rentals in the suburbs she'd seen photographs of were well out of their price range.

Dawn looked down at her sneaker-clad feet, her footwear of choice while commuting. She carried heels in her wine-colored leather tote bag. It would be a long walk up twelve flights, but she gathered from the conversation around her that some people had already been waiting for over an hour. It was already past five-thirty, and she'd like to eat by seven. Besides, Zachary had been alone long enough. Best to begin the trek.

By the time she unlocked her apartment door Dawn felt like she'd gone ten rounds with Laila Ali. If she took those stairs once a day she'd probably lose those thirty pounds she wanted to shed . . . if she didn't have a heart attack first.

"You home, Zach?" she called.

He emerged from his bedroom, relief etched on his young face. "Hi, Mom! You're kind of late tonight."

She could tell he'd started to worry. Staying in the apartment alone after school had been his idea; when school resumed last month he came to her and Milo and firmly stated he no longer wanted to spend afternoons at Georgiana Sanders's apartment until they got home from work. Between the noise made by the numerous other kids there and Georgiana watching her soap operas with the volume way up so she could hear above the din, he said he couldn't concentrate enough to do his homework.

Georgiana, like numerous other tenants in the two buildings, supplemented her family's income by running a day care center out of her apartment, an enterprise both unlicensed by the state and prohibited by the building management. The terms of everyone's lease contained a paragraph stating that apartments should not be used for commercial purposes. Georgiana cared for several small children all day, plus numerous older kids in the few hours between the end of school and their parents' workdays. But Dawn and Milo suspected that Zach's real reason for wanting out of day care was because his friends in the building all went home alone, some of them even responsible for supervising younger siblings, and he didn't want to be teased for being a baby. But that didn't change the fact that he was still only nine years old, city kid or not.

"The elevators are out," she said to him now. "Both of them."

"Really?"

"Yes, from what I heard you got upstairs just in time."

She dropped her purse, tote bag, and jacket on the floor and plopped into a leather swivel chair in the large living room, breathing heavily, her long legs stretched out on the matching ottoman in front of her. She knew she couldn't sit indefinitely, but she would give herself a chance to catch her breath before getting the meat loaf and sweet potatoes in the oven.

Her hand went to her scalp, which was wet with perspiration. At times like these she wished she wore her hair natural, so she could just get in the shower, wash out the sweat, and let it air-dry. Dawn wore her hair in a short pixie cut that required either a wet set or a wrap. The process really didn't take long, but nonetheless she tried to limit it to once a week. She'd always believed that frequent shampoos were for those whose hair didn't require chemical straightening.

She patted her ends, half-expecting to find them dry and brittle, but they remained silky smooth.

After a few minutes she began to cool off and smiled at her surroundings. Dawn loved her apartment. It had good-sized rooms and plenty of closet space, plus great views, although now she hated to look. The Manhattan skyline had been tragically altered just a month ago by those jets crashing into the World Trade Center, on the type of sunny, clear morning she hadn't seen since. Now, instead of the two majestic Twin Towers, a massive cloud of dust hovered around the skies of lower Manhattan. She could see it both from here and when she emerged from the subway in midtown. It made her feel vulnerable, like her life could come to a sudden halt at any moment. She knew from talking to her coworkers that many of them felt the same way.

Dawn wondered if she would ever feel truly safe again. She found herself sneaking glances at fellow passengers on the subway as she rode to and from work. Were any of them packing bombs in their briefcase?

She achieved her greatest sense of safety and security here, in their roomy apartment in Williamsburg. So what if their landlord charged them an exorbitant fee during the summer months because they had air conditioners in the living room and both bedrooms? It beat sweating her hair out and being unable to sleep at night.

Another feature she considered a plus was that, unlike many of their friends' apartments that had back-to-back bedrooms, the bathroom separated their bedroom from Zach's. This arrangement provided Dawn and Milo with more privacy.

But the twin buildings were nearly forty years old and beginning to show their age. With the passage of time the elevators became less and less reliable. The Olympic-sized pool had long since been filled in with cement after the cost of membership privileges soared so high that few residents purchased them, making it too costly to operate at a profit. This had occurred long before Dawn and Milo moved in, and she regretted its having happened. A pool to cool off in during the often unbearable heat of July and August would be the cherry on the sundae.

Dawn loved New York, but sometimes she allowed herself to consider that if she and Milo lived just about anywhere else in the country they'd be able to have a house of their own instead of making their landlord richer with every rent check they wrote. They both made good money—she worked as a payroll supervisor, he as a programmer—but home prices in Brooklyn and the surrounding areas had gone through the roof. They weren't alone in their housing dilemma; all of their family members and friends rented apartments. The waiting list to get into the two buildings of this complex numbered in the hundreds, unreliable elevators or not. Other than some of her coworkers who owned homes in central Jersey or out on Long Island, she didn't know anyone who owned their own home, and she doubted Milo did, either.

But many city residents would consider them lucky, and she supposed they were. They had a good-sized terrace where they had a grill and a few pieces of patio furniture. Many people in New York who wanted to cook out had no recourse but to put tiny hibachi grills on their fire escapes.

By the time Milo staggered in the door she had dinner in the oven.

"That was rough," he said between breaths.

"As best I can tell, the elevators went out around three-thirty," Dawn said.

He collapsed into a chair, throwing his hip-length black leather jacket over his knees. At thirty-eight, he had put on weight in the past year, and the slight paunch of his belly rose and fell beneath the pullover sweater that covered his regulation shirt and tie. "This shit is for the birds. That's the second time this month I had to walk up those stairs. I'm too old for this foolishness." He removed his wire-framed glasses and wiped his face with his palms before replacing them.

"I'm disappointed, too. I'd planned on doing laundry tonight. I can't do it without an elevator."

"We probably ought to see about getting a washing machine. A lot of folks in the building have them, even though it's against the building rules. Dishwashers, too."

The owners of the buildings, like most who owned income-regulated rental units in New York, paid for their tenants' water use, as well as their electricity. But prohibiting these machines had to do with the plumbing, which was as old as the rest of the building, and the concern that draining soapsuds from washers on higher floors could easily clog the pipes at the bottom, creating the need for costly repairs. Quite a few older buildings in the city weren't zoned for individual washing machines including many prewar luxury apartments selling for seven figures. Of course, people who could afford to live in places that pricey had maids to make the trek down to the basement laundry room for them.

"But Milo, where would we put it?"

"It can sit right out in the corner of the dining room. It'll be on wheels, so we can roll it to the kitchen sink when we need it. When they do the annual inspection we'll put it out on the terrace and cover it up with something."

"But if it's out in the open anyone who comes over will see it. And what if Zach's friends from the building come over while I'm washing a load? It's too risky, Milo. Somebody will blab to the management."

"Dawn, I really don't think anyone cares. Look at Georgiana and all those other women who run day care centers out of their apartments. This isn't *Good Times*, where Florida and James are always being threatened with eviction for breaking this rule or that rule. I always thought that was a stupid plot device, anyway. People don't get evicted from the projects unless they've committed a major infraction, like going three months without paying their rent or something."

"This isn't a project, Milo." Her voice came out sharper than she had meant it to, but as a child of the crime- and graffiti-ridden projects of East New York, she didn't want anyone to infer that at this point in her life she still lived in a ghetto.

He looked at her through narrowed eyes. "So it isn't a project. Don't bite my head off, will you?"

"Sorry," she said, and took a breath. "I'm just so annoyed. And I'm a little worried, too, about these buildings going downhill and turning into something just a step or two removed from the projects. The maintenance is really starting to get bad. Remember those times last winter when the boiler wasn't working? Winter is coming, and we'll probably freeze again this year." She sighed. "What we really need is a house."

"We could use the winning lottery numbers, too, if you're granting wishes."

"Seriously, Milo."

"Dawn, you know damn well we can't afford a house. Only rich people can buy houses, at least in this part of the country. People with incomes a lot higher than ours are renting."

"I know people our age at work who have houses."

"Yeah? How many of them are black?"

She hesitated just a moment. "A few."

"Okay. And how many of these black home owners aren't from the Caribbean?"

"Okay, you've got me there." Dawn didn't understand why such a great number of people from places like Jamaica or Barbados or Trinidad managed to amass more than the average African American. Popular culture viewed these islanders as exceptionally hard workers who weren't averse to working two or even three jobs to earn their rewards in life. But she and Milo could hardly be called lazy. She'd worked steadily ever since graduating high school nearly twenty years ago, even putting in full days until her labor pains started with Zach, and returning promptly at the close of six weeks' maternity leave.

Dawn had spent her entire career at the same company, starting out as a receptionist, then moving into payroll and working as a clerk, and finally interviewing for the supervisory position when it became available. Milo's first foray into the workforce was at a paint factory. He'd quickly decided he didn't want to stay on there, doing hard physical labor, the strong odor of paint doing God knows what to his lungs, collecting tiny annual cost-of-living increases until retirement. He enrolled in a community college, learned to write code, and after getting his associate degree he got a job as a junior programmer at an office machines manufacturer. The "junior" had long since been dropped from his title, and he'd done quite well.

But not well enough to be able to afford a home of his own.

"Have you seen the prices of homes lately?" he asked.

She unconsciously jutted out her lower lip, like a child who'd been told she couldn't have the toy she wanted. "Well, I think we ought to start looking. I'm sure there's something out there we can afford."

It looked to her like their building had begun what would likely be a long slide downward, and she didn't want to take the trip with it.

Chapter 2

The Curry Family
The Bronx, New York
October 2001

Camille stirred at the sound of the Lexington Avenue line elevated train. She rolled over and snuggled up to Reuben. He grunted in his sleep and otherwise ignored her.

She stretched lazily, then sat up and turned the alarm clock to the OFF setting. She set it only as a precaution; she rarely slept until it went off, even now that it was mid-October and still dark out when she arose. The return of Standard Time would change that, but that wouldn't happen for another two weeks. She'd be glad to see it come; she much preferred getting up in the daylight. She could open the blinds and let the morning sunlight wake Reuben. He'd pull a pillow over his eyes, but his subconscious would know it was time to get up. She got tired of shaking him every morning like a bottle of soy sauce.

Carrying the underwear she'd laid out last night and wearing a bathrobe, she stepped out into the hall and crossed to the bathroom to take a ten-minute shower. As she scrubbed herself she mentally went over her personal to-do list. The cable bill was due this week. She had to make appointments for Mitchell and Shayla to get their six-month dental checkups. And she needed to see her hairdresser; her roots had grown in as tough as an overdone steak.

No, before she made the hair appointment she'd better remind her sister-in-law, Arnelle, about that fifty dollars she'd loaned her three weeks ago. Camille's expression went momentarily sour when she thought about Arnelle, who usually excused her financial shortages with, "It's hard trying to raise my daughter all by myself. You're lucky to have a husband, Camille."

Camille resented Arnelle for trying to make her feel guilty just for being married. She and her sister-in-law had been quite close earlier in Camille's marriage to Reuben, more like sisters than in-laws, but all these repeated requests for forty dollars here and sixty dollars there, which Arnelle often conveniently forgot about come payday, had begun to put a strain on their friendship.

Camille felt pretty sure that Arnelle had already tried the patience of both her mother, Ginny, and her older sister, Brenda. She usually prefaced each loan request with, "Don't mention this to Reuben, okay?" Well, once Camille got back this fifty she'd start telling Arnelle she couldn't spare any extra. Just because she had Reuben's income to help provide the necessities of life didn't mean that her children didn't need things just like anybody else's kids, or that she should go around looking like a tackhead.

Still, she did feel sorry for Arnelle. Her daughter's father had long since skipped out of New York for an unknown destination and hadn't sent her a fat nickel since. At least Brenda's ex-husband, that is, if they'd ever gotten around to getting a divorce, helped her with the support of their daughter.

Camille scrubbed her back vigorously. She'd just have to stop being such a soft touch . . . and stick to it.

Fifteen minutes later, all dried off and a bathrobe covering her underwear-clad body, she woke the children. When they finished washing up she'd wake Reuben. He hated having to wait to get into the bathroom, something he'd had to do as a child as one of four children, and he insisted it be all clear by the time he got out of bed, so he could get in there right away.

Wouldn't it be wonderful, Camille thought dreamily, if their two-bedroom apartment had *two* bathrooms. The building's owner, who also owned the sheet metal shop that operated on the ground level directly below them, had once lived in this apartment with his family. For that reason he had made a few nice improvements: butcher block kitchen countertops, an attractive laminate vanity cabinet under the bathroom sink, parquet floors, storm windows. She knew for a fact that the duplicate apartment across the hall had no special features, although admittedly it rented for less money. Once the building's owner started making big bucks with his sheet metal business he moved his family to a condo on City Island, which, along with Riverdale, ranked among the nicest neighborhoods in the Bronx.

She and Reuben first heard about the apartment from Reuben's brother Saul, who was working downstairs in the shop. Not long after Saul decided to quit and work at a larger shop near Willis Avenue. At the time Mitchell was just eighteen months old and Camille had just gotten a positive result on a home pregnancy test. They desperately needed something bigger than their one-bedroom in Gun Hill.

Camille, now dressed in a brown wool suit and crisp yellow blouse, her long hair pinned into a French roll to help disguise the fact that she was overdue for a visit to the hairdresser, prepared breakfast for the family in the kitchen. The kids had cereal with sliced banana, and she had a Waldorf salad with sweet apple slices, golden raisins, and chopped walnuts. Reuben didn't eat breakfast on weekdays, at least not at home. He usually grabbed a croissant or one of those fried-egg sandwiches with bacon. Camille kept telling him that all that butter and cholesterol were bad for his heart, as well as making him gain weight, but he didn't particularly enjoy fruit or cereal. "I ate oatmeal for breakfast every day when I was growing up, but my stomach cried out for eggs and bacon," he always said.

At ten minutes to eight Camille kissed her family good-bye and left for work. She sighed when she stepped out into the street. The sunlight that came through her apartment windows was practically obscured by the shadow of the elevated train tracks a block away. She heard the wheezing of the train's brakes as it pulled into the 161st Street station. Employees from the sheet metal shop congregated outdoors, sipping coffee in Styrofoam cups bought at the convenience store down the street, savoring the last minutes before they were due to start work. They would hastily toss their cups at about a minute or two before eight, and nearly half of them would miss the trash can, leaving the ground littered with white cups that would soon be flattened and dirtied by the shoes of passing pedestrians.

She walked briskly in the direction of the train station, suddenly anxious to get downtown. She always felt like this the moment she stepped out of her apartment, always had the same thought. If only she could lift their building and drop it in a nicer area, like Dorothy Gale's house in *The Wizard of Oz*. Only instead of landing on the Wicked Witch of the North, she'd want to land on a nice block on

City Island or in Pelham Bay, where the commercial space would be filled with upscale shops, including a bakery, which would not only be quiet but sweet-smelling.

Ah, if only. This was no way to live, surrounded by all this noise and ugliness. She could stand the noise from the sheet metal shop if she absolutely had to, but the neighborhood had not one single redeeming feature. The kids didn't even have a park to play in. Mitchell wanted a bike, but Reuben said no because there was no place to ride it safely.

And Mitchell was now ten years old, just a leap away from puberty. He really shouldn't still be sharing a bedroom with his younger sister at this stage of his life.

As she huffed her way up the steep stairs to the elevated train— she'd put on twenty pounds after giving birth to Mitchell and another twenty after she had Shayla, losing none of it—Camille suddenly had an idea. She'd call Reuben when she got to work.

No, she thought, better to wait. This needed to be discussed in person.

"Can I be excused?" Shayla asked.

Camille glanced at her daughter's dinner plate. "You didn't finish your lima beans."

The seven-year-old's face promptly wrinkled, like she wanted to cry.

"Don't even try it," Reuben warned. "You can do better than that, Shayla. Come on. Two more spoonfuls."

"You can do it," Mitchell called out, urging her on from the attached living room.

"Tell you what," Reuben said. "Mommy and I have a surprise for you two, but neither one of you are going to get it until Shayla finishes her beans."

Mitchell got to his feet. "Come, on Shayla! We've got a surprise coming. Don't hold it up."

Shayla stuffed the remaining lima beans in her mouth, her cheeks blowing up like a squirrel's.

Reuben leaned forward. "You've got to swallow them, Shayla, not just hold it in your mouth."

"Chew them quick, Shayla," Mitchell urged. "Otherwise they get nasty."

Her mouth full, Shayla mumbled a response that sounded like,

"They *are* nasty." She shut her eyes tightly, held her nose, and swallowed.

Camille didn't realize she'd been holding her breath. She'd never been too fond of lima beans as a child, either, but she wanted her children to eat a balanced diet and never be troubled by obesity, and she'd read someplace that limas were stuffed with vitamins. She figured twice a month wouldn't hurt.

"Okay, Daddy, what's our surprise?" Mitchell asked anxiously.

Reuben pointed his chin toward the vacant chair of the dinette set. "Sit down, Mitchell."

Their son did as he'd been instructed, his eagerness demonstrated by the way he leaned forward.

"Okay, kids," Reuben began. "You know that your Great Aunt Mary passed away last month."

"She was real old," Mitchell said matter-of-factly.

"Yes, she lived a full life," Camille said. "May she rest in peace."

"I'm sure you guys remember how our family used to help Aunt Mary out," Reuben continued. "Y'all used to come along with me sometimes, to bring her to run her errands and things."

Both children nodded, confusion in their eyes. Camille knew they both wondered what the recently departed Aunt Mary could possibly have to do with their surprise.

Reuben promptly cleared up their uncertainty. "Well, Aunt Mary appreciated us so much that she left us some money."

Camille enjoyed the kids' wide-eyed expressions.

"You mean we're rich?" Shayla asked.

Reuben chuckled. "No, not by a long shot. But it does mean that we've got some extra money. And Mommy and I decided that it's high time we got you guys down to Disney World for a vacation."

He and Camille beamed at each other as the children digested this news, jumping out of their chairs and whooping like Indians, clapping their hands over their mouths.

"I'm gonna see Minnie Mouse!" Shayla exclaimed happily.

"When do we go?" Mitchell asked.

"The week after Thanksgiving," Camille said. "You're going to have to miss a few days of school."

She'd suggested to Reuben that they go during Christmas or Easter, but he insisted that the lines would be much shorter if they avoided school vacation times. Besides, he said, in November the weather in central Florida would still be warm.

"I'll make the sacrifice," Mitchell said, trying to hide his grin.

"Will we be there for my birthday?" Shayla asked. She'd been born in late November; Camille had gone to the hospital in early labor just hours after eating Thanksgiving dinner.

"We sure will, and we'll have a nice celebration for you down there," Camille said, beaming. "I want you both to say a prayer of thanks for Great Aunt Mary before you go to sleep tonight," she added. "She's the one who made all this possible."

Their vacations usually consisted of a few days at the Maryland shore or at Six Flags in Jersey, where all four of them stayed in a single hotel room, her sleeping with Shayla and Mitchell with Reuben. It would be nice to get on a plane, rent a car, and stay in a vacation condo where she and Reuben had their own bedroom, with a luxurious king-sized bed. They would actually be able to have sex while on a vacation with their children. As Robin Williams would say, "What a concept."

Mitchell and Shayla disappeared into their room, and Reuben turned to Camille. "Well, I must say they took that well."

She took a deep breath, knowing the time had come to present her idea. "Reuben, I'm glad we're going to Orlando, but we didn't talk much about what we plan to do with the rest of the money." Aunt Mary had left him fifteen thousand dollars of her insurance proceeds, much to the annoyance of her son, Harvey, who didn't feel he should have to share his mother's estate with anyone. Harvey conveniently ignored the fact that he and his wife moved out to Long Island and essentially left his mother to fend for herself from her Bronxwood Avenue apartment. Camille kept waiting for him to move Aunt Mary in with his family when her age advanced and her health declined, but it never happened. Likewise, Reuben's siblings all felt they should have been remembered as well, although none of them had even bothered to send their aunt so much as a Christmas card. Even Reuben's mother, Ginny, made no secret that she was dissatisfied with the twenty-five hundred dollars her much older sister, who had practically raised her, willed to her.

"Well, I thought you and I might be able to take the vacation of our dreams. Maybe go to Europe, or take a nice romantic cruise somewhere exotic, like Tahiti."

She stared at him incredulously. "You want to take *another* vacation?"

"What's wrong with that? The manager of the store takes two

trips every year, one with his kids and one without. A lot of people do. We haven't really been anywhere alone since our honeymoon, and Rehoboth Beach is hardly a dream spot."

"It's just that we're already spending so much on Orlando, between the plane tickets, the condo, and that convertible you insisted on renting. Not to mention that it'll be nearly two hundred dollars for all of us just to get in the park."

"We're only spending a small portion of the money we got on this trip. If you're worried that I'm planning to blow the rest, don't worry. We're going to put most of it into the bank."

Camille suddenly had a memory of her late mother sternly saying, "You'll put it in the bank, young lady," every time a family friend or relative gave her five or ten dollars' spending money. She knew her mother only wanted the best for her, but all it did was make her feel deprived. She told herself that when she grew up she would never go without. It would have been so much better if she could have had even a third of the gift money for herself. Maybe then she would have cultivated the good savings habits her mother wanted her to form instead of being thirty-five years old with just a few thousand dollars in savings, at least before Aunt Mary's bequest to them.

"I've got a better idea," she said.

"Better than you and I taking a really nice trip for once, and probably the only time in our lives?"

"Yes." She took a deep breath and plunged on. "Let's see if we can buy a house."

Chapter 3

The Lee Family
Manhattan
October 2001

Veronica turned around at the sound of a commotion behind her on Amsterdam Avenue. The next thing she knew she felt a tug at her midsection. A kid in a skull cap was going for the purse she had draped across her body. The bag was sturdier than he thought, but she wasn't. She tried to brace herself as she tumbled down toward the hard cement, dropping the brown paper bag she carried that contained bread and milk from the corner store. Her would-be robber disappeared around the corner before anyone could nab him.

Passersby, as well as neighbors she recognized rushed to her aid as she got to her feet. Someone handed her the grocery bag. The plastic milk container had split, and white liquid dripped out of the bag. She quickly pulled out the bread, which, except for some milk on the outside of the cellophane seemed intact, and cradled the milk jug in an attempt to keep it from leaking any more. When she got upstairs she'd pour it into a pitcher.

"It's a damn shame," somebody said. "You can't even go about your business anymore without somebody trying to rob you."

Veronica knew that anyone who tried to rob her would be sorely disappointed, for she carried her license, credit cards, and cash in a secure waist pouch under her scrubs. Her shoulder bag contained little more than a scratch pad, comb and brush, and her keys. She thanked those who had offered help, assured them she was fine, and quickly went inside her building around the corner on 160th Street. Lorinda, her oldest, was only nine. Veronica didn't like the idea of her and her six-year-old sister, Simone, being latchkey kids. She and Norman set their schedules at the hospital so that he could see them off to school before beginning his shift and she could be there when they got home. She worked from six A.M. to two-thirty, managing to get home just before they did.

She tried to rush up the stairs, but the three flights seemed endless, as they usually did whenever she carried anything extra. Maybe at thirty-six, she was getting too old to live in a fourth-floor walkup. She kept thinking how upset Norman would be when she told him what had happened. This wasn't quite as scary as that incident with him last year, but disturbing just the same.

Three hours later, the girls sat at the kitchen table, Lorinda doing her math homework and Simone practicing her printing in a work-book while Veronica made dinner. Norman came rushing in like a high tide, with no visible signs of exhaustion from climbing the three flights. "Vee! Where are you?"

"I'm in the kitchen, where else?" She kept her voice even, but she suspected the reason why her husband sounded so agitated. Someone had told him about her mishap.

His bulky frame filled the doorway. "Baby! You all right?" He took her arms one at a time, checking for bruises.

"I'm fine, Norman." She'd washed her face, combed her side-parted chin-length hair, which had fallen into her face, and inspected herself carefully. A jagged strip of skin had torn off her left forearm when she hit the pavement, and her left wrist, which she'd used to brace herself, ached a little. She'd carefully washed and bandaged the bruised area and applied a splint to control any swelling that might arise on her opposite wrist. When it healed she'd start applying cocoa butter to it to help darken the scar to match her dark complexion.

"You're not fine. Look at this. My God, it must be two inches long!" He lightly fingered her bandage, the edges of which were held down with adhesive tape.

"Norman, please don't lift up my bandage. I took care of it."

His attention moved to her other arm. "And what about your wrist? Do you think we should bring you in for X-rays?"

"No. I'm not having that kind of pain. I'm sure it's just a sprain."

"It could be a hairline fracture." He applied gentle pressure to different parts of the wrist, studying her face carefully for grimacing. Her expression didn't change.

"Duane told me you got attacked in broad daylight," he said.

She nodded. She didn't remember seeing their friend Duane London at the time of the incident; someone must have told him about it. Like her, he worked an early shift at the hospital and probably had come in a few minutes after she did. News spread quickly on this block where they lived, largely due to the elderly residents, who passed the time sitting on the front steps or gazing at the street scene out of their windows and knew everything that happened. "The kid knocked me down, but he didn't get my purse. I guess it pays to have thick straps."

"Don't make jokes, Veronica. This isn't funny."

The girls, sensing tension, watched the exchange with worried looks on their faces. "Mommy, did somebody try to rob you?" Simone asked.

"Yes, but I'm okay. There's no need to worry."

"The hell there's not," Norman said, softly enough so only she could hear. "Have you forgotten about what happened last year?"

She'd never forget that. Norman, home with a stomachache, had walked to the store to get a bottle of Pepto Bismol when someone held him up at gunpoint. He'd had only a twenty on him, but he could have been killed, depending on the mood of the thief. Like the attack on her this afternoon, it had happened on Amsterdam Avenue in broad daylight.

"This neighborhood has gone to hell in a handbasket," Norman declared.

"You didn't say hello to us, Daddy," Lorinda pointed out.

"I didn't, did I? I'm sorry, girls. You know I didn't ignore you on purpose. It's just that I was worried about Mommy and wanted to make sure she was all right." With a wink at Veronica, he said, "She means as much to me as she does to you guys." He crossed over to the white laminate-topped table in the corner of the kitchen and hugged Lorinda and Simone hello. "So tell me, how are my other two favorite girls doing today?"

Veronica poured dried mashed potato mix into the boiling water and margarine mixture on the stove, added a little milk, and began fluffing it with a fork. "Dinner is just about ready," she said. "Lorinda and Simone, let's put those books away and get the table set."

The girls promptly went into action, and Veronica moved the pan away from the heat, covered it, and followed Norman to their bed-room. "I'm all right, Norman," she repeated. "I don't want you to worry about me."

"I do worry about you, and I worry about Lorinda and Simone as well. This neighborhood sucks. Besides, this apartment is feeling smaller and smaller as the girls get bigger. I'm sorry now that we didn't buy that house up in Westchester we looked at."

"Come on, Norman, what would we have done in Peekskill?"

"Lived decently, for one thing. Plus, we would have built up some equity. The real estate market has really taken off in the last couple of years. The kids would be in a better school, we wouldn't have to worry about how much the rent is going up every year, and we'd have a place of our own with a little peace and quiet."

She had to admit he had valid points. Their neighborhood had gotten pretty noisy in recent years. The New York City public schools sucked. They'd just transferred Lorinda to a different fourth-grade class once they realized she was barely being taught. Simone, who was only in the first grade, brought home more homework than Lorinda did. When Veronica went to the school to meet with the teacher and ask why he so rarely gave homework assignments, she instantly recognized the perennially red face and swollen midsection of a serious alcoholic. How could the school so blatantly ignore the signs? The man looked just like W. C. Fields, between his bulbous nose and face covered with gin blossoms. Lorinda admitted that most of the time Mr. Whalen only instructed them to read silently. Veronica felt he shouldn't be allowed to continue teaching unless he dried out, but if more parents didn't complain he'd stay on another ten years and collect a pension.

And, as Norman said, their rent *did* go up every year. . . .

But that made her think of the main reason they'd decided against moving to Peekskill, an industrial town on the Hudson River some thirty miles north of the city. "But would you really want to move somewhere where we don't know anyone?"

"We'll meet people. I'm sorry, Veronica, but not knowing anyone in outlying areas just isn't a good enough reason to keep living in the city and being robbed on the street. If we could afford to live on Central Park West it would be different, but we're just a couple of working stiffs, and we have to go where we can afford."

"It'll cost more to get to work from Westchester," she said quietly.

"We'll have to pay that toll on the Henry Hudson every day, going and coming."

"So what?"

"Day care will probably cost us more, too." Now they used the services of Louise Qualls, a housewife who lived with her husband on the second floor, during summer vacations and school holidays. Mrs. Qualls also cared for her own grandchildren, who lived around the corner. Veronica would see Mrs. Qualls downstairs each school day as she waited for them to arrive in the afternoons.

Norman had an answer for that concern as well. "I'll work the night shift if I have to, so one of us will always be home with them. If we're not in the city I won't worry about you guys being safe at night. And even with that, living in the suburbs usually has more options. Day camp in the summertime, with field trips, rather than hanging out in someone's cramped apartment all day, watching all that sex on daytime TV. We can afford a house, Veronica. We make good money. The only thing I'm worried about is that maybe we've waited too long. We're probably priced out of even Peekskill by now."

She tried not to let her relief show. The house they looked at in the northern Westchester town, while on a nice street, was just a few blocks away from a section that looked dismal and dingy, not all that much of an improvement from Washington Heights. Maybe if it had been in a nicer part of town she would have been more enthusiastic about living there.

"Who knows how far we'll have to go to get something we can afford. But we have one good thing on our side," Norman said.

"And that is . . . ?"

"Our jobs. If we have to relocate too far, we can change jobs. Hospitals are everywhere, and they all need nurses. Who says we have to keep working at Presbyterian?"

At that moment Veronica realized her husband was serious. He really wanted them to leave the city.

As wonderful as it sounded, she wasn't sure it would be a good idea to leave the city where they'd both lived all their lives, and where their families were, to go live in some strange place, miles away, where they knew no one.

Chapter 4

The Youngs
October 2001

Dawn set the ironing board to a comfortable height so she could iron while seated without straining her back. Milo and Zach were out playing basketball at the courts on the property, and she partook in her usual Sunday afternoon activity, ironing in front of the TV with it set to the Lifetime Channel. Today she watched a movie with Jaclyn Smith. Her stack of clothes to be pressed grew higher every week, and it consisted mostly of Zach's wardrobe, since most of her things and Milo's went to the dry cleaners. She'd be glad when Zach got to high school and could iron his own clothes. He'd be old enough to do it before then, of course, but Milo feared that starting him too early would make a sissy out of him. As soon as he turned fourteen she'd buy him his own iron, since teenage boys tended to saturate their jeans with spray starch, which would turn the surface of her good iron black and sticky, and end up ruining her silk blouses.

She'd preferred to iron here in the comfort of her living room than doing the wash in the basement laundry room. Not that she could do one without having to do the other, but she hated having to go up and down the elevator to wash her family's clothes. And heaven forbid if she got tied up with a phone call or something and didn't get back down there before her clothes were done. The people in this building wouldn't hesitate to remove clothes from a washer or dryer that had stopped. She'd seen people do it many a time, not caring if in the process they dropped part of it on the filthy floor. Wouldn't it be nice if she and Milo could afford to live in one of those luxury mid-rise buildings that had a laundry room on every floor? she thought wistfully.

Their apartment would not accommodate both a washer and dryer, unless they paid a premium for one of those stackable units, which couldn't be hidden any more than could a baby elephant. That would cause a headache when management did their annual inspections of each apartment, looking for outlawed appliances.

But Milo was right when he said that many tenants had washing machines. They had them brought in inside large TV boxes so as not to arouse suspicion. They could do the same, and when it came time to dry a load all they'd have had to do would be to get a couple of drying racks and some clothespins and let the wash air-dry on the terrace in the twelfth-floor breeze.

None of their neighbors would tell on them. It was the maintenance men they had to watch out for. There'd be hell to pay if they got caught. Anyone caught with a disallowed appliance was ordered to get rid of it, and management came back to make sure it was gone. The guilty tenants also had to pay a fine.

Dawn continued to iron through the commercial break, but she allowed her thoughts to wander to what she would wear to the concert next weekend. Milo had tickets to Luther Vandross's concert at Radio City. They would be sitting front and center; none of those nosebleed seats in the second balcony for them. The evening also included plans to have dinner in midtown.

She enjoyed these occasional nights out, putting on a nice outfit—preferably a new one—and strolling around the streets of Manhattan, before it got too cold.

She felt it was important for them to go into Manhattan and spend money to help stimulate the economy, which had stalled in the wake of the terrorist attacks. In the days immediately following, all flights were grounded, and even since flying had been resumed tourism had dropped off sharply, with thousands of employees of hotels and restaurants laid off. Less popular Broadway shows closed, while the hits played to sparse audiences. Some of the old folks said the theater world hadn't been hurt this much since the Great Depression.

Everyday life was slowly returning to normal. Stocks were once again being traded on the floor of the Stock Exchange; the late-night comics had returned to the TV airwaves, albeit subdued, the fall TV season had started; and gas prices, after a brief spike, were back down to where they'd been before September eleventh.

Dawn turned her thoughts away from the terrorist attacks, determined to think of something more pleasant. She hummed a few bars of "Autumn in New York" and thought of her upcoming date with Milo. Nights like those were what made living in the city such an exciting experience. Thrilling, glittering, shimmering . . . She and Milo would look like a million bucks and would manage to stand out in the crowd of other well-dressed folks who typically attended these events.

She heard the clicking sound of a key in the lock, and the door to the apartment swung open. "Mom! Mom!" Zach called out, his voice ringing with excitement.

Milo sounded equally urgent. "Hey, Dawn!"

"I'm right here," she called out. "What happened, Zach, did you beat Daddy?" Every time they played Zach always predicted that he would be victorious, a forecast Milo promptly shot down.

"No, that's not it," Milo said. He picked up his glasses from the end table and put them on. "Dawn, I've got bad news. They just brought out Hazel Alston's body."

She rapidly lowered the iron, her wrist suddenly gone weak. "Hazel's body? She's dead? My God, what happened?" She'd always been fond of the divorcée in her late fifties who lived next door, on whose door she would often knock if she found herself short of eggs or milk. "Did she have a heart attack?" Hazel's immaculate apartment had always smelled of the cigarettes she constantly smoked.

"Somebody killed her," Zach said with a dramatic flourish.

Dawn gasped, covering her mouth with her hand. "No!"

"She was strangled," Milo said quietly. "The rumor going around is that it was a break-in. You know how nice she dressed, with that full-length mink coat, plus that reddish brown fur jacket. Those, together with the car she drove . . . Sooner or later the word is going to get to the wrong element. Zach and I already heard rumors that she kept large sums of cash in her apartment."

Dawn's upper body began to shake with a power she couldn't control. To think she'd been sitting here daydreaming about her upcoming night on the town with Milo while poor Hazel lay dead in her apartment. "But she kept her furs in cold storage over on Hall Street, at least until winter. And I don't think she's the type to stash her cash under the mattress. She was an educated woman who knew better." Hazel, a college graduate, had worked in management of a social services agency. When Hazel confided that her promotion put her above the maximum income allowed for single residents, Dawn offered to create a fake W2 for her to show the landlord—just as she did each year for herself and Milo, which kept their rent lower than it would normally be . . . one of the advantages of Dawn's position as payroll supervisor. A grateful Hazel accepted and gave Dawn a hundred dollars for her trouble.

Dawn also knew that Hazel's ex-husband had died suddenly without having removed her name as beneficiary on his life insurance. With just one grown son and no grandchildren, she had no one to spend her money on except for herself. Her apartment was exquisitely furnished, with her living room done in powder blue with antique white French Provincial accent tables. She weekended on Martha's Vineyard in the summer, usually flew to the Caribbean for a week during the winter, and she drove a Lexus sedan.

"Mom, maybe you ought to lie down," Zachary suggested. "You don't look so good."

"Yes, Dawn, at least come and sit down on the couch," Milo urged, taking her arm. "I know this news comes as a shock." He turned his head over his shoulder and said, "Zach, go get your mother a glass of water."

Dawn allowed him to lead her to the olive green sofa. Fear gripped her like a wrestler's arm. In all the years she and Milo had lived here, there'd never been a murder in the building. And when one did happen, it was way too close, both emotionally as well as geographically. "We have to get out of here, Milo," she said quietly. "The elevators conking out all the time, and now this. Who's to say that person couldn't have broken into this apartment and killed all of us?"

"Dawn, we don't know for sure what really happened. For all we know, it could have been someone Hazel knew and willingly let inside her apartment."

Zachary returned with a glass of ice water and handed it to Dawn. "Mom, you should see the hall. Miss Hazel's door has all this bright yellow tape across it, just like you see on TV. I'll bet that inside there's a chalk outline around where they found her."

"Thanks, Zach," Milo said. "But I want you to go to your room for a little while so I can talk to Mom. And hold down the excitement level. This isn't TV. Hazel was our friend."

"Can I go outside?"

"No," Dawn said sharply. "I don't want you leaving this apartment, not with all that's going on. The person who did this might still be out there, for all we know."

"Your mother's right, Zach," Milo agreed. "There's a lot of confusion outside, a lot of rumors spreading from people talking out of the side of their mouths. Someone might be listening in, trying to determine if anyone saw or heard anything. It's too dangerous. Why don't you go online?"

"Okay." Zach headed off to his room and the computer Milo purchased for him after the two repeatedly clashed over the use of the family machine.

"I don't like the way he's reacting to this," Dawn said when he had gone. "He knew Hazel. She was good to him. He should be upset, tearful even, but instead he seems thrilled. I don't want him here if the police come to ask if we heard anything. The way he's acting, who knows what ideas they might get."

"They probably will come knocking on our door, since we live so close. They just haven't gotten to us yet. It's a madhouse out there now. But I'll talk to Zach. I don't care for his reaction, either. I don't think he fully comprehends what murder and death mean. We haven't lost anyone in our families, thank God. But he's used to seeing it on TV and in the movies, where no one ever grieves."

The doorbell rang, and a male voice called out loudly, "Police."

Dawn stood close behind Milo as he answered the door. For the first time she became aware of the voices buzzing in the hallway. She recognized Gloria Hudson's heavy voice carrying above all others. "I loaned Hazel my Crock-Pot and my good casserole dish," she whined. "How'm I supposed to get them back now?" She ended on an indignant note. "That son of hers will probably take my stuff."

Like Hazel would have borrowed anything from you, Dawn thought. *More likely it was the other way around.* Leave it to Gloria to try to find an angle somewhere where she might be able to benefit. She might look like a typical grandmotherly type to the unsuspecting, but the woman was a conniving old bat.

Milo spent a few minutes quietly speaking to the officers, assuring them that they had all been fast asleep and had heard nothing. Dawn nodded when the officers looked at her for confirmation.

"All right, that's over," he said, closing the door.

"But listen, Dawn. This thing with Hazel is awful, but murders do happen in large cities. It doesn't mean that all of us are doomed to become victims."

"Victims," she repeated. "How about all those poor people who went to work on a beautiful Tuesday morning last month with no idea they would die before eleven AM?"

Milo sighed. "I know. Those people didn't deserve to die like that. I don't have an answer for you, Dawn. That line about never knowing when you might get hit by a truck has become passé."

"And how about the elevators? We live twelve flights up, Milo. It seems like one of them is always out of order. I waited almost fifteen minutes for an elevator the other day because only one of them was running. I barely made it to work on time."

"I heard management is going to replace them."

"Oh, that'll be fun, no elevator service for days, maybe even a week. Even if they replace them one at a time, one elevator just isn't enough for a building with eighteen floors."

"Listen, Dawn, I know you're not happy about living here these days, but you're forgetting something very important. If we left here, where would we go? Don't you remember how difficult it is to rent an apartment in Brooklyn? Why do you think the waiting list to get in here is years long? It's also very expensive. First and last months' rent, plus the expense of moving. Are you forgetting that we pay such low rent because you create phony W2s for us each year and understate our income for the rental board? That wouldn't work if we moved into an apartment where the rent is market rate."

"Well, let's see if we can buy."

He grunted. "Sure, there's a couple of brownstones over in Park Slope that will be perfect for us. Only two or three mil." Then he grew serious. "Dawn, I'd love to be able to be a home owner. But it's out of our reach. The only reason we can afford to live the way we do is because our rent is only $720 a month. Do you really think we'd be going to concerts or ordering pizza and Chinese food on Friday nights, eating out on Saturday nights, and taking vacations every year with Zach if we had to pay two or three thousand a month for a mortgage?"

"Milo, I make over fifty thousand dollars a year, and so do you. Our household income is over six figures. I've read financial guidelines that say it's considered correct to spend up to twenty-eight percent of your annual income on rent or a mortgage. That comes to more than $25K, or something like seventeen or eighteen hundred a month. Surely we can find something with carrying charges in that vicinity."

"That would be fine if we lived in Atlanta or Houston, but"— Milo quoted the title of a Roy Ayers tune—"we live in Brooklyn, baby. Besides, there's more expense involved in home ownership than a mortgage payment. We'd have to buy a lawn mower, a water heater, a washer and dryer, all that stuff. And if it's a condo, there's a bunch of fees for maintenance and stuff. You wouldn't be able to go clothes shopping for a very long time."

She cast her eyes downward. All those things added up to thousands. If they had to pay an additional thousand dollars just to keep a roof over their heads, plus buy all that stuff Milo talked about, she'd be wearing the same clothes for ten years. She'd never get to the manicurist again. And forget about going on vacation or trading in their car for a newer one once they made the last payment and received the title. Damn it, Milo was probably right.

"We need to stay right here, Dawn," he said firmly. "I'm as distressed as you are about Hazel, but in a month or two we'll have a new neighbor, and life will go on."

Chapter 5

The Currys
October 2001

"Reuben, I don't know." Camille's voice was low with doubt and disappointment as she and Reuben sat at the dining table studying the real estate listings in the Sunday *Times*. "Look at these prices."

"I thought we were doing pretty good financially until I saw these numbers," he said, equally mournful. "Together, we have an income of about $75K a year, Camille. A lot of people living right here in this neighborhood are getting by on a lot less. But these people want more than a quarter mil for houses right here in the Bronx!"

"It's even worse in Long Island and Westchester." She twirled a lock of newly relaxed hair around her index finger and sighed. "I hate to say this, but our apartment is looking better and better to me all the time. I just wish we could pick it up and move it to a different location." She wasn't thrilled about their children having to share a bedroom, but the unpleasant surroundings truly made her unhappy. She felt Mitchell and Shayla deserved better than the junkyards with their barking dogs, used car lots, and the noisy elevated train. She wanted them to have someplace decent to play, unlike her own childhood, when the only times she got away from the concrete jungle of sidewalk hopscotch games and could actually play on grass were the ten days she spent at camp in Pennsylvania each year.

"It's not fair," Reuben muttered. "Back in the day your average working man could afford four walls and a roof. People who work hard are supposed to be able to get somewhere. I'd like to get more out of life than just having a decent apartment, and I want to give Mitchell and Shayla something to strive for from life. Too many black kids today have no goals other than to drive a nice car. I don't want our kids to start thinking that's all they can achieve."

"Well, let's not give up. I'm sure that somewhere out there is the perfect house for us."

But even as she said the words, she wondered if they were pursuing an impossible dream.

"Camille, c'mere!"

Camille sensed the urgency in Reuben's voice. She rushed to their bedroom, toothbrush in hand and her mouth still full of toothpaste. "What is it?" she asked anxiously.

"Look at this." He reached for the remote control and raised the volume on the TV.

She stared blankly as the camera scanned a neighborhood of well-kept, new-looking homes, all with immaculate front lawns. She felt a pang of wanting in her chest at the shot of children riding bicycles along wide sidewalks bordered by thick, lush grass. Those should be *her* children. . . .

The announcer's voice played as the camera continued to scan the pretty neighborhood. "Arlington Acres, a taste of paradise in the shadow of the Pocono Mountains. Enjoy life surrounded by graceful mountain peaks and peaceful valleys. Swim in our community pool, and indulge in boating and fishing in our lake. Come out to visit us today and arrange for your new home. Why wait? It's affordable. Get rid of your landlord and become a home owner in lovely Arlington Acres, Tobyhanna, Pennsylvania." The picture changed to a dark background with the address and telephone number written across the screen.

She shrugged. Most of her childhood friends had left the city years ago, settling in places like Ohio and Maryland, some alone, others with boyfriends, eventually settling down and purchasing homes in an affordable market. She envied their becoming home owners, but the time had passed for her and Reuben to make a cold move like that. They had careers to think about and two children to care for. "It's too bad they don't have anything like that here." Damn New York for being so expensive.

"Why don't we check it out?"

"What for? Seeing it will only break our hearts."

"I don't want to just look at it. I want us to *consider* it. Let's see what it's really like, see how long a commute would take. It's not that far, Camille."

She stared at him skeptically. "Not that far? It's in *Pennsylvania*, Reuben. I went to camp in the Pocono Mountains when I was a kid. That ride took forever."

"Camille, you missed the first part of the commercial. That man might as well have been talking to us. He asked if we were frustrated over being priced out of the New York suburbs. He asked if we wanted better neighborhoods and schools for our children. He said that hundreds of New Yorkers are moving to eastern Pennsylvania and enjoying the finer things in life while commuting to work. And the best thing of all, he said we can have a beautiful, brand-new home for as little as $740 a month."

Her apprehension melted away quicker than butter on a steaming hot baked potato. They paid more than that for rent now. "Really?"

"I don't know much about what it's about, other than what I saw on the commercial. Maybe there's a catch. But I think that if there's a chance we can buy a brand-new house for less than we're paying in rent, I think we owe it to ourselves to find out."

"So do I, Reuben." Camille made a face, suddenly aware of her taste buds objecting to the gooey toothpaste that lingered in her mouth. "I've got to rinse my mouth."

She rocked her head jauntily from side to side and made little singsong noises in her throat as she finished brushing her teeth. A house note for just a little over seven hundred dollars? They could definitely afford that. They could take what remained of the fifteen thousand dollars Aunt Mary had left them and live happily ever after. . . .

No, she shouldn't get so far ahead of herself. They didn't know a thing about what living in Pennsylvania involved. Regardless of what Reuben said, it was still a long way from New York.

But then again, maybe that bus ride to the Poconos wasn't as long as she remembered.

After all, she'd been only a kid then, who'd never been out of the city.

And if other people could make it work, why not them?

Chapter 6

The Lees
November 2001

"Now, remember, girls," Norman cautioned the children, "Mommy and I are just going to look at a few houses. Nothing is definite, so don't go telling anyone that we're going to be moving, all right? Not even your grandparents or your cousins."

The girls nodded and replied affirmatively. "But I hope we do move here, Daddy," Lorinda said. "I like it. It's pretty."

"I think so, too," Veronica added softly, so that only Norman could hear. He smiled at her and reached for her hand, giving it an affectionate squeeze before returning it to the steering wheel.

They'd seen a commercial last weekend for the Arlington Acres housing development, and it seemed as though the announcer spoke directly to them. They'd both gotten excited at the prospect of affordable housing in what appeared to be a lovely suburban environment. Norman pointed out that nothing really held them to New York, that since they both worked in health care, they should be able to get jobs locally to avoid that long and expensive commute to the city. But Pennsylvania wasn't so far away that they'd feel too isolated from their family members in Washington Heights.

They found themselves talking of nothing else, and before the weekend ended they decided to take off the next Thursday and Friday from work, take the girls out of school for two days, and spend the weekend checking out the area. Their first stop was the human resources department of the local medical center, where they each filled out applications and attached their resumes.

Then they went to the development they'd seen advertised on television, Arlington Acres. It looked just as it had been described: rows of neat houses, some larger than others, with lush lawns of thick green grass, and swing sets and trampolines visible in some of the backyards. In the center of the development sat a large lake, the water looking almost blue in the sparkling sunlight, even though Veronica knew that close up it would appear brown. This was, after all, the Mid-Atlantic, not Martinique.

Lorinda and Simone leaned against the windows of the backseat eagerly. "Mommy," Simone said, "if we move here will we have our own yard to play in?"

"Yes, we will. But remember, girls, we're just looking. We're not sure if this will work for us yet. I wouldn't want you to get your hopes up." Still, Veronica knew how they felt. One glimpse, and she already wanted to live here. This neighborhood came right out of one of those Lifetime Network movies set in Middle America. Amsterdam Avenue seemed a million miles away instead of a mere hundred.

They made their next stop the sales office, which had been set up in the finished garage of a furnished model of one of the larger homes. Prospective buyers sat at each of the three desks. "Let's look at the model while we wait," Veronica suggested to Norman.

His whistle as they walked adequately expressed her own feelings. The exquisitely furnished model contained no shortage of upgrades—extra-long kitchen cabinets; a huge sculpted bathtub plus an oversized shower in the master bathroom; high, gracefully curved faucets; two fireplaces. "It's a cinch this house is more than $125,000," he whispered.

"But it's beautiful," Veronica replied wistfully.

"It's probably the largest model they've got. That makes sense when you're trying to sell houses, to make everyone want the one that costs the most." He watched as Lorinda and Simone inspected a large rag doll that sat on one of the beds in the children's room. "All right. There's no way we can afford this one, but let's go see how they react to a black family expressing interest in one of their smaller houses."

"I don't think it'll be a problem. They showed black people in their commercial, remember?"

"Actors, Veronica. We're about to find out how they *really* feel. They may well be two different things."

She shared his apprehension, in spite of the living-side-by-side harmony displayed in their advertising. Even in the twenty-first century (and, she suspected, it would be the same in a thousand years from now), black people were simply not welcome in certain neighborhoods.

Their salesman, a young blond man who introduced himself as Eric Nylund, certainly seemed friendly enough. He shook their hands and offered lollipops to Lorinda and Simone, "if your parents say it's okay." Veronica liked his methods. She hated it when personnel in doctors' offices or at car dealerships offered sweets to her daughters without first getting her permission. Her own mother always turned down the lollipops they used to offer her at the dentist's office, choosing instead to buy candy at the corner store. When Veronica asked why she did that she said, "Because I don't trust those lollipops in the dentist's office. You just had a cavity filled, and I think they get extra sugar put in their candy to guarantee you'll be back with another."

She, Norman, and Eric spent a few minutes chatting about the differences between city and suburban living, then moved on to their particular needs. Eric gave them floor plans for homes in their price range. Norman and Veronica studied them, and Eric answered their questions, excusing himself twice to take incoming calls on his cell phone. She guessed from hearing his end of the conversation that the first was a social call from a young lady, whom he quickly brushed off with a promise to call back later. The second call, from a client, sounded much more interesting.

"I'm sorry, but I won't be able to hold that lot for you much longer," he said politely. "It's first come, first serve. We're running out of lakefront lots, which means someone will want it soon. We tried to work with you while you sorted out your finances, but we just can't deny it to another buyer on the strength of a maybe from you. I'm sorry."

Eric disconnected the call and looked up at them apologetically. "Sorry about that," he said. "I had someone who wanted us to hold one of the best lots we've got for him while he tries to get someone to finance his loan. He must be crazy."

"How much is a lot on the lake?" Milo asked, adding, "Just out of curiosity. I'm sure it's more than we can afford."

"Oh, they begin at about six thousand dollars."

Norman and Veronica looked at each other, both shaking their heads, before Norman replied, "Like I thought, that's more than we're willing to spend."

"I'd be happy to show one of them to you," Eric offered. "The one I was holding for the buyer who just called is seventy-five hundred, but it's one of the absolute best."

"No, thank you," Veronica echoed. She looked at Norman again, a frown on her face. Hadn't Eric heard them the first time?

"We do have models of all of these within walking distance," Eric said. "We find that buyers prefer to look on their own without feeling pressure from a salesperson. But I want to make sure you understand that we're rapidly running out of home sites in Phase I, and construction on Phase II won't begin until the spring. Putting down a deposit today will guarantee you'll get in Phase I."

"Kind of pushy, wasn't he?" Veronica remarked as they set out to look at the models.

Norman shrugged. "He's in sales. They have to be aggressive to a certain degree. But I did find it ironic that in one sentence he talks about no pressure, and in the next suggests we consider putting down a deposit . . . today."

"Do you think that was a real phone call about the lot on the lake?"

"Hell, no. It was really his mother calling. It might have even been her the first time. Telling people that he'll get back to them might be code for them to call back in a few minutes and let him rant about how he can't hold their lot any longer, like he's talking to a real client."

Veronica nodded. With a smile, she said, "He certainly wasted no time trying to sell it to us, did he?"

"Well, I did nibble a bit. But that's what he was banking on. If he thought we'd be an easy sell, he was wrong."

The smaller furnished models they viewed paled in comparison to the larger one by the sales office, but nevertheless were bright and appealing, decorated with equally stylish furnishings. Still, put off by Eric's tactics, overly aggressive at best and devious at the worst, they decided to look at other developments in the area as well, the ones that hadn't been advertised on New York television. The homes there were just as nice, but the salespeople demonstrated the same buy-fast-or-lose techniques as Eric Nylund that had made them uncomfortable.

"You know, Veronica, the key here is affordability," Norman remarked. "No one says we have to get a brand-new house."

"I guess you're right, but there's something so fresh about a new house where you can still smell the paint on the walls. It's like that smell of a new car." Not that she'd ever had one of those, either—she and Norman always bought used—but she'd ridden in vehicles of friends and relatives shortly after they left the showroom.

"We might be able to find an existing house with an asking price a lot less than what we'd pay for something new. I've got to tell you, I'm not impressed by any of those salespeople at the new developments. I'm glad they treated us well and made us feel welcome, but I don't like all the high-pressure techniques."

"I know what you mean." She mimicked one of the salespeople. "'A price increase is scheduled to go into effect in just two weeks. You can beat it if you sign a contract today, lock in the current price.'" She rolled her eyes. "Why don't we check a newspaper?"

"Better than that. Let's go to a real estate office. Maybe they can set us up to view a few prospects tomorrow. If we don't see anything we like at least they'll be able to watch the market for us and set up appointments to view good prospects."

"We might have to come out here a few times, huh?"

"Yes, but I think that's a good thing. We'll get to know the area better, get a feel for the people. Just don't let the long ride discourage you. We shouldn't have to do it very long."

"This is nice, Norman." Veronica looked approvingly at the bright little house. Just two bedrooms, but it was all brick, and the asking price was just eighty-five thousand dollars—forty thousand less than the smallest new homes they'd seen. She could hardly believe the price—this same house in New York would probably be over two hundred thousand. They could manage just fine with a two-bedroom house. Lorinda and Simone could continue to share a bedroom, especially since the bedroom in this house had considerably larger dimensions than the room they shared in their Manhattan apartment. The house, built in 1928, had three working fireplaces, one in the living room and in each of the bedrooms. A sly smile formed on Veronica's lips as she entertained the possibilities of having a fireplace in her bedroom. She'd buy one of those bearskin rugs and lay it down a couple of feet away from the fire, and she and Norman would make love on it on a cold night, heat from the flames and from within keeping them warm. . . . Mmm.

A pull on her hand from Simone, eager to show her something, jolted her out of that pleasant thought. The house had plenty of other appealing features. An abundance of windows kept the house light, yet it felt well insulated from the brisk early-November weather. The kitchen and bathrooms had been modernized, and the wall-to-wall carpeting still looked new. The house had just one full bath upstairs, but it was accessible from the master bedroom through a pocket door, as well as from a regular door to the hall. The current owners had added a powder room under the stairs. And it had a full, finished basement. Veronica pictured a family room down there, with one of those rectangular flat-screen TVs and big, comfy chairs.

"I like it," Norman said.

"But it does seem to be missing something. I can't put my finger on it."

"I know what it is. It's not furnished, like the models at the new developments, filled with expensive furniture and fixings we can't afford. But it's immaculate, and it's large enough, and it's affordable." He turned to Lorinda and Simone. "What do you think, girls?"

"I like it," Lorinda said.

"Our room is real big," Simone added.

"Only one thing concerns me," Norman said. "I didn't see any black families on this street. It makes me worry a little about how the neighbors will react."

"We know there are black people in town, so if there aren't any on this block I'm sure there's some on the next block," Veronica said.

"I'm going to ask the agent."

She sighed. "Oh, Norman. I think you're making too much of this race thing."

"It's important, Veronica. We know nothing about this community or its people, and I don't want any fanatics burning a cross on our front lawn or throwing bombs through our windows. This isn't Washington Heights."

The Realtor, a middle-aged white woman, knocked discreetly as she entered the house, having given them time to walk through it and discuss it among themselves. "It's a great house, isn't it?" she asked proudly, like it was her own home being offered for sale.

"We like it very much, but we were wondering," Norman began, "what's the racial mix of this neighborhood?"

"About the same as the general population. Mostly white, with a small percentage of blacks and Latinos. A lot of families are moving here from the city because they're priced out of the market there. Plus, we have better schools, cleaner air. . . ."

"And this probably isn't a preferred terrorist target," Veronica said flatly.

"I'd have to agree." The Realtor looked at them curiously. "Were either of you affected directly by the attacks?"

"No, we were lucky," Norman said. "The medical center where we both work is within walking distance of our apartment. It made for a long walk, about twenty blocks, but at least it was doable. A lot of folks who lived in the Bronx or Queens played hell trying to get off Manhattan Island."

Veronica nodded. "A lot of folks slept right there in the hospital."

"We can still see the dust cloud over lower Manhattan," Norman added, "although I predict they'll be finished with the cleanup by spring. They're working really fast."

"Our children didn't sleep well for weeks afterward," Veronica stated, saddened by the memory. "They were afraid someone would crash a plane into our apartment building, even though it's just a walk-up. Their fears are just starting to recede a little." She sighed. "No, I don't think any of us will miss the city at all."

"But yet it's not so far where we can't drive in for dinner and a concert on a Saturday night, or to visit our families," Norman said.

Veronica smiled. "I've got a feeling they'll be wanting to come out to see *us*."

Chapter 7

The Youngs
November 2001

Dawn couldn't believe it. All this, for a price just twenty dollars more than the rent they paid every month? She knew that the source of wealth for many people was the home they lived in. Real estate appreciated; everyone knew that. Mortgage payments, unlike rent, stayed the same year after year provided you had a fixed-rate loan, while your income rose. And look how comfy they'd be in a brand-new house while their net worth soared.

Much as she loved New York, after seeing this lovely suburban neighborhood she couldn't help feeling a little cheated. Living in the world's most exciting city shouldn't mean having to give up on green grass and blue skies unless you were wealthy enough to live in a building with a rooftop garden. Here she was thinking that she and Milo had it so good just because they lived in a spacious apartment, took annual vacations, and traded in their old car for a new one every four years.

Now she imagined Zachary running free on their own property with the pet dog he'd always wanted, or riding his bike with the dog trailing behind him. Her next thought was of how impressed all their family and friends would be when they learned she and Milo were buying a house. Not just buying, but building a brand-new house from the ground up, with new appliances, new carpeting . . . She and Milo would throw a big housewarming party after they moved in.

How fortunate that they'd happened to see that TV commercial last weekend. Living here would be like stepping into one of those TV shows or books that showed black people living on lovely, tree-lined streets, where everyone over eighteen had their own car, the kind of settings that prompted so many people to say scornfully, "Black people don't live like that."

"You guys are in luck," the salesman, a handsome young man in his twenties named Eric, told them. "We're offering an incentive. Anyone making a deposit today gets a free deck and fireplace."

"Really?" Milo exchanged glances with Dawn. "Sounds like a good deal to me."

"But which house do we want?" Dawn hadn't even been this excited the last time they bought a car, three years ago.

"We don't need anything too big," Milo said, "since we only have one child. We probably don't even need three bedrooms."

"Even our smallest model has three bedrooms," Eric answered. "It's the most popular size for a house. You want to think of resale value. Many of our residents telecommute and use the third bedroom as a home office."

"I wish I could do that," Dawn said wistfully. "But my job requires me to be on-site, and so does Milo's. It would be great if we didn't have to make that long trip to New York every day. It's nearly a hundred miles one way."

"One of the politicians has proposed a passenger train to go into New York for our growing population of commuters," Eric said. "It would be only ninety minutes from here to Penn Station."

"Oh, that would be wonderful," Dawn said. "A lot quicker than the bus. You're not at the mercy of traffic patterns."

"Well, why don't I give you two some time alone to look at the models," Eric suggested, handing them a map. "They're all unlocked, and they're all within walking distance, so feel free to go back and forth. And then the available lots we have are on the map of the property in the sales center."

With eyes shining in excitement, Dawn clutched Milo's arm. "Let's go."

Chapter 8

The Currys
November 2001

"It's beautiful here, Reuben," Camille said as they passed a man riding what resembled a small tractor that she quickly realized was actually a riding lawn mower. "I never got to see any residential areas when I came to camp out here. Not that this would have been built up like this back then, anyway."

"All the New Yorkers coming in is making this a fast-growing area. Hey, look at that."

Her gaze followed his pointing finger. A jacket-clad black man puttered around inside the open garage of an attractive, part-brick, part-siding two-story house. The open garage door revealed garden utensils neatly hanging from a wall-mounted holder, a large chest freezer, and various supplies neatly arranged on metal shelving. He even had a small TV on the highest shelf.

Camille breathed softly through her open mouth. To think she and Reuben thought they had it good because their apartment had a few upgrades. Compared to this they had nothing. How many times had she watched a TV sitcom or a movie featuring black people residing in lovely homes in the suburbs and said to herself, *Black people don't live like that*. At least they didn't in New York City and the surrounding areas.

The hundred-mile distance suddenly seemed like less when she considered the change in lifestyle. Here they would have all the wonderful comforts suburban life offered: a lake, tennis courts, a pool. . . .

She could picture Mitchell riding the bicycle he wanted so badly along these smoothly paved sidewalks. Mitchell and Shayla would get much better educations here than they would in the city. They would go on to college and begin successful careers. They'd be able to afford to buy homes on their own, not because someone died and left them money.

That's how it was supposed to be. Children were supposed to do better than their parents had. Mitchell and Shayla would do her and Reuben proud, but she and Reuben would make their bright futures possible by moving them out here.

Reuben took a few minutes to drive around the well-kept streets of the development, getting a better look at the grounds and the people. The adults they saw all appeared to be in their thirties and forties, and there was no shortage of children of all ages in the neighborhood. Eventually he parked in front of the model home that also housed the sales office.

Camille tugged on his arm. "Reuben, I already know that I want to live here. I want our children to know that hard work does pay off, that we're getting somewhere instead of living where nothing ever changes, and having life stop for twenty seconds every time the El goes by."

He chuckled. "Ah, the El. I could definitely get used to living away from the El."

They went inside, where they were greeted by a receptionist, offered bottled water and coffee, and given a brief form to fill out.

Within two minutes of returning the completed form, a toothy young blond man joined them, introducing himself as Eric Nylund. He shook their hands, then invited them to his office. "Ah, you're from the city. Did you have a nice ride out?"

"Nice, but a little long," Reuben answered. "It's about a hundred miles. I'm a little concerned about the commute. That's a long way to travel every day."

"I'm told it's not too bad. Many of our residents have come to us from the city because our homes are affordable. There's a commuter bus that begins running at 3:45 AM, and an express train service is being considered, which would cut your commute to a more manageable ninety minutes each way."

"That's not too bad," Camille said.

Reuben nodded. "I guess I can live with that."

"Did you get to look at the floor plans?" Eric asked, gesturing toward the framed drawings with dimensions plus outdoor views.

"Yes," Camille said. "We liked The Ellsworth."

Eric nodded. "Three bedrooms, two and a half baths."

"Let me ask you this first, Eric," Reuben said. "Your ad on TV said payments of $740 a month, yet you've got different-sized houses with different costs. How does that work?"

"Actually, the figure of $740 is based on the smallest model. But it's all a matter of financing," he added quickly at their crestfallen expressions. "We work with the bank that provides most of our buyers' financing to get them the best deals possible."

He named a major bank, and Camille noticed that Reuben's tense look immediately dissipated. The whole idea of owing six figures to anyone made her nervous, too, but she felt better knowing they would be in the hands of such a prominent lender.

"But of course that's just an average figure," Eric concluded. "I can take you to the model. It's right around the corner."

They got in a golf cart and drove down the street a ways. Camille gasped as she entered the house. The living room actually had a fireplace, a real wood-burning fireplace. Of course, they had to pay extra for that feature, but she felt it would be worth it. They could decorate the mantel with family photos in those expensive ceramic or silver frames. . . .

The kitchen was a dream, all open and airy, with another room connected to it. From the furnishings, it appeared to be what all those TV shows called a den, a place for the family to gather to watch TV and play games. She especially liked the way the decorator furnished this area, with that six-sided card table, a desk with a computer—well, a cardboard creation of a computer—plus a cardboard big-screen TV and a loveseat. To think this was actually someone's job, to simply pick out furnishings and artwork for model homes, right down to picking out place settings for the dining room table and toasters and blenders for the kitchen.

She'd never really thought about the managers and directors at the pharmaceutical firm she worked for, but if a normal working person could live like this for $740 dollars a month, how must someone making big bucks live? She suddenly felt as if she'd been swindled. She and Reuben had been missing out all this time and, even worse, so had Mitchell and Shayla.

Eric discreetly left them alone, excusing himself with the explanation he was going outside to smoke and return a few phone calls.

"Reuben, isn't it wonderful?"

"Not bad. But I always liked the idea of having stairs."

"That's because most private houses in the Bronx are two stories, not that we've ever actually been inside one. But those houses are old. It's a whole different type of architecture out here."

"I've seen houses here that have a second floor."

She knew he was thinking of the black man with the TV in his garage. "Yes, but those are larger houses. They're going to cost more, probably out of our financial league. Besides, isn't this basic model big enough for us to be comfortable in?" She never thought she'd get to live in a house with its own laundry room, tucked away between the kitchen and the garage. She always thought home owners did laundry in their kitchens.

"Let's look at a larger one, just for G.P. Eric said the house next door is a model, too."

Camille broke into a smile. "I guess it won't hurt to just look."

"Wow," Reuben said, whistling. Now, *this* is a house."

"It's lovely, all right." She looked around in awe. This two-story model, which resembled the one where they'd seen that black man in his garage, had a huge master bedroom and bath, with a shower and the largest bathtub Camille had ever seen. The laundry room was upstairs with the bedrooms, which at first struck her as silly before she realized that, except for kitchen dishcloths and towels, everything that got washed would go in the bedrooms or the linen closets.

"This one is a lot nicer," she said, "but I don't think we can afford it."

Eric, apparently through with his calls, joined them inside. "It's a beauty, isn't it? The second floor is especially nice when you're on a lakefront lot. You can get out of bed in the morning and see the sun rising over the water."

Camille began to panic. Reuben, normally so sensible, clearly had gotten carried away by the loveliness of their surroundings plus Eric's aggressive sales pitch. She feared he was about to get them in over their heads. Even the man with the nice garage didn't have a lakefront lot. "I'm sure it's lovely, Eric, but with us having to commute to the city we'll be long gone before the sun rises."

"Eventually we hope to be able to get jobs locally," Reuben explained to Eric. "I manage the grocery section of a supermarket, and my wife is a secretary. I know there's not a lot of industry around here, but they have to have supermarkets, plus some kind of offices, like lawyers or something."

"I'm not a legal secretary, Reuben," Camille pointed out nervously.

He merely shrugged. "Can we see one of those lakefront lots you were talking about, Eric?"

Camille watched, forcing a smile, as Reuben signed a thousand-dollar check and handed it to Eric. "This will hold our lot, won't it?" he asked.

"It sure will. Now we'll work on getting you financed. You wanted the second model we looked at, right?"

"We'd like to see the numbers for both that one and the first house we looked at," she said quickly. "Just so we can decide which one will be best for us financially." The last thing she wanted was for Reuben to commit to a house they couldn't afford. Whatever choice they made they'd have to live with for thirty years, and that was a long time.

"Sure, Mrs. Curry."

"Reuben, the way I see it, we can either go for the smaller house on the lakefront lot or the larger house on an ordinary lot, but not both," she said when they were back in the car on their way back to New York. "That model had a lot of bells and whistles that cost extra, like that Jacuzzi tub in the master bathroom. We'd be better off getting the basic model with a fireplace. We could probably swing having it built by the lake, but I don't see us in anything more than that."

"Camille, stop being so cautious. We have our savings, plus fifteen thousand dollars."

"Our savings isn't all that much, and that money from Aunt Mary is more like thirteen thousand now, after we pay for the trip to Disney. And I don't want to use every dime we have to buy this house. What if the water heater breaks down or something?"

"It's a brand-new house, Camille. It'll come with a warranty."

"Well, what if we have expensive car repairs? We have to have cash available in case of an emergency."

"That's what credit cards are for."

She rolled her eyes. "Reuben, you know good and well that we've always tried to not use our credit cards."

"But that hasn't stopped us from having a balance, does it? You never seem to worry about using our credit card when there's a suit on sale, do you?"

Heat rushed to her face like a home spa treatment. It was true that she dressed well to go to work, but her employer insisted on professional dress, reserving casual Fridays for warm-weather months only. Most of their Visa balance, currently $3,300, came from her wardrobe, with the rest from car repairs and other unexpected expenses.

"I have to look nice for work, Reuben," she said weakly.

He reached for her hand and gave it a quick, reassuring squeeze before releasing it. "I know, baby. I'm not criticizing you or anything. I'm just trying to make a point."

Well, he'd made it, all right. "I just don't want us to get in over our heads," she whined.

"Will you stop worrying, Camille? It's going to be fine. But now that you mention it, it might work out better if we drive to work ourselves than to take the bus, since I can park for free at the store."

She considered this possibility. "Maybe we can take on a couple of carpoolers," she suggested.

"There you go. That's the way to think. We'll get everything to work out just fine. And won't the kids be surprised when we tell them they have a house in the country!"

"Yes, but let's not tell them yet. No one needs to know our plans until we have them finalized ourselves." She couldn't help smiling. "Just think, you and I are going to have a home of our own."

"It's the American dream," he said. "And for us it's a dream that's going to come true."

Chapter 9

The Youngs
November 2001

Dawn and Milo sat side by side at the dinette, going over their complete financial picture. Their net worth wouldn't impress anyone, especially after considering they were in their late thirties and had been in the workforce nearly twenty years.

"I guess we should have put more emphasis on saving," Dawn said sheepishly. "I just never thought we'd be able to afford a house, so why shouldn't we indulge ourselves here and there?" In fact, they indulged themselves regularly, a fact she conveniently chose to overlook.

"Well, we're going to have to come up with some money quick if we expect to get a house now," Milo said. "We've paid our bills on time and we don't have a whole lot of debt, but we only have a few thousand dollars in the bank. At least part of the money we spent on dinners out and vacations should have been put in the bank instead." He tapped the table with his pencil. "I'm seeing things differently now. We should have kept our cars for another two or three years instead of trading them in as soon as they're paid for. All that could have been money put away instead of having car payments that never ended. And we don't really have to have a hundred-and-something cable channels, do we?" He muttered a "Shhh" sound, but stopped short of saying the word. "Now I'm wishing we hadn't taken Zach on that cruise in July."

"But he loved going to Bermuda and playing with all the other kids on the ship. We all had a good time." Dawn felt guilty. She'd been the one to press for the new cars, for the best seats at concerts, for designer labels in their clothes, and to stay at the nicest hotels when they traveled. Milo usually went along because he wanted her to be happy. She'd fallen into the trap of surrounding them with the finest material things they could afford, while doing little to provide for their future, other than generous contributions to their 401(k) accounts.

Now she realized that people who got ahead didn't spend so freely. Couples determined to buy homes would scrimp and save, do their laundry at their parents' homes for free—provided their parents *had* a washer and dryer—instead of paying by the load at the Laundromat, would brown-bag their lunches and vacation at the Jersey shore. Even if they ended up buying a co-op apartment, at least it was theirs. And their investment reduced their withholding tax burden and put them on the road to financial security.

"We had a good thing going, with those fabricated W2s to get lower rent every year," Milo continued. "But we should have banked more of what we saved in rent. A lot more."

Dawn hesitated, almost afraid to hear the answer to the question she was about to ask. "So what do you think our chances are of getting the house?"

"The way it looks right now, not very good," Milo replied in his usual, take-no-prisoners manner. He looked as somber as a funeral director. "But don't give up, Dawn. Remember what Eric said about how the lender they use works with people? As long as they're not talking something outrageous like 10 percent interest, I'm willing to sit down and see what they can do for us."

Dawn listened in on the extension. The loan officer on the other end of the phone knew she was on the line, but since Milo provided answers to all his questions, she really had no need to contribute. She prayed they would be able to work something out. She wanted that house so badly.

She chewed her lower lip as she listened. The loan officer, Jim Brickman, startled them when he announced that he was not an employee of the major bank that Eric Nylund had told them handled mortgage loans for Arlington Acres, but from a lender neither of them had ever heard of. "We're helping the big boys do the legwork, since their loan department is getting overwhelmed," he explained.

"Now, I have the figures you faxed to Eric," he said. "Let me ask you something. Have either of you ever had a previous mortgage loan?"

"No," Milo answered. "We've both lived in Brooklyn all our lives, in apartments."

"Well, you'll be glad to know that we have a special program to help you amass a down payment. I see your rent is $720 a month."

"That's right."

"This is how our program works. You make your rent check payable to us each month for the next six months. In turn, we will deposit that check in a special escrow account, and we will take care of paying your rent. The total of $4,500, give or take a few dollars, plus what you already have to put down, will give you what you need to make the required down payment. In other words, we're advancing you your down payment."

"When do we pay it back?" Milo asked.

"It'll be worked into your mortgage loan, so you'll actually pay it back over thirty years."

Milo looked up to meet Dawn's gaze and gestured to her, encouraging her to ask any questions. She shook her head. She knew all about payroll and withholding taxes because of her work, but she found real estate finances confusing.

"And what's the hitch?" Milo asked. "Because I'm sure there is one, somewhere."

"The hitch is that construction can't begin until all your financing is set, so you're looking at approximately May, or being part of Phase II of construction. But that still means you'll be able to move into your new house by the end of August. Construction tends to move faster during the warmer weather. No blizzards or ice storms to slow down the process."

Dawn recognized disappointment on her husband's face across the room, and she spoke for the first time. "But that's not bad, Milo. At least Zach will be able to start his new school at the start of the semester. If we moved in the spring he would have to change midyear."

"That's a good point, Mrs. Young," Jim said. "You see, we have several programs to offer assistance to first-time home buyers such as yourselves. Based on the numbers and the credit score I'm seeing, this is the one that would work best for you. You see, we want to put you in a brand-new home. And, more than that, we're *committed* to it."

Chapter 10

The Currys
November 2001

Camille closed her eyes and savored the taste of sweet potato pie. Reuben's sister Brenda added coconut to hers, something many people disliked but Camille loved. She looked forward to the holidays every year to get some of this pie. Forget about her diet and the six pounds she'd managed to lose so far. She'd definitely have seconds. And she'd ask to bring a piece home.

Every Thanksgiving the Curry family always gathered to have dessert at Brenda's apartment in a high-rise on Sedgewick Avenue. Camille, Reuben, and the kids had eaten with her father and step-mother in Inwood, and Reuben's brother ate with his girlfriend's family. Besides, with about a dozen members of the Curry family, no one had an apartment large enough to accommodate all of them for a sit-down dinner. Dessert was easier; you just brought your plate to the couch or a chair, or even the floor.

One thing that always struck Camille when she was around her in-laws was that they were one good-looking bunch of people. The siblings all resembled each other, all having been blessed with the best genes of their mother and late father, with straight noses, prominent cheekbones, and distinctively almond-shaped eyes. Reuben and his brother Saul took their light brown complexions from their father, who had shown no signs of a receding hairline, even at the time of his death at sixty-one; while their sisters Brenda and Arnelle were browner, like their mother, Ginny.

"So when do you guys leave for Orlando?" Brenda asked.

"Tuesday. We'll be back Saturday."

Brenda made a clucking sound with her tongue. "You guys are making it hard for the rest of us. All the kids are saying they want to go to Disney World like Mitchell and Shayla."

"We're going to Wet 'n Wild and Sea World, too, aren't we, Mom?" Mitchell bragged.

Camille poked his upper arm and whispered, *"Shh!"* "You'll get there," she said confidently to Brenda.

Saul, Reuben's older brother, spoke up. "Yeah, well, if Aunt Mary left me some ducats I'd be able to take my kids to Disney, too. If I had any kids."

Camille bit her lower lip. She'd been waiting for that. Reuben's siblings were all so jealous that Aunt Mary remembered him and not them, although none of them had done a damn thing for her.

"And take a cruise, and get me a new car to boot," Saul continued. "You guys gonna be drivin' a new Caddy soon, I guess."

Camille knew she should let Reuben answer that, but she couldn't help responding. "We didn't get *that* much." Of course, all three of Reuben's siblings knew exactly how much they'd received, courtesy of their mother, Ginny, who was Aunt Mary's younger sister.

"And we didn't buy a car," Reuben said calmly. "Actually, we bought a house."

His announcement met with a few seconds of complete silence. Reuben's other sister, Arnelle, broke the quiet. "A house?" she asked incredulously.

"Where?" Brenda demanded.

"In Tobyhanna, Pennsylvania," Reuben replied.

"Toby what?"

"Tobyhanna. It's near the Pocono Mountains, about a hundred miles from here."

"Y'all relocating?" Saul asked. "You must be crazy, givin' up that good job at the supermarket. You got security, man."

"Actually, they have supermarkets in Pennsylvania, too, Saul," Reuben said with a smile, "but both Camille and I are keeping our jobs, at least for the time being. We're going to commute to work."

Ginny spoke for the first time. "All the way to New York? Won't that be exhausting for you?"

Camille leaned back in her chair unhappily, determined not to say another word. Her in-laws reacted to their news exactly how she predicted they would. No congratulations, no that's wonderfuls, no you go, guys, nothing but pointing out all the negatives.

"Don't get me wrong, I'm glad for you," Ginny said, "but I can't help being a little concerned. How will you two manage to drive a hundred miles each way, every day?"

"I'm not sure we'll drive in, Mom, at least not every day. They have a commuter bus that runs regularly until they get the train going."

"Well, if you drive, you'd better hope that car holds up," Saul said.

"The Malibu will be fine. It's only two years old."

"So when are you guys moving?" Arnelle asked.

"In the spring."

"Why so long? Surely it doesn't take that long for all the paper-work to get processed."

"The house won't be ready until then."

"What'd you guys do," Brenda asked, "buy one of those real old fixer-uppers that needs a lot of work?" The pleased look on her face suggested she liked the idea of them living in an antiquated dump.

Camille gritted her teeth. She wanted to slap that smug smile off her sister-in-law's face.

It delighted her that Reuben remained so calm. "No, Brenda. It's in a development where all the houses are brand-new. It has to be built from the ground up."

"You mean it's a *new* house?"

Camille grinned at Brenda's obvious flustered state and forgot her vow to not speak. "Brand-spanking, never-been-lived-in-before new," she said proudly.

"How much you pay for it?" Saul demanded to know.

"Saul, don't be tryin' to get in our business," Reuben warned.

"I just wanna know how y'all can afford a brand-new house. What is it, some kinda low-income housing project or something?"

Camille gasped audibly. This was the last straw. A project? How dare Saul say such a thing?

"Of course it's not a project," she snapped. "It's a beautiful two-story house, right on the lake, with a fireplace and a two-car garage and a bathroom inside the master bedroom with both a big shower and a sculpted Jacuzzi tub. And plenty of grass. How many *projects* do you see have features like that?"

"Take it easy, Camille," Saul said, "I was just asking."

"Yeah, in the most insulting way you could. Who the hell moves two states away to live in the projects?" She glared at her brother-in-law. For the first time she felt glad that she'd allowed herself to be convinced to buy the larger house Reuben wanted. Wait until Saul and the rest saw it. Their eyes would get as big as Tracee Ross's.

Ginny spoke out calmly. "All right. No reason for anyone to lose their temper. Reuben, Camille, your house sounds lovely. I just hope . . ."

Here it comes, Camille thought angrily.

". . . you two haven't bitten off more than you can chew."

"We wouldn't have bought it if we couldn't afford it, Mom," Reuben assured her.

"Well, who knows? I might have bought a condo or something for myself if my sister left me enough to do it with," Ginny commented airily.

"Have you gotten a mortgage loan yet?" Arnelle asked.

Camille knew she hoped that they wouldn't get approved, but they already had been. She and Reuben would never announce their intentions if the plan wasn't solid. Still, it hurt to hear Arnelle in particular sound so hopeful that their plans wouldn't work out. How many times had she loaned her sister-in-law money so her lights wouldn't get cut off?

Saul hadn't given up painting a picture of doom and gloom. "What happens if the builders run out of money and can't finish the house? You guys just lose your deposit?"

"They'll finish it, Saul," Reuben replied, unruffled. "They've built hundreds of homes in the area. The developers are multimillionaires."

"Well, just try not to forget about your poor city relations once you're living large in your bright, shiny new house," Saul said.

Arnelle leaned forward and spoke so only Camille could hear. "Now I know why you told me what you did the other week, Camille."

Two weeks ago Arnelle had asked to borrow eighty dollars to pay her cable bill, and Camille had turned her down, saying she and Reuben had begun a tight new budget with nothing to spare. Arnelle had clearly been shocked by the refusal. She whined a little, saying the cable company would cut her off if she didn't pay, but Camille held firm. "You and Tiffany have a roof over your heads and enough to eat," she'd said. "Living without HBO for a while isn't the end of the world." She felt proud of herself for not caving in to her sister-in-law's attempts at manipulation. Even now, sensing an attempt on Arnelle's part to make her feel guilty, Camille looked her dead in the eye and merely smiled.

"Y'all sure are livin' large," Brenda remarked. She paused a beat and added, "Thanks to Aunt Mary."

Camille rolled her eyes, not caring if they saw her. Her family had reacted similarly when she and Reuben announced their plans at dinner, with the general consensus being that they'd gotten too big for their britches. She didn't understand their disapproval. What was so wrong about wanting to improve your life and that of your children? But with the Curry side of the family they also had to deal with snide remarks about how Reuben alone had benefited from their aunt's will. None of them had even so much as picked up the phone to say hello to the old lady, but that didn't matter, they still felt slighted.

Reuben, thank God, handled all the derogatory remarks like a pro. "We'd love it if you guys came to visit us. We'll be moved in just in time for the barbecue season."

"So your house isn't even built yet?" Ginny asked.

"Well, no, Mom. It's a new community. People come in, pick out the house they want and the lot they want it built on, and once they get approved for a mortgage loan they sign contracts and the builders go to work. That's how it works."

Camille wanted to tell him not to bother, that they wouldn't understand.

In truth, sometimes she had trouble grasping the concept herself. Initially she'd worried about whether or not they would qualify for a mortgage. They'd paid some bills late here and there over the years. The bank loan officer advised them to pay down some of their debt before making a formal application, so they reluctantly took two thousand dollars from their savings and complied. Their reward was a reasonably low interest rate.

Sometimes Camille still worried about how they would manage, living so far away from their network of families and friends who also provided babysitting support, but Reuben radiated such confidence she told herself it was foolish to worry. Besides, after the comments she'd had to listen to today, the more distance between them and their families, the better. And surely nervousness among first-time home buyers was a perfectly natural reaction. A home was the biggest purchase a person ever made. Before this she and Reuben had bought nothing more substantial than cars.

Still, what was that Saul said? "I hope your car holds out." Driving two hundred miles round-trip five days a week was an awful lot of wear and tear on a vehicle. Hell, that added up to a thousand miles a week. She wondered if Reuben had thought of that. They probably should forget about any plans to drive and take the commuter bus, at least for now. They'd switch to the train once it started running.

And she would check the want ads faithfully every Sunday. Like Reuben said, surely someone locally would have need for a secretary. She worked in the marketing department now, but she could handle anything as long as it wasn't too specialized, like medicine or law. Surely she'd have to take a pay cut, but it would be worth it if she didn't have to spend over two hundred dollars a month to commute to New York. Just think, if she had a job in Stroudsburg she'd be able to watch the sun rise over the lake behind her backyard every morning.

She couldn't wait.

December 2001

"Okay, here we are!" Camille said. The kids had pestered her and Reuben continually with "Are-we-there-yet?" for the last fifty miles. It reminded her of how she felt during that endless bus ride to camp as a child, wondering if they'd ever get there. At least they wouldn't have to make the round-trip every day after they moved in, unlike Reuben and her.

Mitchell and Shayla were speechless as they took in the smooth paved streets and the children playing in their front yards. Even the sight of partially constructed houses on dirt lots, with builders' materials littering the front yards, and other lots that were completely empty, didn't take away from the attractive neighborhood.

"This is pretty," Shayla proclaimed. "Like in the *Beethoven* movies."

"And this is where our house is going to be," Reuben said proudly. "Look. They've already laid the foundation. I'm glad they got it in before we had any snow, or else our house might not be ready in April like it's supposed to be."

Camille stared at the deep concrete square.

"Will we be able to swim in the lake?" Mitchell asked.

"You have to learn to swim first," Reuben teased. "Actually, this lake isn't for swimming. They have it stocked with fish, and maybe we'll get a rowboat and some fishing poles and see if we can catch anything."

"Cool!"

"But you'll still be able to swim," Camille added. "There's a nice big pool on the property. There's also a playground. We'll drive you past there so you can see it before we leave."

Shayla pulled at Camille's sleeve. "The terrorists won't crash a plane here, will they, Mommy?"

She knelt to be face-to-face with the eight-year-old. Things had changed so much already this century, Camille thought with a touch of sadness. When she was Shayla's age she had no idea what a terrorist was. "Shayla, we never know what's going to happen five minutes from now. None of us is immune, or really safe. But Daddy and I will always do whatever we can to protect you and Mitchell from any harm. All right?"

Shayla nodded. "Mommy, this is even better than Disney World, because we'll be here every day."

The children ran toward the lake, and Reuben and Camille stood with their arms around each other. "Well, I think it's safe to say that the kids are pleased," she said.

"And why not? This is a dream come true for people like us who live on an ugly street in the Bronx." He chuckled. "You know, every time I talk to Saul or my sisters they keep asking if we're still moving."

The thought of her in-laws put a halt to Camille's charitable feelings. "It figures. They probably hope something will go wrong. Honestly, Reuben, your family is like crabs in a barrel, all trying to pull the one who manages to get out back in."

"Actually, Saul is asking if he can rent our apartment when we leave. The landlord will probably go for it. Saul used to work for him, and he left on good terms."

"Why does Saul want a two-bedroom apartment all of a sudden?"

"He wants to get a place with his girlfriend, and she's got a little boy. She lives in a tenement around Tinton Avenue, and he wants to get her out of there. He's actually talking about settling down. Hell, he's avoided it all these years. I guess it's about time." Saul, a year older than Reuben, was nearly forty.

"You know, I confess, I was a little worried when we signed those papers for the larger house, especially since we sprung for a lakeside lot," Camille said. "But now that I can start to picture it, it's going to be just wonderful."

Chapter 11

The Lees
December 2001

"Okay, here's what I figure," Norman said as he and Veronica sat having a discussion at their butcher-block dining table. "You'll probably get hired on at the hospital before me."

"Oh, I don't know about that," Veronica said. "Orthopedics is just as active as surgery." Both she and Norman worked as RNs, she in the postsurgical unit, he in orthopedics.

"We'll see. But I think we should request to work twelve-hour shifts three days a week instead of what we're doing now so that we can manage to have one of us at home. It's going to make for a very long workday with such a long commute, and we won't get many chances to sit down to dinner together, but we can't have Lorinda and Simone at home by themselves from before dawn until seven or eight o'clock at night."

"Oh, that's right," Veronica said. She hadn't thought of that. Norman was so smart. She felt lucky to have him to put her faith in. He knew all the questions to ask: taxes, school systems, and the like. At his insistence they'd even attended a free seminar for home buyers given by their bank. They needed all the help they could get, he said.

No doubt about it, she'd made a good decision when she chose him to be her husband and the father of her children.

"Working different days will stretch our commuting dollars as well," Norman continued. "We can use the same pass instead of us both having to buy one. I know they say they're nontransferable, but as long as it doesn't have our picture we're okay."

"But Norman, do you think the buses run long enough to accommodate a twelve-hour workday?"

"Ah, good point. They probably don't. We probably need to think about doing ten hours, four days a week. That'll give us forty hours."

Veronica frowned. "But we can't get in forty hours each in a seven-day week, Norman, without having an overlapping day. And then what about the kids?"

"I'll work forty hours. That will keep our benefits going. You'll have to cut down to part-time, three days a week. That'll give you thirty hours."

"Well . . ." She couldn't deny how nice that sounded to her ears, making that long trip into the city just three times a week. "I guess I can let the hospital in East Stroudsburg know that I'm available for part-time work as well."

"If they offer you something that's at least thirty hours, you take it. It's the same as you'd be doing at Presbyterian without a two-hour bus ride to get there." He paused. "I'm sorry about the delay, Veronica. I know you really liked that house."

"It's not your fault, Norman." She meant it, but she couldn't deny being sad over the way things had worked out.

"I just can't see getting stuck paying 8 1/2 percent interest when we can pay 5 1/2 if we slow down a little bit and do what we're supposed to," he explained. "Over thirty years three percentage points adds up to a lot of money. But I promise you that every dime I make from this part-time job will go toward paying off the bills so we can get a good mortgage rate. We'll get our house, probably by the summer. It just won't be the one we looked at. I doubt it'll still be on the market by then."

She'd been terribly disappointed when all the lenders they tried said they didn't qualify for the lower interest rates because of the combined effects of high credit card balances and a few late payments. She'd even suggested to Norman that they go ahead with the higher rate and refinance after a few years, an idea he promptly vetoed. "It costs money to refinance, Veronica. Plus we have to plan on higher expenses while we're commuting. There might not be any extra left over to pay down the bills. We have to do this right from the jump. And we definitely have to pay close attention to our bills.

Credit is getting more and more important these days. We can't afford to miss any payments. Credit card companies are starting to charge extra if you pay even one day late, and if you're late paying one bill the others can raise your interest rate."

He'd been right, of course, and now she sought to reassure him. "You're working awfully hard, Norman. Forty at Presbyterian plus another twenty at the nursing home. I think it might be too much for you."

"It's only temporary, and it'll be worth it in the long run. We're talking about our future, and the future of our daughters."

Chapter 12

The Youngs
January 2002

Dawn turned her upper body so she could see her son in the back-seat. "So, what do you think, Zach? Would you like living here?"

"We're really going to live here?"

"Absolutely," Milo replied, his eyes on the road.

Dawn loved the look of wonder in her son's eyes. "I take it you approve."

"Can I have a dog?"

Dawn laughed. "Well, not a pure breed, you understand, but we'll bring you down to the local pound and see what they've got."

"Awright!"

"I always wanted a dog when I was a kid, Zach," Milo said. "We couldn't have one because our apartment house didn't allow them, just like the one we have now doesn't, either. But it's especially nice to have a dog when you have a house. Their barking will let you know if someone is lurking around outside or even approaching."

"I heard a rumor the other day that the Mitchell-Lama agreements for moderate rents on the buildings is set to expire in a couple of years," Dawn remarked.

"What happens then? Surely they can't just throw all their old tenants out."

"No, but each time someone moves out, or dies, they'll rent the apartment at the market rate. I heard they'll start allowing dogs then. I'll bet you that after a certain percentage of tenants are paying market rates it'll go co-op. And that's when they'll start fixing them up."

"Well, by then we'll be long gone," Milo said, "so it doesn't matter to me if they make the tenants buy their apartments or not."

Zach piped up from the backseat. "Where's our house gonna be, Daddy?"

"We'll be in the next phase of construction, which is down the main road and to the right. But right now there isn't anything there. They're knocking down a lot of trees and leveling the land, but they won't start building on it until the spring."

"Oh."

"Don't be disappointed, Zach," Dawn said. "Instead we're going to show you a house here in Phase One that's just like the one we picked out, and in the same type of location."

Milo pulled over in front of a neat ranch house. "There we are. But Zach, you can't get too close to it, because there are people living here. They might think you're a burglar and shoot you."

"Shoot me?"

"Yes. And they'd be within their rights. You don't walk up and peek in someone's windows. It's called trespassing, and it's a criminal act."

"The house next to this one is just going up, Milo," Dawn said. "Let's get out and pretend we're looking at it, and then Zach can get a better look."

"We can always go to the model. This house has just been started, and it's a lot bigger than ours."

"Later. I do want him to see the inside, but I also want him to get the full effect." Holding her head where only Milo could see, she mouthed the words "the lake."

"All right." He backed up so that they were in front of the skeleton of the partially constructed house next door.

Zach hopped out of the backseat of the Volvo and ran toward the incomplete two-story house, his gaze fixed on the ranch house next door. "Where's my room gonna be?" he asked his parents when they caught up to him.

"Your room is the one with the window on the right front, plus the window on the side."

"Which one is y'all's room?"

"On the other side of the house," Milo told him.

Dawn smiled discreetly. They had opted for the larger ranch house with its split bedroom arrangement rather than the smallest model that had been advertised on the TV commercial, where the master bedroom shared a common wall with one of the other bedrooms. This arrangement would give them the privacy they had become accustomed to with their apartment layout, even if that privilege plus the extra square footage came with a price tag several thousand dollars higher. They both felt good about their decision. After all, they weren't building a house so they could have a less-appealing layout than their apartment had.

"So I'll have my own section. But you'll have to come over here to use the bathroom."

Milo patted Zach's back. "Nope. We've got our own bathroom right there in our bedroom."

"Your own bathroom? Wow!" Zach stared at the sparkling water just beyond the backyard. "Is our house gonna be on the river?"

"It's a lake," Milo corrected. "And we thought you'd never notice."

"Wow! A lake in our backyard!"

"Just think how nice it'll be in the summertime," Dawn said. "You'll meet lots of kids here, and you'll be able to have a birthday party in the backyard, with balloons tied to the trees. Maybe we'll even buy a canoe or something, and we can take boat rides."

"Cool!" Zach ran off to see the water close up.

Dawn peeked into the wood-frame house through one of the openings for windows. "What's that in the walls, Milo, insulation?" She pointed to the fuzzy yellow material tucked in between the rafters of the walls. It reminded her of cotton candy.

Milo looked inside. "Yes, that's what it looks like." He frowned. "But they certainly didn't use much of it."

"Maybe they ran out and plan to finish up next week."

"I hope so. Or else the owners of this house are going to freeze come winter. Come on, let's drive over and show Zach the model." He whistled to catch Zach's eye, then gestured for him to come to them.

They got into their car and drove off, passing two signs in front of the house in progress with the poor insulation. One had instructions for the builders, and the other proclaimed, "Future home of The Currys."

Chapter 13

Reuben got behind the wheel of the U-Haul truck, where Mitchell already sat next to him. "Again, Camille, don't worry about trying to stay behind me. It's tricky to follow someone when you're driving on the highway, especially in heavy traffic. But you do know how to get there, right?"

"Are you kidding? Of course I know. Reuben, we've been going out there every week for the last four months." They drove out to the site every Saturday once construction had started, sometimes disappointed to see little or no progress, sometimes thrilled to see their home edging closer to completion. The structure didn't look like much at the beginning, with just the foundation, wood frame, and unfinished roof, but then windows were placed, the drywall went up, the stairs to the basement and the second floor were built and the house took on the shape of the model it mirrored. As it neared completion even Mitchell and Shayla got excited.

"Call my cell if you have any problem," Camille said.

"Will do. Drive carefully, honey."

"I will." Reuben leaned out the window to give her a quick kiss. He patted the large steering wheel. "I'm not looking forward to driving this big ol' thing all the way to Tobyhanna, I've got to tell you."

"It's gonna be fun!" Mitchell exclaimed.

"That's what you say now, Mitch, but wait til we start hitting all those bumps on the turnpike and your butt is bouncing all over the place." Reuben turned back to Camille. "I'll see you in a couple of hours. We'll have lunch in our new house."

Those last three words made Camille's toes tingle. Our new house. Their own house. God, just thinking of it gave her that same rush she got during sex. "I can't wait."

"Bye, Daddy. Bye, Mitchell," Shayla said.

"Bye!"

Camille and Shayla got into the family's white Malibu and drove off. Camille allowed Shayla to insert her *Winnie the Pooh* CD and sing along. Normally she found cutesy songs like that "Christopher Robin" one overly cheerful, but today she didn't care what they listened to. She felt too keyed up. Besides, better *Winnie the Pooh* than hip-hop.

After waiting so many months for construction to be complete, suddenly everything fell smack dab into place. She and Reuben went for a final inspection Thursday morning, closed Thursday afternoon, and now they had the keys to their front and back doors, plus a bottle of champagne, courtesy of the builder. This was it. Instead of looking at their future home and longing for the day when they would at last live in it and then heading back to the Bronx, the future had finally arrived; and they were going to their new home for good.

The moment seemed almost anticlimactic. There was no one to wave good-bye to; Saul and the others who had helped carry their belongings down the stairs had already said their farewells and gone on their way. The sheet metal shop was closed today, so all was quiet for a change. Camille thought it ironic that the banging and slamming that often disturbed her Saturday mornings didn't happen this last morning in their apartment. But a roaring train pulled into the 161st Street station as she headed for the Major Deegan Expressway, a fitting ending to the life they were leaving behind. Now it would be Saul's turn to cope with those damn El trains every ten minutes.

The landlord was happy to offer a lease to Reuben's brother, his former employee, when he learned they would be moving out. It still incensed Camille whenever she recalled telling the landlord that she and Reuben would be giving up their apartment to live in their new house in Pennsylvania. He hadn't bothered to even try to conceal his astonishment. He clearly expected them to remain in the apartment for years and years, raising their rent annually, even though he knew it was too small for them. She'd wanted to ask him, *Do you think you're the only one who wants to improve their life?*

They crossed the George Washington Bridge into New Jersey. Camille felt like they'd gotten away with an extra four dollars, because the toll booths were on the other side, for those entering New York. Of course, she and Reuben would be coming back to the city to work a week from Monday, but on a commuter bus, so they wouldn't have to pay the toll themselves.

To her pleasant surprise, their new neighbors welcomed them as they unloaded the truck, coming over to say hello and introducing themselves. Two of the men, the one next door and the one across the street, actually helped them move in the heavier pieces. One of them took over for her as she and Reuben attempted to place their entertainment center on a wheeled lift, telling her she had no business trying to lift anything so heavy. Imagine getting a complete stranger to help you move your furniture if you were in New York! If they offered, you could be sure they would make careful note of what they saw so they could come back and rip you off, she thought matter-of-factly.

It amazed her that the help they received came from white folks. She'd never lived near white people before; the South Bronx was nearly exclusively black and Hispanic. Their new neighbors seemed like genuinely nice people. To show their gratitude, she and Reuben invited both men and their spouses over for dinner on Tuesday. She wanted a few days to get the house in shape, unpacking and hanging the new drapes and curtains they'd bought, before they entertained their first guests. Besides, the new dining room furniture they ordered wouldn't be delivered until the weekend.

Camille insisted they buy a formal dining room table because their white laminate-top table and Windsor chairs looked way too casual for a separate formal dining room. They placed the existing set in the corner of the eat-in kitchen. She wanted to get the matching china cabinet as well to go with their new table, but Reuben pointed out that they had no china and put his foot down about buying any, so she settled for a buffet server.

Camille knew that as long as she lived she would never forget their first week in the new house. It had been heavenly, just perfect.

The knowledge that they had a home of their own still hadn't completely sunk in. Several times a day she walked through it, sniffing the walls, loving the way the fresh paint smelled. She walked barefoot over the beige wall-to-wall carpet they had chosen, loving its thick, lush feel. She'd lived in apartments where there'd been new paint, but never in her dreams did she ever believe she'd live in a house with a rug so light it was practically white.

Finally, she walked up the staircase, letting her hand trail along the pecan-wood banister, telling herself over and over that this was their home, where they would live from now on. She'd never been a stay-at-home mom, except for a brief period after both Mitchell and Shayla's births when she took off for two months. Now she played the housewife role with vigor, unpacking their belongings while Reuben got the children registered in school. Late April was awfully late in the semester to make a transfer, but they saw no point in paying rent in the city for another two months just so the kids could finish out the year. Besides, this way she could get an idea of how far ahead the Tobyhanna schools were compared to the Bronx—she had no doubt they were ahead—and maybe give the kids some tutoring to help them prepare. She wanted to limit any difficulty they might have to the last weeks of the current semester. By the time the fall semester rolled around Shayla would be ready for the third grade and Mitchell the sixth.

As Camille lined the shelves with contact paper and helped Reuben paint, she wished she could be at home like this all the time.

But she knew she had to work, and she wanted to. Money brought good things, and she wanted good things. Heading her wish list was more new furniture. Their stuff was far from ratty, but it did look a bit tired, and a little chintzy as well, in their brand-new home. She kept thinking of how nice that furnished model looked, everything brand-spanking new and expensive-looking; no assembly-required tables. Ah, but they had plenty of time to redecorate. They'd be here the rest of their lives. When they retired they would sit out back in the proverbial rocking chairs and watch the sun set in the evenings. Mitchell and Shayla would send their children to Grandma and Grandpa's for the summers. . . .

The first prick in Camille's bubble came when, Tuesday evening at dinner, she asked her female neighbors about day care options for the children of New York commuters.

"I don't think anyone stays open past six," Linda Tillman said. She turned to Marianne Willis. "Do you know of any place, Marianne?"

"Actually, I don't." She shrugged apologetically. "Our oldest was fourteen when we moved here, so Jeff and I managed without day care. And now that I have a real estate license in Pennsylvania, I work pretty close by."

"I work from home doing medical insurance coding," Linda said, "so we had no need for day care, either. But I'm sure there has to be someplace."

"Oh, I'm sure there is," Camille replied confidently.

But her subsequent research proved there wasn't, and she began to panic. She hadn't expected to encounter problems in finding day care; she just assumed that since people from New York were pouring into the area that extended day care would be readily available. Was everyone who lived here like Linda and Marianne, with older offspring or work-at-home positions that didn't require them to need child care?

Once she and Reuben returned to work in another week they would be away from home most of the day. They would have to catch the 5:40 AM bus into the city, and take the 5:30 PM bus back, which would put them in Tobyhanna at around 7:30 in the evening. That made for a frighteningly long time for the children to be alone. Not only would they have to get themselves up and off to school each morning, but they would have to get their own dinner upon returning from school. They could hardly have dinner at 8:00 or 8:30 at night. They couldn't avoid the commute, but the schedule bordered on neglect for children as young as theirs.

She talked to Reuben about it. "We'll have to get someone to watch them," he said.

"That'll be expensive, Reuben. I'm not sure we can afford it, especially after what we've already spent." The cost of window fashions alone ran over two hundred dollars, and the dining room another twelve hundred. And Reuben, anxious to start barbecuing in the warm spring and summer weather, had bought a shiny new gas grill from Lowe's; another two hundred gone.

"What choice do we have?"

This seemed like a good time for her to tell Reuben what was on her mind, even though the want ads in Sunday's paper revealed dismal pickings. "I thought I'd try to find a job around here."

"And make, what, eight bucks an hour? You saw the paper the other day. You can't bring home those kinds of wages in the twenty-first century. It won't be enough for us to make it, Camille."

"But if I can find something that pays reasonably well, when you factor in the cost of bus passes and babysitters, wouldn't you want me to change jobs?"

"Yes, but that's a pretty strong *if.* In the meantime we've got to protect Mitchell and Shayla. Maybe get some local kid to sit with them until at least six. By that time they'll have to go home and have dinner themselves, but at least we'll be home within another ninety minutes. Mitchell is almost eleven. I know that's young to be responsible for your little sister and yourself when it's getting dark outside, but I think he can manage for an hour and a half. We'll coach them."

Camille wasn't convinced. "It's such a big house, Reuben. And it'll take us at least a few weeks to find someone. You and I have to go back to work next week."

"Talk to some more of the neighbors. Maybe they can recommend someone."

She felt uncomfortable with the idea of knocking on doors of people she didn't even know. "And if we don't find anyone by the end of the week?"

Reuben shrugged. "They can go to the library after school, and we'll pick them up there. That won't cost anything, plus it's educational. It'll encourage them to study or read even after they're done with homework."

The underlying fear about child care was the only blemish on an otherwise perfect week. On a particularly cool spring night Reuben gathered them all together in the family room and lit a fire. Camille even bought some graham crackers, Hershey's bars, and marshmallows, which they toasted over the open fire, and then made s'mores, a snack new to everyone but Camille, who remembered it from her days at camp.

On the last Saturday before she and Reuben were due to return to work they drove into Bushkill so Camille could show the family where she'd gone to camp as a child. No one was there at this time of year, and she imagined all the buildings were locked up tight, so they didn't even try to go inside the beautiful, high-ceilinged chapel she remembered. Much of the grounds had changed. Not far from the lake a new Olympic-size pool had been built.

She smiled, full of fond memories of learning how to swim in the brown water of the lake with other city kids. Who could have predicted that one day decades later she would be living in a house on another Pennsylvania lake?

"This is nice, Mommy," Shayla said. "Can Mitchell and I come here this summer?"

"How come you and Daddy didn't send us here before?" Mitchell asked.

"Because you're not eligible to come here. This camp was founded to give poor kids from the city a place to get away for a few weeks each summer. My family didn't have much money, and while Daddy and I don't have a whole lot of money ourselves, we do make too much for you to qualify to come here."

"So what're we gonna do all summer?"

"You'll have a great time," Reuben said with enthusiasm. "You'll know all the kids in the neighborhood by then, and we'll probably get one of your cousins out here to keep an eye on y'all."

Camille's head jerked. That was the first she'd heard about *that* plan. When had Reuben decided that? And why hadn't he discussed it with her?

He caught sight of her startled expression and shrugged. "It's just an idea. It popped into my head."

"Any particular cousin you had in mind?"

"Kierra. Mom was saying how Brenda would love to get her out of the city. A couple of girls in the building are having babies already, and Brenda's worried. I can't blame her. Kierra's only fifteen."

Camille didn't respond, but she couldn't help remembering how unkind her sister-in-law had been when she learned about their plans to build a house. Now Brenda had Ginny relaying her worries to Reuben in hopes of securing an invitation so that her daughter would stay out of trouble in the city. Camille found that ironic. They probably had Reuben believing that no teenage girls ever got pregnant in Tobyhanna, where half the parents in town spent five hours a day commuting to offices in New York.

On Sunday evening, after cooking all afternoon so she could get dinner on the table within minutes of arriving home the next evening, Camille packed extra sandwiches and drinks in the kids' lunch boxes. The library was easy to get to from the school, and at least there the children would be safe. But she felt an unrelenting sense of guilt for not researching her options for child care before they moved out here. It was rather irresponsible of her to merely assume that extended day care services would be readily available to people like her and Reuben, with young children who needed supervision in the hours between the end of the school day and their parents' arrival at home. She'd been too caught up in the excitement of owning a brand new home to look into it. Already she worried about their upcoming summer vacation. Reuben's idea of bringing Kierra out to watch Mitchell and Shayla wasn't a bad one, but Camille was still annoyed at Brenda and really didn't want Brenda's daughter coming to stay with them unless she had absolutely no other options.

But the day camps advertised in the newspaper all looked so expensive. Back in the Bronx the kids had attended a low-cost day camp sponsored by their church. She doubted anything like that existed out here, where everyone seemed reasonably well off. Besides, their long weekdays would probably make joining a church difficult. She couldn't picture Reuben getting out of bed early on Sunday morning when he already arose before the crack of dawn Monday through Friday, and she didn't find the idea particularly appealing herself.

But Camille knew that unsupervised kids could get into all kinds of trouble out here in the country. She knew they had to be especially careful with so much distance between them while she and Reuben worked in Manhattan. It could be disastrous if one of the kids fell off their bike and needed stitches or something, with her and Reuben working two states away.

She forced herself to think calmly in the face of rising panic. She still had several weeks before summer vacation began, and a lot could happen in that time. By then she'd probably know more of the neighbors. She'd meet people on the bus once she and Reuben returned to work next week. Surely there had to be a couple of teenage girls in the neighborhood who offered babysitting services. Maybe she and Reuben would let them watch the kids while they went to dinner or something and see how it worked out, then offer them a summer babysitting job if it all went well.

Monday morning the idyllic week came to an end, with a new week starting uneasily. Camille arose groggily at 4:40 after snoozing for ten minutes. To her still-tired body it felt more like 2:40. She wondered if she'd ever be able to get Reuben up at this hour.

She managed, but not without much difficulty. He practically sleepwalked his way into his clothes, but she didn't plan on his being much help, anyway, knowing how he hated getting out of bed in the morning. Working quietly and efficiently, she gathered the lunches she'd packed into microwave dishes the night before and poured juice into thermoses. On the inside of the front door as a reminder to the kids, she posted a note written in jumbo letters: Don't forget your lunch! She and Reuben left the house at 5:25 to drive to the train station. She hated the idea of leaving the house before the children and even the sun had risen.

At 7:00, well after the bus had made its last local pickup and was headed north on the New Jersey Turnpike, she called home to make sure the kids had gotten out of bed. Reuben had already fallen asleep in the seat next to her. She managed to doze off herself. Little conversation could be heard on the bus; except for a few hearty souls working on laptops, just about all the passengers had nodded off.

She peeked at her fellow riders. Surprisingly, only one other black couple was aboard. She expected to see more, but of course this was hardly the only bus to New York. Even one couple could tell them a few things that only other black people would know . . . like the name of a good barber and hairdresser. Reuben, as particular about his hair as any woman, wouldn't even consider going into a Supercuts for a trim, no more than she would want to risk her tresses to an unknown beautician.

The passengers slowly came to life when the bus emerged from the Lincoln Tunnel. Compacts and lipsticks were pulled out, peppermints were popped to freshen sleepy breath, and men and women alike ran combs through hair that had gotten a bit mussed as they napped.

At Port Authority she and Reuben parted ways, he for the subway to bring him to the supermarket's Bronx location, and she for the street, where she would walk to her office on Fifth Avenue near Forty-Eighth Street. *This isn't so bad,* she told herself as she speed walked, swinging her arms as best she could with the weight of her shoulder bag on her shoulder, plus her tote bag in one hand and her insulated nylon lunch bag in the other. *I might even lose a few pounds.*

By the end of the day she wondered how she'd ever survive. She'd already been awake thirteen hours, and she still had a two-hour commute back to Tobyhanna. If traffic was as bad as it had been this morning, it would take more like two and a half hours.

Mitchell called from the library using the calling card she had provided him with, letting her know he and Shayla had arrived safely and were doing their homework.

He called back as she was on her way to Port Authority. "We're all done, Mom. Can we go home now?"

She kept her brisk pace as she talked, not wanting to miss the 5:35 bus, or else she'd have to wait until 6:05. Her breath came out in ragged near-gasps, and her scalp line and upper body felt damp from perspiration. Her dry-cleaning bills would be murder. "I'm sorry, Mitchell, but you have to stay there until Daddy and I pick you up, and the bus doesn't leave until 5:30. We'll be there as soon as we can. Read a book or something."

When Camille boarded the bus she automatically sat next to the black woman she'd seen on the trip in. "Hi," she said. "Don't worry. I don't plan to sit here for the entire trip home. I just wanted to introduce myself. I'm Camille Curry, and my husband and I moved to Arlington Acres a week ago."

The woman smiled. "My name's Tanisha Cole. My husband and I live in Arlington Acres, too. Oh, here he is now."

Camille turned her head toward the aisle. A large, light-skinned man with a shaved head, his tie loosened around his throat, carrying his suit jacket, rapidly approached. "Oh!" Camille said, "I'll move across the aisle." She held out her hand to the man. "Hi, I'm Camille."

He gripped her hand, and she tried not to wince from the pressure, which was well past firm. "Douglas."

She sat across from Tanisha and Douglas and anxiously looked out the window. The bus had arrived at Port Authority from Lower Manhattan a few minutes early, but Reuben had only about two minutes to get here before it set off at 5:35.

She relaxed, letting out a relieved sigh, when she caught sight of him running along the side of the bus.

"That must be your husband," Douglas said to her from his aisle seat.

"Yes. He made it, thank God." If Reuben had missed the bus she would have had to wait at the Tobyhanna station for him to get in, and she wanted to get to the library as soon as she could to pick up Mitchell and Shayla.

She introduced Reuben to Douglas and Tanisha. The return trip proved to be much more lively than the snooze of the morning commute. She found her other fellow commuters as friendly as her neighbors had been. She enjoyed hearing their stories of adjusting to the suburbs—they, too, had been driven out of New York by unaffordable real estate prices. Everyone seemed to love it here, and no one regretted their decision . . . They just wished those train tracks would get laid so they could take a train instead of being at the mercy of traffic patterns.

She noticed one exception in all the praise of suburban living. Douglas and Tanisha Cole, while welcoming, remained conspicuously quiet, concentrating more on each other than on the conversation around them. At one point she even saw Tanisha grip her husband's shoulder, like she was trying to offer him moral support. Maybe, Camille thought, this couple had some kind of crisis situation at home to deal with.

Or maybe the Coles didn't share their neighbors' high opinion of life in Monroe County.

Chapter 14

The Currys
June 2002

Camille formed more hamburger patties than she could count. Their new grill could hold forty hamburgers, and Reuben said he wanted to cook all the burgers, hot dogs, and chicken at one time. She didn't blame him. Who wanted to be stuck in front of a hot grill when you could be socializing with your guests? They'd set up the grill on the deck, which, due to the sloping grounds, looked from the back of the house like it was on the second floor. They'd rented round tables and folding chairs from a local party planner, setting them up on the grass of the backyard.

After delivering the tray to Reuben, she returned to the kitchen to wash her hands. On her way out to join her guests she stopped in the living room to pat the sky blue sofa and two matching striped chairs they'd purchased, along with pecan-wood accent tables. They'd gotten a good price, plus interest-free financing for the next two years. They'd also bought bedroom furniture for Mitchell and Shayla, who for the first time in their lives had rooms of their own. She knew that they probably shouldn't have bought all this additional furniture after the other purchases they'd made, but she wanted their house to look perfect for their housewarming, and she knew Reuben did, too. She still remembered the comments her in-laws had made when they announced their plans to build a house in Pennsylvania, and she wanted their eyes to bug out when they saw it for the first time. Like someone had once said, *Living well is the best revenge.* A room devoid of furnishings didn't fit the image. They'd moved their old living room furniture into the family room. She'd start setting money aside every payday to give to the store when the bill became due. It shouldn't be too hard. When their salaries rose their mortgage payment would remain the same, unlike the rent they had paid in the Bronx. In two years they'd be sitting pretty.

A pang of worry stabbed at the center of her chest. Their mortgage payment ended up being considerably higher than the $740 that brought them out here in the first place, thanks to their selecting a lakefront lot and a larger house with upgrades here and there, like the deck that cost three thousand dollars. But they'd manage. What counted was that today they played host to their families and their friends, both old and new, in their beautiful, brand-new home. Her friends who'd moved south or west of New York in search of a better life had nothing on her now.

She smiled. Her childhood friends always sent her Christmas cards, often with a photo of their families on the steps of their homes. This year she and Reuben and the kids would be able to do the same thing.

The day couldn't have been prettier if they'd ordered it from a catalog. Camille loved weekends, when the morning sun shone over the lake behind their house, making it look like sparkling, dark green seawater.

Curious guests began arriving at the exact time their party began, 11:00 AM. Camille basked in all the oohs and aahs. When the question invariably came up about black families in the neighborhood, she politely replied that there were a number of them. She simply shrugged at comments that she and Reuben had better get a second lock put on their door and some covering on their new furniture to keep it clean. She'd always hated that plastic that people in New York often put over their chairs and sofas. It stuck to the back of your legs when you wore shorts in the summertime, and the rest of the year you sweated.

Her sister-in-law Arnelle pulled Camille aside. "This is a great house, Camille. I love all your new furniture."

"Thanks." Camille kept her voice casual. She still hadn't forgiven her sister-in-law for her snide remarks about their new house, but she did appreciate Arnelle's gracious comment. She certainly seemed sincere. "We like it," she added with a shrug.

"I never saw white carpet before. It's beautiful, but how do you manage to keep it clean?"

"We bought a carpet shampooer. I usually run it every two or three weeks. And the kids have been trained to wipe their feet before they come in the house."

"Oh. One thing I didn't understand. Why are there two living rooms?"

"Uh, the one by the kitchen is a family room, Arnelle." Camille quickly looked around. It would be embarrassing if anyone from the neighborhood—she'd invited a few families from the street, as well as Doug and Tanisha and the new black couple from Mount Pocono who rode the bus with them—heard Arnelle's question. She might have asked the same question herself before she'd come out here, but now that she'd seen the model homes she knew better. Fortunately, no one else had overheard.

"Oh. Well, I'm sure Kierra will have a wonderful time out here this summer."

"Actually, it works out well for us, too. We won't have to worry about who's taking care of the kids all day." Once Camille realized that Kierra represented the cheapest child care for Mitchell and Shayla, she warmed up to the idea of having Reuben's niece here. It solved a large problem and really didn't create any.

"Maybe next year Tiffany can be your babysitter."

Camille kept her expression impassive, but inside she fumed. Arnelle hadn't complimented her about the house out of sincerity; she'd had an ulterior motive for her own daugther. Their relationship had been strained since she'd declined to make Arnelle any more loans. All Arnelle wanted was to put in a reservation for Tiffany to spend the summer out here, and she'd tried to butter her up like an ear of corn.

From the beginning of her marriage to Reuben, Camille had preferred Arnelle's easygoing, almost happy-go-lucky nature to that of her older sister, Brenda, who, when not complaining about this or that being unjust, concentrated solely on trying to make something out of nothing. They could put her picture in the dictionary next to the word "dour." Now the sisters practically seemed like one and the same, friendly only when they wanted something. Brenda had gone way overboard when she arrived with Kierra, greeting Camille like they were best friends.

But in the meantime Arnelle waited for an answer. "We'll see," Camille said vaguely. No way would she get in the middle of what she suspected would be a battle between the sisters. Surely Brenda would want Kierra to return next year, and Camille and Reuben had neither the space nor the need to house two teens. After all, they weren't running a fresh-air camp for city kids. Instead she would refer their mothers to the same camp she'd attended as a child. If she remembered correctly, they had a separate facility for fourteen- and fifteen-year-olds.

She made a mental note to warn Reuben not to commit to anything. She wouldn't put it past Arnelle to try to extract a promise from him that she could hold them to.

She reached for the bags of hamburger and hot dog buns. "Would you bring these out to Reuben for me, Arnelle? He wants to put them on the grill to get them a little toasty."

"Sure."

Camille reached for the dishcloth to wipe a crumb from the counter, then went to check on Kierra, who was unpacking her clothes in Shayla's room, which she would be sharing.

"How's it going?" Camille asked pleasantly. Brenda was with her. She zipped Kierra's large suitcase and removed it from the bed, standing it up against the wall.

"Good, Aunt Camille. We're just about finished."

Camille caught sight of a yellow and blue two-piece swimsuit on top of the pile of clothing Kierra held. "Oh, what a pretty bathing suit!"

Kierra smiled shyly. "Thank you. Mom bought it for me, since you guys have a pool here."

Brenda spoke up. "Camille, did you want me to put Kierra's suitcase in the closet?"

"Sure. There's plenty of room. It's a walk-in."

Brenda carried the empty bag to the closet door and opened it. Camille heard her gasp. "Wow. This is one big closet."

She couldn't help doing just a little bit of bragging. "Yes, the closet space in this house is pretty generous. Reuben and I have two walk-ins in our bedroom." She turned to her niece. "We're very happy to have you with us for the summer, Kierra."

"I'll probably like it so much I won't want to go home."

Camille didn't dare look at Brenda's reaction to her daughter's remark, but she knew Brenda couldn't have liked it very much. "But of course you'll want to go home in August," she said. "You'll miss your mother."

"Oh, I'll probably come out a couple of times to see her between now and then," Brenda said airily. "You know, Camille, this really is a nice house. I never really knew anybody who lived in a house before, other than friends of friends who live out in Queens." She paused a moment before adding, "It's too bad you and Reuben spend so much time commuting to work that you hardly ever get to enjoy it."

Camille felt her jaw tighten. "Well, we'd rather spend two hours on the road every afternoon and come home to this than take a half-hour subway ride home to a too-small apartment in one of the ugliest sections of the Bronx." She conveniently shortened her commute time—the trip took two and a half hours each way—but she refused to give Brenda any ammunition.

The defeated look on Brenda's face told Camille she'd hit her target.

When Camille returned outside, the air was permeated with the scent of barbecued meat. Veronica Lee approached her, plate in hand. "Camille, it was so nice of you to invite Norman and me."

"You're welcome." Camille hadn't known Veronica very long, but felt she and her husband, Norman, would make a nice addition to their barbecue. The main purpose of the party was for her and Reuben's friends and family members to see their new house, but she also wanted them to know that they had met new people. "We black folks have to stick together," Camille said in a low voice. Douglas and Tanisha Cole, who'd also attended, would know what she meant, but she wouldn't want the Tillmans to overhear her; that was the type of comment that would make non-black guests make a beeline for the exit. It pleased her that their neighbors from next door and across the street both accepted their invitation and appeared to be having a good time. It wasn't every white person who could feel comfortable surrounded by black folks.

"Where is Norman, anyway?" she asked.

"He couldn't make it. Unfortunately, Sunday is a workday for him."

"Does he drive into the city on the weekends?"

"No, the bus runs on the weekends. He just has to take a later one; the bus we usually take in the morning doesn't run that early on the weekends. But the hospital has been very nice about letting us tailor our work schedules to accommodate the available transportation." She gave a sheepish shrug. "I think they expect us to stay on with them, but we're going to switch to the local hospital as soon as they make us offers, and I hope it doesn't take long. This commute is killing us."

"I didn't even know the buses run to the city on the weekends."

"Yes. Apparently a lot of people go in on Saturday to shop or have dinner and see a show, and then come back Sunday. People who don't have to make the trip Monday through Friday, I'm sure. But I might swing back with Norman after I pick him up at the station." Veronica held up her plate. "By the way, this macaroni and cheese was the bomb."

"I'm glad you liked it."

"I went back for seconds. I've never had it made with spaghetti before."

"My daughter is a picky eater. She doesn't like noodles. Says they're too thick."

Veronica pursed her lips. "Well, that was definitely my treat for the week."

Camille looked at her incredulously. "Macaroni and cheese is a treat? As tiny as you are you don't have to watch what you eat." The first thing she'd noticed about Veronica was her petite size. She was one of those women who would probably never gain weight, like Jackie Onassis or Audrey Hepburn. Standing next to her made Camille more aware than ever of those forty extra pounds she carried. She could hardly believe Veronica had given birth to two children. Naturally, her husband, Norman, looked like a linebacker. Not all that tall, just big. Those huge types often went after petite women.

"Can I fix you a plate? You're so busy, running in and out of the house but not eating."

"Thanks, but I'm all right. I just want to make sure I spend a few minutes with everyone here and make sure they're all right, and then I promise I'll sit down with a plate." Camille started to excuse herself, then decided she owed it to Veronica not to leave her standing alone. Norman wasn't here, and the only other people Veronica knew were Douglas and Tanisha, whom she didn't even see at the moment.

"Veronica, have you met our neighbors? Marianne and Jeff, Linda and Bob?"

"Yes, I traded relocation stories with them. Nice people."

"And Tanisha and Douglas are here somewhere. I know you know them from the bus."

"Actually, uh . . . I think they left."

"They did?" Camille glanced around at the guests. She spotted Alex Cole, Tanisha and Douglas's ten-year-old who often played with Mitchell, but no sign of his parents. "Well, that's a surprise. They didn't say anything to me about leaving."

"They weren't here long," Veronica remarked lightly.

"Just what I need," Camille said with a groan. "Guests who eat and run."

"Tanisha said something about their son not feeling well."

She rolled her eyes. "I could see if she was talking about Alex, but since he's here, she must mean her older kid, and he's out of high school." She knew from conversations with Tanisha that in addition to Alex, their child together, Douglas had a nineteen-year-old son from an earlier relationship. The young man lived with his mother in St. Albans, Queens, but came out to stay with them from time to time. He obviously didn't work or go to college, and although Tanisha didn't say it, Camille sensed that her stepson's presence was the source of conflict in her household.

Veronica tactfully changed the subject. "Anyhow, everything is very nice, Camille. Your house is gorgeous."

"Thanks." Camille and Reuben had met Veronica and Norman on the commuter bus. The Lees lived in nearby Mount Pocono and had been in Pennsylvania only for a month or so, and she and Reuben both felt them to be nice people. Today Veronica had brought their two daughters along, and they played with Shayla, who delighted in playing hostess to her cousins and other visiting children.

Like most of the other commuters, Veronica and Norman had moved here from the city, in their case Washington Heights. But the Lees worked untraditional hours. Both RNs, they worked ten-hour shifts at the Presbyterian Medical Center in upper Manhattan. Camille and Reuben saw the Lees only during the afternoon trip to New York; they took the first bus out to get to work before 7:00. Camille envied their work schedules. Norman worked four days a week and Veronica three. They never rode the bus at the same time;

they'd worked it out so that one of them would always be at home with their children. Not only did they have no child care expense, but they got to share a single bus pass.

She wished she and Reuben could cut the cost of their commute in half. They shelled out nearly five hundred dollars a month for two bus passes, which hurt more than a toothache. And as if that wasn't bad enough, Reuben also had to purchase a MetroCard weekly to get to work in the Bronx from Port Authority. The Lees had to buy MetroCards, but with buying just one bus pass the expense seemed more bearable.

Again she experienced that stabbing discomfort. It felt like some-one had jabbed a needle directly into her rib cage.

"I'm looking forward to redecorating our place," Veronica said now.

Camille's fears melted away. This was no time to be nervous, not when she'd just been complimented. Best relax and enjoy it, like the clear, fresh scent of the lake and the lingering aroma of the food Reuben had cooked. "It's fun, buying furniture," she said. "You just have to be careful to make sure you love what you buy, since you'll be looking at it for years."

"I'm afraid we need more than just furniture. Our kitchen and bathrooms need updating."

Camille's brow wrinkled. "Updating? In a new house?"

"Our place isn't new. It was built nearly forty years ago." Veronica shrugged, a sheepish expression on her face. "We didn't buy in one of the new subdivisions. We did start to buy in Arlington Acres. Their ad on TV is what brought us out here in the first place, but the salesman was so aggressive he turned us off. We think he even staged a phony telephone call to try to get us to spring for a lakefront lot, like this one. We told him we couldn't afford to build by the lake, but he kept pushing."

Camille swallowed hard. "What was your salesman's name?"

"Oh, I don't remember. Elvis? No, that wasn't it. But I do think it started with an 'E.' He was a young man, reminded me a little of Brad Pitt. Tall, blond, and very handsome, if a bit on the skinny side. But we ran into the same problem at the other subdivision we visited. Everybody tried to get us to buy right away, or else, they said, we'd lose out. All that high pressure made us very wary. We decided to look at existing houses for sale." She glanced at the lake, and then at the back of the Curry house with a wistful smile. "But now that I see how lovely your property is, it makes me wish Norman and I could have afforded something like this."

Camille knew Veronica meant to praise her and Reuben's taste, but privately she felt mortified. What would Veronica say if she knew that Reuben had been unable to resist Eric's ploy to upgrade both their house and the lot it stood on? The Lees probably pulled in close to a hundred grand, if not more, and Veronica made no bones about the fact that they couldn't afford a lakefront lot. If the Lees couldn't afford it, how could she and Reuben?

In spite of his assurances to the contrary, she still wasn't convinced they hadn't overextended themselves on this particular house. Last month they barely squeaked by after paying their monthly expenses plus commuting costs and their electric bill, which, now that school was out and Mitchell and Shayla would be home with Kierra all day, would be even higher. The central air would have to run continuously to keep the house bearable. Back in the Bronx they had room air conditioners in the bedroom windows, but it wasn't bad, even with Con Ed billing at higher rates from April to October, a ridiculous extension of the summer months in a not-all-that-warm Northeast climate. Here, on the other hand, having central air meant they had to pay to cool the entire nineteen-hundred-square-foot house, not just selected rooms.

And this month, with the money they'd spent on food, beer, and wine for their housewarming party, they'd be lucky if they had anything left at all.

That stabbing feeling returned, and this time she knew she wouldn't be able to shake it.

"So, Lance, what do you think of the place?" Reuben asked, genially patting his friend Lance Howard on the back. By 7:30 most of the guests had left to return to the city, with Lance himself about to embark on the long drive.

Camille waited confidently for their friend's response. Lance had worked construction in New York for fifteen years, and he knew a thing or two about buildings. His endorsement would affirm her and Reuben's decision to move here and quiet everyone's criticism once and for all.

"Nice layout," Lance replied. "I like the way they put the laundry room upstairs."

"Layout? You're kidding, right?" Reuben wore an amused expression that matched his body stance of arms held slightly out, bent up at the elbow and his palms facing outward. "Who cares about the layout? How's the house *constructed,* man? You're the expert."

"Hey, I'm no expert."

Reuben clearly didn't buy it. "Whattaya mean, you're no expert? You know enough to probably build a house yourself, from foundation to roof."

Lance's seeming reluctance to answer puzzled Camille. Why the hesitation?

He finally answered. "Listen, I've been in construction for nearly twenty years, and I've got to tell you I'm not too impressed with the way they built this house."

Reuben drew back his head on his neck, clearly taken aback by Lance's words. "Whatchoo talkin' 'bout, Lance?" he demanded, unintentionally sounding just like Gary Coleman during his *Diff'rent Strokes* heyday.

"Nails are sticking out all over your siding, especially in the back of the house," he explained. "That suggests carelessness to me. I wouldn't be surprised if your siding started peeling within two years. And worse, I didn't see any signs of sealant under the siding," he said, "and when I tapped on the walls they sound hollow. I don't think the builder did a good job of insulating. But I never claimed to be an expert. The real test will be when it gets cold."

Camille's eyes went to Reuben, who looked as dazed as she felt. Then she looked at her brother-in-law, Saul, who wore an amused smile. Fortunately, both Brenda and Arnelle had already left with Ginny, although she knew Saul would be sure to tell them all about Lance's comments.

Camille squared her shoulders in defiance. She wouldn't have expected it of Lance, but he was acting just like the others. Just about every one of their friends, and certainly her in-laws, first praised the neighborhood and the house, then finished with something negative, along the lines of Brenda's comment about their long commute limiting the amount of time they had to enjoy their new home. Saul said he would feel uncomfortable living around so many white people. Arnelle said she would never allow her children to go in a pool with no lifeguard on duty.

She'd suffered through comments of that ilk all afternoon. Even her mother-in-law, Ginny, gave a backhanded compliment. "I'm glad you two put my sister's money to good use," she said.

Camille knew jealousy lurked behind all the negativity. Still, she thought Lance, one of Reuben's closest friends and the best man at their wedding, was above all that.

As far as she was concerned they could all go back to New York and never come back. She and Reuben would be better off without them.

Chapter 15

The Youngs
August 2002

Dawn's shoulders twitched with excitement. She had never dreamed she would one day experience this happy situation. She and Milo signed paper after paper, and in a few minutes they would be given the keys to their new home. She felt not only happy but proud.

"And this is a breakdown of your monthly payment," the broker said, showing them the latest in the dwindling stack of papers they still had to sign.

Dawn gasped. Her eyes automatically went to the total at the bottom of the page, which was $1,020.

Milo saw it, too. "I don't get it," he said. "What's all this extra stuff? I know we bought a larger model and got some extras, but even with that we were told we'd only be paying $850."

Dawn's mind swirled. She only half-heard as the agent explained about the escrow account, from which their home owner's insurance and taxes would be paid. All she knew was that it meant an extra $170 each month they hadn't planned on spending. They already had to shell out $480 a month for bus fare. On top of that, they'd visited the local Thomasville Furniture Gallery in Scranton and bought new furniture for their bedroom plus sets for the living room and dining room. Everything was scheduled to be delivered just days after they moved in. It cost over four thousand dollars. For the first time she felt a sense of alarm. Where would all this extra cash come from?

"Well, this comes as an unpleasant surprise," Milo said with a grunt. "Another $170 every month. You really shouldn't go around advertising affordable mortgage payments and then tell people at their closings about an escrow account."

"There certainly was no secrecy involved. We clearly advertised $740 for mortgage principal and interest," the agent clarified, sounding just a tad defensive. "Most lenders open escrow accounts for their mortgagees to pay their taxes and insurance. If not, the mortgage holder has to pay them directly themselves. There's no escaping death and taxes." He chuckled at his little joke, but neither Dawn nor Milo cracked a smile.

Instead Milo held his pen still over the paper, staring at the number on the bottom.

"Uh, Mr. Young. I can understand this comes as a shock if you didn't know about it previously, but is there a problem?" the agent prompted.

Milo looked at Dawn, and she gave him what she hoped looked like a reassuring smile.

"No, I guess not," he finally said. He signed the page and then handed the clipboard to her.

They left the closing, Dawn clutching the bottle of champagne given to them at the conclusion by its neck. "I don't know, Dawn," Milo said. "I guess I should have done some homework before contracting to have this place built. I don't know escrow from enchiladas."

"I didn't know, either, but what could we do? It's not like we can talk to any of our friends about it. They wouldn't know any more than us. And I wouldn't want to ask anyone at work. I don't want those people in my business." Or to know how little she really knew about this whole home-buying thing. The only thing they'd looked into ahead of time was the cost of bus passes and parking at the station. It occurred to her that she could have gone to the library and read up about home ownership, but now that they'd officially taken ownership there seemed little point in doing it now.

"We've already got the added expense of bus passes to get to and from work, Dawn. When you add in the cost of parking at the station all day, that's over five hundred dollars a month by itself. Now we've got this extra payment for escrow. We already know we'll have to pay an electric bill and buy a washer and dryer and a lawn mower.

All these extra expenses add up to a lot of money. I'm not sure if we're going to be able to make it."

"Of course we'll make it, Milo. We shouldn't have to commute into the city for long. We'll get jobs in Pennsylvania, eventually, and we can drive to work like a lot of people in the suburbs do."

"Work in Pennsylvania? Where, at Wal-Mart? Dawn, have you looked at a map recently? Tobyhanna is in the middle of nowhere. There isn't even a McDonald's in town, for heaven's sake. The nearest one is in Mount Pocono."

"Milo, most of America is made up of small- and medium-sized towns. Everybody doesn't work at Wal-Mart or McDonald's. If anything, it might be harder for me to find a job, but you're a programmer. You can't tell me that no one in Scranton or Wilkes-Barre has a need for programmers. And those cities aren't that far away, maybe twenty-five miles. That's a reasonable commute."

"Well, maybe. But somehow I doubt it."

She tried again. "Look. Even Newark is closer than going all the way to the city, and they already have vans going there. Both of us might be able to find something closer, and the commute won't only be cheaper, it'll be shorter."

Milo's thoughtful look told her she'd accomplished her goal of trying to get him to feel better. After all, they'd just closed on their house and been given the keys. Tomorrow they would load up the rented truck and drive to Pennsylvania. Their good friends Donald and Carmen Triggs would help them load up, drive down with them, help unload the truck, spend the night, and then drive back on Sunday. Because of the new furniture they'd bought, most of their belongings were simply boxed up.

Dawn looked forward to having Carmen keep her company during the long drive. Zach would ride with Milo in the rented truck, and Donald would drive the family car with their son, who was just one year younger than Zach. The two boys had been friends all their lives.

"This is such a beautiful house," Carmen said with admiration.

Upon arriving at the house, Dawn and Milo gave them a tour. "It even *smells* new. And to think it's all yours."

"Thanks, but we can't take credit. It's actually the bank's house," Milo joked.

"I can't wait to see your new furniture."

Milo grunted, and Carmen looked taken aback.

Dawn jumped in. "It's going to look fabulous. It'll be delivered next week." She hadn't told Carmen about the escrow account or the argument she and Milo had after learning about it. He'd suggested they cancel their furniture order, and she pointed out that all their living room seating—the sofa, loveseat, and chair—was being created with the upholstery they had chosen and they could hardly stop it at this late date. He countered that they should cancel everything but the sofas and chairs. She insisted on going ahead as planned, that they would manage. Things got pretty ugly before he finally relented.

She expected him to eventually give in. Milo had always seen to it that she got whatever she wanted, but he still felt uneasy about the decision. Even now he expressed doubts. "Yeah," he said, "my wife thinks our last name is Rockefeller, not Young. She picked out new everything. You won't recognize this place next time you see it. The only furniture we're keeping besides Zach's room is our living room. It'll go in the den."

"Well . . ." Carmen obviously sensed she'd touched on a sensitive topic. "It all goes together, doesn't it?" she asked brightly. "Brand-new house, brand-new furniture."

"I would have been happy with just a washer and dryer."

"And a dog!" Zach added gleefully.

Milo chuckled. "That's right, Zach. Next week you and I are going to pick out a nice dog who needs a good home."

"Your own washer and dryer," Carmen said wistfully. "I'm really envious of you guys. I'll think of you, Dawn, every time I go to my building's laundry room and find that someone has taken my clothes out of the dryer and dropped them on the floor while doing it, usually in a puddle of dirty water."

Dawn laughed. "Well, we'll probably get a few more new things, like curtains and bathroom towels."

She ignored Milo's dubious look and hoped he wouldn't open his mouth. Their worries about paying the bills should be kept private. If he objected to her buying a few towels, that would really make them look bad in front of their friends.

Fortunately, Carmen didn't appear to notice the tension. "Did you see the stunned look on Gloria Hudson's face when she saw us carrying out the furniture and you told her y'all had bought a house?"

The memory made Dawn smile. Gloria had immediately fired off about ten questions, but Dawn politely blew her off, saying they had a lot of work to do and not a lot of time.

"That woman is a busybody," Milo said with a grunt. "Wants to get into everybody's business so she can tell all she knows."

"They ought to give her a bugle and let her stand on the corner and make announcements on the hour, like an old-fashioned town crier," Donald said, laughing.

"I'm just glad you didn't tell her anything, Dawn," Milo said.

Carmen made a grunting noise. "Not knowing any details won't stop her from talking. What she doesn't know she'll just make up. I wonder if she ever got back the housewares she claimed she lent to Hazel? She must have told everyone in the building about that."

Dawn took a moment to say a prayer for her late neighbor, whose murder remained unsolved after nearly a year.

Dawn waved to Milo, then yawned deeply as she half-stumbled onto the bus. Something hadn't felt right when she opened her eyes in response to the alarm. Quickly she realized that it was pitch-dark outside. Just as quickly she had another thought, one much more sobering.

This is how it would be from now on.

Now she wished she hadn't taken all those stray vacation days earlier in the year. Milo had decided to take two weeks off for the move, but she took only one. She wanted to save some time to take around Thanksgiving and Christmas. So he had another week to enjoy getting acclimated to the area, and she embarked on what would become a five-day-a-week commute to the city. At 5:40 in the morning. She'd had to get up at the ungodly hour of 4:15 AM. *No one should have to get up that damn early unless they're anchoring* The Today Show *for six million a year.* Of course, Milo had to get up, too, to get her to the station, but he could drive back home and go back to bed, and of course that was precisely what he would do. What else was there to do at that hour?

Dawn found her fellow commuters to be a friendly bunch, asking her if she was new to the area and introducing themselves, seeming genuinely welcoming. Among them was another black couple about her own age, Camille and Reuben. She made it a point to remember their names.

As she expected, within thirty minutes into the trip the bus grew completely quiet as the passengers dozed off. The bus, which originated in Tobyhanna, made stops in Mount Pocono and Stroudsburg before getting on the highway for the remainder of the trip. It finally pulled into Port Authority a few minutes after 8:00, which gave her plenty of time to get to her office before nine. She'd spoken with her boss, who agreed to allow her to leave a few minutes before five, provided she got in before nine. If she missed the 5:35 bus back to Pennsylvania she had to hang around Port Authority until the next one left at 6:05.

She decided to walk to the office to save carfare. Good Lord, wasn't she spending enough on commuting expenses without having to shell out another two bucks for a MetroCard?

She headed toward the Forty-Second Street exit, behind the woman named Camille from the bus. She couldn't see her face, but she recognized the two-piece short-sleeved print dress Camille had on, the short skirt falling above her knees and showing off shapely legs, probably the high point of her pudgy figure. An animal print canvas bag hung from one of her hands, a white blazer was draped over the bend of her arm.

Dawn had walked nearly two blocks behind Camille when she decided it was silly not to say anything to her. Better to walk with someone than alone. Besides, she was anxious to meet other people who lived in Monroe County. She could probably learn a few things. She watched as Camille's hair, falling slightly past her shoulders in a shiny cascade, bounced as she walked. Dawn wore her own hair in a short cut, but she'd love to know who in Monroe County relaxed Camille's hair so she could make an appointment there herself.

She quickened her steps and caught up with Camille, who moved with typical midtown Manhattan briskness. "Hi there. I'm Dawn, and I met you on the bus. I hope you don't mind. I figured we might as well walk together if we're going the same way."

The woman smiled. "Yes, please join me. My name's Camille Curry. You work over this way, Dawn?"

"Yes. I've been behind you for a couple of blocks now, and I finally told myself this is silly. How far are you going?"

"Fifth and Forty-Seventh."

"I'm at Madison and Forty-Third."

Camille smiled. "About the same distance, give or take. But it's nice to have someone to walk with."

*   *   *

By the end of the week Dawn could easily match names with faces of all the regulars on the bus. Like her and Milo, they all came from New York and had at least one child, and they all had the desire to become home owners, despite the impracticality of working so far away. But she felt a special bond with Camille and Reuben Curry and Veronica and Norman Lee. She'd met the latter couple, one at a time, on the afternoon bus. Neither couple had lived in the area for more than a few months, but they still provided a wealth of information for her and Milo while they learned their way around Toby-hanna.

The following Monday she shook Milo awake after she finished in the bathroom. He replied with his customary, "Ten more minutes." It didn't worry her; he always dressed in a flash anyway.

In the kitchen she gathered the hero sandwiches she'd made the night before and placed them in insulated soft nylon lunch bags, along with fresh bagels and nonleak thermos bottles filled with juice. She dropped dollops of cream cheese into small plastic containers. Just because they had moved into their house didn't mean they should stop the money-saving habits they'd developed while amassing their down payment. That unpleasant surprise they received at the closing was an excellent impetus for trying to conserve cash. Besides, Camille made lunch for herself and Reuben every day.

Dawn's efforts to cut back made her feel a lot less apprehensive about meeting their obligations. Carrying breakfast and lunch four days out of five saved a small fortune, but to keep from feeling deprived they agreed to allow themselves one day each week to buy meals out.

Before she and Milo left the house they both stopped in Zachary's room. "Zach, can you hear me?" Milo asked. When the sleepy boy nodded, he said, "Your mom and I are leaving now. We'll call and make sure you're up, and you call the cell if there's any problem. After you walk Stormy and you're ready to leave for school, all you have to do is make sure the latch is on the door." During Milo's week off he had driven Zach to the local pound, and they came home with a bulldog Zach promptly named Stormy. "Do you remember how to do it?"

"I'll hear it click," Zachary mumbled.

"That's right, son." Milo rubbed his shoulder, and Dawn bent to kiss his cheek.

"I don't like this," Milo muttered as they left the house. "He's just turned ten. He's too young to be left alone in the middle of the damn night."

"It's not really the middle of the night, Milo. Zach gets up at seven. That's less than two hours from now. And Stormy is in the house with him. She'll bark like crazy if anyone shows up." Dawn felt reassured by her own words, even if she did feel that Stormy was the ugliest creature she'd ever laid eyes on. "He'll be fine."

Milo grunted in response.

She proudly introduced Milo to all their fellow commuters, and to Veronica Lee on the return trip. Norman Lee, who worked Thursday through Sunday, and Veronica, who worked Monday, Tuesday, and Wednesday, took the first bus out in the morning, which left at 3:45 AM, to allow them to work ten hours a day.

Milo promptly fell asleep, waking up just as the bus rolled into Port Authority. Dawn affectionately covered the back of his hand with her palm. The one week head start she had had made her feel like a pro, but her husband looked like he ought to still be at home in bed. "You all right?" she asked as he rubbed the sleep from his eyes.

"Yeah, I'm okay. This commute is going to be murder."

"You'll get used to it. It's a routine, just like anything else."

"I don't know, Dawn," he said, reaching for his lunch bag. "I just don't know."

Chapter 16

The Currys
September 2002

Camille promptly picked up the receiver when her buzzer sounded, praying her boss wouldn't want anything urgent twenty-five minutes before quitting time. She liked to rush out at the stroke of 5:00 to make sure she caught her bus. "Yes, Mr. Stephens."

"Camille, please come in."

She rolled her eyes. Her boss knew she left work promptly to make sure she got to Port Authority before 5:35. He'd already made her miss it once with a last-minute urgent assignment. By the time she got to Port Authority the last bus of the day, the 6:20, had just departed. Not only did she have to sleep on her father's couch in Inwood, but she had to buy a new outfit to wear to work the next day. Thank God she managed to find something on sale. She hated the thought of spending forty dollars she really couldn't afford, but at her office employee wardrobe held high importance. An account executive whose wife had left him began showing up for work in shirts that looked like he'd slept in them, and not long after he lost his job. Even secretaries were expected to wear suits or at least tailored separates. If she showed up wearing the same outfit on consecutive days, the gossip would have her living on skid row.

She enjoyed her work in the fast-paced environment of marketing, and George Stephens was as good a boss as any.

Notebook and pen in hand, she entered his office. "Here I am."

"You won't have to write anything down. Have a seat."

Apprehension filled her belly. She'd been called in to the boss's office at 4:30 on a Friday. Could she be about to lose her job? How could that be? George had always been satisfied with her work, or at least he claimed to be. She'd worked here longer than he had, staying on after her old boss went to a competitor. She'd only worked for George a little over a year. Maybe he wanted to bring in his own secretary?

No, she decided. He couldn't be giving her the ax, not with that big Jimmy Carter grin on his face. If anything, maybe he'd accepted a better position and he wanted her to be the first to know of his impending departure. And she'd be left to break in a new boss. Ugh. Just what she needed, another idiosyncrasy-plagued personality to cope with. And would this one like or dislike the use of serial commas in his documents? How would he want his coffee, black or with sugar? And, most important of all, would he be understanding of her schedule or would she be relegated to going home on the 6:05 from now on? A half an hour extra was a big deal with a workday as long as hers.

"Is something wrong?" she asked tentatively.

"Camille, I'm being promoted."

"You are! To what?"

"They made me a director. I'll be moving upstairs."

To the thirty-sixth floor with the senior management, she knew. The department had been buzzing about what management would do to fill in the vacancy resulting from the retirement of one of the vice presidents and the subsequent placement of one of the directors into that position. So ol' George had been made a director. She wished *she* could move up in the organization, but there was no place for her to go, not with just a high school diploma.

But this was no time to think about herself. "Oh, how wonderful for you!" she exclaimed, effectively masking the sadness she felt. "It looks like I'll have to begin work with a new manager." She sighed. "It's happened before. Just when I get used to someone's personality and habits they move on."

"Not this time, Camille. I'd like you to come along."

Her mouth fell open for a second, then formed a somewhat bashful smile. "Me? Working up on thirty-six?"

"Why not? You're bright and efficient. Why shouldn't you be up there?" He smiled at her warmly. "It would mean a salary increase for you, too, if you accept."

A salary increase? *If* she accepted? Was he crazy?

"I accept."

"The executive level, huh? Well, I guess all that money you spent on your suits will pay off after all," Reuben said with a broad grin when she told him the good news.

"He said he's going to try to get me 15 percent, to bring me in line with what the other secretaries on that floor are getting."

"That sounds good, Camille, but don't go redoing our budget yet. Wait until you know for sure what you'll get."

"I think it's a reasonable request. I'm sure *he's* getting at least 15 percent."

"Yes, but he's a director. You're just a secretary."

She could only shrug at that. She wished she'd become more than just a secretary, but no one had stressed the importance of a college education to her. Her high school guidance counselor had mentioned career options like beauty school or fast food management. Even her own mother, who had died of an abdominal aneurysm when Camille was nineteen, used to tell her to choose a husband carefully, as if that would solve all her problems. The negative comments from Reuben's relatives when they announced they were building a house had roots in jealousy of Aunt Mary's bequest, but her own family had accepted and even embraced the status quo. Her father, stepmother, and brother had no expectations from life, content to know they'd never go hungry and would always have a roof over their heads—a rented roof. She'd never be able to convince them that upward mobility wasn't a sin.

She ended up enrolling in a secretarial school after she had gotten her first job as a receptionist, knowing that unless she did something she'd be greeting clients until she got old and gray. She'd been impressed with Reuben's associate degree when she first met him at a downtown club when she was twenty-two, but now she knew that two years of college meant nothing in today's tough job market. Mitchell and Shayla would both get bachelor's degrees, and maybe even master's. Just let some white guidance counselor try to steer Shayla toward doing nails or Mitchell toward working at McDonald's, like they'd done to her. She'd tell them in an instant that they were full of shit, that her kids *were* college material. Now that she was thirty-five instead of sixteen, she had a pretty good idea that her counselor had made recommendations along ethnic lines, steering white students toward college and black and Hispanic students to trade schools. She never claimed to be the brightest bulb in the class, but she was certainly smart enough to go to college and earn a degree.

Look at that Dan Quayle. The man had the brains of a bag of hair extensions, he'd managed to get a law degree and become vice president of the United States, a heartbeat away from the most powerful job in the entire world. But he was white and wealthy. Dawn bet no guidance counselor had tried to get *him* to flip hamburgers while he learned the fast food business. The old double standard at work again. People like Britney Spears and Barbra Streisand could spell their first names different from the standard and be considered unique, while when a black person does that, people say they can't spell.

Every now and then Camille toyed with the idea of enrolling in college on a weekend program, but decided she'd waited too long. In five years she'd be forty. Besides, now that she spent so much time going to and from work she really had no time for sitting in a classroom or studying. Reuben did well at the supermarket, and with her raise they'd do fine.

Two weeks later Camille found out that a 10 percent increase had been approved for her. She'd initially been disappointed, having hoped for the 15 percent George had said he'd request for her, but office scuttlebutt had it that the cost-of-living increases being given hovered around 4 percent, so at least she'd gotten two and a half times more than the standard. It just went to show that Reuben had been right; she shouldn't start spending the extra money until she knew exactly what she'd be getting.

One thing for sure, they certainly could use the extra income.

Chapter 17

The Youngs
October 2002

Dawn always felt rejuvenated when the bus reached Mount Pocono, the next-to-last stop of their commute. About half of the remaining commuters got off here.

She looked up curiously as Veronica Lee climbed aboard the bus as soon as the door opened. Veronica usually drove to the station to pick Norman up—like most transplants from the city, they were a one-car family—but simply waved to them from outside as she waited with their two young daughters. Something special had to be happening.

Norman moved to stand behind her at the front of the bus. They made a cute couple, with Veronica so petite and Norman so strapping, although he was more beefy than tall, standing maybe five-ten.

"This will only take a minute," Norman said to the driver before addressing the remaining riders. "Good news, everybody," he announced. "Veronica and I have both accepted positions at the Pocono Medical Center. Another two weeks and we won't be joining you for the ride home."

Applause and wild shouts broke out. Even the bus driver applauded.

"We're going to have a barbecue to celebrate, and you'll all be invited," Veronica said generously.

The Lees shared congratulatory handshakes with the riders getting off, then moved forward to accept the good wishes of their fellow riders. Dawn and Camille congratulated them, as did Milo and Reuben. "How about stopping by the house tonight for a drink to celebrate?" Camille offered.

"Thanks, Camille," Veronica said, "but the girls are in the car, and Norman and I need to go over some things. It's sweet of you to invite us. Maybe another time." She shrugged. "It's hard to get an evening out when you don't have anyone to watch your kids for you."

"I'm sorry we didn't get to know each other better, Veronica," Dawn said, feeling a little sad.

Veronica feigned indignation. "This isn't good-bye, Dawn. I hope we'll see each other often. And I certainly expect to see you and Milo at our party."

Norman pulled at her sleeve. "C'mon, Vee. We don't want to hold up the bus. Everybody wants to get home."

Dawn beamed. "Thanks, Veronica. We'd love to come, and we're happy to be included, since we're the new kids on the block."

As the bus pulled out of the station Dawn watched Veronica and Norman walking to their car with their arms around each other. They looked so happy, and why wouldn't they be? No more getting up at three in the morning to get the first bus of the day and getting home after seven at night. Even done just three or four days a week instead of five, it had to feel a little like getting out of jail.

"I wish that was us," Dawn said wistfully to Milo as they drove home. "Two weeks from now they'll be able to drive a half hour or so to work while we're still getting up to catch that damn bus. And listen to all those retired folks singing show tunes on matinee Wednesdays."

"I wish it was us, too."

"Why don't you look and see if you can get a job at that hospital? Everybody needs programmers. Hell, I'll check their Web site myself. They might need someone to run their payroll department." But even as Dawn spoke she knew the low likelihood of getting a decent position, as she had no previous hospital experience. The most she'd probably be able to get would be a clerical position, and she'd be crazy to take that kind of pay cut. Plus, she wasn't sure she'd want to work a full-time schedule squeezed into three or four days a week.

The Lees

Each week Norman attended the free do-it-yourself workshops at the Home Depot in Stroudsburg, and Veronica and the girls had come along this time. She had already picked up a few things at the Target in the shopping center out front, bought the kids ice cream at the snack bar, and was now enjoying herself as she walked along the aisles of the home improvement store looking at all the modern fixtures. How nice it would be to have a kitchen with nice light-colored cabinets instead of those dreary dark brown cupboards they had now that made the room seem so dim, even in bright sunshine.

When the girls tired of looking at model kitchens and pedestal sinks, Veronica led them to the paint and wallpaper area. They selected a wallpaper runner for the girls' room. Their room was painted lilac, but the floral runner would provide a nice break in the solid walls. Norman had probably learned enough by now to be able to glue it to the wall without it being crooked. He'd really benefited from those free classes. He'd already put in a beautiful new faucet in the kitchen. Today he was learning how to do flooring. Maybe they could tear up that dreadful burnt-orange shag carpet themselves and put down hardwood and area rugs.

Their house, while certainly well-built, comfortable, and up to all codes, needed cosmetic updating to look more twenty-first century. After slashing expenses to the bone to pay down much of their credit card debt, they'd been happy to find a house with three bedrooms for the same money they would have paid for the two-bedroom they initially fell in love with. The house they bought was newer, although it hadn't been modernized, like the first house they wanted. Veronica regretted that it had no fireplaces—her dream of making love to Norman on a bearskin rug went up in smoke—but she had to agree they would get more use out of a guest bedroom. Plus, she liked the way the house was laid out, with the entire second floor dedicated to the master suite, including a full bath.

As their sales agent had pointed out, the Cape Cod structure had great potential. They'd already done quite a bit with paint, and to get more decorating ideas she went to open houses and model homes. At her suggestion, Norman changed all the doorknobs on the bedroom doors from those old-fashioned knobs that looked like oversized faux diamonds to gracefully curved brass handles. That small step went a long way toward a more modern look.

She just wished they could do the whole house over right away, especially after seeing what Camille and Reuben had done to their place. The Currys had such a lovely home, all modern, with brand-new furniture. She had mentioned it to Norman on the way home from the barbecue, and he remarked that they'd probably bought all those new furnishings on credit. "Remember, misusing our credit almost prevented us from buying a house in the first place. We don't want to use credit anymore unless we absolutely have to," he reminded her. "In the meantime, our stove might be old, but it cooks food just fine."

"So how'd it go?" Veronica asked when Norman emerged from the workshop.

"Pretty good. I want to pick up some supplies before we leave. I thought I'd start by tearing up the carpet in the dining room and laying down hardwood."

"Can you get that done this weekend?"

"If I can't, so what? I'll finish it next week, or the week after that. That's the beauty of doing the work yourself. Not only is the price right, but you can work at your own pace."

"But we're having a party next weekend, remember? Duane is coming, and so are our sisters." They hadn't seen any of them since they'd moved. "We want the house to look nice for company, don't we?"

"Lucy and Valerie are family, and Duane might as well be. As far as our guests are concerned, they'll understand that we're working on the house. It's not like we'll have lumber piled up in the middle of the living room, Veronica."

He had a point, she decided. It would probably look better for them to be in a state of updating than to give the impression of being perennially stuck in a time warp thirty-five years behind the times. Of course, Norman, being a man, didn't care about such things, but she did.

Several other guests danced to the old tune by Stevie Wonder in the Lee's basement, but Dawn sat it out, nursing a Rum and Coke and sneaking peeks at her surroundings.

Camille leaned toward her and whispered, "Are you as surprised as I am?"

Dawn flinched. She hadn't thought anyone would notice her look of disdain, and it embarrassed her to have been noticed, but in truth she *was* surprised. She'd known Veronica and Norman had bought a home in Mount Pocono, but she'd thought it was in a new development, like Arlington Acres. The Lee's home was easily thirty-five years old, maybe even older. The carpets were actually shag, burnt-orange upstairs and multicolored, like confetti, here in the basement. The kitchen appliances clearly dated to the seventies, in that avocado green color so popular at that time. The hall bath was actually done in pink—pink tiles, pink sink and toilet, pink tub. She felt like she'd died and gone to Graceland.

"I expected something different," she admitted, speaking just as quietly. "It's not Arlington Acres, that's for sure."

"Hey, Vee, we need more ginger ale," Norman yelled from the foot of the stairs.

Camille laughed. "Norman, I'm sure she can't hear you. I'll go up and tell her."

"I'll go with you," Dawn said. "Maybe we can help her with whatever she's doing. I'm sure she can use a hand."

They walked past a dancing Norman and climbed the stairs, Camille leading the way. They emerged in a corner of the kitchen. "Veronica, Norman says he needs more ginger ale," she said.

"Can we help you do anything?" Dawn offered.

"Thanks, but I'm just about ready. I wanted to put out the food and punch." Veronica had lined the white speckled Formica countertops with large, foil-covered lasagna pans, also made of foil. She reached into the refrigerator and pulled out a two-liter bottle of ginger ale. "Would one of you mind bringing this downstairs? And tell Norman to let everyone know they can eat."

"Sure, I'll do it," Camille said.

She took off down the stairs, bottle in hand.

"What can I do, Veronica?" Dawn offered.

"Can you get the salad dressing out of the fridge?"

"Sure." Dawn opened the refrigerator, which, like the stove, dishwasher, and range hood, looked ancient. The cold air that instantly chilled her hands told her that, old as it was, it did its job of keeping their food fresh. Several different flavors of salad dressing were on the door. "All of them?"

"Yes, so there'll be something for everybody's taste. Let's see . . . We'll need butter, too, for the rolls, and mustard. It's all in there."

"Okay, I'll get it."

"We're going to update the kitchen in a couple of months," Veronica said suddenly, just as Camille reentered the kitchen after her quick trip to the basement.

Dawn bit her lower lip guiltily. Had Veronica been reading her mind?

Camille's breathing halted for a few seconds. What would make Veronica make a statement like that out of the blue? Surely Dawn hadn't revealed the content of their private conversation when she thought she was alone with Veronica . . . ?

"I can't wait," Veronica continued. With her petite build and casual attire of T-shirt and jeans, her relaxed hair parted on the side and falling to just above her shoulders in a slight flip, she looked like a high school kid. "This house was built in 1966. We knew it needed modernizing when we bought it, but for us it made sense. The house is solidly built—the wiring, plumbing, foundation—and the roof was replaced two years ago. All the appliances work fine, so we can replace them at our convenience. Norman wanted to wait until after we got our transfers, when we wouldn't have to buy bus passes anymore."

Camille had held her breath as long as she could, and now her shoulders relaxed. There'd been no breach of confidence; Veronica was merely making conversation with Dawn. Maybe she felt she needed to defend this pleasant but old house. Camille doubted Veronica had been a guest at the Young home—she had yet to be invited there herself—but she'd seen model homes at Arlington Acres and knew how nice and modern they all were. Maybe Veronica even suspected that she and Dawn would privately wrinkle their noses at her house, which, of course, they had.

Camille felt that same twinge of uneasiness she always got when she thought about the larger monthly mortgage payment for the lakefront lot and larger home they'd chosen. Maybe the feeling that their champagne taste would lead to trouble would go away once and for all now that she'd gotten her raise. Like Reuben had said, it would all work out.

She hoped.

"I think that's smart, Veronica," Dawn was saying. "I wish Milo and I could get good-paying jobs locally."

"Maybe you will."

"I doubt it. Besides, I've worked for the same company for so long ever since I finished high school. Part of me would be scared to leave, unless I really felt I had a secure future." She slowly shook her head. "And who feels secure after 9/11?"

"And that mess at Enron," Camille added.

"I feel terribly sorry for those people who lost their pensions. And every time the bus pulls into Port Authority, or when I get on the subway, I say a prayer asking to get out of there alive," Veronica admitted.

"You're lucky you won't have to do it anymore." Dawn wiped some crumbs off the counter and dropped them in the trash. "Hey, do you guys have to pay for trash collection out here? This isn't a subdivision, is it?"

"It's not a subdivision, but we do pay for trash collection. The service picks up once a week."

"But you don't have any association fees or anything like that, huh?"

"No, none of that stuff. That was one reason Norman liked the idea of buying outside of a subdivision."

"Y'all knew about all the fees beforehand?" Dawn asked, surprise in her voice.

Veronica's face wrinkled in thought. "Now that you mention it, I don't think any of the salespeople brought it up. But Norman and I knew from a home buyer's workshop we attended at our credit union in the city that most developments charge for upkeep of common areas, so we asked about it." She shrugged. "We looked at a couple of subdivisions, and I wonder if any of them would have told us about it if we hadn't asked. I'm inclined to think not. They were all a bunch of eager beavers, anxious to make a sale, especially the guy at Arlington Acres." She snapped her fingers. "Eric Nylund, that was his name. Funny how it just came to me this second. Remember, Camille? We talked about him before, but I couldn't remember his name."

"You had Eric, too?" Camille asked. "He must have been gunning for salesperson of the month, the way he was pushing those lakefront lots. And of course, Reuben and I ended up buying one."

Dawn chimed in. "Us, too. Eric greeted Milo and me the moment we walked into the sales office like he was thrilled to see us," she recalled. "He said we would get a free fireplace and deck if we agreed to buy that day. Milo and I felt we hit the jackpot. We'd barely been in Pennsylvania for an hour, although we'd planned on spending the day out here looking around."

Veronica stared at them incredulously. "You mean that you and Milo bought a house the first day you were out here?"

"Uh . . . yes." Dawn's face wore a "What's wrong with that?" expression. "We figured it would be either too good to be true or something we could manage, and it wouldn't take anymore than one day to figure that out." She paused. "Didn't you?"

"Norman and I took a three-day weekend to check things out. Lorinda and Simone came with us."

Camille shrugged. "We bought in one day, too. When Reuben and I saw the commercial we talked about it for hours. We decided that we would go for it, provided the houses really were as affordable as the commercial said. Our only concern was about the kind of reception we'd get from the white folks out here. That turned out not to be a problem." She giggled. "It's a cinch the neighbors wouldn't have been that happy to see us in, say, Riverdale."

"Norman was worried about that, too, especially when we started looking here in Mount Pocono," Veronica said. "But, as it turns out, there are more of our people out here than in Tobyhanna."

The door to the basement opened. "I hear y'all got good eats up here," one of their fellow commuters said cheerfully. Rich Wellington, a normally conservative accountant, had clearly consumed a few drinks.

"Yes," said his wife, Donna, playfully slapping his arm, "and you need to line your stomach with some of it to soak up all that alcohol."

"Well, everything's out and waiting for you," Veronica said. "We were about to send a search party for you, but I had a feeling the music had something to do with it."

"Couldn't think about eating until we finished getting our groove on," Reuben said, swinging his hips for emphasis. "But now we're ready to chow down."

Veronica went to stand next to Norman as their guests helped themselves. He looked at the plentiful spread. "You did good, Vee."

"Thanks. I think it's going well, don't you?"

He kissed her cheek. "Absolutely."

She felt proud, of both herself and of Norman. A successful party meant good music, and good food and drink, which were easy to provide; but most of all it meant good people, which were far more difficult to obtain. Fortunately, they'd met nice people on the bus, couples their own age, and while they came from different ethnic backgrounds, they all wanted the same things out of life: a piece of the American dream for themselves and their children.

Even their friend Duane London had come out from the city with his latest girlfriend to spend the night. So did Norman's only sister, Lucy, and Veronica's sister, Valerie, who brought her twelve-year-old daughter, Essence. Lucy and Valerie would bunk on the pull-out sofa in the living room, and Essence would sleep on a trundle bed in the girls' room.

She watched as Duane teased Valerie about her ability to eat chicken down to the bone so it didn't look like there had ever been any meat on it. Duane was on the thin side, but his six foot three height next to Valerie's petite five two frame almost made him appear like a bully. Only Valerie's good-natured dismissal of his ribbing prevented the scene from looking like harassment.

"Have you ever thought about entering one of those hot dog eating contests?" Duane asked Valerie. "You'd probably walk off with first prize."

"And win, what, a lifetime supply of hot dogs for my indigestion? Forget it. Besides, just because I can clean chicken bones doesn't mean I can wolf down twenty hot dogs in a minute."

Duane's girlfriend, whose name Veronica couldn't remember, tugged at his arm. "Duane, I think you should leave her alone."

"Aw, it wouldn't be the same if I didn't tease Valerie a little. She'd think the real me had been invaded by body snatchers or something."

Veronica smiled. Duane's latest flame clearly felt threatened by his easy camaraderie with Valerie. Duane and Valerie had known each other for years. One thing Veronica felt certain of—this woman would be gone from Duane's life in another month or so. If anything, her clucking would shorten her tenure as his lady of the moment. She no longer felt badly about hardly remembering any of their names.

Duane, who had helped them move their belongings from New York, would be their first overnight guest to sleep in their spare room. He had driven back to New York the afternoon they moved, since they hadn't yet shopped for a bed to put in the third bedroom. Veronica couldn't think of a person she'd rather have for that distinction. He'd been a good friend for many years. It was Duane who'd heard about the opening in their Washington Heights apartment building when they were desperately looking for a larger place. He'd helped with that move, too.

She accepted the compliments of their guests as, one by one, they fixed plates and descended the stairs with them. She and Norman were fortunate to have met such nice people here in Pennsylvania. They had so much to look forward to. She'd always loved entertaining. She felt more than a little sad when Norman put his foot down after their last party, at which the strangers nearly outnumbered familiar faces. "To hell with people we invited showing up with three and four of their friends, passing them off as neighbors or people they've known for years. What do I care how well they know them? They're complete strangers to us. Can't anybody go anywhere by themselves nowadays? We had so many people in here we've never seen before that poor Duane didn't even want to take off his coat."

She agreed. The house party had become a rarity in New York— many a host had been turned off by drug-abusing guests—but now that they had a house of their own she intended to do a lot of entertaining. She daydreamed about how she'd furnish their basement, which now just held some folding chairs and secondhand accent tables. Part of it was dedicated to laundry, but even with that they still had plenty of room down there. She couldn't wait to buy furniture and make it a true rec room.

All she could do for now was entertain the possibilities. Norman insisted they pay for the furniture in the guest room before buying anything else. Eventually she'd be able to shop. All they needed was enough money. Hell, all *anybody* needed was enough money.

For now, she had this weekend all planned. Tomorrow morning they'd have a nice leisurely breakfast here at home with Duane, his girlfriend, Lucy, and Valerie. She'd do the pancakes, bacon, sausage, and home fried potatoes first and keep them warm in the oven while she cooked eggs to order for everyone. She had chilled pineapple juice, as well as orange, and would use those new glass pitchers she'd bought at Target. Finally, she'd grab those frozen biscuits she'd bought at BJ's Wholesale Club and pop them in the microwave just before they all sat down. Everyone would have a nice chat about the party and relax until it was time for them to drive back to the city.

Then, on Monday morning, she and Norman would begin work at their new employer, just thirty minutes away from home. They'd secured the same schedules they had last year at Presbyterian before changing to their shortened workweeks in preparation for the move. She would go in at 7:00 AM and Norman at 9:00, so he could bring Lorinda and Simone to school in the morning and she'd get home in the afternoon around the same time they did. She'd be working an extra ten hours from the thirty she'd been putting in, which would make for a bigger check. Best of all, all four of them would be able to sit down to dinner as a family every night, something they hadn't done since the days immediately following their move, during the period of unpacking before returning to work. They'd even be able to join a church, where they'd meet more people.

The fact that their house desperately needed updating seemed a lot less important now. From the conversation she had just had with Dawn and Camille, Veronica got the impression that neither the Youngs nor the Currys had done much homework before plunging into home ownership. Whoever heard of buying a house an hour after you arrived in town, or to come to town with the expectation of making such a substantial purchase in one day? Hadn't Eric's buy-fast-or-lose-out techniques made them wary? She doubted that either couple had even looked at the other subdivisions in the area, much less considered a house already standing. Dawn had even sounded a little concerned about the costs of owning in Arlington Acres, if the questions she asked were any indication.

Veronica couldn't help thinking that Dawn wouldn't mind changing houses with her, even if it meant having a pink bathroom.

Chapter 18

Dawn folded her arms in front of her in annoyance. This shit happened every Wednesday. Retired folks from the area joined them for a ride home after seeing Broadway matinees. Apparently their taste leaned toward musicals, and on the way home they often sang the more catchy parts of the scores of the shows they'd just seen. Loudly.

She'd been taking the bus to work for three months now. The return trip home to Pennsylvania usually included talk and laughter, but these damn sing-alongs really got on her nerves. All they needed was a screen with the words and a bouncing ball, like she'd seen in film shorts on the classic movie station. This group of eight possessed particular verve; they began performing songs from other shows they seen, dating back nearly sixty years. She'd already suffered through "There Is Nothing Like a Dame" from *South Pacific* and "Put On a Happy Face" from *Bye, Bye Birdie*. Now a white-haired man with a big baritone voice led the group in a lusty performance of "They Call The Wind Mariah."

"Hey, that fellow's got a good voice," Milo remarked. "I wonder if he ever sang professionally."

"Look closely. Maybe it's Robert Goulet, taking the bus into the city a couple of times a year from his home in the Poconos to catch the latest Broadway musicals."

He looked at her curiously. "You're in a lovely mood this afternoon."

"Milo, you'll always find more vocal talent in any church across America than you would at the top of the music charts. Lots of everyday people can sing well. But doesn't it get on your nerves, these sing-alongs every week?"

"No, I rather enjoy it." He lowered his voice. "It's better than all the complaints we usually have to listen to."

The theatergoers, perhaps having developed throat soreness from all that tonsillar strain, finally quieted down as the bus approached the southern half of New Jersey. As Milo predicted, someone began a conversation about the usual commuter woes. At least this was easier to ignore. She only half-listened, having heard it many times before.

"So has anybody heard when the train is coming?"

"I wouldn't hold my breath if I were you."

"I wish they'd get those tracks laid. This commute is killing me. I spent all this money for a house and I don't have time to enjoy it, except on the weekends."

All right, so it's a long commute, Dawn thought crankily. *Tell me something I don't know.* She wondered if anyone else had found that living in the country was more expensive than they had bargained for.

She and Milo never had an electric bill when they lived in Brooklyn, only a surcharge during the summer months for air conditioners. Not only did they have an electric bill here, they had to pay for their water and their sewer service, plus trash collection. She wanted to ask, but didn't want it to look like she and Milo were in financial trouble. You had to be careful about things like that. People were always so quick to misinterpret the meaning behind a complaint . . . and equally quick to spread rumors about how so-and-so were in dire straits. That could be why no one wanted to bring it up.

She mentioned it to Milo on Friday night at dinner, after Zach had been granted permission to leave the table. "Do you notice that all anyone complains about is how long it takes to get to the city? But no one complains about all the stuff you have to pay for out here."

"That's because they don't want people to think they're having trouble paying their bills. Or maybe," he added, "we're the only ones who went out and spent almost four thousand dollars on new furniture we couldn't afford." He yawned. "Damn, I'm glad it's Friday. I'm going to sleep all weekend."

Dawn initially felt she was at fault for at least part of their predicament, for she'd been the one to insist they get the best furniture they could afford . . . even if they really couldn't afford it. But she forgot about that when he said he planned to sleep all weekend, which she found distressing. "Milo, the grass needs cutting."

"I'll cut the grass, Dawn. That's just a figure of speech."

No, it's not, she thought. Last weekend, too, he just laid around the house. They'd agreed to clean out the garage together as their weekend project, but she'd ended up getting the job started herself. That was in addition to her regular weekend chores of washing and ironing. They'd bought one of those new front-loading, water-conserving washers. It had been expensive, but at least it used considerably less water, a convenience that for them no longer came free of charge. After all the money they'd spent on furniture, Milo gave her a choice—either a less-expensive, old-fashioned washer and dryer, or for the same money only a front-loading washer, with a dryer to come when they could afford it. Dawn thought about it, and the desire for the more modern won out, even if it meant that until they could afford to buy the matching dryer she had to line-dry the wash.

The Arlington Acres Homeowners Association frowned on this practice, but Dawn rose early to do the wash, and all but the heaviest items were usually dry by early afternoon. In addition to the line, they also had two drying racks, because she liked doing all the laundry on Saturday, leaving Sundays free for ironing. The drying racks couldn't be seen by anyone from the street, but Dawn told Milo that she found it a little embarrassing that all their neighbors knew they didn't have a dryer.

He did not back down. "We just charged four thousand dollars' worth of furniture, plus a lawn mower, and that patio furniture you insisted on getting for the deck," Milo said. "We have to stop buying on credit unless it's a real emergency."

Dawn knew he was right. Their excessive spending habits caused them not to save sufficiently, and if it hadn't been for the deal they'd worked out with the builder they'd still be living in Williamsburg. She knew that, but she also wanted a dryer. It was a lot easier to merely pop wet clothes into the dryer and press the START button than it was to pin them to a clothesline or drape them on a rack, which required each item to be handled separately.

Still, she felt grateful for having her own washer. She continued to marvel every time she filled the cylinder with dirty clothes and started the wash cycle without first having to put six quarters into it. This phenomenon so amazed her that she didn't even mind having an increase in laundry. When they lived in Brooklyn she used to send Milo's tailored shirts out for washing and pressing with medium starch. Now she did them herself in a cost-cutting measure. She didn't particularly care for the ironing part, though. And she couldn't wait to get a dryer.

"I'm going to come to bed early myself tonight, so don't get all spread out," she said to him now. "I want to get up early and get the laundry done so I can finish the garage."

Milo grunted. "You know, that's the second dig you've made on me in the last five minutes. First you tell me to be sure to mow the lawn, and next you point out how you've been cleaning out the garage by yourself. I'm telling you now, don't let there be a third." He tossed his crumpled napkin on his plate and left the table. Minutes later Dawn heard the door to their bedroom slam shut.

She sighed. All right, maybe it *had* been a mild dig. But what worried her was the way he'd changed. The Milo she knew never used to be grumpy like this. His entire personality had changed. The commute had done it to him, she knew. Five hours a day was a heck of a lot of time to spend traveling back and forth to work. But it wore her out, too. She wished he would realize that. Many a weekend she didn't feel like doing anything, either, but if she indulged herself in being lazy their beautiful new home would look like a trash dump, and it wouldn't smell so good, either.

She carried their plates to the sink, rinsed them, and stacked the dishwasher. Dishwashers used more water and certainly more electricity than washing by hand, but, damn it, after making dinner and trying to straighten up she was too tired to wash dishes. She used antibacterial wipes on the countertops where she'd prepared the flour mixture to fry the pork chops and sprayed a degreaser on the stovetop. She frowned as she jiggled the electric coil burner. She hated the way she could never get them to stand straight from the very first time she lifted them to wipe them down. All her pots leaned slightly, which made it difficult to fry evenly. Even her pancakes came out misshapen. If she had to pick one thing she missed from Brooklyn, it would be her gas stove. No way would those heavy cast iron burners lean to one side. She already conceded that she would need to buy an electric griddle to cook pancakes in, and maybe a large electric skillet for other foods, and just use the stovetop for food items that wouldn't be affected by lopsided burners, like boiling pasta or making gravy.

By the time she got to their bedroom after sweeping the floor and starting the dishwasher cycle, Milo was already snoring. He'd stripped down to his underwear and in spite of her warning not to hog the bed lay stretched out across their king-sized mattress, which meant she'd have to nudge him to move over. He'd put on weight since their move, probably from falling asleep right after eating dinner every night. Her own clothes had grown a little snug around the waist. Eating before bedtime was the worst thing a person could do in terms of weight gain, but what choice did they have?

Still, she'd better come up with ways to eat earlier. Even before she'd ever heard of Arlington Acres she'd been trying to take thirty pounds off of her five eight frame. Half the weight she'd picked up over the years had probably gone straight to her butt. She estimated she'd gained at least five pounds in the three months she'd lived here. Her height helped hide the extra weight, but if she didn't halt this weight gain she'd soon eat herself out of a perfectly good wardrobe, something she definitely couldn't afford to do.

But right now she was too tired to worry about that, or anything else.

Dawn gasped at the amount due on their electric bill. Had they really used that much heat? It wasn't even winter yet. Milo would have a cow when he found out.

She took a few minutes to fondly remember their comfortable apartment in Brooklyn, the apartment that they'd paid $720 rent for, including all utilities. They never had to worry about the price to pay for keeping warm, or for taking long, steaming showers.

Instantly she felt guilty. Had she forgotten so quickly how often they'd been forced to go without heat and hot water because of old boilers in disrepair? What about that exhausting trek up twelve flights of stairs when the elevators conked out simultaneously? And what about poor Hazel, strangled to death right next door to them in a crime still unsolved? She couldn't let one high electric heat bill make her wish they still lived there.

But they faced long months of winter weather, and she had to get this bill lowered. Damn it, she'd *told* Milo not to set the thermostat so high. He was used to being all warm and cozy and not having to pay the bill for it, but he had to stop thinking like a renter and start thinking like an owner. They were responsible for the bill. He'd just have to put on a sweater. Maybe she'd buy a couple of colorful throws and drape them across the couch and chairs so there'd always be something handy to bundle up in.

But first she'd turn down the heat to sixty-eight degrees, maybe even sixty-five during the days when they were at work and Zach was in school. Their house came equipped with a programmable thermostat. She'd set the timer so that the house would be reasonably warm for Zach when he came home after school. Milo said he'd set it, but clearly he hadn't.

She sucked her teeth in annoyance. Damn it, did she have to do *everything* around here?

Chapter 19

The Currys
November 2002

"Reuben, how do you feel about inviting Dawn and Milo to join us for Thanksgiving?" Camille asked. She sat at her vanity brushing her hair, while Reuben did opposing knee-to-elbow crunches on the carpeted floor. He'd decided he was getting too pudgy and started a workout regimen of push-ups and crunches, which he followed religiously every evening. She wished she had the discipline to exercise like he did. All that walking she did between Port Authority and her office left her exhausted and had minimal effect on her waistline. In six months she'd lost maybe five pounds. Reuben had dabbled in a little tennis with Bob Tillman and Jeff Willis last summer . . . maybe next summer she would take it up herself. Running after a flying tennis ball seemed like fabulous exercise.

"Do you really think they'd come? I would think that if they didn't go to the city they'd have company come out, like us."

"No, Dawn said it would just be the three of them." Camille wished *their* families would stay in the city, and in the end her relatives decided to do that, but her in-laws were coming en masse. Not only would they be dinner guests, but they expected her and Reuben to put them up for the night. They'd had to go out and buy an air mattress to provide room for all of them. She wasn't crazy about the idea of having wall-to-wall Negroes sleeping all over the place and having both Mitchell giving up his room to his grandmother and Shayla sharing her double bed with both of her teenage cousins,

Tiffany and Kierra. The thought of three people sleeping in a double bed brought to mind images of the poorest of the poor, and she wanted none of it.

At least Saul and his girlfriend had sprung for a room at a local hotel, even if they planned to leave her little boy with them. Camille would put him and Mitchell on the air mattress, which she would set up in the family room. Brenda and Arnelle would share the sofa bed.

Unlike the Lees, whose basement gave them additional living space, their basement was more like a cellar. It had climate control, but the walls were unfinished and it had no carpeting. She could hardly send anyone down there to sleep; it would be like banishing someone to a dungeon.

Eventually they could probably fix up the basement—Linda and Bob Tillman had done theirs quite nicely—but it wasn't practical to think about that now, not while she was trying to save for the kids' Christmas plus host a Thanksgiving dinner for more than a dozen people.

"How will we fit three more at the table?" Reuben asked.

"We'll manage. The kids can eat in the kitchen. We'll move the card table in there and cover it with a tablecloth for extra seating. There'll be enough room for the adults to sit at the dining room table if we put both leaves in."

"Fine with me. Mitchell will probably be thrilled to have their kid come over, since his cousins are all girls and Saul's girlfriend's son is so young. What's the Young's kid's name again?"

"Zach."

"Yeah, that's it." Reuben counted four more crunches aloud before letting his body go limp on the floor, where he laid for a few minutes, breathing audibly. "I'm going to take a shower."

Camille smiled. In spite of the high monthly cost to maintain their home, she did love having their own private bathroom within their master suite, and so did he. Never again would Reuben have to wait in line to use the toilet or take a shower. Sometimes late at night on weekends when the kids were asleep they both got into the oversize tub for a romantic bubble bath complete with glasses of Chardonnay, and after relaxing for a few minutes they'd turn on the Jacuzzi jets for a water massage.

Yes, she still found it hard to believe that they actually had a home of their own.

She recalled that sinking feeling she'd always gotten when their vacations drew to a close, especially their most recent one in Orlando. Who wouldn't feel a little down after spending a week at a beautifully decorated two-bedroom furnished apartment and riding around in a brand-new convertible, and then having to check out, return the car, and go back to their own apartment and vehicle? But she'd never have to feel that way again. Shayla said it best: living here was like being on vacation all the time.

Lord, she wished weekends lasted as long as the workweek. She loved being home, and not only just to enjoy her surroundings. Camille even enjoyed doing housework, grocery shopping, laundry . . . and, most of all, making love to Reuben, something they were often too tired to indulge in after long days traveling back and forth to the city, except for those quick sessions that ended within ten minutes. She felt especially happy now because she'd be home all next week, preparing for their first holiday season in the new house.

She would begin holiday shopping during her time off. The kids had a scaled-back Christmas last year because of the upcoming move, but this year she wanted to go all out. They'd roast marshmallows in the fireplace and sing Christmas carols. Over the long Thanksgiving weekend they would decorate the outside of the house with Christmas lights, something she suspected many of the neighbors would do as well. Their street would look like a winter wonderland if everyone decorated their home. She'd already bought their decorations at the big BJ's Wholesale Club in Stroudsburg. The lights along the edge of the roof, plus the 3-D Santa and reindeer set meant they'd have a larger electric bill, but it would be worth it.

She hoped they would have snow for Christmas. That would make everything absolutely perfect.

Her raise in salary made life a lot more pleasant and eased some of her worries. Even better than that, she and Reuben had found a young neighbor girl to sit with Mitchell and Shayla until 6:30 in the evening. The kids were overjoyed not to spend hours after school at the library anymore. Camille had bought a large Crock-Pot and used it often, so the kids could have a hot meal before she and Reuben returned home just before 8:00. Mitchell was already a husky kid, and Camille didn't want him to gain weight from eating just before bedtime.

She shivered. Funny, it was always so cold in the house, almost like she had a window open, putting out the welcome mat for the November chill to come in and get comfy.

She got up and stood in front of the window. Yep, she could definitely feel a draft. They'd bought oil-filled radiators for the bedrooms to help keep warm, especially overnight, but those didn't do much good in large, open spaces, like the kitchen and family room. Even with drapes covering the windows, those areas still tended to be cool.

Impulsively she pressed her palm to the wall at a spot well away from the window. The wall felt cold to her hand. Suddenly she remembered Lance Howard at their housewarming party last summer predicting they would freeze in the winter because their house had poor insulation. She'd attributed his remarks to jealousy; they had a house, while all he'd ever be able to do was build homes he could never afford to own. As far as she was concerned, their house being chilly in spots was nothing more than mere coincidence. Lance didn't know what he was talking about.

Besides, she thought with a sly smile, her husband would keep her plenty warm the moment he emerged from his shower.

Chapter 20

The Lees, the Currys, and the Youngs
November 2002

Veronica happily ran an antibacterial cloth over the new toilet in the downstairs bathroom. And as for the new pedestal sink, she could sit and stare at it all day long; that's how pretty it looked. They'd even had movie-star lights installed on top of the mirror that the girls especially loved.

She grabbed some tissues from one of the white wire stacked cubes, which they'd put in here to assist with holding necessities, and wiped hair from the sink. Lorinda and Simone liked to brush their hair in front of the mirror, but she'd tell them not to stand so close to the sink. She and Norman wanted to avoid having to pay any high plumbing bills if the drains became clogged with hair.

How nice to have sleek white fixtures and tile instead of that hideous, antiquated pink. After Norman had finished removing the tile and sanding the walls, they replaced the bright pink paint with a pale peach color the paint manufacturer called Egg Cream. Then he laid fresh new linoleum. Finally, the plumbers had come today and switched out the old pink tub, toilet, sink, and vanity for new white fixtures, leaving them with a brand-new bathroom. Veronica had wanted to have it wallpapered, but Norman said they could do that after their private bath and kitchen were completed. "There's no hurry, Vee," he'd said. "We're going to live here the rest of our lives."

They received special, no-interest financing from Home Depot for up to a year. As soon as the bill for the materials and installation was paid off, in two or three months, they planned to redo their private bathroom upstairs, and after that would come the big job, the kitchen. The latter project would have to be financed, but Norman said that was good debt. The value of their home would increase.

She would have loved to have had all the work completed before they hosted Thanksgiving dinner, but she knew Norman's plan to avoid debt was the right way to go. Working within their budget was more important than trying to impress people. Still, it had been hard to see undisguised shock, followed by condescending smiles, on the faces of Camille Curry and Dawn Young, with their shiny new houses in Arlington Acres. She feared she would see the same looks on the faces of her parents and Norman's brothers, all of whom were coming to dinner from the city. This would be the first time any of them had been out to see them. Her brothers-in-law and their wives had decided against attending their job-celebration party because there wasn't any room for them to sleep in the house.

Norman's sister, Lucy, had already been out several times, but she would not be joining them for the holiday. Instead she would remain home in Harlem to make Thanksgiving dinner for a grieving friend who had just lost her mother. Her own sister, Valerie, decided to stay in the city because she had to work on Friday.

Veronica had to work Thanksgiving Day and the day after as well, but she took a long lunch break and drove home so she could be there to greet the family, although they might arrive before she got home. They planned to ride out in a caravan, following each other all the way from the city. She appreciated the consideration her brothers-in-law showed her parents, who would almost certainly get lost if left to their own devices.

It pleased her that they were finally coming out for a weekend visit. Anyone would think she and Norman had moved to the moon from the way her parents repeatedly stated, "If only you hadn't moved so far away."

Only now, pulling up and seeing three cars with New York plates in her driveway, did she realize how much she'd missed her parents. But at least they didn't feel abandoned. Valerie still saw them frequently and often left Essence with them while she pursued an active social life on the weekends. Phyllis and Franklin Mills hadn't been thrilled when the unmarried Valerie had announced her pregnancy fourteen years ago, but they loved their firstborn granddaughter fiercely.

It pleased Veronica that they'd all arrived before she did, since she couldn't stay very long. She found everyone gathered in the living room. Her mother exclaimed that they'd just arrived less than ten minutes before.

She hugged both her parents hello, holding on to them longer than she usually did. Her mother actually had tears in her eyes. "Veronica, the children look so happy. And your home is beautiful."

"We miss you, but we think you did the right thing," her father added. "It's a much better environment for the girls out here."

"Thank you, Daddy." She wiped happy tears from the outer corners of her eyes with the back of her hand.

"Hey, Veronica! Can you wish somebody Happy Thanksgiving, or what?"

She laughed as she moved to greet Eddie, the firstborn of Norman's family, and by far the most boisterous. "Happy Thanksgiving, Eddie, and welcome."

Veronica greeted Eddie's wife, Michelle, and then Norman's other brother, Charles, and his wife, Germaine. Both brothers brought their children, all of whom were older than Lorinda and Simone, and none of whom were anywhere in sight.

"Where's the kids?" she asked.

"I think they're outside," Norman said. "Vee, look what everybody brought. Macaroni and cheese, cornbread stuffing, and pies galore."

"And I'll make the gravy," her mother said. "That turkey smells wonderful, Veronica."

"Thanks, Mom, but I can't take credit for it. Norman seasoned it and put it in the oven, since I had to get to work early this morning. I still have to go back and put in a few more hours, but we'll eat as soon as I get home."

"That's all right, Veronica," Michelle said. "Germaine and I brought some cold cuts. We're going to make sandwiches now, and that'll hold us for a couple of hours. We knew you had to work today, and we don't think it's right for us to rush to eat the moment you walk in the door after working all day."

"Veronica, I'm admiring your kitchen," Germaine said. "It's twice as big as the one in our apartment, and imagine having a window over your sink that looks out on your own backyard."

The mention of her antiquated kitchen made Veronica feel embarrassed. "Uh . . . we're going to remodel it by next summer."

Michelle seemed stunned by that. "Remodel it? Why, for heaven's sake?"

"Well, we're going to get new appliances, a nice side-by-side fridge, in a different color—"

"If these work, why bother?" Germaine said.

Veronica laughed. "You sound like Norman. But wait til you see it when it's finished. It'll be much brighter and better."

Their first Thanksgiving in their new house turned out to be a smashing success. Dawn and Milo Young had already accepted an invitation to dine with Reuben and Camille Curry when Veronica asked if they would join them for dinner. So she asked them to stop by in the evening for dessert, and to bring their children. Both couples showed up alone, Camille explaining that most of their guests plus the kids, including Zachary Young, had gone to the movies.

Veronica's parents, as well as her brothers-in-law and their wives, clearly found it fascinating that these two other couples from the city had also become home owners here in Pennsylvania at about the same time. When Reuben Curry mentioned he and Camille had had their home built, they were deluged with questions. What did they do for a living? What was their house like? Veronica felt that it was intrusive. She caught Norman's eye and sent him a signal to stop the interrogation.

"Guys, a lot of folks build homes out here," he said. "There are new developments all over the place. Milo and Dawn moved into a brand-new home, too."

"Really?" Eddie asked. He turned to Milo. "So what kind of work y'all do?"

Veronica lowered her head to hide her exasperation. Norman meant well, but all his comment had done was turn the focus to the Youngs. The pleased looks on Dawn and Milo's faces told her they found the admiration as flattering as the Currys had, but she didn't want their families bombarding them with too many questions, or to ask anything inappropriate. Already Germaine had asked, "And your note for a brand-new house is reasonable?"—which was a veiled way of asking the amount of their mortgage payment.

"Maybe we should start the movie now," Veronica said pointedly.

Conversation temporarily came to a halt when Norman put the rented DVD in the player, but when the movie ended once more they discussed living in Pennsylvania. "How are the schools out here?" asked Germaine.

Dawn seemed happy to reply. "Oh, much better than in the city. The kids here were way ahead."

Germaine sighed. "If we didn't have good jobs in the city we'd consider moving out here. Our son already asked if we could."

"There are plenty of people living here who commute to New York, but it takes a lot out of you," Veronica cautioned.

"Yeah, I guess it would be tiring."

"It's just as draining on your wallet as it is to your body," Milo declared. The others chuckled and seconded his statement, except for Dawn. Veronica likened the look on her face to someone who'd just learned they had to *pay* at tax time when they expected a refund, although she seemed to recover quickly.

Norman nodded. "Vee and I were thrilled when the hospital here offered us jobs."

"But there's a lot to consider when changing jobs," Camille said. "I've worked at the same company for nearly ten years, and this summer I received a promotion. I get three weeks' vacation leave every year. If I switched jobs I'd have to start all over at the bottom of the food chain including my salary."

"I know what you mean," Dawn said. "I called about a job in South Jersey that was advertised in the *Times,* but I would have had to take a substantial pay cut, so I said forget it."

"Well, that was a nice way to spend the evening," Camille remarked as they drove away.

"Yes. I like Veronica and Norman. They have nice families, too."

She inadvertently wrinkled her nose, just for a second. "But are all those people actually staying with them?" Here she was complaining about hosting three extra adults and three children. Heaven help Veronica if she had such a large number of people staying under her roof.

"No, just Veronica's parents. Norman's brothers and their families are staying at the Holiday Inn."

Like I wish your sisters would do, she thought. Aloud she said, "That makes it easier for Veronica."

She rested a palm on her belly. The desserts Veronica served had been wonderful, plus earlier she'd had a slice of Brenda's famous sweet potato pie. The holiday season was no time to worry about one's weight. After New Year's she'd cut back on her calorie intake.

She busied herself by looking at the passing scenery during the ride home. Virtually all the businesses were closed for the holiday, except for a gas station here and there and the video rental stores. Most homes they passed either had empty driveways or several cars in front of them.

Their lives had changed so much since last year, when they spent Thanksgiving defending their decision to buy a home here in Pennsylvania, first to her family, and then to Reuben's. This year, for the first time ever, the entire Curry family had been able to sit down together as a family and give thanks, something they'd never have been able to do if she and Reuben hadn't bought their house. Funny how nobody pointed out how nice it felt to do that, now that someone had the space to accommodate everyone, although she felt certain they'd all thought of it.

But, of course, no one, from Ginny down to Arnelle, would ever bring up anything positive.

Reuben turned the Malibu onto their street. "I wonder if everyone's back from the movie."

"I'm sure. Your mother and Brenda are probably up by now, too." Both women had fallen asleep after dinner. "Hell, it's after nine. If anything, they're probably having turkey sandwiches or more dessert before they get ready to go to bed for the night."

They pulled into their crowded driveway and parked at the very end of it, just managing to fit in the small space remaining before the curb. Dawn and Milo, following behind them, parked at the curb. Zach had asked to go to the movie with Mitchell instead of accompanying his parents to the Lees', and Milo said they would pick him up on their way home.

Dawn and Milo, sleepy after eating several heavy desserts at the Lees', didn't linger long after retrieving Zach. Camille felt sleepy herself. She checked on Mitchell and Shayla, talked with Ginny, Brenda, and Arnelle for a few minutes, then retired to her bedroom after going over the sleeping arrangements with everyone and making sure they had sufficient blankets and clean towels.

She noticed a strange pair of glasses on top of her dresser. Frowning, she reached for them. The rectangular wire-rimmed half-frames looked familiar. But since she didn't wear glasses and neither did Reuben, where had they come from?

She thought about it while showering, deciding that maybe Ginny had picked them up earlier and brought them in here, thinking they were hers. Her mother-in-law might have thought she wore glasses to read or something.

She had dozed off by the time Reuben came in. "I thought you said you'd be right in," she said teasingly, her voice muffled with sleepiness.

"Just wanted to make sure everybody was comfortable. I turned up the heat some; you know how easily Mom gets cold."

Camille sat up, the covers falling to her waist. "Did anyone say anything to you about being cold?" She recalled Lance Howard's prediction that their home would be drafty in the winter. She did find the house to be on the cold side, and although she didn't put stock in what Lance had said, it wouldn't surprise her if Reuben's family complained, alerted in advance by Saul.

Saul had been the only family member who heard Lance's declaration, and also the only family member who'd opted to get a hotel room. She pictured him discussing his plans with the others and saying something like, "Hell no, I ain't staying in that cold-ass house and freezing my nuts off."

Reuben shrugged as he kicked off his shoes. "Just Arnelle. Kierra and Tiffany sat on the loveseat with one of those throws over them while they watched TV. Arnelle's been bundled up in a heavy sweater all day and said she couldn't get warm. She made some hot chocolate, and when I made a fire she sat close to it and said she felt much better. Mom said she was pretty cozy, but she already had a throw wrapped around her. I was going to ask if you'd mind if I bring the electric radiator in here out to the family room so Brenda and Arnelle won't freeze."

"I doubt it'll do much good, Reuben. Those things work best in a room where you can close the door and lock in the heat. The family room is too open. It didn't work very well when we tried it in the living room, remember?"

He didn't reply right away, as he was in the midst of pulling his shirt over his head and replacing it with the old sweatshirt with torn-off sleeves that he usually slept in during the winter. "Yeah, that's right. I forgot about that. They'll just have to manage with an extra blanket, that's all."

Camille, wearing only a spaghetti-strapped nightgown, felt a sudden chill and hastily pulled the covers over her skin. The heat was on, but she still felt cold. She couldn't understand why. "Reuben . . . You don't suppose Lance could have been right about what he said about our house, do you?"

He knew exactly what she meant. "Not for a minute. Camille, builders can't just slap houses together. They have inspectors who come out and have to evaluate every aspect of a home's construction, from the foundation to the plumbing to the insulation, and everything else. If they didn't there'd never be a decent house built anywhere."

"Yes, but haven't there been cases where inspectors have been paid off to look the other way?"

"If it's happened here, nobody's been caught yet. If anything comes out about any scandals, I'll be the first one to question how they built this house. But I don't want to suggest to anyone that bribery might have been involved in the construction. I've asked some of our neighbors if their houses feel cold in the winter, and they said no."

Camille considered that their neighbors' homes were already standing before construction began on theirs, and that they probably needed to seek out someone whose house had been built around the same time, which would probably mean involvement of the same workers. But that wouldn't be easy; houses went up all the time in Arlington Acres.

She dismissed the idea in favor of another thought she had. "You didn't mention Brenda. Did she have any complaints about the temperature?" Maybe he didn't want to tell her. Knowing Brenda's complaining nature, she'd probably carried on as if they lived in Siberia and it was thirty below in their living room.

"No. She kept her pullover sweater on, but she didn't complain about being cold. I think she was too busy trying to find her reading glasses."

Camille's eyebrows arched. "Her reading glasses?"

"Yeah, apparently she misplaced them someplace." Reuben pulled on a pair of flannel drawstring pants and slid into bed next to her.

She shook his upper arm. "Reuben, I found a pair of women's glasses on top of my dresser. I meant to ask you if you'd put them there, maybe for safekeeping." She already knew what his answer would be.

"I never picked up any glasses," he said as he fumbled with his pillow. He stopped suddenly, as if he were an electric device and someone had pulled the plug midoperation. "Wait a minute. What the hell were her glasses doing in *here?*"

She sat up. "That's what I'm saying."

"Show me exactly where you found them."

Camille threw back the covers and got out of bed. She pointed to an area on the right-hand side of her double chest of drawers. "Right about there."

"Don't you keep the bills and the papers for the house in your top drawer?"

She gasped again. Quickly she yanked open the top drawer. The blue vinyl envelope they'd received at their closing could be seen through the holes of the dividers she used to separate her panty hose and knee-hi nylons.

"Is that where you left it?"

She nodded, closing the drawer and opening the small one in the center, where she stored the bills and bank statements. "Everything looks all right, but she had plenty of time, Reuben. We were over at the Lees' for over two hours. And Brenda didn't go to the movies."

"Yeah, and here I was thinking it was a good thing that she decided to stay at home with Mom," Reuben said bitterly. "Instead she goes on a fucking snooping expedition."

Camille thought for a moment, but no ideas came to her. "What do you want to do about it?"

"I'm going to give her her damn glasses back and ask what she was doing in our bedroom. Put on a robe or something. I'm gonna bring her back in here. No need for Mom or Arnelle to know anything about this."

"What if she's gone to bed?"

"She's still up." Reuben tightened the drawstring of his pants. "I'll be right back."

Two minutes later Brenda followed Reuben into the room, looking like a child who'd eaten all the beef strips out of the pepper steak, leaving just pepper and onions for the rest of the family. "What did y'all want to talk to me about?"

Camille held up the wire-rimmed glasses. "Reuben tells me you're looking for these."

Brenda brightened. "My glasses! I'll be able to read a couple of chapters of my book before I go to sleep. Where'd you find them?"

Her sister-in-law's innocent reaction brought one word to Camille's mind: *Glib*. "On top of my dresser," she said flatly. "They weren't there when Reuben and I left to visit our friends, Brenda. I came in here before we left to brush my hair, and I stood right in front of my mirror. But they *were* here when we got back."

Reuben spoke up. "So that means that you were in our bedroom while we were out. What were you looking for, Brenda?"

"I wasn't in here. One of the kids must have seen my glasses someplace and brought them in here, thinking they were yours, Camille."

Camille's expression remained unforgiving. "I doubt it."

"Brenda," Reuben said, "I don't know if you're making that up or if that's what really happened, but I'm telling you now so there's no misunderstandings. Our bedroom is off-limits to you, Arnelle, and both your daughters."

"I'm sure Kierra didn't put my glasses in here. She'd know from looking at them that they were mine. Maybe Mitchell or Shayla."

Camille rolled her eyes. "My kids know I don't wear glasses, Brenda."

"Well, maybe it was Lebron."

Saul's girlfriend's little boy, whose name both she and Reuben had trouble recalling. Brenda was so full of it, Camille thought. That little boy wouldn't even know where their bedroom was. "I doubt—" she began, but stopped when Reuben gestured at her to do so.

"Good night, Brenda," he said in a tone of dismissal.

"Good night. And thanks. But I'm telling you again, *I* wasn't in here." She rushed out of the room, closing the door behind her.

Camille pounced on Reuben the moment the door closed. "Why'd you tell me to stop? You know she had to be lying. That kid has never even been in our bedroom. He wouldn't know to put her glasses in here."

"You're probably right. I can't believe Brenda would stand there and deny with such sincerity that she was in here."

She put her hands on her hips. "What'd you expect her to say, 'Oops, I'm busted'? Reuben, as you said, the papers from the house are in my drawer. So are our bank records, and our bills, even our pay stubs. Your sister had plenty of time while we were out to look through it all. Your mother dozed off, and nobody else was here. She probably knows exactly what we paid for this house, how much we put down, exactly how much our mortgage is, what we owe, how much we make, and exactly how much we have in the bank. And that pisses me off."

"She knows you're pissed. I just think it's gone far enough. I don't want you to say anything that might cause a permanent rift between you two. Trust me, Camille."

She glared at him, and then, without a word, removed her robe and slid back between the sheets.

On her side, with her back to him.

"Well, that was a nice way to spend a couple of hours," Milo remarked as they drove back to the Curry house to retrieve Zach. "Be sure to tell your family about the nice holiday we had. I've got a feeling they're in Brooklyn saying among themselves that we probably wish we were there with them instead of so far away with no one we know."

"You can bet I plan to let them know we had dinner with one set of friends and dessert with another," Dawn said. "You're right, I'm sure they're thinking we haven't met anyone and we're here all by ourselves—and I want to set them straight." She paused. "Milo, do you think our families will ever come out to see us?"

"I'm sure they will eventually. We've only been here three months. Even Don and Carmen haven't been out to visit since they helped us move. But I doubt anyone will come out during the winter."

"Maybe we should consider ourselves lucky," Dawn said thoughtfully. "It seems like Veronica and Norman always have company. That must get old after a while."

"Well, from what I see they can afford to have frequent visitors."

Dawn knew he was referring to the Lees' remodeled bathroom. It did look awfully nice. She could hardly believe that just a few short weeks ago it had been a pink eyesore. "Maybe so. Or maybe they charge a fee. Personally, I can't see how anyone can stand having guests so often." She paused, uncertain if she should voice her thoughts or just let it go.

She decided that keeping quiet would only increase her annoyance. "But I do wish you hadn't said what you did about the commute."

"What'd I say? That it's a drain, both physically and financially? Hell, the Lees know that. So do the Currys. It's Norman's sister-in-law who wanted to know."

"I know, Milo, but the way you said it. Couldn't you tell how impressed everybody was that we'd built our house new? Then you made that crack, and it came out sounding like . . . Well, it sounded like we're hurting or something."

"I've got a news bulletin for you, Dawn. We *are* hurting. Maintaining this house, plus the cost of getting to work, has turned out to cost a lot more than we bargained for."

She shrugged, unable to argue with his statement. Of course, they could have saved thousands by not buying a lot on the lake and by sticking with one of the basic models. Instead of pointing that out—after all, she'd been all for it—she might as well bring up the other matter on her mind. "I was hoping we'd be able to have a New Year's party."

"A party? Are you kidding? Do you know how much that'll cost?"

"Milo, we've been guests at Veronica and Norman's a couple of times now, and today we had dinner at Camille and Reuben's. We've got to reciprocate."

"Fine. Invite them over to watch a movie or something and put out some munchies. We'll serve some beer and wine. I'd like for us to be able to get out of this house once in a while, Dawn."

She sighed softly. She understood what he meant and even agreed with it. She didn't want their entire social life to revolve around home activities. Things like travel were still important. This was the first year they hadn't taken a vacation, and even though they felt that moving into their own home more than compensated, they nonetheless missed packing a bag and going to the airport, or even driving to their destination.

She'd already begun contributions to a vacation club for next year, although something along the lines of that seven-day cruise to Bermuda last year was out; no way could she put aside that much. Maybe they'd take a nice drive to the Delaware shore and spend a few days relaxing on the beach.

Still, she felt they owed it to their new friends to invite them over for something nicer than potato chips and beer. She didn't want to get a reputation among their friends of always being a guest and never a host or, worse, being a crummy host. It shouldn't be expensive to provide dinner to four extra people. She just had to catch them on a weekend when they weren't having any visitors.

And with the revolving doors at both the Lee and the Curry homes, that might be more difficult than it sounded.

Chapter 21

The Lees
December 2002

Veronica tooted the horn as she pulled in the driveway after work. She couldn't wait to share her good news with Norman.

"Guess what!" she exclaimed when she saw him in the house. "I was asked today if I'd consider working the night shift, 9:00 to 7:00, four days a week."

His forehead wrinkled. "I don't get it. You don't want to work nights, do you?"

"I never really thought about it before, but there's a nice shift differential in it. Plus, I'd still get to be at home with the girls after school, so we won't have to pay for day care. I can sleep during their school hours, and take another nap to refresh after dinner." His face remained impassive, and she tried again. "More money in our pockets is always a good thing, Norman. We can certainly use it. Doing the kitchen over is going to be expensive."

Then she casually added what she'd been thinking about for weeks. "And we really need a second car." She waved him off when he opened his mouth to protest. "I know we're getting by with one, but we want to do more than just get by, don't we? We don't live in Washington Heights anymore, where we can walk a few blocks and catch the subway at 158th or 155th. Public transportation out here is lousy. You know that." When they first began working locally, Norman spent a miserable three weeks taking the bus to work until he began participating in ride share. With his usual selflessness, he insisted Veronica take the car. "Having one car while working third shift means I'd be stuck in the house all day while you're at work, when I could be going to the bank and Wal-Mart, taking advantage of those markdowns they make on meat that has to be sold soon. They do it in the mornings, and it's gone by afternoon. This way I can buy it and freeze it." He didn't look swayed, she noticed, so she tried another tack. "Why do you think so many of the houses here have two-car garages? Certainly not for storage; that's why we have basements."

"We have a one-car garage, Vee," he said with a smile.

She laughed. "Only because our house was built in the sixties. All the newer houses have two-car garages. Some of the larger homes even have *three*-car garages."

He good-naturedly held out a hand. "Will you stop already? None of that has anything to do with us. But I guess we'll need to get another car eventually. I just want you to know it can be very difficult to get used to working all night long. I know; I did it when I was in the service. Sometimes your body resists staying awake when it's accustomed to sleeping, and the older you get the harder it is." At her crestfallen expression he added, "But if you want to give it a try I don't have a problem with it. Just don't feel badly if it doesn't work out and you want to go back to days. We'll still get the things we want. It just might take a little longer, that's all."

She grinned. "I have a feeling that the money will be a nice incentive for me to get used to it in a hurry." Suddenly she threw her arms around his neck. "Norman, you're my prince. You handled this whole house-buying thing so well, and I know you want me to have everything I want."

"And don't you forget it," he grumbled.

"I won't." She removed her arms and grabbed his hand.

February 2003

Veronica cuddled up to Norman in bed. She could think of no better activity on a cold winter night than making love. "As James Brown would say, 'I feel good.'"

Norman chuckled. "I'm going to sleep good tonight, that's for sure."

"Well, before you go to sleep, let me run something past you. In honor of my working hard on the third shift for the past two months, and since Valentine's Day is coming up, do you think we might be able to get away for Valentine's Day weekend? I'm sure Camille or Dawn would keep the kids for us, provided they don't have plans themselves. Maybe we can go to one of those romantic inns in the Poconos with the round beds and a Jacuzzi big enough for two."

"Uh, Vee, I meant to tell you. Eddie and Michelle asked if they could come out that weekend, and I told them they could."

"You told them—but, Norman, they were just here for New Year's. Charles and Germaine, too. And they all stayed with us."

"But on Thanksgiving they didn't stay here; your parents did. My brothers stayed at the Holiday Inn."

"Fine. Let them stay at the Holiday Inn for Valentine's Day." She felt like her in-laws were taking advantage of them. It might have taken them a while to come out to visit, but now they never wanted to stay home whenever a holiday came around.

"Come on, Vee. You know how hotels raise their rates for Valentine's Day, just like they do on New Year's."

She and Norman had given a New Year's party and invited some of the neighbors, as well as the Currys, the Youngs, and a few people from the hospital. Of course they'd invited Norman's siblings and their families and her sister. Lucy had plans in the city, and they offered the guest room to their friend Duane and his girlfriend—a different one from last fall. Valerie and the guy she was seeing took a room at the Hampton Inn, while Essence stayed at the house with Lorinda and Simone in their room. Veronica had presumed that her brothers-in-law and their wives would stay at a hotel, too, like they had over Thanksgiving. It came as a shock when they asked to stay at the house. When she mentioned it to Norman, he said the hotels probably raised their rates to something outrageous just because of the date. She told him they had no more beds, and he said they'd offered to buy air mattresses and sleep in the basement.

Veronica couldn't believe that the wives of her brothers-in-law would agree to such a thing. For one, the basement was all open, so they would have no privacy. And because heat rose it tended to be a little chilly down there. But no one wanted to miss the New Year's Eve party. In the end she'd gone along, trying to see it from Eddie and Charles's point of view. It cost so much to go out anywhere for New Year's, and it came just one week after all the expense of Christmas. And they were family, as much as her sister Valerie was.

Valerie's boyfriend, without the expense of a family, could probably afford a couple of nights in a hotel, even with a surcharge. Eddie and Charles really couldn't. How could she say no? At least their children stayed with other family members who lived in the city.

Still, she sensed a potential problem on the horizon. "Norman, I know Eddie and Charles are your brothers, but do you see a pattern forming here? With the holidays?"

"If you mean am I worried about my brothers wanting to come out for Easter, no."

But I'll bet they'll want to come out for Memorial Day, July 4th, and Labor Day, she thought.

Norman turned on his side and stretched his hand out across her middle. She shrugged and closed her eyes.

If he wasn't worried about Eddie and Charles and their wives, then she wouldn't either.

Chapter 22

The Currys
April 2003

Camille read over the letter she'd just composed. Positive that George—as she thought of him, even though she addressed him as "Mr. Stephens"—would like it, she inserted letterhead into her printer and sent a command to print. Before George got promoted she had to share a printer with three other secretaries, and somebody was always walking off with her stuff. Now she had her own.

She liked being on the thirty-sixth floor.

George kept her busy, too. Camille had always thought that many executive secretaries didn't do anything but make reservations for lunch or travel plans for their bosses, with plenty of time to file their nails or read the latest novels, but she had very little idle time. George clearly expected her to work for that 10 percent raise he'd gotten her. He used to write out his own correspondence and give it to her to type. Now he merely told her what to say and who to say it to. He hadn't liked her early efforts, but after a while she'd learned to do it the way he wanted.

No doubt about it, she had what it took to work on the thirty-sixth floor.

Reuben called as she walked out of George's empty office after laying the letter on his desk. "Hi!" she said happily. The sound of his voice always came as a welcome sound to her ears. "What's going on?"

"Is there any way you can get off a little early today? We have to talk about something serious, and I'd rather do it before we get on the bus with everybody."

"Uh . . . I don't think it'll be a problem. But I'll have to clear it with George, just in case he has something he wants me to do before I leave. But what's going on, Reuben?"

"I'll tell you when I see you. Let's meet at that coffee shop across from Port Authority at 4:45." He paused. "Trust me, it's best this way."

Fortunately, George gave the green light for her to leave at 4:45. She spent the rest of the afternoon wondering what Reuben wanted to talk to her about.

Reuben wasted no time. The moment he approached the coffee shop where they agreed to meet he took both her hands in his. "I've got bad news, Camille."

She tensed. "What is it?"

"My store is closing."

She drew in her breath. "The whole chain?"

"No, just my store. In three months."

She stared at him blankly. "But . . . You've worked for them a long time. Surely they have a job for you." *My God, without Reuben's income we'll sink faster than the Titanic.*

"They did offer me something, but it's out on Long Island. I had to turn it down, Camille. It'll take forever to get out there, and I'm already spending five hours a day going back and forth to work. Plus, it'll cost more if I have to get a pass for the LIRR in addition to the bus from Tobyhanna, and I wouldn't be making any more money than I am now." He ushered her inside, where they sat at a booth in the back with Cokes he ordered.

She sighed. He was right—Long Island wasn't feasible for daily travel. Of course, if they still lived in the Bronx . . .

But they didn't, and she tried, unsuccessfully, not to let the panic she felt show. "So what are we going to do? You know that even with my promotion I don't make enough to pay the mortgage and the rest of the bills."

"I'll see what I can find. But I might not be able to get work as a manager. I might have to stock shelves or something, at least at first."

"Yes, for minimum wage," she said bitterly. Thank God she'd been able to get off early. By the time she had to board the bus she wanted to be calm, not have her appearance give away the fact that her world had just collapsed. She could pretend to be asleep if she felt like she couldn't bear to listen to Dawn Young and the others, with all their talk about their vacation plans and their home improvements. She'd simply have to be strong enough not to burst into tears at the mere thought of what the future might hold for *her* family.

"Listen, at least we know we've got ninety days. And they're going to give me a severance package that will last at least another two months. They'll give that to me even if I leave sooner because I've found another job. At least that will get us through the summer. We can take a little vacation, like we planned. It'll be the end of October before we really have to worry."

Camille thought about last year's heating bills. They'd been high, but the heat never seemed to completely warm the house. Everyone had worn bulky sweaters all season long, and even with that they usually curled up with throws when using the computer or watching TV. The constant chill had affected the kids in particular. Shayla had a runny nose from January all the way through March, and Mitchell's cough got so bad that Camille had to take him to the doctor.

She desperately wanted to work closer to home like Veronica did, but in a year no local jobs had materialized, at least nothing that paid worth a damn. She couldn't simply give up her current salary, especially after her promotion last fall, to work locally for ridiculously low wages like four hundred dollars a week. It wouldn't be worth it, even if it did eliminate the cost of commuting, especially now that Reuben's employment days were numbered. Her one solace came from knowing Reuben wouldn't be out of work tomorrow. A lot could change in five months.

But she couldn't stop worrying about how they'd manage after October.

Then she thought of something else. "It won't make sense for you to spend all that money to travel to New York to work, Reuben, if you're just stocking shelves for six or seven dollars an hour."

"Oh, I wouldn't look in New York. I'd look near home, like in Stroudsburg. We can probably arrange for you to ride to the station with Bob or Jeff."

Camille's jaw went taut. The thought of him getting to sleep past daylight and driving a mere half hour to work, while she continued to rise at 4:30 in the morning to get to the bus station before 5:45 made her want to weep. She'd thought *she* would be the one who'd work locally. It made much more sense for her, the woman of the house, to be the one with the short commute. *She* was the one who prepared dinner. *She* was the one who washed and ironed the clothes, did the grocery shopping, picked up around the house, and ran the carpet cleaner every two weeks on that high-maintenance white carpet she now regretted having chosen. Reuben would probably still expect her to make dinner the night before so they could eat as soon as they arrived home.

Camille knew she was being unreasonable—Reuben always sought to work with her as a team—but she couldn't help it. The way she saw it she hadn't been hit with one bombshell, but two.

Chapter 23

"Dawn, we've got a problem."

She looked up from the inside of the refrigerator door, which she was cleaning with diluted all-purpose cleaner in a spray bottle. Milo looked so serious. "What?"

"C'mere, and I'll show you."

She put the sponge and spray bottle on the counter and followed him outside to the back of the house. A definite fault line had appeared at the rear, extending from the lake and headed straight for the house. "Ugh. This looks like it could cause a problem."

"Damn straight it can. A break in the soil underneath the house can probably cause our foundation to crack, and the deck wouldn't be all that stable, either. And then we're up a creek."

"What do you want to do, notify the home owners association?"

"Not the association. The builder." He held out his arms on either side of him, index fingers pointing. "You see how our neighbors' lots are higher than ours in the back? That's what's causing this to happen. Every time it rains or snows their water runs into our yard to drain because it's lower. We might have to put up a wooden fence to keep it from happening."

"I think a fence would be a good idea anyway, for privacy. It'll be good for Stormy, too." Dawn had hoped the Willises and their neighbors on the other side would put up fences, which would automatically give them privacy in their backyard without having to pay for it. She suspected they, in turn, hoped she and Milo would do it first.

"We'll see what you say when we find out how much it'll cost. Would you rather go down to Virginia this summer or put up a fence?"

She quickly reconsidered, not wanting to raid her thriving vacation club account to pay for home repairs. Virginia wasn't exactly her dream vacation spot, but it beat staying home. "I guess it would be all right if we got the association to give us some dirt so that our property is at least as high as the neighbors."

"Screw that. I want us to be higher. Let water from our yard drain on *their* property."

To their great dismay, the builder refused to repair the problem when Milo called them. "But my house is warranted," Dawn heard him say. Then, there was a pause, followed by, "It did? You don't? But that doesn't seem fair. Our house was built on a lower lot than the ones on either side. That means y'all knew this would happen after a year or so."

Dawn braced her shoulders through the next long pause as the builder spoke.

"What do I know?" Milo said. "I'm a first-time home buyer from Brooklyn. You guys are the experts. It's not fair to palm this off on me, to say I should have said something before. I didn't notice it until now. But I'm sure your construction crew saw it. *They* knew what would happen down the road."

He made a few more grunting sounds, then closed with, "Well, we'll see about that."

That last remark didn't sound very promising, but when he hung up Dawn nevertheless asked him, "What did they say?"

"They essentially said 'tough tit.' They said if we had noticed that the ground was low while the house was being built they probably could have done something, but that the warranty, which expired after one year anyway, only covered the house and the deck, not the lot."

"Well, that really sucks. Milo, we can't afford to have that fixed."

"We can't afford *not* to fix it. It's headed toward our foundation, remember?" He muttered under his breath.

"Why don't you call the association next week? Maybe they can do something to help us."

"I doubt it, but I'll call them, just to let them know I'm not happy." He walked to the window and looked out at the backyard. "Shit. This is how sinkholes start. We'll have to pay somebody to drop a load of dirt out front, and then we'll have to spread it over the yard ourselves. We can't afford to pay someone to do that, too."

"What about the grass?"

"We'll have to put down new grass. I doubt the old stuff will grow through the dirt. It might happen eventually, but in the meantime every time it rains we'll have a muddy mess in the yard."

"Damn. This is starting to sound more and more expensive." Dawn hoped they would eventually be able to invest in home improvements, like one of those new retractable awnings for the deck. She hadn't planned on spending good money to correct something that should have been done properly in the first place. It wasn't fair.

Who was she kidding? No way could she and Milo afford any home-improvement projects, not with all the money they had to shell out every month for basic expenses. She estimated that the mortgage, their utilities, parking at the bus station, and those damn bus passes ate up more than half their net income. Dawn never claimed to be a financial expert, but she did know home ownership wasn't supposed to work like that.

She sighed. She also knew that home ownership couldn't be all goodness and watching sunrises over the lake. Now she knew how the owners of their old apartment house must have felt whenever she called and said the bathtub had a clogged drain or the front of the kitchen drawer had broken off from the sides. Repairs cost money and cut into their profits.

But they'd deal with it. They had no other option.

In the end they spent $175 to get a dump truck full of dirt placed on their front lawn so they could raise the height of their lot. They drove over to the Home Depot in Stroudsburg, bought a wheelbarrow, and learned it would cost about two hundred dollars for enough square feet of sod to cover their entire backyard. "Forget it," Milo said. Instead he bought two bags of grass seed, paying for that and the wheelbarrow with a credit card.

"Uh . . . Are you sure you want to do that?" Dawn asked in a low tone at the checkout counter.

Milo swiped the plastic card. "Do you have any other ideas?"

All she could do was shake her head. They'd just paid another high electric bill and, as had been the case all winter, there hadn't been a whole lot left over. She looked forward to the coming warm weather. How did other people manage to pay all these utilities? Out here they even had to pay for the water they used. Dawn quickly became aware of her wasteful water habits, like washing dishes under a constantly running stream of hot water. She learned to turn off the tap while she brushed her teeth, and she instructed Zach to do the same.

Dawn and Milo began working with the dirt right away and worked all weekend, but they only had one wheelbarrow, and even with Zach helping, a ton of dirt would take some time for two adults and a preadolescent boy to move.

Monday evening they came home from work to find a note from the home owners association reprimanding them for the unattractive mountain of dirt on their front lawn. Milo went into a rage, cursing the builder and association alike. Dawn felt like she'd been slapped in the face. After Milo's angry phone call last week they knew the situation. They could have at least given them another week to move the dirt.

"We won't be able to do anything with it during the week," she pointed out. How could they? They left the house before light, and by the time they got home it was dark again.

"I'll call and leave them a message that this dirt will sit right here at least through this weekend, and probably next weekend, too," Milo said, shouting in agitation.

Dawn wanted to give him something pleasant to think about, but she wasn't sure if this was the right time. Her usually even-tempered husband had become a miserable sourpuss. "Milo, when we're done moving the dirt we really should think about inviting the Currys and the Lees over," she said. "We can have some fun, and we still haven't been able to return the hospitality they showed us."

"That's not our fault. We've invited them."

"I know." She and Milo had been secretly pleased when Veronica declined their invitation rather than bring along their houseguests, one of Norman's brothers and his wife. "It's hard for them to be social because their families come to see them a lot, especially Veronica and Norman. Between you and me, Veronica's not too happy about it." She giggled. "Maybe there are advantages to having your family feel you live too far to go and see."

"That's what they get for having their extra bedrooms set up as bedrooms. If we didn't have exercise equipment in ours, we might be overrun with weekend guests ourselves."

Dawn didn't reply. She didn't believe that was it at all. She believed that not visiting was their families' way of punishing them for getting ahead.

But if given a choice, she supposed she'd rather be banished than be inundated every weekend with visitors.

Chapter 24

The Lees
May 2003

"Veronica, my sister wants to have a fortieth birthday party."

She'd been scrubbing a stubborn stain on the kitchen floor with a brush and some cleanser, but at hearing this she immediately perked up. Her posture relaxed a little, a dreamy smile on her face. "That sounds nice. I guess we'll plan on spending the night at a hotel in the city, huh? I know hotels in midtown are expensive, but I'm sure if we use the Internet we can find something affordable. Maybe we can get Camille Curry to keep the girls overnight. They enjoy playing with her Shayla."

The idea of a weekend in the city excited her. They hadn't been to New York since Christmas Day, and then they only stayed for the day and drove back that night. It seemed that everyone wanted to come and see them, and unfortunately for longer than an afternoon. She remembered joking to Norman about it when they first started looking at houses eighteen months ago, but the situation had become very unfunny. Veronica was tired of Norman's brothers and her own sister acting like they were running a bed-and-breakfast.

She found her sister's behavior particularly disturbing. Valerie had made it her life's mission to find a husband, and in Veronica's opinion she'd gone way overboard, exposing her daughter to a parade of short-term lovers and often wanting to bring them out here for a weekend.

Just last weekend there'd been an ugly scene. Valerie and her new companion, Michael—it seemed like every three or four weeks she had a new one—rode out last Saturday, Essence in tow. They intended just to spend the day, but they had a few drinks too many and Norman suggested they sleep over rather than try to drive home impaired. Valerie stated that she wanted to sleep with Michael, astonishing Veronica and Norman, and prompting Veronica to ask her privately if she slept with men at her apartment in the city while Essence was at home. "Of course not," Valerie had said, but Veronica remained unconvinced.

She thought about asking her niece directly but decided against it. A question like that about what went on at home would put Essence on the spot, and she also felt it crossed the line. Valerie would be furious if she found out. Instead she'd asked Valerie, "Then why do you feel it's okay to sleep with a man in *my* house when Essence is here?"

Valerie's response of, "Because it's not the same thing. Essence doesn't have to know where Michael slept," struck Veronica as a lame attempt at rationalization.

Norman refused to allow it. "It sets a bad example for Lorinda and Simone. They're both impressionable kids, Vee. Valerie can do what she wants in her own home, but she's not doing it here. Hell, if I haven't had a few too many myself I would have driven their drunk asses to a hotel. I'm trying to be nice here, but I don't know that dude Valerie brought with her, and I don't really like the idea of a strange man sleeping in my house. I also don't want Essence riding with someone who's intoxicated. And just because your sister is sleeping with him doesn't mean she knows a whole lot about him, either. He might be a fucking serial killer, for all I know."

In the end Valerie and Essence slept in the guest room and Michael bunked on the sofa bed. Valerie sulked about it, and Veronica knew that if Valerie hadn't been her sister Norman wouldn't have held back his temper.

They discussed the situation behind the closed doors of their bedroom. "I'm beginning to wonder about your sister," Norman said incredulously. "I think she's turning into a slut."

"Norman!"

"I'm sorry if that offends you, Vee, but there's no nice way to say it. How many fellows has she brought out here in the last couple of months? It can't be good for Essence. Valerie is setting a terrible example for her. I know it can be difficult being a single mother and all, especially since Essence's father isn't in the picture, but Valerie shouldn't be exposing her daughter to all these men."

"I agree. I'll talk to her in the morning."

Veronica pulled Valerie aside last Sunday and pointed out that the man she had with her this weekend was about the third guy she'd been involved with in as many months. She suggested as delicately as possible that it probably wasn't a good idea to introduce Essence to every man she went out with. Valerie had been furious, telling Veronica she didn't know anything and that it really wasn't any of her business how she raised her daughter. Veronica knew they'd eventually make up, but she doubted it would happen anytime soon.

Veronica discussed the confrontation with Norman, and his response gave her new hope. "I'm thinking that maybe we should put a lock on the revolving door our families have been coming through. I understand that people like to get out of the city once in a while when the weather's nice, but between Eddie and Michelle, Charles and Germaine, and Valerie and whoever, we're practically being invaded."

She had quickly agreed with him.

Veronica felt that last weekend's fuss had put a permanent halt to her family and in-laws' constant visits, but that feeling of being safely cocooned far away from their families in New York ended abruptly with Norman's next words.

"Uh . . . Actually, Lucy was hoping she could have the party here."

She looked at him in disbelief. *"Here?"*

"Yeah. She wanted to do a barbecue. You know, during the daytime."

Veronica decided that the spot on the floor could wait; this was more important. She got up, leaned against the kitchen counter, and said, "I don't like the idea, Norman. We just talked last weekend about stopping our open-door policy."

"Yeah, but Lucy hasn't taken advantage of us the way my brothers and Valerie have."

She couldn't argue with that. Lucy hadn't been out to Mount Pocono since their celebration when they changed jobs last fall. "That's true, but think about it, Norman. We don't know Lucy's friends. Doesn't the idea of having a lot of strangers roaming around our house make you uncomfortable? It's like having that guy Michael times fifty."

"No, it isn't. None of them will be sleeping under our roof. They don't even have to go inside the house unless they need to use the bathroom. It should be all right. We'll lock the bedroom doors."

She chuckled. "Remember when we had that New Year's party in the city and Duane didn't want to take off his leather jacket because he was afraid somebody would steal it?"

"Oh, I remember. We had everyone just throw their coats on our bed. But he said, 'It's my only coat.'" Norman laughed at the memory.

"And I hung Duane's coat in the back of my closet, behind those drapes my mother gave us. But it was kind of sad, when you think about it. You shouldn't have to worry about somebody walking off with your coat when you're a guest in their home."

"That was the source of the problem," Norman pointed out. "Friends of ours brought friends of theirs, and we didn't even know half the people there. Duane didn't give his coat a second thought when he came to the party we had last fall, or again on New Year's. And I'm pretty sure he still has just one coat." He laughed.

Veronica didn't even smile. "That friends-of-friends scenario is what I'm afraid of if we let Lucy have her party here, Norman. Everybody likes the idea of getting out of the hot, sticky city in July. We might end up with seventy or eighty people here. And what'll we do with them all if it rains?"

"We'll move the party to the basement. I understand your apprehension, Vee, but I'd really like to do this for Lucy. All she's asking is to use our grounds."

She felt trapped, knowing she had no way to refuse without sounding bitchy. Norman had always been close to his only sister. As the two youngest children in the family, they'd been allies growing up. Lucy even had a scar on her knee from a childhood fight she'd gotten into in defense of her little brother, who at the time was small for his age.

Norman, sensing her reluctance, tried to reassure her. "We'll set some ground rules, the first being that she'll have to limit the number of guests to, say, forty."

"I can live with that. And the forty-first person who tries to get in will be thrown out on their ear." She giggled.

Norman reached for a pad and paper and began writing. "Forty-guest limit. Let's see, what else?"

"Let's tell her what time the party will end," Veronica prompted. "I don't want people thinking they can hang out here until all hours.

The neighbors will have a fit if we're playing music late, and we want Lorinda and Simone to get to sleep."

"Since it's a barbecue, it'll be held during the day, anyway."

"So they can leave by nine. That's plenty of time, don't you think?"

Norman nodded. "They probably won't even stick around that long, if they've been out here all day."

She grew quiet as she thought some more. "I assume Lucy is providing the food?"

"Of course."

"Humph. She'd better have plenty. She'll have to provide both lunch and dinner."

"Don't worry about that, Vee. It's not our problem."

She wished he felt as apprehensive as she did about hosting this party, but she didn't want to be a killjoy, especially where Lucy was concerned. She could still see them comforting each other at their mother's funeral six years ago. She wanted Norman to preserve his close relationship with his sister.

She sighed. "I guess, but I want you to make it understood that the only thing we're supplying is the yard and the grill." ·

Chapter 25

Dawn filled everyone's glasses while Milo prepared for another game of PO-KE-NO. The Lees and the Currys had come over this Saturday night, and the six of them were playing for twenty-five cents a pot while their children played in the backyard, although they'd be coming in soon because the sun had finally set. She'd made a pitcher of Strawberry Daiquiris, and they also had Miller Genuine Draft on ice.

Milo seemed to be enjoying his role of host, which made her happy. What a nice change to see him having fun instead of complaining about the high cost of living in the country. He got up and turned up the volume on the stereo. An old Earth, Wind & Fire CD spun in the player, and Milo did an imitation of Phillip Bailey, clutching at his throat in mock pain as the singer's pitch soared. They'd have to do this more often, Dawn thought, but it was awfully difficult to catch Veronica and Norman on a weekend when they weren't working. Both of them worked as much overtime as they could get. Dawn wished she could make some extra cash, but even if she had time to put in extra hours she didn't receive overtime pay because of her management supervisory position.

"So how's everybody on the bus?" Norman asked.

"Same old shit," Reuben said. "Everybody complains about how long it takes to get to New York and asking when the hell the train is coming."

"Puh-leese. It hasn't even been proposed yet," Camille said with a dismissive wave of her hand. "If you ask me, we'll be bussing it for a long time to come."

"Oh, Dawn, I love pigs in a blanket," Veronica said, reaching eagerly into the dish Dawn placed on the table.

"Good. I do, too." The pay-per-view boxing championship Milo had ordered didn't begin until 9:30, so instead of dinner Dawn served snack food and hors d'oeuvres.

She reclaimed her seat at the dining room table, hungrily eyeing the Four Corners and Four of a Kind bowls, both of which nearly overflowed with quarters. Unlike the Center and PO-KE-NO bowls, which had winners every game, these two had gone unclaimed long enough to practically become jackpots, albeit small ones, maybe forty or fifty dollars. Winning a pot would certainly prolong Milo's good spirits. Hell, it would be enough to pay for the extra cable charge.

"You ready, Dawn?" Milo asked.

"Go ahead."

Dawn looked up expectantly as Camille returned to the dining room, where the women had remained after they had stopped playing PO-KE-NO and the fellows took over the family room to watch the fight. "Kids all right?"

"Yeah, but a little tired, I think. We'll probably leave soon, but everything was lovely, Dawn."

"Thanks!" She appreciated Camille's compliment, but inside she felt like a victim of bad luck. Damn it, why couldn't she or Milo have won one of those PO-KE-NO pots? Veronica had won the Four Corners and Reuben the Four of a Kind, so she and Milo came up empty.

"Yes, it was," Veronica agreed. "But good luck trying to pry Reuben away from that TV. You'd better hope for a quick knockout."

Veronica and Dawn laughed.

"Ah, this is nice," Dawn said. "I wish the weekends were three days instead of two. This is the only time Milo and I get to really enjoy our home."

"I know what you mean," Camille said. "Veronica, you and Norman don't know how lucky you are not to have that problem anymore."

Veronica shrugged, looking slightly embarrassed. Dawn decided that Veronica probably felt a little uncomfortable because she no longer had to make the long commute to New York while she and

Camille did. After all, she'd done it and knew firsthand what a pain in the ass it was.

Dawn searched for something to say to change the subject and put Veronica at ease. "I'm glad Milo and I managed to find a Saturday when both you guys could come over," she said.

"Well, Norman and I decided we were having too much company on the weekends," Veronica said, "but trying to get the point across to our families turned out to be harder than I thought it would." She lowered her voice, although they were well away from the family room. "You won't believe what happened last week."

"Tell, tell," Camille said, rubbing her palms together eagerly, like a child who'd been promised a surprise.

"Norman's brother Eddie called and asked if he could come out with his wife and kids this weekend. I told him it wasn't a good time because we'd been invited somewhere, and he merely said, 'That's all right. Y'all go ahead. Michelle and I and the kids will do our own thing.'"

"Well, what'd you say?" Dawn asked.

"I put Norman on the phone and let him deal with it. Norman told him as nicely as he could that we're not able to accommodate weekend company as often as we have in the past. I don't expect to see either of his brothers until the barbecue." She remembered she hadn't yet told her friends about Lucy's birthday party. "That reminds me," she said—before they could ask "What barbecue?"—"Norman and I are letting his sister have a barbecue at our place. She's celebrating her big 4-0. I hope both of you can make it, and bring the kids. It's the weekend after next."

"It's sure nice of you to give a party for your husband's sister," Camille remarked. "If I were to give either of Reuben's sisters anything, it would probably be . . ."—she paused to think before concluding—"whooping cough."

"You give me too much credit, Camille. We're not giving the party for her. She's doing it all herself—the food, the beer, the music. She's just using our house. But Norman and I laid down some conditions, and one of them included that we could invite a handful of people." Again, she lowered her voice. "You know, Dawn, I'm thinking you and Milo had the right idea by putting your computer and exercise equipment in your third bedroom. Maybe if we hadn't bought new bedroom furniture for our extra room, we wouldn't have had this problem."

Camille took a sip of her Strawberry Daiquiri. "Reuben and I don't even *have* a spare bedroom, but it hasn't stopped his family from coming out pretty regularly. We actually had to buy air mattresses for them. I guess the thought of staying at the Holiday Inn never occurred to them. It was just, 'We're coming out for Thanksgiving,' or 'We're coming out for Memorial Day. Please make sure everyone has a place to sleep.' Like they're making fucking hotel reservations or something," she concluded, exasperation tingeing her voice.

"I can top that," Veronica said. "My brothers-in-law both brought their *own* air mattresses when Norman and I gave that New Year's party, so they wouldn't have to stay at a hotel. They slept in the basement. And my sister-in-law Michelle told me confidentially that not having a room of their own didn't stop Germaine and Charles from having sex right there. Can you imagine? Michelle said it was like running a porn movie with just the sound."

They all laughed uproariously at that, from both Veronica's tale and the effects of multiple drinks laced with rum.

"Having your in-laws visit constantly is hard to take, even if you like them," Camille declared, sounding a little tipsy. "Which I don't. Of course, Reuben's brother and sisters all said that our moving out here means we think we're better than everyone else. So I guess we won't have to worry about them beating a path to our door on a regular basis, unless there's a holiday and they want someplace to go, like Memorial Day a couple of weeks ago and the Fourth of July a couple of weeks from now."

"I don't think that's the right way to be," Dawn said. "Families are supposed to be happy when someone accomplishes something special, like when they have their first college graduate. Maybe I shouldn't say this, but maybe they're just jealous."

Camille leaned forward slightly, resting her elbows on the table. Dawn noticed her eyes were a little teary. "No doubt about that."

"Milo and I have lived here since last August, and our families have always made excuses when we invited them out," Dawn said. "They finally agreed to come out July 4th."

Veronica grunted. "Hopefully it won't be the beginning of your not being able to call a weekend your own."

"It doesn't sound like it, if it took them this long to get out here," Camille pointed out.

"Don't let that fool you. It took Norman's brothers months to get out here for their first visit, but they've certainly made up for it."

Dawn spoke up. "Veronica, I know you don't have this problem, but, Camille, what do you plan to do with Mitchell and Shayla over summer vacation?"

"Last year we had one of Reuben's nieces come out from the city and watch them. It actually worked out rather well, except for the two-week gap in between when school lets out here and when school lets out in the city. I had to take a leave of absence from work so I could stay home with them before Kierra came, and I'll do the same again this year, I suppose, even though we can't really afford it. But now Reuben's other sister wants *her* daughter to spend the summer."

"Ooh, sticky. How do you plan to handle *that?*" Dawn asked.

"The same way Veronica handled her in-laws. I'm leaving it up to Reuben to sort out."

"Sounds like everybody wants to stay at The Curry Country Club," Veronica said with a laugh.

"We're thinking about enrolling Zach in a day camp," Dawn said. "He's a good kid, usually happy playing computer games, but he's still too young to stay home alone all day." She didn't want to point out the high expense associated with day camp. She feared she and Milo wouldn't be able to pay for it and keep up with their other bills. All right, so Camille had bluntly stated that she couldn't afford to take two unpaid weeks off, but that was probably the alcohol talking. She'd downed those Strawberry Daiquiris like they were Kool-Aid. Tomorrow she probably wouldn't even remember what she'd said.

"Anybody have any exciting vacation plans?" Veronica asked.

"Milo and Zach and I are going to drive down to Virginia for a week. We'll see Colonial Williamsburg and go to Busch Gardens, maybe spend some time in Virginia Beach," Dawn said.

"Reuben and I haven't really talked about it much," Camille said. "Whatever we do, it'll be someplace we can drive to. We did the Disney thing while the house was being built a year and a half ago. Plane tickets, rented condo, rented convertible. We won't be doing anything like that again soon. It cost a fortune, although I can't say it wasn't worth it. Mitchell and Shayla are still talking about it."

"I'll bet," Veronica said. "Our girls are asking us to bring them to Disney, but Norman wants to put them off until we can finish the kitchen remodeling, unless we can get a really good discount in the interim. He says that things probably get pretty sluggish around the parks after New Year's and stay that way through Spring Break."

"I think that's very wise," Camille said. She downed the rest of her drink and immediately poured some more.

"I'm so glad you girls came along with Reuben and Milo," Dawn remarked. "I would have been bored stiff listening to them watch that fight."

"Maybe we can form a reading group or something and have a discussion while the fellows are watching sports," Veronica suggested.

"What a great idea!" Dawn exclaimed.

"Yes, it is," Camille agreed. "I'm always reading during the commute. Did you want to keep it among us three, or would you be willing to invite a couple of other women?"

"Oh, not too many other people. I'd like it to be more of an informal group rather than an organized club, so we can meet when we feel like it, instead of every month like clockwork. Of course, most of the people I know from church live in Mount Pocono. The only folks I can think of from Arlington Acres are that couple who lives down the street from you and Reuben, Camille. What were their names?" She snapped her fingers. "Tanisha and Douglas, that's it."

Camille made a face. "Oh, them. I'd advise against it. They're not very friendly." She'd barely seen the Coles since their hasty exit the day of the barbecue she and Reuben gave, and when she did run into Tanisha she never seemed like she wanted to talk.

"I know who you're talking about," Dawn said. "I saw her buying meat at Wal-Mart and asked if she lived here in Arlington Acres because I thought I'd seen her there. She brushed me off like dandruff. Said she was sorry, but she had to get right home because her son was there by himself." She paused. "You'd think I had TB or something. She might have *said* she was sorry, but she didn't sound like it."

"I know of another couple who might be a better fit," Camille suggested. "The Kings. They've lived out here for four years. He works for the post office, and she works for one of the social service agencies. We met them at the pool." She chuckled. "We passed their house the first time we came out here." She still remembered that crisp autumn day a year and a half ago, when she and Reuben caught a glimpse of Lemuel King in his well-equipped garage, looking like the very definition of suburbia. Like Veronica and Norman, the Kings initially worked in the city but managed to get jobs locally. "They're nice people."

"Do they have children?" This from Dawn.

"Yes. A son in college and twins in high school, a girl and a boy."

"Why don't you talk to her and see if she'd like to join us?" Veronica suggested.

"Yes, do that, Camille," Dawn said. The odd look that briefly crossed Camille's face told her she'd sounded too eager.

But she had her own reasons for wanting to meet the Kings.

Dawn and Milo waved goodbye to their guests, whose sleepy children heavily leaned on them as they walked to their cars.

"Well, that was fun, wasn't it?" Dawn asked as she closed the door behind them.

"Wasn't bad. It would have been even better if we'd won those big pots." He yawned. "Damn, I'm tired."

She started to suck her teeth in annoyance, but caught herself before doing so. That was the last thing she expected Milo to say after such a fun evening. Sure, it was late, but he could sleep in tomorrow. She knew better than to hope he'd help her clean up, but would he actually be too tired for sex *again?* This was Saturday night, for crying out loud. Last night he'd fallen asleep on her, waking her in the middle of the night for a quickie, which seemed so impersonal to her.

"I guess I shouldn't have drunk all those Strawberry Daiquiris," he said apologetically. "They tasted like punch going down."

He'd never been much of a drinker. Her irritation began to soften. "I think Camille had a few too many, too," she said, chuckling. "She seemed to be slurring a bit. Thank goodness Reuben had Mitchell to help with Shayla, since he had to hold Camille up."

"They're all good people." He put his arm around her as they walked toward their bedroom.

Dawn took a quick glance over her shoulder. No light showed from beneath Zach's door. He'd already gone to bed.

"I agree," she said. "I feel a kind of kinship with them. We're all about the same age, we've all got kids, and we all moved out from the city within months of each other."

"Humph. I wonder if they're having as rough a time adjusting as we are."

"I think they are."

"Why you say that?"

"Well, Camille came out and said that she'd have to take two weeks off without pay after Mitchell and Shayla's school lets out.

That's because Reuben's niece is coming for the summer to babysit and her school gets out later than theirs. She said she can't afford to do it, but she has no other choice. And Veronica said she and Norman want to finish remodeling their kitchen before they take a vacation." Dawn reached up and covered his hand with hers. "So it's not just us, Milo. Imagine, having all our expenses plus trying to redo our kitchen."

He grunted. "Don't knock it, Dawn. Norman and Veronica have an older house that's not on a lake. They probably didn't pay nearly as much for it as we did for ours. A lot of houses out here are under a hundred grand. Their mortgage payment is likely a heck of a lot cheaper than ours. Plus they don't have the expense of commuting or child care, either, with Veronica working nights and being home during the day. Too bad neither of us has a niece or nephew old enough to take care of Zach."

"It doesn't matter. With the way our relatives have acted since we moved, I wouldn't want to give them the satisfaction of letting them know we're in a bind." Milo went into the bathroom and stood in front of the commode.

Dawn followed him, leaning in the doorway. "But Veronica suggested that we females start a reading group, and Camille said she knew someone who might want to join us. Somebody from over there in Phase I. A woman with a daughter in high school." She stared at him meaningfully, the corners of her mouth turned up in a slight smile.

"Ah, I get it. You plan on offering the daughter a job watching Zach."

"If she doesn't already have a summer job lined up, absolutely."

"Well, good." His hand wandered down from her shoulder to squeeze her breast. "Come on to bed. If you make me wait you'll be disappointed."

Now you're talking, she thought happily.

The kitchen needed to be cleaned, but the hell with it. This wasn't an apartment building in Brooklyn, where a plate with crumbs on it left out would attract an army of cockroaches from adjoining, less clean apartments.

She pushed him down on the bed and climbed on top of him, her fears forgotten as his hands slipped beneath her blouse to caress her back.

Thank God for Saturday nights.

* * *

"It costs *how* much? Dawn, are you nuts?"

"It's for our son's welfare, Milo. How can you take the attitude that we're throwing away money? He has to be safe while we're at work!"

"Listen, I'm all for doing our best for Zach, but for crying out loud, we already bought him a house in the country and a dog, both of which he gets to enjoy a hell of a lot more than we do, and we have jobs. Now you want to send him to this expensive-ass day camp." He shook his head.

"This was the cheapest one I could find. They're all expensive."

Whatever happened to that neighbor of the Currys you were going to talk to? Did the girl already have a job?"

She shook her head. "The Kings' girl? I don't know. I haven't met her mother yet. I was hoping Camille would arrange something soon."

"Dawn, you know most of the kids on this block. We were one of the first families to move in. What about that studious kid two doors down?"

"He's a sweet kid, but I don't know. He seems a little effeminate to me. I'd be afraid he'd try something with Zach."

"Forget him," Milo said vehemently. "I guess a girl would be more responsible for child care, anyway. Isn't there anyone else who could be depended on to keep an eye on Zach? They don't have to sit here with him all day, just pop in on him every couple of hours and make sure he's okay."

"He probably won't be cooped up in the house anyway, Milo. He can ride his bike with the neighborhood kids, play with Stormy. Come to think of it, maybe he wouldn't need to go to camp. The association sent out a flyer saying that they'll have some activities for the kids during summer vacation at the clubhouse; movies and game days. And they're hiring two lifeguards to work afternoons so kids can't swim unattended."

"I'm glad they're offering *something* for that six hundred dollars we had to pay them in dues."

The association dues remained a sore spot, just another expense they hadn't known about until the invoice came in the mail last fall with a due date of January thirty-first. The letter enclosed with it stated that the money would be used to maintain the public areas of Arlington Acres including the playground, the tennis courts, the clubhouse, and the pool. Apparently, the salaries of the two lifeguards came out of this fund as well, plus the cost of any social events and snow clearing during the winter.

"Anyway," Milo continued, "it's an easy way for a kid to make some spending money.

Just call Camille and tell her to ask Mrs. King if she thinks her daugther would be interested in the job. You can't wait for her to introduce you. School will be out in a few weeks. And I don't want to pay for that day camp unless there's no other option."

Chapter 26

The Lees
July 2003

Veronica and Norman looked at each other quizzically when the doorbell rang the Saturday morning of Lucy's party.

"It must be one of the neighbors, or maybe one of the neighborhood kids for Lorinda," Norman said.

"Wasn't Lucy planning on getting here early?"

"Not *this* early. It's only a little past 11:00. The party doesn't start until 2:00, so 1:00 is plenty of time for her to get out here and let me get some meat cooking so we'll have some hot dogs and burgers ready when her guests arrive. Not that anybody'll be here promptly at 2:00, anyway. You know how people are. Maybe 2:30, or even 3:00."

She followed him to the front door. "Who is it?" he called out.

"It's me, Lucy."

He opened the door. "Hey, Happy Bir—" He broke off when he noticed the two other cars in front of the house and the people getting out of both the front seat and backseat. Veronica, her face hidden by Norman's arm, frowned.

Lucy followed her brother's gaze. "Oh. A couple of people were afraid they'd get lost, so they asked if they could follow me out."

"But the party doesn't start for another three hours, Lucy," Veronica said. "We weren't expecting guests so soon. I'm still cleaning the house." She'd actually finished her housework an hour ago, but she and Norman hoped to get in a little R & R before Lucy and her guests arrived. Norman would be working the grill, no small task for forty people.

Damn it, she hated how people took advantage. She and Norman had agreed to open their home from 2:00 until 9:00, seven generous hours, but these folks expected to be let in at 11:00.

"It's no big deal, Veronica. I'm sure the house is spotless." Lucy turned to the people behind her and began making introductions.

Norman immediately went into host mode and greeted the guests warmly, while Veronica barely managed a tight-lipped smile. "The bathroom's at the end of the hall, if anyone has to go," he said.

One of the women immediately headed in that direction. Veronica followed, intent on closing the bedroom doors and instructing the girls to stay in their room, at least for now. She didn't want a bunch of strangers snooping around.

As she walked, a man behind her said to Norman, "Y'all got anything to eat? We had to leave so early I didn't have time to eat breakfast."

Her mouth dropped open in amazement. *He shows up three hours early and has the nerve to ask someone to feed him?*

"I'm afraid we won't have anything ready for a while yet," Norman said easily. "The party doesn't officially begin until 2:00, you know. That's still hours away."

"Oh. Right. Where's Mickey D's, then? I'll go out and get something."

"There's no McDonald's in this town. All we have here in Tobyhanna are pizza places. The fast food franchises are in Mount Pocono, about ten, fifteen minutes from here."

"You mean I have to drive a half hour round-trip just to get a hamburger?"

Veronica, having closed the doors to the girls' room and the guest room and now halfway up the steps toward the master suite, covered her mouth with her hand to keep from laughing. She would have loved to go back down so she could hear Norman's response, but she didn't want to risk someone seeing her eavesdrop. She continued to the top of the stairs and slipped past the open closet bars and shelves that lined either side of the stairs—her clothes on one side and Norman's on the other—and closed the double doors of her bedroom behind her. Only then did she let out the laughter she'd been holding in.

As her laugh faded she noticed her jewelry box sitting on the corner of her dresser. Other than her engagement and wedding rings, which stayed on her finger permanently, she owned no really good jewelry, the kind that required storage in a safe; but Lucy's friends didn't know that. They'd likely be curious about what lay at the top of the stairs. She'd better lock this room so she wouldn't have to worry about anyone trying to sneak up to look around and possibly help themselves. After all, she didn't know any of these people. She'd pull Norman aside and let him know. They kept the keys to each bedroom on the ledge of its door frame, but she doubted any of Lucy's guests would discover that.

She locked the doors, then went down to see Lorinda and Simone. "Girls, your Aunt Lucy is here," she said. "Go and tell her Happy Birthday. And when you leave your room be sure and close the door behind you."

"Why, Mommy?" Simone asked. "We don't usually close our door."

She groped for a response. "Uh . . . It'll be easier for Aunt Lucy's friends to find the bathroom if it's the only door left open."

"Okay, Mommy."

Smiling, Veronica watched as her daughters affectionately greeted their aunt with birthday wishes and hugs.

"Damn, I wish I'd known there would be kids here," Veronica heard a woman say. "I'd a brought mine."

"Lucy said no kids, remember?" her companion replied. "These are her brother's kids. Her other brothers are bringing their kids, too. But it's different when you're family."

Veronica felt somewhat consoled to know that at least one of her sister-in-law's friends had some consideration, even if she had no problem showing up so damn early.

"Still," the first woman said, "I had to leave my kids with my mama and gave them all McDonald's money for lunch, plus money to buy a pizza for dinner. I just know these folks are gonna have plenty of food. I mean, this is a nice house. I could have kept my money in my pocket and brought my kids out here to eat. Hell, what are they gonna do, send me all the way back to New York because I brought three kids along?"

"You're bad, girl. But Lucy's brother isn't providing the food. Lucy is. It's her party. They just said she could use their house."

"Well, I'm sure if Lucy didn't bring enough her brother will back her up. It looks like he can afford to."

All Veronica could do was shake her head. And wish 9:00 would hurry and get here.

Lucy's friends brought in the food and beverages from their cars. Lucy asked Norman if he would fire up the grill so they could make some lunch with the meat she brought, and he said, "Lucy, it's a gas grill, and I've got to have my gas tank refilled because it's empty. I wasn't expecting to start cooking for another two hours or so. I would have told you that if you'd mentioned your plans to come so early."

Ten minutes later Lucy and her friends took off in search of something to eat. Norman turned to Veronica. "Can you believe this shit?"

"No, I can't," she said calmly. "Now you see why I didn't want to host this party in the first place. What nerve, expecting us to feed them before noon. They all knew what time the party's supposed to start."

"I'm very disappointed in my sister, asking me to get to cooking right away like I'm the damn butler or something."

"Nor am I the maid. Norman, she just handed me large packages of ground beef, but it's not formed into hamburger patties. I'm wondering if she expects me to do it."

"I don't give a shit what she expects. You're not going to do it. Let her friends help her make the burgers when they get back. It'll give them something to do." He shook his head. "Vee, I'm beginning to think you were right. It might have been a mistake for us to open our home to these people."

"Oh, that reminds me. I locked our bedroom door. It's kind of isolated up there, and someone could easily sneak up." The master bedroom and bath took up the entire second floor, which was smaller than the lower level but still spacious.

"Good idea."

"I've also told Lorinda and Simone to keep the door to their bedroom closed, whether they're in it or not."

"All right. With Lucy putting her stuff in the guest room, I guess she'll automatically keep that closed." He sighed. "Let's relax a while. We'll have to be on our toes from the time they get back until they leave. It's going to be a very long day."

*   *   *

Veronica turned at the sound of her name. She already knew Lucy's best friend, Francine. "Having a good time?"

"Oh, yes. Everything is very nice. But is there someplace I could lay down for a bit?"

She hesitated. Francine wanted to lie down? It was a party, for crying out loud, going full swing in the backyard, with music and laughter. Why would anyone want to lie down? "Aren't you feeling well?"

"Just a little tired. It was a long drive."

Oh, fine. If Francine, who had been one of the early arrivals, felt tired, what was to say the rest of that crew wouldn't feel the same way? The last thing she wanted was to have people stretched out all over her house. "Well, Francine, we've got the bedrooms closed off . . ."

"Just for a little while. I'd feel so much better."

Veronica thought quickly. "All right. You can lie down in the girls' room."

After getting Francine settled Veronica sought out Norman. "I just wanted you to know, Lucy's friend Francine asked if she could take a nap, so I put her in the girls' room."

"Take a nap? You don't come to a party so you can go to sleep. Maybe she should have stayed her ass home, or at least slept later and not come out until 2:00 like she was supposed to."

She stared at him incredulously. Where did he get off acting like she'd done something wrong? "What was I supposed to tell her, Norman?" she hissed. "I didn't want to have this party in the first place, remember?"

"All right, all right. I guess it'll be okay. But I'm going to let Lucy know I think this is ridiculous."

"And that we won't do this again."

"Believe me, I won't have to tell her that part. By the time I get finished she'll know not to ask."

"Can I help you with anything, Veronica?"

"Oh, no thanks. I've got everything under control." How considerate of Dawn to offer help, Veronica thought. Not one of Lucy's friends had, and not even Lucy herself. If anything, her sister-in-law looked shocked when she returned from lunch and Veronica reminded her that she had to make patties out of the pounds and pounds of hamburger she'd brought. Her startled expression told Veronica that she had expected her to take care of it, even after

Norman had stressed to her that their roles were limited. All right, so Norman had volunteered to do the barbecuing, but only because Lucy didn't have the slightest idea about how to grill meat. That didn't mean they would actually form dozens of hamburgers.

And those people she'd invited! The majority of them barely spoke to her and Norman. Good thing she'd invited Dawn and Milo, and the Currys as well, or else they'd have no one to talk to.

She had just turned down what she felt was an excessively loud volume on the boom box providing the music when she noticed Anita, one of Lucy's friends, come out of the house wearing a swimsuit and matching sarong that covered her to midthigh. Anita's statuesque build reminded Veronica of Dawn, who'd been gaining weight recently. She'd worn shorts and a sleeveless knit sweater when she'd arrived, so obviously she had changed clothes. What was up with that?

"Beautiful outfit, Anita," Veronica remarked as she passed by, "but you do realize that we don't have a pool."

"Lucy said your friends have a pool where they live and we could go in that."

"She said *what?*" Veronica shook her head. "No, I heard you. I guess I just can't believe it. Excuse me." For Lucy to treat her and Norman like they were servants was bad enough in itself, but to expect *their* friends to shuttle *her* friends to the Arlington Acres pool was carrying bad behavior too far.

She started to approach Lucy, but changed her mind and looked for Norman instead. Let him handle Lucy. She was *his* sister.

She didn't see Norman outside. Milo, who stood scrubbing the bars of the grill with a brush, said he thought he saw Norman going in the house. "He's about to put on the chicken. Maybe he went to get it from the fridge."

Veronica glanced at her watch. It was 5:15. That was about right. They'd be able to have dinner served by 6:30. She turned toward the house and bumped into Simone. "Sweetie, you've got to watch where you're going, all right?"

"I wanted to get the ball from my room."

"I'm going in. I'll get it for you."

"Is the lady still sleeping?"

"I believe she is. I haven't seen her out here." Francine had been asleep for over an hour now. Maybe she really didn't feel well.

"So you have to be very quiet so you don't wake her up."

"I will." Veronica held her index finger to her lips. Every time either of the kids went to their room to get something they left the door open. Veronica didn't feel like making a big stink over it; after all, they weren't used to having to close their bedroom door. But she'd make sure both bedroom doors were closed, to give the message that these rooms were off-limits.

It surprised her to see the door to the girls' room closed. Lorinda and Simone must not have come back inside lately, or else they remembered to close the door out of consideration for the sleeping Francine.

She opened the door carefully. She heard grunting noises the moment she stepped in the room. She gasped. There, on top of Lorinda's white paneled bed, lay a couple in the throes of passion.

"My God," she exclaimed aloud.

All movement on the bed stopped. The man turned around, and she recognized the embarrassed face of another one of Lucy's friends, not one of the early arrivals, but one who had driven out from the city with his wife. His *wife,* who sat out back with friends, blissfully unaware of her husband breaking a commandment like it meant no more than a cheap drinking glass.

The anxious-looking female beneath him raised her head just high enough to peek out, but Camille recognized her face, too.

Francine. Who'd been so tired.

The last straw.

"I'm sorry. I'm really sorry," the man said as he rushed to pull up his pants.

He didn't even know her name, and she couldn't remember his, either. But she didn't *have* to know his name. He, on the other hand, should have made it his business to know whose home he was in. "I'm sure you are," she said with as much dignity as she could muster, considering she'd just seen his naked ass. "I expect to see both of you outside in the next five minutes." She turned and left the room.

Outside an eager Lorinda ran to her. "Mommy, where's the ball? Simone said you were getting it."

She slapped her thigh. "I forgot it. I'm sorry."

"I'll get it."

"No!" The startled look on her daughter's face made her soften her tone. "You guys can find another game to play that doesn't require a ball. I don't want you going in the house until I tell you it's all right. And that goes for Simone, too. Now, Mommy has to talk to

Daddy and Aunt Lucy about something important." She placed a finger under Lorinda's chin. "Remember, now, no going in the house for *anything* until Daddy or I say it's all right. Understand?"

"Okay, Mommy."

"You make sure your sister knows that. I'm counting on you, now." Veronica gently pinched Lorinda's cheek, then went off to find Norman.

She spotted him talking to Milo as he repositioned chicken quarters on the grill surface with a long-handled spatula. Eddie and Charles had both come to the party, but, probably smarting over having their weekend visits all but eliminated by Norman, mingled with Lucy's guests rather than with their little brother. "Excuse me," she said. "Norman, I need to speak to you right away."

His curiosity showed on his face. "I'll take over," Milo offered.

"Thanks." He gestured for Veronica to lead the way. "What's up?" he asked when they moved out of hearing range.

She told him what she'd just witnessed in the girls' room.

"They were doing *what?*"

"Shh. Sex, Norman. They were doing it right on top of Lorinda's bed. Didn't even have the decency to turn down the bedspread. Which I'll have to wash," she added, making a face.

"The hell you will. Lucy made this mess by inviting these lowlifes to our house, and she'll clean it up. What did you say to them?"

"I told them that I expected them to rejoin the party right away."

"I don't want them here at all. They disrespected our house big-time, Veronica. They need to go home."

She knew he meant business by his use of her full name. "That'll be a little embarrassing for him, since he'll have to give his wife a reason. And now that I think of it, I think she's here with someone, too."

"After you walked in on them, they can't possibly be any more embarrassed. I want them off my property."

"Norman, don't you think Lucy ought to be the one to tell them? They're her guests."

"That's fine. She ought to know about the disgraceful way her friends behaved in someone else's house, anyway, so she'll know why we'll never host another party for her. But if she doesn't want to tell them they have to leave, *I'll* tell them."

"Hopefully they'll realize they should go anyway, under the circumstances."

"There's Lucy now. Come on, let's fill her in, and then all three of us will go talk to those adulterers."

Lucy appeared stunned at hearing what had transpired. "I thought I saw a little flirting going on between Francine and Lyman—"

So that was his name, Veronica thought.

"—but how dare they use your home to start an affair, and right under the noses of his wife and her boyfriend." Her eyes darted around the yard. "Are they back out here with everybody?"

"Lucy, we don't want them back. We want them out of here right now."

"Out? But Norman, that's not fair. What'll they tell their partners if you throw them out?"

"It's not my problem, Lucy. They should have thought about that before they decided to have sex in my house, on my eleven-year-old daughter's bed."

"You've got to admit that takes a lot of nerve, Lucy," Veronica said. "Especially when his wife or her boyfriend could have come looking for them at any time."

"They were in my daughters' room," Norman repeated. "Lorinda or Simone could have walked in on them."

Veronica nervously chewed her lower lip. She didn't mention that Lorinda had been about to retrieve a ball from her room; it would only serve to infuriate Norman even more.

Lucy cast an incredulous stare at Veronica, then at Norman. "I understand they showed horrible judgment, but you actually plan on telling them to leave?"

"No," Norman said calmly. "*You're* going to do it."

"Me? It's not *my* house."

"No, it isn't. But they're *your* guests. Veronica and I sure as hell didn't invite them." Norman took her arm. "Come on, Vee, let's go."

Lyman and Francine, now fully clothed, stood quietly talking in the living room, looking up expectantly at the sight of the threesome approaching them.

Lyman spoke first, and with his words Veronica knew Francine had coached him on their names. "Norman, Veronica, Lucy," he began. "I can't tell you how sorry we are about what happened. It wasn't planned, believe me. It just happened. We got caught up in the moment." He met Norman's eyes. "You know how it is when you get the urge."

"I may know how it is, Lyman," Norman said coldly, "but I'm

not into cheating on my wife. And even if I were, if I were in some-one else's home and my wife was right outside I'd manage to cool it until a more appropriate time."

"I'm sorry, too," Francine said, practically crying. "Honestly."

"I believe you," Lucy said. "But what were you two thinking of?"

"Uh, you didn't mention anything about this to Barbara or Danny, did you?" Lyman asked.

"No. I'm not interested in doing that," Norman answered in an unfriendly tone. "I just want to make it clear that my wife and I won't tolerate certain acts being committed in our home."

"In that case, it might be best if we just forget the whole thing," Lyman suggested. "I'd like to get back to Barbara before she comes looking for me."

Norman and Veronica's eyes both focused on Lucy, who said nothing.

"Wait, Lyman," Norman said. "Since my sister doesn't want to say this, I will. I'm sorry, but I think the best thing to do is for both of you to leave."

Their distress showed on their faces. "Leave!"

"We think it's best," Veronica said firmly.

"But that puts me in a bad spot. What am I supposed to tell Barbara?" Lyman asked. He caught Norman's stone-faced expression and sighed in defeat. "Go on out now, Francine. Tell Danny you're still not feeling well. At least you'll have an excuse for leaving. I'll come up with something, but we shouldn't do it at the same time."

Francine nodded. "I'm really sorry," she repeated weakly to Norman and Veronica before leaving.

When she left Lyman tried again. "I wish you wouldn't do this," he said. "You've really put me in a spot."

Veronica spoke quietly. "I think it's a little late to worry about that."

He stared at her. She saw Norman's eyes narrow, as if he dared Lyman to say something to her. She held her breath, fearing a physi-cal altercation between the two. But "Yeah," was all he said.

"I think we should all go outside now," Norman suggested. "Our guests are going to start to wonder what we're up to in here." He turned to Lyman and made a sweeping gesture. "After you."

Head shaking as if to chide himself for his own stupidity—or per-haps out of annoyance at Norman for forcing him to leave mid-party—Lyman headed for the back door.

"Well, that's over," Veronica remarked.

"Maybe for you," Lucy said, "but neither one of them will probably ever speak to me again."

Norman turned to her. "I don't see why you're upset, Lucy. You didn't tell them to leave, even though I still think it would have been better if it came from you. So your reputation is still intact." Sarcasm radiated from his last sentence.

"Norman, you're not being fair."

"Incidentally, Lucy," Veronica said, "I've decided to switch your room. I'm going to let the girls sleep in the guest room and put you in their room, so you might want to wash the linens on Lorinda's bed before you sleep in it tonight." She took a moment to savor the discomforted look on her sister-in-law's face before taking Norman's arm and leaving with him.

By this time Camille and Reuben had gathered around the grill with Dawn and Milo. Both of the men tended to the chicken. "Thanks a lot for watching the meat for me, fellas," Norman said. "Hope I didn't put you out too much."

"Hey, this is good practice for me," Reuben replied. "I'm still trying to master the art of grilling chicken."

"The last time he tried it the insides came out pink," Camille said with a laugh. "I had to put them in the oven to finish cooking."

"Tattletale," he shot back playfully.

"Milo makes great chicken," Dawn stated, pride in her voice. "We used to grill all the time on our terrace in Brooklyn."

"Tell me, guys," Veronica began, "were any of you approached by any of the guests and asked to bring them to your pool?"

"Our pool?" Dawn repeated quizzically.

"You must mean the Arlington Acres pool," Reuben said.

"Why would anyone ask them that?" Norman asked as Veronica nodded. Then she saw his shoulders stiffen. "Don't tell me that Lucy—"

"Did you notice that swimsuit her friend Anita was wearing? When I reminded her we don't have a pool she said Lucy told her that they'd be able to use the pool where our friends live. I never got a chance to ask Norman to look into it."

"Well, nobody said anything to me," Camille said.

"Me, neither," Dawn added. "And no one can even get in the pool without a key. I certainly wouldn't give my key to anyone. They charge twenty-five dollars to replace lost ones. Maybe Lucy's friend just wanted an excuse to walk around in that outfit. I did see her in it. It's fabulous," she said admiringly. The kind of outfit that she would have bought in a heartbeat in the days before they bought their house. How long had it been since she'd bought something new? "Besides, how would they get over to Tobyhanna?"

"Don't ask," Veronica said quietly. "But I'm glad no one said anything to either of you."

"Hey, there's a buzz going on about something," Reuben remarked.

Veronica looked at the guests and saw groups of people whispering among each other and pointing with their chins. Others covered half-open mouths with their fingertips. She knew gossip when she saw it. Francine had already taken leave with her date, and she guessed that word had circulated that Lyman and his wife were leaving as well. The rest of Lucy's friends undoubtedly found that strange. Veronica wondered how many of them had seen Lyman slipping into the house while Francine was allegedly asleep. Her own strained expression when she and Norman brought Lucy to confront the two might have been noticed as well.

"Gee, I can't imagine what they're talking about," she said sweetly.

Chapter 27

As they were about to leave Arnelle's Bronx apartment, Camille stopped to give Reuben's niece one more affectionate hug. "I hope you had a nice summer, Tiffany. Reuben and I really enjoyed having you with us, and so did Mitchell and Shayla."

"Thanks, Aunt Camille. I had a lot of fun. I wish Mom and I could move out there. I like it out there a lot more than I do here."

"Well, you feel free to come and visit us anytime." Camille meant what she said. Tiffany had been a joy. Not that her cousin Kierra wasn't welcome, but Kierra had some habits Camille didn't care for. For one, she was a slob. Second, she seemed to make a concerted effort to get into their business, asking inappropriate questions like how much their mortgage payment—she called it "rent"—was each month and hanging around when Camille and Reuben had candid conversations with each other. Camille didn't feel that she and her husband should have to limit their semiprivate conversations to their bedroom.

Tiffany, on the other hand, had as little interest in what she and Reuben said to each other as Mitchell and Shayla did. She made friends in the neighborhood including Destiny King, Denise and Lemuel King's daughter who kept an eye on Zachary Young. The girls often brought their charges for afternoons at the community pool. When it came to Mitchell's playmates, Camille much preferred Zach to Alex Cole, who lived around the corner. She had nothing against the kid, but something about his parents, Douglas and Tanisha, didn't seem quite right.

They weren't particularly friendly, for one thing. Actually, their behavior bordered on rudeness. And after Veronica told Camille she'd seen the Coles leaving their barbeque without saying good-bye, their relationship with their new friends had gone downhill. Then the Coles had stopped taking the commuter bus in favor of a carpool that left from southern Jersey, and after that the two couples barely spoke.

Tanisha and Douglas's near animosity made Camille uncomfortable whenever Mitchell went over there to play with Alex. Reuben said she was overreacting, that it broke no laws for people not to make small talk.

She wondered if someone had offended them at the barbecue, since that seemed to mark the beginning of their change of attitude. She considered her in-laws as prime suspects. Saul, Brenda, Arnelle . . . any one of them could have said something insulting. Reuben, however, said the Coles were just strange folks, and if they acted like they didn't want to be bothered she should follow their lead. But Camille had had high hopes for a lasting alliance with the first black couple she and Reuben had met in Tobyhanna, and it disappointed her to see their fledgling friendship go the way of the Betamax. Fortunately, it didn't matter so much anymore, not now that she had Veronica and Dawn as friends.

Besides, now she had other things to worry about. Reuben's job had ended in late July, but they chose not to say anything about it to the children until after Tiffany went home. Even though the chain that employed Reuben was in the Bronx, its location wasn't near the apartments of his mother or siblings, so they had no reason to know the store had closed and he was out of a job. They merely told everyone, even their own children, that Reuben was taking some accrued vacation time. The timing worked well. He'd been home only one week when they returned Tiffany to Arnelle.

Camille turned Tiffany over to Reuben while she said good-bye to Arnelle.

"Thanks so much for letting my daughter stay with you guys this summer," Arnelle said.

"We loved having her. She was a big help. Uh . . . how's Brenda?" Reuben's other sister had been angry when Reuben told her that he felt that Arnelle's daughter also deserved a summer in the country.

Kierra, Brenda said, had been looking forward to spending another summer in Pennsylvania.

Arnelle shook her head. "Still not speaking to me."

"I'm sorry to hear that, Arnelle," Camille said.

"Don't worry, sis," Reuben urged. "She'll come around. You want me to talk to her?"

"No, Reuben. It's between her and me. But thanks."

For a moment Arnelle seemed like her old self, the sister-in-law who had been more like a sister to Camille. She found herself hoping the two sisters would make up soon.

As Camille and Reuben left the apartment and walked toward the elevator, rap music blared from several of the apartments. "God, that's loud," she remarked.

"You've forgotten how noisy life is in these big buildings. Even when we lived in the city, we only had one neighbor across the hall. No one upstairs."

"But all that noise downstairs from the sheet metal shop and from the El," she said with a smile. Then she wrinkled her nose as she breathed in a variety of food odors: frying chicken, sautéing onions, tomato sauce, and frying fish. Separately they would be pleasant. Together they were anything but, especially in an enclosed hallway that received virtually no ventilation.

Her stomach did a little dance. To get her mind off the combined odors, she concentrated on the graffiti surrounding the three elevators, some in blue ink, some in black marker. She recognized dried paint strokes, sloppy attempts to cover previous markings. The paint splotches here and there gave the walls a spotty appearance. The elevator doors themselves were free of markings, but their windows had been covered with a metal plate in a crisscross pattern to guard against breaks.

An elevator stopped, and they stepped inside. It held no other passengers. A sticky mess of purple liquid sat in one corner, with chewed pink bubble gum on top. Camille's stomach already felt a little queasy after all those conflicting food odors in the hallway. Now she made a gurgling noise as she fought back a sudden rising of bile in her throat.

"Camille, you okay?"

"I'll be all right. I just need some fresh air." She forced herself to look away from the mess on the floor. Thank God her family didn't live on top of each other in a twenty-story apartment building, riding this cage up and down. Thank God they didn't have to listen to what everyone on the floor played on their CDs or smell what they were making for dinner.

"I know what you're thinking," he said. "And I'm glad we don't live in the city anymore, too. This environment is what both Brenda and Arnelle wanted to get their kids away from."

Camille had sat next to Reuben two months ago when he called Brenda to give her the bad news. In Brenda's excitement her voice rose, allowing Camille to hear every word.

"Reuben, Kierra is looking forward to spending the summer at your house. Why should my daughter be penalized just because I was quick enough on the draw to arrange for her to have some protection against being at home alone all day? It never even occurred to Arnelle to ask about Tiffany until after Kierra was out there."

"I'm sorry you feel Kierra is being penalized, but they're both my nieces," he replied evenly, "and I don't play favorites. I'd like to help both of them. Kierra can come back next year."

At that Camille turned away and made a face. She hoped Kierra never came back. The girl was too nosy. She wouldn't be surprised if Brenda put her up to trying to find out as much as she could about their personal business and report everything she saw or heard. Wasn't it enough that Brenda had looked through their financial records last Thanksgiving?

Besides, what would Brenda and Arnelle have done to occupy their daughters if she and Reuben hadn't moved to Tobyhanna?

Camille felt relieved when the elevator doors opened. She practically ran through the double sets of doors to get outside. She breathed deeply, then took Reuben's arm. "There are many beautiful places in New York City," she said, "but few of them are in the Bronx."

He chuckled. "In August it's all ugly, except for the botanical gardens." His good humor faded at the sight of two teenagers sitting on the hood of their car with a boom box between them. The youngsters promptly got up when they realized Reuben was the driver of the car they sat on, moving to the hood of the car parked in front of their Malibu.

"I know what *you're* thinking," Camille teased, "but I guess you've forgotten how kids in the city sit on people's cars."

"Damn punks." He buckled his seat belt, then started the ignition. "Okay, so we'll pick up the kids from Dawn and Milo. Now that Tiffany's gone I think we ought to sit them down and explain to them about me losing my job."

"I don't want to frighten them, Reuben. Maybe it should wait until we get back from our trip." They planned to spend a few days at the Maryland shore, their first trip since moving to Pennsylvania. "Are you sure we should even go?"

"Why not? I'm still getting paid. I think that telling the kids I'm out of a job and then going on vacation like we planned will be good for them. They probably won't be concerned at all. It'll seem like everything is normal, business as usual. And as soon as we get back I'll start looking for a job locally."

She sat silently and let it sink in. Reuben's commuting days were over.

But hers would go on. Indefinitely.

Her eyes narrowed and her lower lip protruded. It wasn't fair.

Chapter 28

The Youngs
September 2003

"Hey, it looks nice in here," Milo said approvingly, looking at the freshly painted master bedroom. "No wonder you wanted me to lay down in Zach's room. These colors look great, Dawn."

"Mom did most of it, but I helped," Zach said with pride.

"Yes, Zach did all the edging, and he helped cover the baseboards with blue painter's tape," Dawn said in agreement. "As for the colors, they say that blue and green are the most soothing." Hands in pockets, she took a deep breath of satisfaction, proud of her accomplishment. The four walls of their bedroom were now a deep blue, and the ceiling a sea green.

She'd gotten the idea to paint the ceiling a different shade from a picture in a home-decorating magazine while browsing at a Barnes & Noble near her office. Having a house should mean more than just moving in your furniture and enjoying your yard. She wanted a real home, one they could decorate any way they pleased. The long list of rules at the apartment in Brooklyn included no painting walls colors other than those provided by the management: white, off-white, tan, pale blue, and mint green, all light and boring hues. Next weekend she and Zach would paint his room cranberry with an orange ceiling.

It made her feel good that Milo complimented her work, but she would prefer it if he offered to help. It seemed like all he ever wanted to do on the weekends since they moved in was to sleep in and then later nap for several hours on the couch in the afternoons. She knew he worked hard, and so did she, but he never wanted to have fun anymore. She had to practically drag him out of the house to get him to bring her to the movies. Reuben Curry tried to get Milo to join him at tennis, but he had yet to pick up a racket.

He reminded her of the father on an old TV commercial whose family took a vacation that he slept through. Wherever the setting—a deck chair on a cruise ship, a hammock at a secluded beach, stretched out on a towel under an umbrella on a busy beach—he sat snoring, oblivious to the sounds of his family frolicking nearby.

When Dawn asked Milo about helping her to give the house more personality, more life, he'd simply shrugged and said, "We're going to be here a long time, Dawn. We'll make changes and improvements, sure, but we don't have to do it all right away."

He had a point—this house was comfortable enough size-wise where she imagined them living here the rest of their lives, even after Zach left for college, but she couldn't help being anxious to get started, especially after seeing what Veronica and Norman had done to their place. She and Milo had spent last Sunday afternoon at the Lee home, and Veronica had proudly shown them their newly re-modeled master bathroom upstairs, with its rust-colored marble countertops and dual raised sinks in burnt orange. Milo commented that the sinks reminded him of mixing bowls, but Dawn found the look sleek. Even the faucets looked futuristic. And soon the Lees would begin work on their kitchen.

That house she and Camille Curry had privately snickered about was turning into something quite attractive. The pink bathroom in the downstairs hall was a thing of the past, having been replaced months ago. Plus their house had come with a completely finished basement with insulation. The houses in Arlington Acres came with what they called an "English basement," meaning it had climate control but unfinished walls and floors. The overall effect reminded her of a storm cellar, someplace where you stored unused belongings or hid in during violent weather.

Dawn knew from conversations on the bus that some of her neighbors had put up paneling and laid down flooring or carpets in their basements, improvements that likely transformed it into more of a rec room.

One thing for sure: she and Milo wouldn't be finishing their basement any time soon. The only projects she could consider were the ones that she could handle alone, or with a little help from Zach.

Still, the improvements the Lees made to their house made her want to do more to hers than just paint. She wondered where Norman and Veronica had gotten the money to pay for everything. Clearly they'd spared no expense, with their marble countertops and those great-looking twenty-first century sinks. Could buying an older house mean that much lower a mortgage payment every month?

Dawn quickly realized there was more to it than that. The Lees didn't live in a subdivision, which meant they had no association dues. Nor did they have the expense of paying for bus passes into the city. Lucky them.

She had another reason for wanting to fix up their home a little. Their friends in the city had already begun asking if she and Milo would be giving another party. No one had been out since the large housewarming they threw last fall. She didn't want to give the impression that they only entertained if it meant getting gifts. Everybody had a great time last year, and if they did it again she wanted to have made noticeable improvements to the house and grounds. She'd held off on asking Milo about it, but she believed he might go for it. After all, they had saved a small fortune on Zach's care over the summer by paying Destiny King to look in on him instead of sending him to day camp. They wouldn't have to buy a lot of liquor for their friends, just some beer and wine. No point serving mixed drinks to people who had a hundred-mile drive home.

She liked it when they entertained. It reminded her of the old days back in Brooklyn. Even Milo perked up. He'd been a different person when they had the Currys and the Lees over for PO-KE-NO and that boxing match on pay-per-view. It sure beat listening to him grouse part of the time and snore the rest of the time.

Milo stretched. "You and Zach worked hard today, Dawn. What say I reward you two by taking you both out to dinner?"

She grinned. "I'm all for it, and Zach will be, too. Just give me an hour to get cleaned up."

"Sure. I'll move the furniture back while you get ready. It's dry now, isn't it?"

"Let's wait until tomorrow morning to give it a chance to get completely dry. We'll have to sleep with the bed in the middle of the floor tonight." Already Dawn wished she'd gone ahead and done this months ago instead of waiting for him to help her. Her little initiative might have sparked a change in him. She couldn't remember the last time he had suggested he take her and Zach to dinner, and as far as his offer to move the bedroom furniture back against the wall . . . that represented more activity than he usually did around the house in a month. Hmmm . . . This might be a good time to ask about giving another party for their friends.

He winked at her. Leaning over and speaking in her ear so only she could hear, he said, "In that case, why don't I help you get cleaned up?"

She turned to their son. "Zach, go take a shower and change your clothes. We'll go to Applebee's for dinner in about an hour."

"All right! Barbecued ribs!" Zach high-fived Milo before running toward his room.

She closed the door behind Zach and turned to see her husband grinning at her in a way she hadn't seen in far too long. As she walked into his arms she wondered, could something as simple as new colors on their bedroom walls bring about such a positive change in him? Hell, if that was all it took she'd cheerfully paint the whole damn house!

They had an enjoyable, tasty meal and returned home and ordered a pay-per-view movie. Dawn didn't like all the bad language in it, but she knew that she couldn't protect her son forever. At eleven, he was growing up, and he had to know the way some people spoke.

She snuggled on the sofa with Milo, her head resting on a pillow in his lap, while Zach sat on a floor pillow with Stormy at his side.

After the movie Zach announced he was going to bed. He hugged Dawn good night, and then Milo. "Come on, Stormy," he said. The dog dutifully followed him. She would spend the night at the foot of Zach's bed, as usual.

"Well, that was unusual," Dawn remarked. "I don't get hugs like I used to from Zach. I figure it's because he's growing up. Now he's hugging both of us. I wonder what brought that on."

"He's happy," Milo said. "He had a good day, plus a pleasant evening. He hasn't had too many days like this lately." She had moved into a sitting position to embrace Zach and stayed there, and Milo reached for her hand. "Dawn, I know I haven't been spending as much time as I should with both of you. My system is having real difficulty adjusting to that long ride every day, and by the weekend I'm worn out. But I'll promise you I'll try to do better."

"I guess I can't ask for anything more than that," she said softly, stroking his fingers.

With his other hand he rubbed her shoulder. "Let's go to bed."

Dawn, asleep contentedly in Milo's arms after the most romantic evening they'd had in months, jerked at the loud noise that sounded frighteningly near. "What was that?"

Even he looked startled. "It sounds like it came from the closet."

She relaxed. At least no one had broken into the house. "Something must have fallen over."

Milo put on his glasses, then threw back the covers and walked to the closet, Dawn hovering close behind him. He hesitated at the door, then pushed it open in one motion. "Oh, shit."

Dawn gasped. A beam had collapsed in the back corner of the closet, its weight taking down one of the clothing racks. Clothes now littered the floor of the previously neat space, both those that had been hanging as well as the baseball caps and sweaters from the shelf above.

"This would happen now, damn it," Milo said. "Our warranty expired just last month. Bastards must have timed it to last just over a year."

"You mean this isn't covered by our home owners insurance?"

"Hell, no. That policy is for things like fire and theft and damage from falling trees. We'll have to pay to fix this shit ourselves. Damn." He slammed the door shut and shook his head in disgust. "I'm going back to bed."

Dawn could think of no comforting words. She began picking up the fallen items, then realized she had nowhere to place them. She'd have to wait for Milo to rehang the rack. She hoped to God he would do it later today. She didn't want to have to ask him and have him accuse her of nagging, especially after the nice time they had had, but how could they possibly manage with their clothes on the floor?

Instinctively she knew that the brief respite of contentment with his life had passed.

Milo not only rehung the white wire rack that day before she had to prompt him, but by Tuesday he arranged to have the beam replaced. "It's there for a structural reason," he told Dawn. "If we just let it stay down, we're likely to have a cave-in, and that'll *really* cost us." He shook his head. "I can't believe how much we have to pay to have this fixed. What the hell did the builder do, slap this house together like a deck of cards?"

Dawn thought of the expense they'd incurred last spring to raise the height of the lot that their house stood on and she wondered the same thing.

"I'm getting tired of shelling out all this cash for this or for that," Milo continued. "I never thought I'd ever have to pay for a septic system or for someone to collect our garbage, for Christ's sake."

"It's all part of living in the suburbs, Milo. It's pretty and clean here, but it can't be free. Somebody has to pay for it."

"Yes, but it would have been nice if we'd been told about the price tag before the bills showed up in our mailbox. We might have decided the cost was too high and stayed in Brooklyn, where we could flush our toilet and put our trash down the chute for free."

She remembered Veronica saying about how she and Norman had attended a home-buyer's seminar, where they learned about things like home owners association fees and septic systems and snow clearance. Of course, Dawn knew all about these things now, but that knowledge came from learning the hard way. The Lees had definitely been better prepared to buy a home in Pennsylvania than she and Milo had.

Still, the thought of continuing to live in Brooklyn next door to an apartment where a friend had been murdered made her twist her mouth in distaste. "I'm glad we're out of there."

"You make it sound like we lived in a tenement, Dawn. Yeah, there were some maintenance problems in the building, but they're being fixed."

They knew from their friends Carmen and Donald Triggs that the elevators had been replaced, one at a time; and that residents had been encouraged not to let strangers past the locked vestibule of the building, but instead let them call the apartment they were visiting and be buzzed in. Signs to this effect had been put up. Hazel's murder had prompted this action, as review of the security tapes showed a strange man being let in by a resident at eight PM the night she was murdered. The grainy image still hadn't led to an arrest, and Hazel's apartment had been cleaned out and rented to an unsuspecting new tenant, but the police felt certain this man had committed the murder, as he was shown leaving around the time of Hazel's death.

"We had a good life there," Milo concluded.

"You can't deny it isn't nicer here," she said stubbornly.

"No, I can't. But when do we really get a chance to enjoy it? I only get fifteen personal days a year, plus maybe seven holidays. Weekends don't count. By the time I've rebounded after commuting all week it's time to go back to work again. So not only am I broke but tired, too. I'm sorry, Dawn, but living here isn't like I thought it would be."

She sighed. Life in Pennsylvania hadn't panned out to what she wanted, either. She found the bills just as staggering as Milo did. But they lived here now. They had to make the best of it.

Chapter 29

The Currys
September 2003

Camille slammed the car door and wearily fastened her seat belt. "God, I'm beat. The kids okay?" Usually Reuben brought Mitchell and Shayla with him when he came to the station to pick her up.

"And hello to you, too, Camille."

"Oh, I'm sorry. Hi."

He started the car. "The kids are fine. I left them home so I could talk to you. I had some good news today. I've got a job at FedEx."

Camille immediately brightened. "They pay good, don't they?"

"Yes." He named an hourly rate. "Not bad for loading and unloading packages on trucks."

"Well, that'll certainly help. Actually, with no commuting expenses, it'll help quite a bit." Referring to Reuben's lack of a commute still left a lump in her throat, but she forced herself to think about the positive effect one fewer bus pass would have on their budget. "They have good benefits, too, don't they?"

"Uh . . . I heard something about tuition reimbursement and discount travel."

Her eyes widened. She and Reuben certainly deserved a vacation—without the kids—after all they'd been through. Maybe they could go somewhere romantic for a few days, like Charleston or Savannah. Hell, maybe they could even go to Vegas, a place she'd always wanted to see. Did they really have slot machines in ladies' rooms and supermarkets, like people said?

She could barely keep up with her thoughts, which had gotten on a runaway train. They should be able to get Brenda or Arnelle to keep the kids, returning the favor they'd done by having Kierra and Tiffany stay with them for an entire summer.

"But there's something you have to know," he said quickly. "I do get some benefits, but my job is only part-time. Twenty-five hours a week." Seeing her crestfallen expression, he quickly added, "It's better than nothing, Camille."

She felt like a deflated tire. "But it's not what you were making at the store. And with just working part-time—"

"I'm sure I can get another part-time job at the supermarket here. That'll bring in more money and, besides, I won't have to buy a bus pass to ride into the city. I can even arrange my hours so I'll be there for the kids when they get home from school."

Her mouth set in a hard line at the second reminder in a minute's time that Reuben no longer had to commute to the city. Except for the part about working a second job, he would have the life *she* wanted. It wasn't fair. "How nice for you," she said rigidly.

"Camille, I know you're annoyed that you still have to get up so early and make that long trip and I don't. I know you wanted to get a job here in Pennsylvania. You still can, if you can find one that pays decently. But you haven't been able to in a year and a half, and you've gotten a promotion and are making even more money. Right now we're just not in a position for you to take a pay cut."

She sighed. "I'm tired, Reuben. Let's talk later." To herself she added, *I spend five hours a day going back and forth to work, a problem* you *don't have anymore.*

At home she wearily climbed the stairs to her bedroom, stopping to look in on the children. "Mom, didya hear about Daddy's new job?" Mitchell asked with excitement.

"Yes, I did. It's wonderful news."

"We won't lose our house now, will we?"

She looked at him sharply, not even sure she'd heard him correctly. "Mitchell, what a question to ask!"

"Well, Alex had to move back to the city. His parents didn't have enough money to pay the bank for their house every month. They didn't even know where they were going to sleep when they left."

Camille lowered her chin to her chest as she studied her son. Now that he mentioned it, Alex hadn't been around lately, nor had she seen Douglas or Tanisha in passing. "Did Alex tell you this?" she asked curiously.

"No, all he said was that his parents didn't like it here and they were going back to the city. But he didn't want to go. He said he likes it a whole lot better here than the city. He told me that last week, and the next day he was gone."

"So where did the rest come from, about them losing their house?" She figured someone had started a rumor. For all anyone knew, the Coles might have had a family emergency and would be back in a few days.

"I heard about it from Mike Willis. He said he heard his parents talking at night."

Marianne Willis sold real estate, so she'd be sure to know the status of the Cole house. Camille's shoulders slumped. Unfortunately, it sounded like the story had merit.

That would explain a couple of things. Now she understood why Tanisha Cole never had much to say and sometimes even sought to avoid her. *Hell, if I were about to be thrown out of my home I wouldn't feel like grinning at people, either.*

It made her uneasy that Marianne knew the truth behind the Coles' abrupt departure. She'd probably told everybody on the block about it. Everybody except her and Reuben, that is. All the white families were probably buzzing about the blacks who'd been foreclosed on. Camille didn't want to think badly of her next-door neighbors. Marianne and Jeff Willis had been kind to them from the beginning. Jeff even helped move in their furniture. Still, she would have loved to have been the proverbial fly on the wall to overhear the private conversations of the other home owners on the block. It wouldn't surprise her if the words "dumb niggers" came up.

Camille had no fantasies about how her neighbors perceived black people. Sure, they were friendly, and careful to never consider using any racial slurs in front of her and Reuben, to whom they'd shown only cordiality. But let a person of color cut them off on the highway and see how fast that word came out of their mouths. Camille believed that everybody had a touch of Archie Bunker in them; that no one, no matter what ethnic group they belonged to, was immune to using a racial slur when they felt wronged by a person of identifiable ethnicity. The standoffishness Tanisha and Douglas demonstrated had done little to endear them to any of the other families on the street, and she suspected that many of them privately celebrated the Coles' downfall. She wondered if anyone made the connection between their behavior and the fear they must have felt.

They'd probably lived in fear and dread for a long time, possibly as long as she'd known them. Foreclosures didn't happen overnight. The Coles might have been struggling for years, possibly from the day they'd moved in. Maybe they, too, hadn't done their homework, or had gone overboard with decorating, or both.

Now Camille felt guilty for wishing Mitchell had a playmate from a more cordial family, and for resenting the Coles for eating and running at the barbecue she and Reuben gave for their families and new friends. A free meal for your entire family must be pretty appealing when you were behind on your mortgage.

But that bit about them not knowing where they would sleep, that had to be pure fiction. No way would Marianne and Jeff Willis know something so private. The Coles certainly wouldn't have confided in them. Either that son of Marianne and Jeff's had embellished, or he had heard his parents making presumptions about the Coles' plight.

"Mitchell," she said, "Daddy and I are *not* going to lose our house. We'll have to cut back on some things, but we'll have a roof over our heads, enough to eat, and you'll never have to worry about having a place to sleep."

"But Alex's parents lost their house and they both still had jobs."

Mitchell was twelve years old, but suddenly he looked about six. He'd really been worried that the same thing would happen to them that had happened to the Coles. She chose her words carefully. "You know, Mitchell, just because Mike Willis told you the Coles couldn't pay their mortgage doesn't mean it's true. Maybe they really did go back to the city because they didn't like it here, like Alex told you. I understand that Alex didn't want to go, but it's the grown-ups who get to make the decisions, not the kids."

She spoke to Reuben about it after the kids were in bed. Poor Douglas and Tanisha, having to make a quick departure without a word to anyone, probably in the middle of the night when no one could see them. "How do you suppose that happened? Like Mitchell said, they didn't have an unemployment problem like we do."

"Camille, we don't know *what* kind of problems they had. Do you think that if one of them were out of work they would have told us about it? Those people barely said fifty words to me the whole time we've lived out here. Douglas told me about a good barber, and that was it. If their little boy didn't play with Mitchell we wouldn't even know they weren't still around."

"Yeah, I guess."

"Then again, maybe they just didn't plan well," Reuben remarked. "There's a lot to take into consideration when you move all the way out here from the city. To be very honest, you and I could have done a better job of it ourselves. Remember how we just presumed that there'd be a day care center that stayed open until eight o'clock to cater to New York commuters?"

"Yes, I remember." She had a flash of the funny looks she used to get from the librarians on duty when she and Reuben finally arrived to pick up the kids after seven-thirty at night. It was like they were saying, "*We* know what you're up to." Nor could she forget Veronica's incredulous stare when she learned that they had driven to town for the day with the intent of buying a house, then turned around and drove back to New York without doing any research on the area. Reuben was right; they could have planned better.

"Do you think Mitchell is still worried?"

"No, I think I reassured him." Camille looked around at their comfortable bedroom, which had the same black lacquer furniture they'd had in the Bronx. How frightening, she thought, to lose the roof over your head. Where did you go? Many city dwellers lived in cramped quarters already without taking in an entire family.

When she knelt to say her prayers that night, she included a prayer for the Cole family. She felt a strange vibration in her chest, like a motor running, that she recognized as stress. She really didn't know the Coles, so she didn't understand why she felt so troubled by their misfortune.

Then, as she felt Reuben climb into bed beside her, it suddenly hit her.

There but for the grace of God, go I.

She went eagerly into Reuben's embrace, thrilled to be able to make love to her husband in the privacy of their bedroom. Tanisha and Douglas Cole might not be able to have this private time together, not if they were sleeping on someone's pull-out sofa bed.

Chapter 30

The Lees
October 2003

The reading group had their first discussion on a Saturday night in October. Veronica, who offered to host, scheduled it to coincide with a boxing match on cable TV. Camille felt a little funny, like she should have been the one to host, since it had been her suggestion to bring Denise King into the group, but Veronica pointed out that it had been her idea to start the group in the first place.

What Veronica considerately didn't mention, and the reason Camille felt so awkward, was that the change in Reuben's work status would make entertaining a strain for them. Camille suspected that Veronica and Dawn had discussed the situation privately among themselves, probably with a "poor Camille" or two thrown in. She hated the idea of anyone feeling sorry for her.

Camille didn't want to make too much out of it, but she would have preferred to provide a meal for eight adults plus assorted children—even if it was just chicken, hot dogs and baked beans—now than later. Right now they were doing fine, with Reuben getting paid from his part-time job plus a full check every two weeks as part of his severance package. In a few weeks his severance would be all paid out, and he would have only the income from his part-time job. She'd insist on having the next get-together at her house, just in case things got sticky down the road.

Reuben planned to inform his mother about his job loss after he received his final paycheck. Ginny, of course, would inform his siblings. Camille dreaded having them know her business. She would talk to them over the phone, but she could practically see the smug smiles on their faces as they tried to project real concern, asking if they'd be able to manage on a reduced income.

As part of Veronica's organizing the group, she searched a book list until she found one all of them had read. They agreed to discuss it at their first meeting, but, seated around the Lees' pecan-wood dining room table while the guys gathered in the family room, Veronica had barely had a chance to make opening remarks when Denise King said, "Did y'all hear about Doug and Tanisha Cole?"

"What about them?" Dawn's flippant tone suggested she was still smarting from Tanisha's snubbing her.

"They don't live in Arlington Acres anymore."

Veronica looked surprised. "They sold their house?"

"In a matter of speaking. The bank sold it for them."

Dawn drew in her breath. "They were foreclosed on?"

"I'm afraid so." Denise turned to Camille. "You knew about it, didn't you, Camille? You lived closer to them than me."

"Yes, I knew," she said reluctantly. Talking about a family who'd lost their home while worried about her own family's future held little appeal, but Veronica and Dawn both seemed fascinated to know more. "They left without saying anything to anybody, except their son told Mitchell that his parents didn't like it out here and they were going back to the city. But a couple of our neighbors said they'd been foreclosed on. I thought they might have been talking out of school, but then I saw the sign in their yard saying FORECLOSED PROPERTY FOR SALE."

"That's too bad," Dawn said. "Tanisha really pissed me off that day at the store, but I hate to hear anything like that happening to anyone. At least now I understand why she didn't want to stop and chat."

"I barely knew them myself," Veronica said. "They didn't talk much to me, either. Essentially, they said hi and good-bye."

"They never said much to anyone," Camille said. "But I can't fault them for that. In hindsight, I think they've been having difficulties for a while now. People just don't lose their homes overnight."

"You know, I saw an article in the paper that said the foreclosure rate in this area is higher than in other cities," Denise said. "Naturally it also mentioned all the African Americans and Hispanics moving out from the city, like one has something to do with the other. I hate it when the media presents our people as being dumb."

"So do I," Veronica said with a shrug, "but there might be a connection. When you think about it, there's a lot working against us. First, moving so far away from our families, trusted neighbors, and established babysitters means you have no support system. Then, you have to travel to the city five days a week to keep earning New York money to pay for Pennsylvania real estate. I know I don't do it anymore," she added quickly, "but it was hard, even just three days a week. I'd be exhausted when I got home, and I barely had a half hour to spend with my daughters before their bedtime."

"It's hard for your children, too," Dawn said. "Zach couldn't have been happier to have his own yard and have a puppy, but he had a hard time getting up to speed at school."

"We had an advantage because we came out before the school year ended," Camille said, happy to be discussing something other than foreclosure. "I met with the kids' next-year teachers to find out where they should be, and we had some home lessons over the summer."

Dawn nodded. "I didn't have that luxury, because we came out during the summer. But I agree with Veronica. We've got a lot of strikes against us. It's not all that hard to go under. Milo and I weren't even told about half the expenses we would have. We were shocked when we got that bill for the home owners association dues. And as far as jobs are concerned, it's practically impossible to find a position in this area that pays comparably to what you make in the city."

"I had to take a pay cut," Denise said. "But for me it was worth it. I couldn't stand that damn commute."

"That's one saving grace for Reuben and I," Camille said. "At least with him working near here, he doesn't have to buy a bus pass." She chuckled, but it didn't quite come out right. "Y'all say a prayer that he'll find a full-time job soon. Or else next year you three might be sitting around the table talking about how the Curry family lost *their* house."

Chapter 31

The Youngs
November 2003

Dawn and Milo both arranged to take off from work the week of Thanksgiving. They had felt as tired as they usually did on the Friday morning before vacation started, but the picture changed completely when they met at Port Authority for the return trip. They both felt nearly giddy at the prospect of being able to sleep in for a week.

Dawn savored her vacation time, which allowed her to enjoy all the benefits of suburban living. She and Zach rode their bicycles while Milo lounged. But even Milo did some work around the house, puttering around in the garage and installing a new kitchen faucet when the cheap one the builder put in began to require more and more effort to turn the water completely off.

"Good job, Milo," Dawn said with admiration. "That's a pretty faucet, too, isn't it?"

He shrugged. "As faucets go, I guess it's all right."

She playfully flicked a dish towel at him. "Stop making fun of me."

"Ah, I'm just messin' with you. Actually, I've got a surprise for you."

"A surprise? Tell me!"

"I've got tickets for the Michael McDonald show at Radio City Friday night."

"You do?"

"I figured it'll keep you out of the stores on the biggest shopping day of the year. Besides, you're always playing his new *Motown* CD."

"Oh, Milo, that's wonderful! Now, what am I going to wear . . . ?"

"You don't need anything new. Your side of the closet looks like a fashion showroom as it is."

She made a face at him. "All right, all right. I'm going to check."

Milo grinned. He knew Dawn had been unhappy with his lack of energy in the fifteen months they'd lived in the new house. In recent weeks he'd really made an extra effort not to be so dull. Hell, many a man had left his wife for being an old stick-in-the-mud. Dawn was an attractive woman, and she still turned heads, in spite of her self-criticism that she'd put on weight. If he didn't get on the good foot soon someone might be willing to take his place. He'd already noticed the eyes of both Lemuel King and Reuben Curry lingering on her curves. Norman Lee, on the other hand, was the type who saw no one but his own wife. Milo didn't mind if other men looked—as long as they didn't touch.

He glanced out the kitchen window. Zach was throwing pebbles into the water, Stormy at his heels. Stormy's devotion to Zach reminded him of Kevin Hooks's dog in that old movie *Sounder.* As he'd told Zach, he'd always wanted a dog when he was a kid, but their apartment house didn't allow pets. It made him proud to be able to provide an environment for his son to have one, even though Stormy had grown into a full-sized boxer, and the cost of her checkups with the vet cost more than his copays at the doctor's office.

He tinkered with the newly installed faucet, turning it on and off. In spite of the baleful look he'd given Dawn when she'd said how nice it looked, he had to admit it was an attractive fixture.

He did like living here, loved having a piece of property to call his own, but the daily commute to New York was a killer. He slept on the way in and usually dozed off on the way home as well, yet he always felt tired. His body cried out for eight hours of sleep in his own bed, not snatched Z's while riding. What good was having a home if he had no time to enjoy it?

Plus, he and Dawn really had to struggle to pay their monthly bills. He became acutely aware of this while listening to his neighbors talk on the bus. This one was going into the city for dinner, a show, and an overnight stay; that one was having their patio enclosed; the other one was going to Vegas for four days. He and Dawn couldn't even afford to drive to the city to see a damn show and drive home again.

She'd probably kill him if she knew he'd charged the concert tickets, but how else were they supposed to have any fun? He'd bet their neighbors all funded *their* vacations with plastic. He and Dawn had already put out thousands this year alone, considering the cost of raising their backyard, having their closet repaired, and giving that party last month, on top of all the other expenses.

The way Milo felt, if he could afford to pay for the necessities, they should be able to enjoy some of the desirables as well.

"Hey," Milo said on Tuesday afternoon, "I'm in the mood for a bloomin' onion. Anybody want to go to Outback?"

"Outback, yeah!" Zach said. "Can we go, Mom?"

Dawn hesitated. "Uh . . . I guess. But aren't they kind of expensive?"

"Where do you want to go, Mom, McDonald's?"

"You know better than to talk to me like that, young man," Dawn said sternly.

"I'm sorry."

Dawn looked questioningly at Milo. They'd spent so much repairing their bedroom closet; in fact, they hadn't yet paid off the charge. Outback for three people would probably come to sixty or seventy dollars. Even though Zach was only eleven, he'd long since outgrown the children's menu. But Milo's confident grin told her that perhaps she was being overly thrifty. "All right, let's go."

Wednesday Dawn baked pies and a pound cake. The three of them would have a quiet Thanksgiving dinner at home, but they'd invited the Currys and the Lees over for dessert, plus any of their guests. She'd invited Lemuel and Denise King as well, but they were having dinner with family in New York. Camille said that this year her family was coming for dinner, instead of her in-laws, and that they would be leaving a few hours later. That left the Lees, who as usual had a bunch of people coming, most of whom had gotten hotel rooms. Veronica said that only her parents, sister, niece, and Norman's sister were staying at their house. Still, Dawn wanted to be prepared in case some or even all of the Lees' dinner guests came over for dessert. In total they numbered over fifteen people.

*   *   *

By Friday Dawn's good spirits held. Camille kindly agreed that Zach could spend the night at her house. He and Mitchell would have a good time together. Dawn and Milo set out for New York at three o'clock.

Finding a parking spot wasn't as difficult as it usually was, possibly owing to the fact that many folks had the day off. Dawn slipped her arm through Milo's as they walked east along Fiftieth Street.

"So what do you feel like eating?" Milo asked.

"Oh, I'm open to whatever you want." She squeezed his arm. "You know, I'm still surprised that you included dinner with the concert. It reminds me of the old days in Brooklyn when we used to do it all the time."

"Yeah, the good old days."

"Now, Milo, don't start that again. Isn't it nicer, knowing that after the show is over we'll be going back to our own home?"

"Yeah, I guess."

In spite of his attempt to be blasé, he hadn't been able to conceal the beginnings of a smile at that thought. She caught his eye—they were nearly the same height when she wore heels—and puckered her lips into an air kiss. "I knew we would get to this point one day."

"Well, that day hasn't arrived just yet. We're still paying on the furniture and the dryer, plus we spent five hundred dollars on that table, chairs, and umbrella for the backyard just two months ago, remember?"

"But we got such a good deal on it, being that it was the end of the season. Besides, the set we bought last year for the deck only seated five, and we needed more seating for the party. And everybody who came said how nice it looked."

"Yes, they did. But we need to cool it, Dawn. We've been spending a lot of money, and we don't want it to bite us in the ass."

She frowned thoughtfully. "I'm puzzled about something. If things aren't getting any easier for us, how is it we can afford orchestra seats for the concert and have dinner out twice in one week?"

"We can't. I paid for the Outback in cash, but everything else is pure plastic."

She stopped walking. "You charged it? Why didn't you tell me, Milo?"

"Because I feel you and I are overdue for some good times for a change." He pulled her arm. "Come on, let's keep moving. It'll be all right, Dawn."

"But I thought we wanted to stay away from credit cards. We don't have a lot of cash to spare after all the bills are paid as it is."

"You didn't think of that when you bought that outdoor furniture, did you?" he retorted angrily.

She instantly regretted bringing up the matter. She had no argument. She'd seen the patio set for eight at BJ's Warehouse and just had to have it. When she called Milo and told him about it he told her if she wanted it that badly to go on and get it.

"You're right," she said. "I did buy that furniture without even thinking about the bill." No point trying to kid herself. She'd whipped out her credit card quicker than a juggler could toss balls in the air. "It's not right for me to criticize you for wanting us to go out and have some fun." They did everything they were supposed to, didn't they? Sent Zach to the dentist and the optometrist, brought Stormy to the vet, paid their bills on time. Surely they couldn't be expected to do all the right things and nothing else. They *did* deserve to have a night out on the town once in a while.

"You know what?" she asked, tightening her grip on his arm. "Let's find a seafood restaurant. I could really go for a good paella."

He grinned. "Now you're talkin', baby."

Chapter 32

The Currys
January 2004

"Mom, can't you make us dinner?" Shayla pleaded. "I'm tired of spaghetti and hot dogs."

"At least Daddy can make those right. When he tried to make meat loaf it came out all lumpy," Mitchell said. "I had to fill up on mashed potatoes and biscuits."

Camille put an arm around each of her children. "I'm sorry, kids, but your mom is worn out when she gets home. Daddy is going to be your chef for the time being." At the sound of their groans she added, "But I'll make some extra food this weekend so you can have leftovers. Daddy can fix that casserole I always make."

Shayla brightened. "Ooh, the one with the biscuits on top?"

"That's the one. All he has to do is add vegetables and potatoes. It's absolutely mess-up-proof." Camille was glad that the kids liked her all-purpose casserole for leftover chicken, beef, and pork. She kept it as fresh as possible by changing the vegetables it contained and by sometimes using sweet potatoes instead of white, especially when the meat was ham or other pork. Shayla didn't even complain about the lima beans when she used mixed vegetables. Any way she made it, it was economical. And at this point everything revolved around saving money. Reuben's severance pay had ended three months ago.

* * *

Sitting at the kitchen table, Camille added up the column of numbers one more time, hoping she would get a lower total.

She didn't. She really hadn't expected to, but desperation gave people foolish hopes. She shut her eyes for a moment, then opened them and turned to Reuben, who sat a few feet away in the family room, watching ESPN. The sports network was abuzz with predictions about tonight's Super Bowl. Later this evening they would be going over to Lemuel and Denise King's to watch the game. Denise, Camille, and the other book club members had worked out a menu, and each agreed to bring two dishes for a potluck meal. They would be discussing another book, at least until just before the spectacular halftime show, which the women would watch and then leave, since tomorrow was school for the kids and work for them. Poor Veronica had to go in at eleven that night.

Camille took a deep breath and then said the words she'd been dreading. "Reuben, we don't have enough to pay the bills this month."

"Do what you've been doing for months. Take what you need from savings."

"Reuben, we've been doing that since November, and you know we haven't been short an insignificant sum like fifty dollars. There wasn't a whole lot in there to begin with. Another month or two and it'll be empty."

He took a deep breath. "I'll bring home my first check from the supermarket next week." He'd put in applications months ago, but hoards of high school students had beat him to it, taking all the available jobs. No one had called him until after New Year's. At least he'd been able to get in more hours with FedEx during the busy holiday season.

"Reuben, even with two part-time jobs and working forty-five hours a week you're not making as much as you did in New York. And my check is a lot less now, too. I had to pick up medical and dental insurance for us, remember?" They had been getting their health insurance coverage through Reuben's job. She toyed with the idea of not carrying insurance at all, but quickly abandoned it. Anything could happen to any of them at any time. She had to make sure her family was protected. Family coverage cost a fortune these days, but not carrying it held too big a risk.

"How much do we have left?"

She told him.

"All right. Hopefully next month we won't need to take as much. If we're really strapped, we can start taking money from our retirement account."

She prayed it wouldn't come to that. She could cope with being broke at thirty-seven, but by the time she was sixty and considering retirement she hoped to be well fixed. She hated the idea of taking from that security, but if Reuben didn't find better-paying work soon they would have no choice.

As had become their custom, the women sat down with their plates to chat about the latest news before beginning their book discussion.

"I'm happy to announce that Norman and I, at long last, have had the work started on our kitchen," Veronica announced.

"That didn't take too long," Dawn said. "You haven't been in the house two years yet, have you?"

"It'll be two years in the spring. I guess it seems longer because I wanted it since before we moved in."

"I can't wait to see it when it's finished," Denise said eagerly.

"You'll all be invited over for the grand unveiling. All I want to do now is live through it. I'm told it's hell to live through a remodeling."

Camille forced a smile but remained quiet. She wished she and Reuben had enough money to redo their kitchen. Not that their kitchen needed redoing, but they could take that amount and spend it on basic living expenses, taking some strain off of their rapidly diminishing savings.

"And that's not all," Veronica continued. "We're getting new carpet in the house, and Norman is going to put new flooring down in the basement."

"Well, aren't you full of news!" Denise exclaimed.

"I'm very excited about it." Veronica's dark brown skin glowed with happiness.

"I have some news, too," Dawn said. "Next month, during Zach's winter break, Milo and Zach and I are going on a cruise."

The others made squealing noises. "Where to?"

"It's five days, and it stops in Cozumel in Mexico and Grand Cayman Island. The only bad part is that we have to drive all the way down to Tampa to board the ship."

"Ooh, send us postcards," Veronica said.

"To hell with a postcard," Denise declared. "I hear liquor is real cheap in the Cayman Islands. I'd love it if you could bring me back a bottle of that Hypotiq Lemuel and I like. I'll reimburse you for it, of course."

Camille knew the others would think it strange if she didn't say anything. "Veronica, Dawn, I'm happy for both of you." She spoke honestly. She knew everything was fine in Veronica's world, but she'd thought Dawn and Milo were struggling as much as she and Reuben were. How nice to hear that the Youngs' fortunes looked better these days.

It gave her hope that the future held promise for the Currys.

Chapter 33

The Youngs
February 2004

"Milo!" Dawn said in exasperation. "What do I have to do to get you away from that slot machine, use a crowbar?"

"Not now, not while I'm winning."

She sighed. "Honestly, Milo. We spend all this money to take a nice cruise and you want to spend the entire time in the casino." She wondered how much money he had spent between the slots and the poker and blackjack tables, then tried to chase that thought away. She wasn't supposed to worry about those things, not during a vacation that should be strictly fun.

There'd be plenty of time for that after they returned home.

"I'll be done in fifteen minutes. I swear."

"All right. I'm going to take my book up to the deck. Come and have a drink with me."

"Where's Zach?"

"He's with the kids' group. The counselor keeps them pretty busy. I doubt we'll see him until dinner."

She headed for their cabin, furnished with a double bed, a desk and straight-backed chair, plus an oversized upholstered chair that the stewards converted to a twin bed for Zach at night. She picked up her sunglasses and the paperback that the reading group planned to discuss.

Fifteen minutes later she was lounging in the sun on the ship's deck, a fresh ocean breeze cooling her shorts-clad legs. A waiter brought her a Strawberry Colada, and after signing her name to the receipt she sat back and took a long sip. The alcohol surged through her body, relaxing her instantly. This, she thought, was the life. Zach occupied all day, Milo happy and smiling, and her enjoying the food that the ship's crew constantly served and the equally plentiful shopping, two of her favorite activities. Both of those pastimes helped make up for the temporary shelving of another favorite activity while she and Milo shared a cabin with their son.

She fought weight gain from the extra food and alcohol intake by joining in on the brisk walk-around-the-deck exercises in the mornings, and yesterday she and Milo played several sets of volleyball. Milo had even volunteered a couple of times to go down to the deck below and retrieve a ball that had gotten knocked out too far. Of course, Milo also did a fair amount of sitting, like he was doing right now, warming a chair in the casino for the past hour and a half.

They were now about halfway through their trip. The ship was sailing toward its final destination of Grand Cayman, where it would dock later this afternoon. Dawn had done some research on the island's shopping, and planned to treat herself to some nice jewelry and real perfume while there.

They'd gotten a good rate on this late-winter cruise through a discount-travel Web site. Still, with the purchase of three tickets it was still expensive. But Dawn and Milo had never taken a vacation without Zach. He was their only child, and it didn't seem right to them to leave him behind. If he had a sibling things would have been different, but they'd wanted only one child, feeling that more would limit their ability to provide the way they wanted to. Zach, not yet twelve, lived a life that many other children would envy. In just a few short years, when he reached college, he'd probably prefer to travel with his friends than to go anywhere with his parents, which would be tough to accept. Whenever she heard of a fortyish woman having another child ten or twelve years after their last one she nodded in understanding while others often scoffed. It was like getting a second chance at being a parent, eighteen more years of joy.

She and Milo agreed it would be best to drive down to the pier in Tampa, which, although inconvenient, saved the cost of three round-trip air fares. Two of their cruise tickets, if not the accompanying port charges, were covered by her surprise bonus check this year, a thousand dollars. Her attempts to run her department more efficiently—something she'd had to come up with so she could make her bus home every night—had been cited by management.

Milo's bonus was only five hundred dollars, but he received it every year and considered himself lucky to get it. He'd long stated that the programming industry in the U.S. was in trouble, threatened by lower-paid workers in Asia, and predicted much lower wages for those just starting out and low salary increases for established workers like him.

For their shipboard spending, Milo set up a sign-and-go account for them. Even Zach had the ability to pay for his Sprites by signing his name to a receipt. In addition to Dawn's daily consumption of tropical drinks, she'd made some purchases in the ship's boutiques, and she'd had a wonderful massage yesterday in the spa, cheerfully paying for it all and signing with a flourish. Already in the back of her mind she dreaded seeing the tally.

Dawn chased that thought out of her mind with a long slug of Strawberry Colada. They'd all remember this trip for a long, long time, and that's what counted.

Two days later, the three of them struggled to carry their luggage plus all the merchandise they'd bought: Perfume and jewelry were lightweight, but that onyx chess set and sculptures, Zach's colorful baseball bat from Mexico, the boxed bottles of Mexican Kahlúa and various liquors from Grand Cayman, and all the T-shirts from both destinations added both weight and bulk to their luggage.

"Good thing we didn't fly after all," Milo remarked as he placed the chess set on top of the luggage in the Volvo's trunk. "We would have had to pay extra to check all this stuff, and they wouldn't have let us on with this." He held up Zach's baseball bat. "It's considered a weapon, and it's too damn long to fit in any of the bags."

"You forgot the liquor bottles, Dad," Zach said.

"They're not going to fit in here. You'll have to share the back seat with them, buddy."

"Oh, it was a wonderful trip," Dawn said contentedly as she settled into the front seat. "I wish we could turn back the clock and do it all over again."

"Now back to the frozen north," Milo muttered.

"I can't wait to see Stormy," Zach said.

"We'll stop at the kennel before we go home. We should get in early tomorrow. They'll still be open." Milo started the engine. "I kind of miss the old girl myself."

"Bye, Florida," Zach called out.

Dawn turned her head toward him. "We'll be in Florida another couple of hours, Zach."

"And then Georgia, and then . . ."—he stopped to think for a moment—"South Carolina, and then North Carolina, Virginia, Maryland, and then Pennsylvania."

"You forgot Delaware," she said with a smile.

"Oh, that's right."

"That's forgivable," Milo said, "since we're only in Delaware for maybe twenty minutes before we cross into Pennsylvania."

"How far are we gonna go today, Dad?"

"I'd like to make North Carolina, but I don't know. We might only get as far as South Carolina this afternoon. It'll take about four hours just to get out of Florida."

"Let's not wait too late to stop, Milo," Dawn suggested.

"It's 9:45 now. We'll go until 6:00 and stop wherever we are at that time."

"Uh, did you get the folio for our charges?" she asked.

"Yes. But don't ask. You don't want to know."

She stared out the passenger window at the rapidly passing landscape, content to take his word for it.

But the time had come to start worrying.

Chapter 34

The Lees
March 2004

Veronica rushed into the hospital where she had worked for years. She didn't have to ask for directions to the emergency room; she knew how to get there.

She burst into the double doors. Her mother sat in the waiting room, leaning forward with her eyes cast downward, Valerie on one side of her and Essence on the other.

"Aunt Veronica is here, Grandma," Essence said.

Phyllis Mills looked up and broke into a feeble smile. "Veronica. I knew you'd come."

Veronica bent to embrace her. "How is he?"

"We don't know yet. It's awful, this waiting."

"Was there any warning?"

Phyllis shook her head sadly. "He just collapsed. I heard a thump and went to see what happened. There he was, lying on the kitchen floor. I called the ambulance right away."

"Pop has never had any kind of heart trouble before," Valerie said hopefully.

"No, but his father—your grandfather—died of a heart attack when he was seventy-three."

Valerie's shoulders slumped in defeat. "I didn't know, Mom."

"You'd have no way to know, dear. Franklin's parents lived down in Virginia, and you girls didn't really see them a lot. Mostly in the summer and at Christmas. You were still young when he died. You didn't really understand what death meant."

Essence thoughtfully moved over a seat so Veronica could sit next to her mother. For about five minutes they sat silently. Then a nurse came out. "Mr. Mills is resting comfortably," she said.

"Oh, thank God." Phyllis dabbed at her eyes. "I've been sitting here praying."

Glancing at the four of them, the nurse added, "Two of you at a time may visit him. We're waiting for lab results to determine what happened, but my guess is he'll be admitted."

"You and Valerie go, Mom," Veronica urged. "I'll wait here with Essence. "We'll take turns visiting with Pop."

Phyllis, leaning on Valerie's arm, seemed much older than her sixty-three years this afternoon, almost feeble. Her parents had been married over forty years. No doubt the thought of losing her life's partner had terrified her. Still, she'd done well, with the presence of mind in what had to be a frightening situation to call for help instead of standing over her unconscious husband, bawling.

Veronica turned to her niece. "Have you been here long?"

"About two hours."

"Did you have lunch?"

Essence shook her head.

"I'll bet you're hungry. Tell you what. I want to give Norman a quick call and let him know what's going on, and then you and I will go to the cafeteria and get some lunch."

"What about Mom and Grandma?"

"Oh, I'm sure they'll figure out where we went. It'll be all right to slip away for a few minutes, now we know Grandpa's doing okay. You have to eat, Essence. Grandpa would want you to."

In the cafeteria Essence ordered a typical teenage meal of cheeseburger, fries, and soda. Veronica settled for the hospital's chicken salad sandwich; she liked it.

"Try not to worry about Grandpa," Veronica told her niece. "Even if he did have a heart attack, I don't think the Lord is ready for him yet." Her attempts to cheer up her niece raised her own spirits, although uneasiness about her father's health had worked its way into her blood.

"Do you really think Grandpa is going to be all right?"

"I think it's a very good sign that he's alert. I know you've prayed for him this morning and afternoon, but be sure to say another prayer that he recovers tonight before you go to sleep."

"Why didn't Lorinda and Simone and Uncle Norman come with you, Aunt Veronica?"

"Oh, I thought it might be best if the girls stayed in school. They can always come with Uncle Norman if—" she broke off, not wanting to say, "If there's a real emergency." That sounded too ominous. "I called Uncle Norman right after your mom called me, and he's going to leave work early so he'll be home when they get home from school." She smiled across the table at her niece, who at almost fourteen had become a lovely young lady, if a little on the chubby side. She had a sweet shyness about her and thus far hadn't demonstrated any of the rebellious behavior so common in teenagers, particularly those who, like Essence, had less than ideal home lives.

"So how is everything with you otherwise?" Veronica asked.

Essence looked down at her food for a few moments. "Aunt Veronica, do you think I might be able to come and stay with you and Uncle Norman for a while?"

Veronica's forehead wrinkled. "You want to stay with us? What's wrong, Essence? Aren't you happy at home?"

"It's just that sometimes I think I'm in Mom's way."

"In her way? How?"

"Because it seems like she wants to spend all her time with her boyfriends. She doesn't spend much time with me."

Veronica hated the forlorn look in Essence's eyes. She would like nothing better than to wring Valerie's neck for putting it there. Her sister needed to stop chasing men long enough to realize the devastating effect it had on her only child.

"Essence," she said, "you're always welcome at my home, provided it's okay with your mother. But the way you feel is very serious, and your mother should know about it. Have you discussed it with her?"

"I did talk to her about it."

"What did she say?"

"Oh, that I'm being silly, that nobody means more to her than me, stuff like that."

Veronica had the sense that if Essence hadn't been so respectful of her mother she would have said something like, *All that bullshit.* "You didn't believe her?"

Essence twisted her napkin. "All I know is that I don't *feel* like the most important person in her life, no matter what she says."

Veronica made up her mind right then and there. "If your mother says it's okay, of course you can come stay with us. But I think it might be best if you waited until summer vacation. The schools in Tobyhanna are ahead of the ones in New York. You might have trouble catching up." Summer vacation still lay several months away. Maybe her sister would come to her senses.

But she doubted it. As soon as she had an opportunity, she would get Valerie alone for a talk.

When Veronica and Essence returned to the emergency room, they stayed with Franklin while Phyllis and Valerie went to get something to eat. Lab tests revealed that Franklin had indeed suffered what they termed a myocardial infarction, which Veronica, an RN, knew meant heart attack. The four of them continued to take turns sitting at his bedside in the ER bay until he was ready to be transferred. As the orderly wheeled Franklin's gurney toward his room, they followed behind.

Veronica walked alongside her mother, holding her hand. "He'll be all right, Mom," she assured her. "This is one of the best hospitals in the city. And I'm not saying that just because I used to work here."

"Veronica, it's so sweet of you to stay all day like this. But don't you have to go to work tonight?"

"I've already called in and explained that my father had a heart attack in New York and that I won't be in. They're lining up someone to cover at least part of my shift."

Her mother looked distressed. "I hate for you to take off work."

"Don't worry about it, Mom. I'm getting paid. That's what personal days are for. And I'll be back here on my day off."

"I want you to get home before dark tonight. Valerie will bring me home."

"Mom, there's nothing wrong with my night vision, but I am a little tired. I'll probably be leaving soon."

They waited outside Franklin's room while the orderly and a nurse transferred their newest patient from the gurney to the bed.

Veronica yawned. "Excuse me."

"You probably need to think about setting out for home," Valerie said. "It'll take you nearly two hours to get there, won't it?"

"Give or take. I'd like to see if I can get a jump on the rush hour traffic. Uh . . . Valerie, can I talk to you for a minute?"

"Sure. Mom, Essence, we'll be right back."

They walked down the hall toward the elevators, stopping when they spotted two unoccupied chairs in a corner.

"I know what you're going to say," Valerie began. "You want me to keep a close eye on Mom. Don't worry, Veronica. I'm on it. I know you can't get here very often."

"I'm glad to hear that, Valerie, but actually I wanted to talk to you about Essence."

"Essence? What about her?"

"Let me say first of all that I'm not trying to get into your business. Essence volunteered some information to me." The last thing Veronica wanted was a rehashing of the unpleasant episode in Mount Pocono when Valerie accused her of just that after she and Norman refused to allow her to sleep with Michael at their house.

Valerie's eyes narrowed suspiciously. "What'd she tell you?"

"She asked if she could move in with me. It seems she's feeling rather unloved lately because your attentions lie elsewhere."

"Oh, *that*. It's nothing but a bid for attention. We already talked about it."

"I'm worried about her, Valerie."

"It's *nothing*, Veronica. Essence is trying to manipulate you into feeling sorry for her. She told me she wishes we lived in the country. It's all those teen shows she's been watching, where all the kids in the suburbs hang out at the mall and the drive-in hamburger place."

Veronica didn't believe it. Essence was just looking for the love her own mother should supply. God only knew what path her search would lead her down. "I told her that if it was okay with you, she could come spend summer vacation with us."

Valerie shrugged. "It's all right with me."

Her instant approval confirmed for Veronica that her suspicions were correct. *You didn't even have to think about it, did you?*

It was nearly six when Veronica returned home. An anxious-looking Norman and the girls greeted her and sat her down to a dinner of spaghetti, salad, and breadsticks they'd prepared themselves in their messy but still operational kitchen. She'd had to send the workmen home this morning when she received a frantic call from Valerie.

"How's Grandpa, Mommy?" Lorinda asked.

"He's resting comfortably. We'll see how he does the next few days."

"Can we go see him?" Simone asked.

"I'll bring you girls into the city on Sunday, when I'm off," Norman told them. "Of course, hopefully he will have been discharged from the hospital by then."

"They don't need to go to a hospital, anyway," Veronica said. "When I was your age, girls, children weren't allowed to visit patients. You had to be at least twelve, I think."

"I'm almost twelve," Lorinda stated proudly.

Simone made a face. "Oh, you won't be twelve til August. *My* birthday's next month."

"Yeah, but you'll only be nine, so shut up."

Veronica and Norman exchanged smiles. Their once-close daughters had reached a point where they had become competitive, which would probably go on through their early teenage years until they became close once more. It wouldn't be easy, but at least her daughters knew they were loved. Poor Essence felt like she'd been pushed to the background in favor of a parade of men.

Veronica had forgotten to tell Norman about that. But it wasn't a suitable discussion for the dinner table, so she'd have to talk to him about it later.

Chapter 35

The Youngs
April 2004

Dawn stood observing the multiple cracks in the backyard with slumping shoulders and a hopeless feeling. That expense she and Milo took on just last year, all for naught. The dirt, when they'd finished packing the hole and spreading the rest of it, didn't add the height they'd hoped it would. On top of that, the grass seed they planted didn't seem to have any roots to it; it didn't hold the dirt together. A hole had formed in the same spot and begun to spread in spidery lines, and now their yard had more cracks in it than the top of a molasses cookie. The recent rains only made it worse. Once again, the breaks in the soil ran toward the house and were perilously close to the wood columns that held up the deck.

She dreaded having to show this to Milo, but of course she could hardly keep it from him.

"Goddamn it!"

Dawn stood mute, allowing Milo to rant, the way she knew he would.

"Fuck!" he shouted again, clearly not caring if the neighbors heard him. Then he spoke normally. "What did we spend to fix this, two, two hundred and fifty dollars? We might as well have taken that money and thrown it in the damn lake. Look at this shit." His face contorted into a scowl.

"What do we do now? More dirt?"

"I'm not sure. But we'll have to do something quick. It's moving fast, and if we get more rain it'll be at the house in no time. Hell, it's already reached the back of the deck."

"Milo, what are we going to do?"

"I don't know squat about yard work, Dawn; I'm a city boy. But I do know when it's time to call in a professional, and that's what I'm going to do."

"What kind of professional?"

"A landscaper. They'll come out and take a look and recommend what we should do to take care of this once and for all. And once we agree on a price, I'll let him do it."

She thought of the bills that would be coming in any day now. The tally of their shipboard expenditures alone came to over five hundred dollars. It seemed impossible they could have spent that much in five days, at least until she thought about it. Her time in the spa alone accounted for twenty percent of the total. The rest of it added up easily. All that soda Zach consumed, her and Milo each ordering two or three five-dollar mixed drinks a day, the e-mails Zach sent to his friends at two bucks a pop, and her purchases in the ship's boutiques. And then there were those endless photographs they had taken at dinner and when disembarking the ship in port—every one of them remarkably flattering, like the photographer had a magic lens or something. She hadn't been able to resist. She *had* to have them for their family collection.

Dawn estimated that their port shopping came to even more than that. In addition, Milo confessed that he'd taken a three-hundred-dollar cash advance to fund his gaming at the slot machines and poker tables. They'd managed to turn what had started as a reasonably priced cruise into a major financial outpour.

Plus they still had payments to make on the furniture. It had been almost two years. Would it ever be paid off?

"That sounds expensive," she said haltingly.

"It will be, but it's got to be done. Our do-it-yourself attempt didn't amount to much more than a Band-Aid."

She had to agree.

Chapter 36

The Currys
April 2004

Reuben got out of the car. "See you later," he said.

He left the driver's side door open but didn't wait for Camille to get out of the passenger side to take the wheel. In the old days he would have leaned over and kissed her, waited for her to come around and closed the driver's door for her. Now they barely spoke to each other unless they had to. It took almost fifteen minutes to get to the supermarket, and they'd said maybe the same number of words during the trip.

As far as he was concerned, he just followed her lead. She was the one who'd started the whole mess, getting into the car when he picked her up at the train station and not even saying hello. He knew she blamed him for their predicament, and he didn't feel that was right. He'd had nothing to do with the company's decision to close the store. And even if he had, Camille was his wife. She was supposed to support him, be on his side, no matter what happened. Instead she went around sulking and slamming doors like a little kid.

"Bye," she said flatly and with more than a little touch of sarcasm. He was already six feet away. No wonder the kids chose not to take a ride to get out of the house this dreary Sunday. The tension between her and Reuben was as impenetrable as an inch of steel. The endless clouds and periodic rain did little to help.

On the way home Camille pulled over when she saw Denise King tending to the large plant containers that flanked the entrance to her house. Camille would have indulged in some gardening herself, if she had the time. But that part of her dream, working perhaps a half hour from her house, had failed to materialize.

She stopped because she'd seen a new FOR SALE sign prominently displayed in their neighbor's yard, and Denise was sure to know why they'd decided to sell, even possibly their asking price. This seemed as good a time as any to find out.

She looked up at the sky as she approached Denise. It looked like rain would start at any moment. She hadn't seen the sun since Tuesday, five days ago.

"Hi," she said to Denise, then got right to the point. "I see your neighbors are selling their house."

"Yeah, they went right into action when they saw that article in last Sunday's *Record*."

Camille shook her head, not knowing what Denise meant. "What article?"

"The one about a brewing scandal involving the builder. How he made some of these houses out of material not much sturdier than Popsicle sticks, overvalued them, indulged in shady lending practices, the whole nine yards. Personally, I don't blame the folks next door for trying to unload their place. I think they got one of the lemons. Their basement has flooded twice. But I say, lots of luck trying to sell the sucker. Water stains are hard to conceal."

"I didn't see the article," Camille confessed. "We usually pick up the *Times* every Sunday and look at the local paper just to read the want ads and to see what's playing at the movies." Denise's talk about the builder's dishonesty made her think of how cold their house got in the winter. She already knew about the problems Dawn and Milo Young had had with their bedroom closet and their backyard last year, but at least those problems had been fixed. Her family would always have to bundle up for five months out of every year.

Did the Kings have similar problems, she wondered. "Have you and Lemuel noticed anything, well, not quite right about your house?"

"No, not at all. I think we had a good, thorough construction crew."

"Lucky you. Our house tends to be cold in the winter. One of our friends who works construction said it wasn't properly insulated. But Reuben says that every major step in the building process has to pass inspection, or else they can't continue."

"Not in Pennsylvania they don't."

"They don't?" Camille asked increduously.

"No. They just proposed legislation to start doing that because a lot of people have been complaining that their houses don't seem to be built all that well. It'll probably become law around July or so, they said."

It embarrassed Camille to know so little about what went on in local affairs. Denise had just given her two important pieces of information that she, as a property owner, should have known. "By the time I get home the news is over, and I'm usually asleep before the late news comes on."

From the look on Denise's face, Camille knew what she was thinking. *What does Reuben do all day?*

She had the same thought herself as she told Denise good-bye and got back in the car. Her first impulse, admittedly a bad one, was to drive back to the supermarket and berate him for not watching the local news. Their relationship had been deteriorating along with their fortunes, but so far they'd managed to keep their troubles private. But going to his place of business and creating a scene would just embarrass them both and make them the topic of gossip.

But he had no excuse to be so uninformed. Hell, he finished at the supermarket at 11:00 AM and then worked at FedEx from noon until five. He could easily catch the evening news.

According to Denise, her neighbors planned to stay in the area after they sold their house, just in a different house. They'd told Denise and Lemuel they'd probably get one of the older houses around town, not in a subdivision.

Hearing that made Camille think of Veronica and Norman. The Lees seemed to be doing just fine. They might have only a one-car garage, but they now had two cars. Veronica tooled around town in a little red Neon. Not that she did much tooling these days, unless it was to go to New York. Her father had had a heart attack there a couple of weeks ago.

Much as Camille loved her house, she wished that she and Reuben had taken the same route as the Lees had. Their life would have been so much easier if they'd bought a less expensive house. Even if they didn't want a house as old as they were, they could have resisted Eric Nylund's sales techniques and purchased the basic model with a principal and interest payment of $740 a month. How much easier that would have been to maintain now with Reuben's income sliced in half. By the time they paid the monthly note for the larger house and lakefront lot they'd bought, it cost considerably more than their rent back in the Bronx.

Even as Camille had the thought, she knew the blame for their predicament didn't lie entirely with their salesman. Their own desires for something grand had gotten the best of them. The sad truth was that they lived in a house they simply couldn't afford. Before she had gotten her promotion they barely had fifty dollars leftover each month. In the past two years she'd bought maybe four new suits, charging them to her Visa.

It troubled her that they seemed to be trailing behind their contemporaries, struggling while their friends were thriving. She didn't include Denise and Lemuel King in her assessment, only the Lees and the Youngs. The Kings were a little older than the rest of them, plus they had lived here longer. She'd expect for them to do well.

Part of the reason could be income, she considered. She suspected that both Veronica and Norman and Dawn and Milo made more money than she and Reuben even when he still worked at the Bronx supermarket. And, of course, the Lees didn't commute to the city, a savings of nearly five hundred dollars a month. That would explain why they flourished like those May flowers that would pop up everywhere after this month's rain.

In a rare moment of cohesion she'd asked Reuben for his thoughts on how Veronica and Norman could afford to have their kitchen redone plus buy a second car. Reuben guessed that they had refinanced their house and gotten cash from it. "They haven't been in it very long, but those improvements they made to their bathrooms probably went a long way toward increasing its value," he explained. Sensing she was about to ask if they could do the same thing, he said, "We, on the other hand, haven't done anything to our house, not that we needed to anyway, since it's new. And we probably haven't been in it long enough for the value to increase a whole lot on its own. Not that we'd qualify for a loan now, anyway."

Just like him to bust her bubble, something he'd developed a real talent for lately, she thought bitterly. But the Lees had been smart. They'd bought a house for less money that would appreciate faster. One that was no doubt constructed much better than their own.

As for Dawn and Milo, she could easily understand how money might be a little tight. They had only one child and a house smaller than hers and Reuben's, but they had awfully expensive taste. Their furnishings were exquisite, and all new. Camille estimated they'd cost as much as a used car. She already knew how much they paid for all those upgrades in their house—the forty-two-inch kitchen cabinets, the titanium kitchen appliances, the tile flooring in their kitchen and bathrooms, the fireplace in their bedroom, the ceiling fans. She and Reuben had considered and then quickly decided against purchasing at least a few of those same upgrades for their house. But even with all that, Dawn and Milo still managed to go off on a Caribbean cruise, and bring Zach along at that.

In the two minutes it took her to drive from the Kings' house to her own the skies had opened up. Camille activated the garage door opener—one of the few upgrades she and Reuben had purchased—and drove inside. She cut the engine and took a deep breath as the door came down behind her. This morning she caught herself being short with the kids. Just because Reuben was getting on her nerves didn't give her an excuse to yell at Mitchell and Shayla.

"I'm home," she called out as she entered the house.

"Hi, Mom!"

The kids were watching a movie in the family room. Now that Mitchell had just turned thirteen she didn't mind leaving them alone for brief periods during the day.

"Miz Young called while you were out, Mom," Mitchell said.

Camille slapped her thigh. "Oh, that's right. I'm supposed to drop off her book."

Dawn had been nice enough to offer to let Camille read her copy of the next book their reading group was to discuss. She'd been grateful not to have to put out fifteen dollars, and had managed to read a lot of it last week during the ride back to Tobyhanna and during her lunch hours. By Friday she still hadn't quite finished, but she'd promised to return it this weekend to Dawn, who hadn't read it yet. Surely that had been the reason for Dawn's call. Good thing, too. In her annoyance at Reuben she'd completely forgotten.

"Kids, I'm going to drop something off at Miss Dawn's. I'll be back in a few minutes. Will you be okay?"

"Yes, sure," Mitchell replied absently, his eyes glued to the TV.

"Mommy, will it rain all day?" Shayla asked.

"They say it's supposed to clear up this afternoon. We'll have to wait and see."

"I wish it would stop so I can go skating," Shayla said with a pout. "I've been stuck in the house all weekend. Can't we rent a video?"

"No, Shayla, we can't. Instead of complaining all the time maybe you should be grateful that you have so many TV channels to watch." Sometimes she wondered about her children. Had Shayla been such a little brat when they lived in the Bronx, or had suburbia affected her badly?

Shayla's shoulders slumped, and she sulked on the couch.

Camille left without another word. She heard Mitchell say, "You should have kept your big fat mouth shut, Shayla. Don't you know we don't have much money since Daddy lost his job?"

She paused in the kitchen, hidden from their view, to continue listening.

"But Daddy has two jobs now. Doesn't that mean we have *more* money?"

"No, nitwit. He doesn't make as much with two jobs as he did when he had just one. I asked him, and he told me. So stop whining. All it does is make Mama mad. At least we won't be like my friend Alex. His parents couldn't pay for their house, and they had no place to live. But Mama and Daddy told me that won't happen to us."

Camille lowered her head, tears filling her eyes. Mitchell had never forgotten the fate of his friend. And she and Reuben had a promise to fulfill.

Her head jerked as she suddenly looked up, blinking furiously. She just wanted to get this book back to Dawn and get home as soon as she could. Maybe she could actually do a little relaxing until it was time to go get Reuben. She hadn't needed to keep the car today, but if she hadn't she never would have seen Denise King and found out about that newspaper article, nor would she have been able to drive over to Dawn's to return her book. Dawn would rightly be annoyed if she had to come and get the book from her, especially in this weather.

Five minutes later Camille rang the Youngs' doorbell.

"Who is it?" an adolescent male voice asked.

"It's Mrs. Curry, Zach."

The door opened to reveal a beaming Zach. "Hi!" He looked past her. "Did Mitchell come with you?"

"No, dear, I'm afraid not. I wasn't going to stay anyway. I just wanted to see your mom for a minute."

"Sure. C'mon in." He closed the door behind her, then turned and bellowed, "Mom! Miz Curry's here!"

Dawn hurried into the foyer. "Zach, how many times do I have to tell you not to shout like that? Don't you know your father is taking a nap?"

"Sorry." Zach promptly headed up the stairs.

"Hi, Camille," Dawn said. "Don't mind Zach. All this rain is making him stir crazy. It's times like these that I think maybe Milo and I should have given him a brother or sister. At least Mitchell has Shayla to play with."

"You can still have another baby," Camille said innocently.

"Girl, shut your mouth," Dawn said with a laugh.

"Mitchell told me you called. I brought your book back. Sorry I forgot to do it yesterday."

"Thanks, Camille." Dawn gestured toward the living room. "Why don't you come in and sit a while? Milo's asleep. For once I can't blame him. If there's nothing on TV and you don't have anything to read, what else is there to do on a weekend like this?"

"I know what you mean. Sure, I'll stay for a minute. I don't want to leave the kids too long." She followed Dawn into the elegantly furnished living room and sat down. The voice of a female singer came from a Bose Wave radio on a corner table, sounding so clear she could have been performing in the corner. Camille wondered how much Dawn and Milo had paid for it. Talk about high-maintenance black folks. The Youngs had some nice stuff.

"I talked to Denise this morning," she said chattily. "She mentioned that her next-door neighbors are selling their house because of an article in last Sunday's paper about a building scandal."

"Really? I didn't know that. I'm afraid that I'm a true New Yorker. I'll pick up the *New York Times* before I will that local paper. I've given up finding a decent-paying job in this area, so why bother?"

"I know what you mean. But I thought of how cold my house gets in the winter and how you and Milo have had problems with your place."

"You don't know the half of it, Camille. Our bedroom closet is holding up fine, but our backyard looks just as bad now as it did a year ago. That same problem we had with erosion happened all over again."

"Oh, no! What're you going to do?"

"Milo says he'll get a professional landscaper to look at it and then fix it. It'll probably cost a fortune, and that on top of what we spent trying to fix it last year." Dawn rolled her eyes. "All I can say is, I'm glad we already took a vacation this year."

"Vacation," Camille said wistfully. "I wonder if I'll ever get to go on one of those again."

"I'm sorry. I shouldn't have said that, not with Reuben's situation."

Camille suddenly felt an urge to confide in Dawn. Her closest friends had all left New York years ago for greener pastures like Maryland and the Carolinas, and the combination of years and distance had slowed their friendship to a trickle of birthday greetings and Christmas cards, maybe an occasional phone call. She couldn't simply pick up a phone, call, and start telling them her troubles. Her father and brother wouldn't understand, and she'd never been particularly close to her stepmother.

Her mother-in-law Ginny would probably be sympathetic, but would also relay anything she said to Brenda, Arnelle, and Saul, all of whom, she suspected, would get a perverse enjoyment from hearing about her and Reuben's difficulties.

"Things are bad," she admitted.

"I'm sorry to hear that. Is there anything I can do?"

"Not unless you can get my husband a job managing the grocery section of a supermarket." She gave a rueful chuckle.

"Hang in there, Camille. I'm sure he'll find something."

"He hopes a department-manager position will open up at the supermarket he's working at, but it hasn't happened yet. In the meantime, he's working twenty hours a week for minimum wage, stocking shelves." She wrung her hands. "I'm sorry, Dawn. I shouldn't be talking about this."

"Everybody needs someone to talk to, Camille. I know it's hard. Well . . ."—she shrugged with embarrassment—"maybe I *don't* know. Milo and I have never had to deal with unemployment or . . . I guess you'd call it underemployment. But we've had our hard times, regardless." She lowered her voice to a tone barely audible. "I'm not sure if moving out here was the best thing for us to do. I mean, Zach loves it, but it's been a drain on us. Poor Milo has never adjusted to those long hours of commuting. And it costs a lot more than we thought it would." Once more Dawn glanced at the entry to the living room. "We got the shock of our lives at our closing when they told us how much we had to contribute to our escrow account. If we'd known that we would have stuck to the basic model on an ordinary lot and skipped all the upgrades."

"Oh, yeah, the escrow account." Camille nodded. "We were surprised, too, but it came before the closing. Reuben asked the loan officer what P&I meant, and that's when we found out we'd be paying extra every month for the insurance and taxes. By that point I wished we could downgrade to a smaller house and I think Reuben did, too, even though he kept up a brave front. It was too late to change anything by then; contracts had been signed and they'd already begun building."

"I find myself thinking more and more that things weren't all that bad back in Brooklyn," Dawn admitted. Right about now they'd be entertaining friends by cooking out on the terrace. Milo would be standing over the grill, carefully moistening steaks for the adults and burgers for Zach and whatever kids had come, with soaking-wet corn still in the husks cooking on the other side of the grill. She'd have baked potatoes in the oven, French fries for the kids. If she closed her eyes she could smell the food cooking, hear the sounds of the city twelve stories below. . . .

"I wonder what happened to Tanisha and Douglas," Camille said suddenly.

Dawn blinked away her daydreaming and looked at her curiously. "Where did *that* come from? Camille, you don't think you and Reuben will be foreclosed on, do you?"

"Oh, no," she said quickly. "We still have money put away that'll last us for a good while." She wasn't really lying; they did have money. Their retirement funds. They weren't supposed to dip into it and would probably pay dearly, but at least they had it. That was a lot better than *not* having it.

"What's that song?" Dawn asked, anxious to change the subject, then paused a moment to listen. "It's called 'The Edge of a Dream.' Nice song. Minnie Riperton sang it. Remember her?"

"I've heard of her, yes. They say she could hit notes that could shatter glass."

"I think she could hit notes that only dogs could hear," Dawn said with a laugh. "She died really young, barely thirty. Breast cancer, if I'm not mistaken."

"That's too bad." Camille listened to the song's lyrics, about a paradise visualized but not quite real, and felt like Ms. Riperton could have been singing about her own situation. For the past two years she and Reuben had lived here in Arlington Acres, pleased with the quality of life it brought to them and their children. Now that lifestyle was threatened, and she wondered if they'd merely been sitting on the edge of this life she'd dreamed of rather than actually living in it.

Chapter 37

The Lees
May 2004

"When are Grandma and Grandpa coming, Mom?" Simone asked.

"They'll be out the end of June," Veronica said, beaming. "I'm glad you girls are so excited. They might be with us for a while."

Her father's recent health crisis had prompted both her parents to retire, something they'd been thinking about doing for some time. In a surprise announcement, Phyllis and Franklin announced they would move to Monroe County. Veronica was thrilled about having them so close. They would stay with Veronica and Norman while they searched for a place to live. Home prices were low enough where they could buy for the first time in their lives. They were leaning toward a condominium, if they could find one with low maintenance fees and no stairs. Franklin's doctor advised him to avoid the extra strain that climbing steps would put on his heart.

"Just two weeks until the end of school," Lorinda announced at the dinner table. "I can't wait."

"Oh, I forgot to tell you," Veronica said. "This year you'll have a special surprise. Your cousin Essence is coming to spend the summer. This way instead of waking me up if you need something she'll be able to take care of the problem. Won't that be nice?"

"Cool," Simone said as Lorinda agreed.

"Essence will help me with Grandma and Grandpa, too," Veronica said happily. Then she noticed Norman's frown. "Is something wrong?"

"When did all this happen, Vee?"

She didn't like the look on his face. He looked indignant, like she'd just insulted him or something. "Two months ago, when Daddy had his heart attack. I told you about it, remember?"

"No, you didn't."

She tried to remember that day. She'd been so tired when she got home. Norman and the kids had had a spaghetti dinner waiting for her when she'd arrived.

She drew in her breath. Now she recalled that at dinner she had reminded herself to discuss the situation with Norman later, but she was so tired she went straight to bed. Between preparing to return to her night-shift schedule the next evening and continuing concern about her father, she'd forgotten all about it.

"You're right," she said. "Now I remember that I fell asleep that night. I'm sorry I forgot to tell you, Norman."

"I know you didn't do that on purpose, but we've got a problem. I told Charles that Chucky could come for the summer."

"What?"

"He really liked it out here. Apparently he's been asking Charles and Germaine to buy a house out here. Charles told him that wouldn't work, but that he'd ask us if he could spend the summer at least." Norman's stricken expression changed to one of embarrassment. "I guess I forgot to mention it to you. I didn't see any problem."

"What are we going to do, Norman?"

"I don't know. I hate to tell Chucky he can't come. He's a good kid."

She thought so, too. A bright boy who liked to read as much as he liked to play softball, the entire family expected great things from Chucky. He was the kind of kid who'd been made to live in the country but had spent his entire life in an urban environment.

Norman's entire family had moved to the New York area from the South, and Norman and his siblings grew up with no grandparents or other family to spend summers with. Veronica felt they'd missed a lot. She and Valerie used to spend a few weeks with their grandparents in southern Virginia every year before they died. It was such a wonderful change of scenery from the city atmosphere of Washington Heights to run along the quiet rural streets, to scream at the top of their lungs in the fields.

She knew that reneging on Chucky would only antagonize his parents, Charles and Germaine. Norman hadn't shared with her anything that anyone in his family might have said, but Veronica had a sneaking suspicion that both Norman's brothers and sisters-in-law felt she'd been behind putting the brakes on their frequent weekend visits. Relations between them had been somewhat strained recently, and she didn't want an already tense situation to worsen.

"We still have a few weeks to come up with a solution," she said now. "Our kids will be out of school earlier than they get out in the city. We'll think of something, Norman."

The Youngs

Dawn opened her eyes at the sound of a child's playful yell punctuated by a loud splash. She'd drifted off as she read while stretched out in a lounger by the pool.

She liked to relax here whenever she could. The association dues she and Milo paid each year entitled them and any guests they had to use it as well as the clubhouse. Even Milo enjoyed it. He was in the pool now, at the shallow end, since, like her, he'd never learned to swim.

She put down the book and walked over to him, sitting on the lip of the pool with her legs dangling in the water. A spell of unusually warm weather for late May had hit, sending many of the home owners here to cool off or, in the case of the white folks, to get rid of that fish-belly pallor and get a little pigmentation on their exposed body parts. Sometimes it amazed her at just how *white* white folks were.

Milo came to join her, hoisting himself out of the water with his hands. He kicked up a not-too-large splash her way. "You can't get cooled off by just getting wet from the knees down."

"I know. I thought about going in all the way, but it's supposed to be hot again tomorrow, so I thought there's not much sense in ruining my hair today. Hey, where's Zach?"

"Riding his bike."

"I thought he'd be here. I see some of his friends, like Mitchell Curry."

"I don't think he likes the water."

She shrugged, wondering, but concerns over Zach were quickly forgotten as she enjoyed a sense of camaraderie with her husband. Moments like these, when they just sat and relaxed together in easy companionship, had become rare. Too often they bickered over their financial burden and his unwillingness to do anything around the house. Afternoons like this were to be savored.

The mercury returned to seasonal readings during the week, but by the following weekend it had returned to the upper eighties. Dawn did her shopping and cleaning early. After she tossed the last of the laundry into the dryer they'd finally bought last year she changed into a swimsuit. Milo had laid down for his usual Saturday afternoon nap. She expected he'd show up at the pool when he awoke. She might take a nap herself, but it would be in a lounger by the pool.

"Hey, Zach, are you planning on hitting the pool? It's going to go up to ninety today," she said.

"Nah. I'm gonna ride my bike."

She wondered if he had reached the self-conscious stage of adolescence where he didn't want to expose his thin physique to the neighborhood girls. Then she decided it was silly to wonder and asked him outright. "Zach, we've lived here for almost two years, and you went in the water maybe twice when we first got here. Don't you want to go swimming?"

"Mom, you know I can't swim."

"It's a figurative term, Zach. I can't swim, either, and neither can your father, but we still get in the water. And I see your friends in there all the time."

"That's just it, Mom. All the kids around here know how to swim. If I go in and they find out I can't they'll mess with me."

"Son, why didn't you tell us sooner? Maybe we could get you some swimming lessons."

"Oh, Mom, I know you and Daddy don't have much money left after you pay the bills for the house. I'm managing okay."

Dawn bit her lower lip. Of course Zach knew about the hard time she and Milo had keeping up. They'd had several arguments about it since the bills started coming in for the concerts they'd attended, theater tickets, dinners out, and pricey New York hotel rooms they stayed in when they were too tired to drive back to Tobyhanna afterward. Equally substantial were the purchases they'd made in Grand Cayman and Mexico during their cruise, and the landscaping project to raise their backyard, which, in addition to the landscaper's fee, involved buying sod to cover the entire area and keep it from buckling again. But that didn't mean Zach should have to make excuses to his friends for not joining them at the pool when he really wanted to. She wasn't so old that she didn't remember how important it was to fit in. Damn it, they would just have to get him lessons, that's all.

"Zach, I'll talk to Daddy. Let's see if we can get you in for lessons at the Y. The summer's just beginning, so you should be able to get in and do some swimming by next month."

"Sure, Mom."

He didn't brighten like she'd expected him to. Instead, he seemed doubtful. Dawn felt her heart break. How had they gotten to the point where her child thought she would lie to him?

"No, Dawn."

She and Milo spoke in the privacy of their bedroom, but she was careful to keep her voice down. If she had her way, Zach would never hear another argument between them. "What do you mean, 'no'? Zach needs to know how to swim. He *deserves* to know how to swim. Why should he be the only one who can't?"

"I agree that he shouldn't, but Dawn, we can't afford it, and that's that. Maybe next year, after we get some of this stuff paid off."

She sighed. She knew they had stretched themselves to the limit, but she hated for Zach to be without anything he needed. "What if I take it out of the vacation club?" she suggested. "That way I can pay cash and we won't be contributing anything to our debt."

"All right, go ahead. It's a cinch we won't be going on vacation anytime soon."

Dawn felt like a professional as she applied the relaxer mixture to Camille's new growth. She worked quickly—Camille had a lot of hair, and she had to make sure she covered the whole head in the allotted time. It should be a snap for Camille to do her short hair right after this was done.

What a great idea Camille had had, suggesting they touch up each other's relaxers. A six-dollar kit from the drugstore sure beat paying forty bucks for the beautician to do it. The woman Dawn had gone to in Mount Pocono hadn't done a bad job, but she still preferred her former salon in Brooklyn.

She used to get the full beauty treatment: hair, eyebrows, manicure, pedicure, even an occasional facial. Now she had only her eyebrows and fingernails done, both at the local Wal-Mart, and her nails were her own, not the acrylic overlays she used to get. Once you started with that you had to keep it up or your fingers looked like shit. If she didn't feel like devoting the time to having her nails done professionally at the salon she could do them herself at home and blow cool air from her blow dryer to hasten the drying process. They might not come out looking quite as nice as they did when she went to the salon, but at least she could work at her own pace and in the comfort of her own home.

Milo was right. They didn't get enough time to enjoy their house. Virtually all their free time was spent riding either to or from the city. When you factored in the commute, their workweek was sixty hours. She didn't want to spend her weekends sitting in a chair at the salon. Having to grocery shop was bad enough.

"Is it burning?" she asked Camille when her shoulders jerked.

"Just a little. I caught myself scratching the other day. Just keep going; I can take it."

"Okay, if you say so. We've got another eight minutes. Let me know if it gets unbearable."

"I will. This is such a convenience, Dawn. I really can't afford to go to the salon. As it is I have to buy some new clothes."

"Your old clothes look fine to me."

Dawn, who generally didn't impress easily, found herself admiring many of Camille's outfits. Of course, most of the secretaries at her firm dressed real sharp, too. She always considered secretaries to be necessary but overpaid employees. Any idiot could keep a schedule, make travel arrangements, arrange for meeting rooms and catering. But many of those at the top levels made more money than professionals who, in her opinion, would be much more difficult to replace. Secretaries were a dime a dozen. How many people could come in off the street and supervise the preparation of a complicated payroll?

"I've lost some weight, and I'm not sure all of my things can be taken in."

"I thought your face is looking slimmer these days. What's your secret?"

"Stress."

Dawn didn't know how to deal with such forthrightness. "Oh," was all she could say.

After Dawn combed the leave-in conditioner through Camille's long tresses, and then wrapped the outer portion and wound the center on jumbo rollers, the women changed places. Dawn sat on the step stool, and Camille put a towel around her shoulders and smoothed Vaseline around her hairline to guard against burning.

Camille hummed as she applied the relaxer, stopping abruptly when she recognized the melody as that old Minnie Riperton tune Dawn had on in her CD player the other week. She couldn't get that tune out of her head. "Dawn, it's too bad I don't know anything about cutting hair. Your hair has such a defined style; you'll probably lose some of it because it's grown out."

"Oh, I'll probably go in for a wash and set just before I'm due for my next touch-up, and I'll ask her to reshape it."

"How often do you touch up your hair, anyway?"

"Every four or five weeks. I know they recommend waiting six, but for me that's a long time, probably because my hair is so short. It's hard to hide that new growth, and if my hair starts to look like it needs a touch-up, that means I've waited too long."

"I know what you mean. I usually wait six weeks, but I can go five if that works for you." Camille didn't want these home treatments to be a one-time thing; she wanted to do it on a regular basis. Wearing the same suits for two years was one thing. Walking around with nappy roots was something else. As a secretary to a director, she had to look her best going to work. She was desperate to pull it off without having to pay a fortune to do it.

"Mommy, Daddy's home!" Shayla yelled.

"Whoop-de-doo," Camille said softly. She could tell from the way Dawn's eyebrows shot up that she'd heard her comment, but she didn't care.

A minute later Reuben tapped on the open bathroom door. "Hey, what's goin' on here? You two starting a beauty salon?"

"Hi, Reuben," Dawn said pleasantly. "We're giving each other home treatments. It's a lot more convenient than spending hours in the beauty salon."

"And cheaper, too," Camille added, "since we can't afford to pay a hairdresser to relax even two strands of my hair."

Dawn looked on with embarrassment as Reuben's cheerful demeanor dissolved into a mask of stone. She rushed to say something pleasant. "It's a harmless experiment, Reuben. A little mutual back-scrubbing that'll benefit us both."

"Harmless," Camille repeated. "We're not doing anything devious, like plotting how to murder our husbands."

Dawn frowned. What the hell was Camille's problem? Why was she deliberately seeking to embarrass Reuben?

"Camille, when you've rinsed Dawn I need to see you," he said, amiably enough. Dawn saw him nod in the mirror. "Good to see you, Dawn. Excuse me."

"Good to see you, too, Reuben."

Camille finished the application and rinsed and shampooed Dawn's hair thoroughly. Wrapping a towel around it, she said, "Dawn, if you can give me a minute I'll go see what Reuben wants."

"Sure, go ahead." Dawn kept her expression impassive, but she already *knew* what Reuben wanted. She wondered if she should make a quick exit. She could easily wrap her own hair at home, and she didn't want to be an ear-witness to a shouting match.

She pulled the towel off her head and poured conditioner over her hair and combed it through. In less than five minutes she had the longest strands at her crown rolled and had brushed the outside of her wet hair into a smooth circle. She covered it with a wrap net, fastened the Velcro, and began straightening up the bathroom. The sound of raised voices could be heard coming from the master bedroom. Just as she thought, Reuben was on Camille like pigeons on bread crumbs for making insensitive remarks designed to belittle him in front of her.

This wasn't the first time Dawn had heard Camille make disparaging comments about Reuben. She always had something unflattering to say whenever his name came up during the long rides to and from the city. Dawn could only imagine how frustrated her friend must be. She and Milo had it hard enough trying to meet their monthly obligations while retaining their income, but Reuben had lost his job nearly a year ago. He worked more than forty hours between his two part-time jobs, but he couldn't be earning very much. Still, she felt Camille's statements were inappropriate, and that it would be only a matter of time until the things she said got back to Reuben. Milo had once remarked that somebody ought to cover her mouth with some duct tape.

Dawn quickly gathered her purse and keys and hurried out, stopping outside to ask Shayla to tell her mother that she had to leave. As she drove home it occurred to her that life in the Curry household was as rocky as in her own.

Chapter 38

The Currys
July 2004

Camille carried her summer suits into the house. She'd lost so much weight that she'd had no choice but to visit a seamstress and have them taken in. Buying a new wardrobe was out of the question. The bills were now due for the new furniture they'd bought two years ago on a deferred payment plan. She'd had a special account set aside to pay the bill in full and not have to pay any interest, but she panicked and raided it when their savings ran out a few months back, so they'd gotten slammed with two years' worth of interest payments for their furniture. Withdrawals from their 401(k) accounts now kept them afloat. She hated to think what that would mean for them at tax time.

She'd been notified of her new salary increase, which sucked. She'd nodded politely at George when he'd informed her, but inside she fumed. What the hell was she supposed to do with three and a half percent? He'd probably gotten a lot more than that, and a bonus to boot. But it was the little people, like her, who had to get by on crumbs while the big shots got the bulk of the loaf.

Once again she recalled her mother telling her to choose a husband carefully and to be sure to get someone who would be a success, someone who could support her. Here she was, just a few years away from forty, married to a man who didn't make enough to keep a roof over their heads. What would happen when their retirement funds ran out? Why couldn't Reuben find a damn job?

The Lees

Veronica proudly showed off her new kitchen. From the amazed looks on the faces of Camille and Dawn, she knew they could hardly believe it was the same room that they'd first seen when she and Norman gave that party to celebrate being hired by the hospital in Stroudsburg nearly two years ago. She couldn't blame them; she had trouble believing it herself. Those room-dimming, dark wood cabinets had been taken down and replaced with white extra-long ones like Dawn and Milo had, with four shelves instead of three. One cabinet, in which they displayed their fancier drinking glasses and most colorful bowls, was made of glass with a wood trim. They'd bought sleek black appliances, including a stacked wall oven and microwave. A smooth surface, five-burner cooktop sat on one end of a large island. The old brick-print linoleum had been replaced with gleaming white tile. The stark black-and-white color scheme contained splashes of red—including a toaster, blender, and coffeemaker. A red ceramic holder held cooking utensils.

Their new carpet had also been installed, a sea of maroon so thick that you could see your footprints. They'd selected an attractive linoleum for the basement and accented it with throw rugs. She felt it unlikely that their basement would flood, but Norman pointed out that the area sometimes had days of heavy rains and that it didn't make sense to spend a lot on flooring there. It looked pretty good, considering they'd done the work themselves. A few seams showed here and there, but it was a huge improvement over that old shag carpet.

"Ooh, it's so lush," Denise King said as she wiggled her bare feet on the carpet.

Her husband Lemuel poked Norman with his elbow. "Yeah, man, now I know why you're always working overtime."

"Whenever I can get it," Norman admitted. "And that won't change anytime soon. Gotta pay for all this."

"It's worth it, if you ask me," Dawn said. "Milo will love this."

"I hope he feels better tomorrow," Veronica said politely.

"I do, too. He hated to miss it, but he said he'll be over soon."

Camille, who'd been quiet, spoke up. "Reuben said he'd try to stop by after work, but he's usually pretty tired when he gets home."

Veronica didn't expect him to show up. The Currys had pretty much withdrawn from the social group the four couples had started, and she feared their marriage might be collapsing under the strain of financial problems caused by Reuben's layoff. Camille made no secret of the fact that she'd run out of patience, but Veronica felt she was being unfair. Reuben worked so hard. He'd even quit his part-time job at the supermarket for a more lucrative one at the hospital in maintenance Norman had told him about.

"I can understand that," Norman said. "He works a lot of hours."

Camille could only grunt.

"Norman, you should put the chicken on," Veronica said, glancing at her watch. She'd agreed to cover a shift for one of her coworkers tonight. An extra eight hours would be very tiring, but it would also mean overtime pay.

Lemuel King kept Norman company as he grilled chicken quarters in the backyard. The four women sat around a round patio table with its umbrella positioned to keep the late-afternoon sun out of their eyes.

"Oh, it feels good to sit down for a change," Veronica said. She rolled her head back on her neck and then from side to side, eyes closed.

"You've really had a house full, haven't you?" Denise asked empathetically.

"All summer. It hasn't been easy, especially with the work we had done."

"Living through a remodel is hard enough without having extra people in the house," Denise commented.

"Cooking has been a challenge," Veronica admitted. "We've probably used the grill three or four times a week. I just couldn't face the mess in the kitchen."

"How's everything going with your niece?" Dawn asked.

Veronica smiled. "She's a joy. So is Norman's nephew. We ended up having to put him in the basement, because I forgot to mention to Norman that I'd invited Essence to spend the summer and he forgot to mention to me that he'd invited Chucky. But he's a good kid, and he's never complained about being stuck down there."

"That makes for a lot of extra people, when you include your parents," Camille remarked.

"Tell me about it. It's doubled the size of our family. When I'm not cooking for eight people I'm doing the laundry. But Essence is a big help with that, and so is Lorinda." She sighed. "Still, I have to admit I won't be sorry to see the kids go home and my parents in their own place. Norman and I made a pact to never commit to any company without clearing it with the other first."

"Have your parents found a place yet?"

"Yes, they found a ground-floor condo they like, right here in Mount Pocono. They'll probably close the latter part of next month." Her shoulders sagged in fatigue. "Then Norman and I will have to get them moved in."

Camille raised her chin defiantly. "Well, one advantage to being broke is that no one has asked for us to keep their kids this summer."

"Uh . . . How does Reuben like working at the hospital, Camille?" Veronica asked, wanting to change the subject.

She shrugged. "He says it's all right. At least he makes more than at that supermarket. I kept telling him he was wasting his time, but it wasn't until they hired a produce manager from outside instead of promoting him that he was ready to chuck it. And I like the fact that he's home more during the week with the kids and gone all day Saturday and Sunday, when I'm home."

Veronica rolled her eyes. There was just no getting Camille to shut up. She could understand the financial strain Camille must be under, but did she have to knock her husband every chance she got? It only made everyone uncomfortable.

"Again, Veronica, I think your kitchen and your new carpeting look wonderful," Dawn said in what Veronica suspected was another attempt to change the subject. "And I hope you're not overdoing it by entertaining us this afternoon and going to work tonight."

"No problem. That's why we made it an early evening. I'll lay down at seven and sleep for a few hours." She shrugged. "A woman's gotta do what a woman's gotta do. After all, these improvements all come with a price tag. But just eighteen more years and it'll all be ours."

"Eighteen years?" Dawn's facial expression reflected her puzzlement. "Is that all?"

Denise nodded knowingly. "You must have gotten a twenty-year mortgage."

"Yes, when we asked the bank to do the math it wasn't much more each month than a thirty-year, so we went for it. This way we'll own the house free and clear before we turn sixty."

The Youngs

"So how was the great unveiling of the masterpiece?" Milo asked.

His question surprised Dawn. She hadn't expected him to even acknowledge that she and Zach had gone over to the Lees', not after he'd flatly said he just didn't feel up to having Norman and Veronica's brand-new kitchen shoved in his face.

"Hey, they're good people, and I'm glad for them. They're not show-offs or anything like that," he said, "but I just can't cope with it right now, not while this fucking house is bankrupting me. I'm sorry."

She'd been terribly disappointed. Spending time with their friends was one of the few times Milo truly relaxed. These days he walked around more tightly wound than an unused garden hose.

"It was gorgeous," she said now. "Their kitchen is right out of a magazine. It's all black and white, with a few touches of red."

"Sounds nice. But you're home awfully early."

She nodded. "Veronica's working an extra shift tonight, and she wanted to sleep for a few hours before going in. She and Norman both work overtime whenever they can."

He grunted. "Sure they do. It helps them pay for all that work they're doing."

"Zach and I are going to the pool, since it's still early. He likes to practice his stroke just before the lifeguard goes off duty." She remembered something she'd made a mental note to share with him. "Milo, I learned something interesting tonight. Veronica mentioned that they have a twenty-year mortgage, not thirty."

"They could probably afford to do it. A forty-year-old house isn't going to cost as much as new construction, Dawn."

"I understand that, but I wondered if we should have looked into doing that. Veronica said it only came to a few more dollars every month, and they'll own their house ten years earlier."

"Well, it's too late to do anything about it now, isn't it?"

His sharp tone annoyed her. "You don't have to jump down my throat, Milo. I was just wondering." She left the room, wanting to put some space between them.

In her private bathroom she splashed cold water on her face. Why hadn't they considered all their options instead of rushing in to the first deal that came along? If they'd moved a little slower, they might now be sitting as pretty as Veronica and Norman instead of struggling to get by month after month. Milo was probably right: most likely the Lees' house had cost a lot less than her and Milo's. All right, so when they first moved in, the house looked awful, but all older houses weren't as outdated. Lots of owners modernized their kitchens and bathrooms and put down new carpet before selling. Dawn wished she and Milo had considered an existing house instead of building this new one on the lake. They'd never even thought about it.

But the Lees hadn't gone out and spent thousands on new furniture for every room, like she and Milo had. Her usual expensive taste had resulted in more debt for them. She asked herself, if she had the option of financing over ten fewer years and making do with the same furniture they used back in Brooklyn, would she have done it?

In her heart she knew she wouldn't have. She liked nice things too much.

When she came out of the bathroom Milo sat on their bed. "I'm sorry I snapped at you, Dawn."

"I accept your apology." She held his gaze, knowing he had something else to say.

"It's just that I'm not happy living here. It's nice and everything, but it's much more draining than I thought it would be. Nobody told us about all these extra expenses. When they're not being evasive, they just outright lie. First they said the bus takes about two hours each way, when it takes two and a half. That alone takes an hour out of my day when there aren't a lot of spare hours to begin with. Then they said a train is coming. We've been here over two years. Where is it? We get a bill for upkeep of the common areas, our taxes are higher than we thought they'd be. . . . It just goes on and on." He shook his head sadly. "I've got nothing against Norman and Lemuel, they're both good men. But they're making it work, and we're hurting. I'm tired of feeling like I'm lacking."

She felt she had to say something, come up with a valid reason why their friends were doing so much better than they were. "That's only because they both have jobs here, Milo, and so do Veronica and Denise. If you and I didn't have to spend all that money to commute to New York we'd be doing okay, too."

"Dawn, don't you get it? The reasons don't matter. I'm not interested in making excuses. All that matters is the result, and that's what I'm not happy about. We're barely breaking even." He held her gaze. "But if you want to talk about the reasons we're having such a hard time, there's more to it than just not having local jobs, Dawn, and you know it. We shouldn't have gone out and spent all that money to build on the lake and then to furnish the entire house. There wasn't anything wrong with the furniture we had in Brooklyn. If we'd taken it slowly, we wouldn't be thousands of dollars in debt now."

He'd said nothing she hadn't already considered, but hearing him say it nevertheless made her wince. She tried to come up with something comforting, a way to cheer him up that didn't have a price tag attached.

"Why don't you come swimming along with Zach and me?" she finally suggested. "We can cook out when we get back." This time of year, at the height of summer, it stayed light out until about nine, but they also had lights on their deck for grilling after dark.

"Maybe tomorrow. I think I'll just stay in and watch TV."

Uh-oh, she thought. *That sounds bad.* Usually Milo enjoyed splashing around in the water. He almost seemed to forget about all their problems while enjoying the pool. As comfortable as their old apartment had been, it hadn't offered a pool to cool off in on a hot summer day.

A knock sounded on the door. "Come in, Zach!" she called.

He entered the room, dressed in swim trunks and a decorative T-shirt from Mexico. "Are you ready, Mom?"

She looked uncertainly at Milo.

"Go ahead," he said. "I'll be here when you get back."

"Give me a couple of minutes to change," she said to Zach.

"Okay." He left, closing the door behind him.

Dawn walked to her dresser to get out her bathing suit. She felt Milo behind her even before he said, "Come here."

She went into his embrace, content just to feel his arms around her.

"I'm sorry, Dawn," he repeated. "Don't mind me today. I guess I'm just in a bad mood. It's not easy being the ones who are struggling to get by. We never had this problem until we bought this house."

Her head rested in the nook where his neck met his shoulders.

"But we're not the only ones struggling, Milo. Look at Camille and Reuben. He didn't even stop by the Lees' today, and he gets off at 4:30."

"I wouldn't have either, if I were him. That Camille acts like their predicament is his fault, the way she's always criticizing him. What was that she said on the bus last week? 'If I met a rich guy I'd drop Reuben like he had the bird flu.' Hell, people get laid off every day. I'd be tempted to slap her if I was him." He mumbled something unintelligible under his breath. "But at least they have a good reason for having it rough. We really don't, other than we should have been better informed and been prepared to crawl before we walked. And now I'm hearing that the bus company is going to raise their rates."

"That figures. The price of gas is going up. It's cutting into their profits. Besides, there hasn't been a fare hike in two years, so I guess they're due." Dawn deliberately did not address the first part of Milo's comments. She felt they shouldn't have had to crawl. This year she'd turn forty and he'd turn forty-one. Crawling along at a snail's pace was for people in their twenties. But she kept her thoughts to herself, certain Milo wouldn't be able to appreciate the sentiment.

He didn't appreciate her opinion on the bus company's rate increase, either. "Nice of you to be so understanding of their motives," he said in a voice drier than hay.

She moved her head so they stood face-to-face. "I didn't mean it that way, Milo. Of course I'm not happy about it. But I understand why they're doing it."

He leaned forward and kissed her lightly on the mouth. "You'd better get changed."

"I wish you'd come with us, Milo."

"I promise that if it's nice tomorrow I'll go with you. It's probably better if I stay home tonight, anyway. Didn't you say you were going to tell Veronica that I wasn't feeling well?"

"Oh, yes, that's right." It wouldn't look right if Milo suddenly showed up at the pool after not going to the Lees' just a few hours ago. Norman and Veronica wouldn't see him, since they didn't live in Arlington Acres, but Denise and Lemuel might, or one of their kids. Dawn wouldn't want anyone to feel she'd lied to them, even though it was just a little fib.

Milo squeezed her arm. "Go ahead, have fun. And like I said, don't pay me any mind. This, too, shall pass."

She wondered if it would.

Chapter 39

Veronica yawned as she removed clothing from the dryer. She'd just washed two loads, but the clothes sorter still held oodles of dirty clothes. She'd be glad when her niece and Norman's nephew went home, and when her parents got into their condo. This laundry situation had her exhausted.

She turned at the sound of footsteps. Essence's petite frame came into view. "Aunt Veronica, I emptied out the dishwasher and swept and mopped the kitchen floor, like you asked. Can I help you do anything else?"

She thought quickly. "If you can help me get these clothes folded, I'll be finished that much sooner."

They worked separately to fold shorts, T-shirts, underwear, and towels. Working together, they folded flat and fitted sheets.

"Oh, thanks, Essence," she said gratefully.

Essence pointed to the assorted socks on the folding table. "We still have to do the socks."

"No, I save those for Lorinda and Simone to take upstairs. They put away their clothes plus all the linens, and they sort all the socks. All I do is carry upstairs my clothes along with your uncle Norman's, plus Grandma and Grandpa's, so Grandma won't have to come down here." Veronica gathered two piles of folded clothes. "You might as well get your things now," she said to her niece over her shoulder. "Chucky will get his things when he comes down."

After Veronica had given her mother her clean clothes and gone up to the master bedroom to put her own things away, she returned to the kitchen and poured some sweetened iced tea. "Would you like some?" she offered to Essence when she entered the kitchen.

"Yes." The fourteen-year-old grinned. "I guess we had the same idea at the same time."

Veronica poured another glass and handed it to Essence. She placed an arm around her niece's shoulders. "Well, Essence, next week you'll be going home, and in a few weeks you'll be starting ninth grade. Are you excited about the new school year?"

To her surprise, the teen merely hung her head. "Essence? What's wrong, sweetheart?"

Essence raised her head and looked at Veronica imploringly. "Aunt Veronica, I don't want to go back home. I want to stay here."

The plea flustered Veronica and made her temporarily speechless. She hadn't been at all prepared for this reaction. "But there's school, dear," she said.

"Can't I go to school here?"

Veronica tried a different tack. "Essence, I'm glad you like it here, but what about your mother? I know she misses you, and you miss her." Valerie had driven down twice during July, sometimes alone and sometimes with a girlfriend, but there was no evidence of any men. Veronica lauded her efforts.

"I do miss Mom, but I'd rather live out here and go to school."

Veronica fought a rising panic. Essence staying here would cause all kinds of familial problems. Lucy had been scarce since her disastrous fortieth birthday party, but Norman's brothers were sure to create a ruckus if her niece moved in while they were allowed only occasional weekend visits. And on her side of the family, Valerie would swear she'd put Essence up to this.

Instantly she felt ashamed of her selfish behavior. Here she was, thinking only of herself. Essence wouldn't be asking to stay if she wasn't deeply unhappy at home. She had a familial duty to find out why.

"Essence, you have to give me something here. Why don't you want to go back to New York?"

"It's so much nicer here, Aunt Veronica. New York is ugly. Here they have grass and everything."

Veronica nodded. Grass was a rare commodity in Washington Heights outside of a park setting. What little there was was usually roped off, to be admired only from a distance, like a priceless painting.

Suddenly she recalled Valerie telling her that Essence had gotten into a fight last spring with another girl from the building. "Essence, tell me the truth. Does your wanting to stay here have anything to do with that fight you got in before you came here? Are you afraid that if you go back you'll get hurt?"

Essence scoffed. "Me, afraid of Zena Hawkins? If anything, *she's* afraid of *me*. I was whipping her butt, and I would have finished the job if Mr. Inniss didn't pull us apart."

Veronica believed her; she looked too serious. But she didn't understand the reasons behind Essence's request. Surely it couldn't be simply because the suburbs had more visual appeal than the city.

"Essence, I think there's something you're not telling me," she said. "Before we can go any further with this, you'll have to tell me the whole truth. Come on." She led her niece through the back door, and they sat together on a double-width covered swinging chair. "Okay, let's have it."

Essence still seemed reluctant to talk, and Veronica suddenly had a terrifying thought. What if she'd been molested by one of Valerie's boyfriends? That would account for her reluctance to talk about it. Just because Valerie hadn't brought any men along with her during her visits didn't mean she'd stopped her frantic dating pattern. *My God, if Essence has been abused, there'd be hell to pay.*

Essence began to speak, staring at the grass at her feet. "Aunt Veronica, the reason I jumped on Zena Hawkins was because she called my mom a whore. She said her mother told her my mother has a different man every night, and sometimes two." She choked back a sob. "Aunt Veronica, I had to beat her up. But I couldn't tell Mom what she said, could I?"

Veronica swallowed hard. So that was it. "No, I guess you couldn't." *But somebody should,* she thought.

What a mess. But at least Essence hadn't been messed with. Valerie's dating habits being noticed and talked about by her neighbors, even if they were exaggerating, wouldn't do Essence any good.

Veronica fell silent as she thought. She couldn't tell Essence it would be all right, for she had no idea if it would or not. It wasn't her decision to take her niece in. Essence was Valerie's daughter. Valerie would have to approve any change in her living arrangements. And so would Norman.

"Essence, I can't make you any promises," she said, "but I'll see what I can do."

Veronica's spirits dropped at the apprehensive look her niece gave her, but it was the best she could do for now.

The Youngs

Dawn watched from a lounge chair as Zach swam laps across the width of the pool. He'd worked so hard to learn to swim, and although he joined his friends in the water he still practiced every chance he got, usually in the last hour the lifeguard was on duty, between 7:00 and 8:00. Dawn insisted that he never swim alone, even after he became experienced, and forbid him to go in the water when the lifeguard wasn't present.

She walked over to the cement lip of the pool as he approached from the other side. She stood and applauded lightly, more like a gesture than an actual clapping noise. "Bravo!"

Zach grabbed the edge and hoisted himself up with folded arms. "Am I getting good, Mom?"

"You've gotten great! Who knows, Daddy and I might take lessons next year ourselves." It pleased her that he smiled in response instead of doubting her. Between her managing to pay for his swim lessons and being careful not to exchange cross words with Milo in Zach's presence, she felt she'd been successful in putting a halt to his worries.

"Hi there!"

She looked up and saw Reuben Curry with his daughter Shayla. "Hey, Reuben. Hi, Shayla."

"Mr. Curry, look at me!" Zach turned to his stomach and shoved off, moving his arms in even strokes, his hands cupped.

"Looking good, Zach. What're you doing, training for the Olympics?"

"Just practicing." Zach stopped swimming and began to tread water in the five-foot-deep water. "Summer's almost over, and I don't want to forget the things they taught me at the Y about the right way to swim." He paused, probably realizing he'd given something away. "I wasn't doing it right before. That's why Mom sent me there."

"Ah, you won't forget. Swimming's just like riding a bike. Once you know how you can't forget."

"Daddy, come on!" Shayla called from the shallow end.

"Excuse me, folks," Reuben said. "I'm giving Shayla some coaching."

He walked to the shallow end. Zach resumed doing laps, and Dawn returned to her lounger. She watched as Reuben instructed Shayla on the basics of swimming. He seemed to know what he was doing and seemed to be good at it. She considered that maybe she should have asked him to teach Zach to swim. Look at all that money she could have saved. She would have paid Reuben, of course, but not nearly as much as she'd paid the Y for his membership and lessons.

Once more her gaze went to her son, who was now practicing a different stroke. She decided in an instant that she'd done the right thing. Zach liked doing his practice laps so late because the pool was practically empty, except for an occasional late commuter taking a quick dip before a typically late dinner. Zach would have been embarrassed if Reuben knew he hadn't been able to swim. Mitchell Curry would have found out, and the news would spread to every kid in the subdivision. Her son's pride was worth paying extra for.

Zach had gotten surprisingly good. He'd begun lessons just six weeks ago, and she doubted he'd become a strong swimmer, but he did have good form. The only reason she got to watch him tonight was because she'd taken a couple of vacation days. Milo, who'd gotten a ride with Camille, would probably be home by the time they drove back to the house.

They found Milo at the kitchen table, eating his favorite chicken and rice casserole that she'd taken out of the oven before bringing Zach to the pool. "Damn, I love this," he mumbled, his mouth full of food.

"Me, too," Zach said as he ran toward his room to change into dry clothes.

"It feels good to be able to make dinner in the afternoon rather than cook a couple of meals on Sunday," Dawn remarked as she fixed a plate. Soon she joined him at the table. "Zach has really become a good swimmer, Milo. He's gotten a lot better since the last time I saw him in action."

"Maybe he can teach us how to swim next year," he joked.

She chuckled.

"Our anniversary is coming up next month," he remarked casually.

"Yes, I know." She wished they were in a position to do something about it, but with all their bills that was mere fantasy. "Maybe we can go to dinner someplace nice." *That* shouldn't break the bank, she thought.

"I was thinking along the lines of something a little more festive. How would you like a long weekend in New Orleans?"

She looked at him incredulously. "I'd like nothing more, but you know"—she broke off, realizing that a referral to their current predicament would only serve to antagonize him—"I mean, it isn't practical right now."

"To hell with being practical, Dawn. We've been married fifteen years. That's considered a milestone. Besides," he added with a sly smile, "I've already booked the reservation. I found a deal too good to pass up. You'll have to take off that Wednesday, Thursday, and Friday. We'll be back Saturday. I know how difficult it is for you to miss Mondays." Monday was the day Dawn submitted the payroll, and taking off that day often presented problems for her.

Still, how could he go out and charge airline tickets and make hotel reservations when he knew they were still paying for their expenditures on the cruise? And what about that brake job on the car just a few weeks ago? She'd been late paying two of the credit cards in May, making double payments in June, and both creditors promptly raised their interest rates to a whopping 29 percent. To add insult to injury, both the furniture store they'd bought from and a department store where they had an account began charging them higher rates as well. When she called to object, saying they'd always paid them on time, representatives at both companies told her that they looked at how she and Milo paid their other bills as well, not just the ones from them.

Milo knew about all this, yet he'd gone ahead and booked a vacation on credit? She just couldn't fathom it.

She didn't want to tell him how little she thought of his idea. He took everything so personally these days, and she didn't feel like putting a damper on the day with yet another money argument. Instead she searched for an excuse. She couldn't claim an issue with her job, he'd already avoided any complications by scheduling the trip for the latter part of the week.

"We really shouldn't take Zach out of school so early in the semester," she said.

"We won't have to. I talked to Camille, and she said Zach can stay with them and go to school with Mitchell."

"Camille! Milo, she and Reuben are barely making it as it is. When she was here a couple of months ago she mentioned that couple who lived over by her, the ones who lost their house. She never would have brought them up if she wasn't worried about foreclosure herself."

"Dawn, what do you think I am, some kind of insensitive oaf? Of course I wouldn't ask Camille and Reuben to take in our son without offering them compensation."

"Oh." She paused before asking curiously, "What're you giving them?"

"Never mind. It was a business deal between Camille and me."

"What about Reuben? Is it okay with him, too?"

"Camille spoke for him. If I know her, she didn't say a word to him and he'll find out the day Zach shows up with his suitcase. You know, she's really looking good these days since she lost all that weight, but if you ask me she's become a real bitch. But how she treats her husband isn't my concern. I don't have to live with her. As long as Zach is taken care of, then I'm good to go."

Dawn wished he would tell her how much money he'd offered Camille to take care of Zach for four days, three of which he would spend in school. Milo's keeping so mum about it suggested he'd paid through the nose. No doubt Camille needed the money, but they had to watch their pennies, too. Plus, she didn't know how the Currys' diet had been affected by Reuben's job loss. For all she knew, Zach might be eating nothing but macaroni and cheese for three nights.

That thought made her a little uneasy, but it was only for four days. They'd be back Saturday, and they'd take Zach out to dinner to help make up any dulling of his taste buds.

In the meantime, she and Milo could truly enjoy their fifteenth anniversary. Plus they'd be helping out their friends the Currys.

She began to feel better about the plan. Besides, she'd never been to New Orleans. . . .

Chapter 40

The Lees
December 2004

The streets of East Stroudsburg were deserted at 7:00 AM Christmas morning. Still, Veronica wished she could drive through the red lights she encountered so she could get home faster. She wanted to see how Norman had arranged the girls' gifts around the tree. Lorinda and Simone routinely awoke early on Christmas morning in anticipation of what they would receive, and she hoped to be there to see their first reactions.

This year there were no big-ticket items, no fancy electronics or expensive toys, just a lot of clothing and some inexpensive fun things. Their biggest surprise would come in an unexpected form.

She unlocked the front door and stepped into the slightly re-arranged living room, with a six-foot pine tree in one corner. Norman sat on the loveseat across from the tree, admiring his handiwork. He jumped up to greet her.

"Merry Christmas," they told each other before sharing a sensual kiss. "Ooh, Santa," she said, reaching out to touch his erection through his scrub pants. "What have we here?"

"Something you probably need to forget about, at least for the time being. The kids'll be up any minute, and your parents, Valerie, and Essence will be here at 9:00."

For a moment Veronica regretted inviting her family over to have breakfast and to open gifts together. She wished she could have just a

half hour alone with her husband, but she had to start mixing pan-
cake batter. It was already past 7:30.

"I want us to have breakfast first before anyone opens any gifts,"
she cautioned as she whisked the eggs.

"Come on, Vee. The girls are excited. It's Christmas. Let them at
least open something small. They'll still have plenty left."

"Oh, all right."

Lorinda and Simone opened their gifts, each one accompanied by
excited squeals. Essence, too, appeared happy—probably in part because her mother was there and she didn't have to share her with the
man of the moment.

Veronica was proud of Valerie, who, after great initial resistance
and the urging of their parents, agreed to allow Essence to stay with
her grandparents in Mount Pocono. She had enrolled in school there
and was thriving, with good grades and lots of new friends.

It hadn't been easy for Veronica to tell her sister the reason Essence
had gotten into a fight, but she sensed, rightly so, that it would be
her trump card in changing Valerie's mind. Eventually Valerie admitted, albeit reluctantly, that the arrangement was a success. Mount
Pocono represented a much better environment for Essence than
Washington Heights, and their parents loved having their firstborn
grandchild stay with them.

Simone threw her arms around Norman. "I had a nice Christmas,
Daddy."

"Me, too," Lorinda said as Simone moved to thank Veronica.

"Ah, but we have one more gift for you," Veronica said, gesturing
with her head to Norman.

He went to the coat closet and pulled out a large package. "This
is for our girls from Mommy and me," he announced.

Lorinda and Simone eagerly attacked the package, which turned
out to be a navy and gold floral suitcase. They looked at their parents questioningly.

"If they were grown, they'd be saying, 'What the hell is *this* supposed to be'?" Valerie quipped from her seat. She'd been filled in
ahead of time about the girls' surprise.

"Open the bag and you'll find out what it's all about," Norman
instructed.

Lorinda took over, unzipping the suitcase. Simone grabbed the paper inside. " 'This is the suitcase that Lorinda and Simone Lee will carry with them when they go to Disney World in three weeks,' " she read. Lorinda let out a playful yelp, and Simone quickly joined in. The girls ran to Veronica and Norman, practically knocking them over with bear hugs.

"You're welcome, my little princesses," Norman said.

"Yes, you are," Veronica echoed. Because of their upcoming Florida vacation, she and Norman had exchanged modest gifts; a nightgown and matching peignoir for her, a hip-length leather jacket for him. She'd just earned time and a half for working a holiday shift, and Norman would go in at noon and work until 4:00 to cover part of a coworker's shift. He'd be back in time for dinner.

She glanced first at the colorful torn paper that littered the living room, then at her watch. "Norman, will you collect all the wrapping paper? I've got to get the turkey in the oven."

"Help me out, girls," he said. "Let's get this mess cleaned up quick so I can lay down for an hour or so before I have to leave for work. I've been up since 6:00." He punctuated the request with a yawn.

He showed up in the kitchen while Veronica stood washing the bird at the sink. "I'd say they were surprised, wouldn't you?" he asked.

"I certainly would. And I echo Simone's sentiment. It's a nice Christmas. But I'm sure it's not easy for you, being around all these females."

"Hey, before we got married you warned me that girls run in your family, so I wasn't surprised when our two both turned out to be females. At least I've got your father to keep me company." He paused. "I'm real glad he's okay, Vee."

"Me, too. He had all of us scared to death when he had his heart attack. But he's doing well, thank God. And how about my little sister? I can't remember the last time I saw her when she wasn't either looking for a man or trying to hold on to one." She noticed a knowing look come over his face, like he knew something she didn't. "What?" she demanded.

"I'm not supposed to tell you."

"You're keeping a secret from me? From *me*, your wife?" She put the turkey down in the sink and wiped her hands on a paper towel. Playfully she lunged at him, wrapping her hands around his neck and pretending to squeeze. "You aren't allowed to have any secrets I don't know about, Norman Ellis Lee."

He clutched his throat and spoke in a raspy-sounding Donald Duck voice. "All right, all right. I'll tell you." When she let her hands fall to her sides he said, "I know that Valerie has been seeing someone, and I know who it is."

"You do? Well, don't just stand there, Norman." Veronica suddenly frowned. "Wait a minute. How would *you* know who Valerie is seeing? Don't tell me the rumors have gotten all the way back to our old block!" Their friend Duane London would have passed on whatever he might have heard to Norman, with caution not to tell her, especially if it was something unpleasant.

But wait a minute. If it was some unsavory bit of news, why was Norman grinning?

"Okay, what's the scoop?"

He turned around to make sure no one had entered the kitchen. "She's been spending time with Duane."

Her lower lip dropped. "Duane? *Our* Duane?"

"That's the one. But Vee, don't say anything to her. She might become self-conscious if she knows you know."

"I won't say a word. Now you go get some rest. You've barely got time to lay down for forty minutes." She sent him on his way with a kiss.

While cleaning, seasoning, and stuffing the turkey, Veronica allowed herself to daydream about the possibilities of their longtime friend dating her sister. Like Valerie, Duane had never been married, but he was quite a ladies' man. Maybe the two of them would find something in each other that had eluded them elsewhere.

Veronica was very much aware of the plight of many black women who looked without much success for suitable husbands. She always considered herself fortunate to have met Norman when she did. They started work at Presbyterian on the same day and went through orientation together. The group contained other black men, but she'd found out from the word exercises they'd done in class that they were barely literate. She was no snob and knew she was just a nurse and not a research scientist, but she couldn't picture herself married to someone who disposed of hazardous waste or who transported patients on gurneys down to the hospital's X-ray department.

She and Norman began dating after orientation, and after a few months she brought him to meet her family. Valerie had scoffed, saying that Norman wasn't handsome and that in ten years he'd probably weigh four hundred pounds. But Norman scored high marks with her parents, both of whom said he appeared to be a fine man.

It was true that Norman's prominent jawline prevented him from being conventionally handsome; and it was also true that even when they dated Norman was never thin, but she'd had the last laugh. Norman had been a wonderful husband to her and father to Lorinda and Simone. The weight gain Valerie predicted had never materialized. Norman more than satisfied her in bed. And he always led their family down the right path. Veronica had all these happy years with Norman, while Valerie was still trying to catch the eye of the cover model-types who only wanted to get her into bed.

She put the turkey in the oven, marveling at the convenience of having an oven at a comfortable level. It beat having to bend over while carrying a twenty-pound bird.

Secretly, Veronica felt glad to be making dinner for only four extra people. She'd had more than her fair share of company the past year. Norman's brother Charles and family, along with their sister Lucy, were all having dinner at Eddie and Michelle's. They'd all asked if she and Norman planned to give a New Year's Eve party, but she'd said no, this year they would be guests. She hadn't lied. Denise and Lemuel King had invited them over to their place to see in the new year.

Veronica didn't harbor any strong feelings against her in-laws, but she was content to not see them very often.

The Currys

Camille awoke with an unusual feeling, a mix of satisfaction and apprehension.

She closed her eyes to block out the strong morning sunlight that filtered in from between the open blinds. It looked like a nice crisp winter day.

She closed her eyes, and suddenly she remembered the reason for her satisfaction. She and Reuben had had great sex last night . . . twice. Not the sex of people who loved each other but sex just for pure release, for no other reason than they both needed to get laid. They pounded against each other like strangers passing in the night, never to see each other again.

She glanced over to the other side of the king-sized bed. Reuben had already gotten up. She wished she could lie here all day. Even covered by a quilt stuffed with simulated down fiber, she still felt a draft.

The door to the bathroom opened, and Reuben emerged.

She shivered under the covers. "Hey, Reuben, now that our builder is in trouble, can't we sue him for giving us insufficient insulation or something? It's freezing in here."

"Good morning to you, too."

She shrugged with next to no embarrassment. Hell, if he had a schedule as grueling as hers he would overlook the little niceties as well. Okay, so he worked two jobs and an extra five hours. She'd gladly change places with him if it meant she wouldn't have to commute five days a week.

"Actually, you should skip the 'good morning' and try 'Merry Christmas,'" he said caustically.

That got a reaction from her, in spite of her determination not to let him get to her. She made a gasping sound. How could she forget this was Christmas morning? No wonder she had awakened with such an apprehensive feeling. Bad enough that she and Reuben had been making withdrawals from their retirement fund all year, she'd paid for Mitchell and Shayla's Christmas with credit cards. Reuben had been adamantly against that; he said they were in deep enough financial trouble without running up yet another bill. Camille didn't like it, either, but they'd always had generous holiday celebrations with plenty of gifts, and she didn't want them to go without. They ended up having a big fight, but lately they fought about everything, so it really didn't matter.

She'd spent nearly five hundred dollars on clothes and computer games, and already she was worrying about the bills that would arrive next month. That explained her uneasiness. The queasy feeling in her stomach was becoming routine; she walked around in a perpetual state of worry and dread. She felt like a deer trapped between a grizzly bear and a busy highway. They could probably sell their home at a decent profit, but then where would they live? Getting a cheaper house, like Denise King's neighbors, wasn't an option. No way would they qualify for a mortgage, not with Reuben's work situation.

And renting wasn't feasible. Apartments had gotten so expensive; the monthly rent for a three-bedroom apartment wouldn't be much less than their mortgage payment. What would be the point of moving? At least with a house they had something of value.

She just prayed they'd be able to hang on to it until Reuben found a good job.

The Youngs

Dawn went back to the buffet and loaded her plate with shrimp. The hotel restaurant where they decided to eat served an impressive Christmas dinner. She hadn't eaten this much since her trip to New Orleans in September.

This marked their first Christmas with only the three of them, and the first time they'd eaten out on the holiday. She thought they might drive into the city to visit their families, but Milo had been against it. "We can have a perfectly nice holiday with just the three of us," he'd said. "I'm tired of everybody in Brooklyn acting like we moved to Pluto. If you want we can drive in between Christmas and New Year's and see everybody, but I think we ought to get used to the idea of you, me, and Zach against the world."

Dawn knew that relations between Camille and Reuben had deteriorated to the point where their Christmas would likely be tense and strained, but she envied Veronica and Norman, who would enjoy a homey celebration with her parents, sister, and niece.

It seemed like everything went well for Veronica, she thought with a touch of bitterness. Why did some people get to live charmed lives, while others struggled? Would she have to live out her life, die, and then come back as a different person before she got a chance to be one of the lucky ones?

At least they had had a nice holiday. Milo had bought Zach the newly released version of his favorite computer game, and she'd bought him those new gym shoes he wanted, plus some boring necessities, like underwear and socks. She'd even bought Stormy some gourmet dog biscuits, which the canine loved.

Milo surprised her with an earring and pendant set in black onyx and gold. She gave him a couple of shirts that she'd matched with snazzy tie-and-hanky sets.

She'd paid for everything with proceeds from her Christmas club savings, and Milo paid for his purchases with his annual bonus. She knew they would have to either stop spending or pay cash for everything. They'd already maxed out two credit cards and were running up the balance on a third.

That would be her New Year's resolution, she vowed. No buying anything on credit unless absolutely necessary. If they tightened their belts they would win this battle of the budget.

Something told her that 2005 would be their year.

Chapter 41

Camille stared at the number in disbelief. She suddenly found it hard to breathe, and blood rushed to her head. "Reuben, we owe the IRS eleven thousand dollars."

"What?"

"Eleven thousand dollars," she repeated. It sounded even worse the second time. She could feel her heart racing in her chest. It felt like it would jump out at any moment and bounce around the room. "Because of the money we took from our retirement fund. Early withdrawal penalties. Plus, we have to pay tax on the amount withdrawn." Her eyes filled with tears. "What are we going to do?"

He was at her side in an instant, gathering her in an embrace. "Camille, don't cry."

"What else am I supposed to do?" she asked between sobs. "What are *you* going to do?"

He took a deep breath. "I've wondered if we should sell the house."

"And then what? Live on the streets?"

"That's where I get stuck," he admitted. "I'm not sure what to do. I don't know how long it'll be until I can get a better-paying job. I keep telling myself that when it happens I'll keep working at FedEx to help us get out of this hole. But I don't know when that'll be."

She pulled back a little to look up at him. "And this is supposed to help me feel better? Hearing you talk about what you hope will happen? You're the head of our family, Reuben. You're supposed to take care of us."

He winced at her words. Instantly she wished she could take them back.

"Reuben . . . I'm sorry. I shouldn't have said that. It's not your fault. I know it isn't." She looked down, suddenly ashamed to look him in the eye. "I wish I could take back what I said. I didn't mean it, I swear." She looked up slowly when he began to speak.

"At least I'm bringing home more money since I started working at the hospital. Plus we don't have the expense of two bus passes."

This only made her cry again. "Just one," she said between sobs. "Reuben, I'm so tired of commuting every day. It's gotten to the point where I absolutely hate Sundays because I know I have to start all over the next morning."

"I know you're tired, Camille. But we've got so much at stake here. We're talking about our family's entire way of life. I wish . . . No, it has to be more than that. Camille, we've got to work together. That's the key. If we do that, we'll manage."

"How, Reuben?" Her voice came out sounding like a whiny child, but she couldn't help it. All last year she'd had an idea of what lay ahead, but now that it had actually happened, it meant they'd run out of time.

"First of all, wait until April fifteenth to actually file the return. That's six weeks from now. That'll give us time to do a little finagling and maybe get the amount we owe down. Then ask to set up an installment agreement with them," he said.

"And what happens when we default on it?"

"We don't. This is at the top of the list, right after food, the electric bill, and your bus pass."

"I notice you didn't say the mortgage."

"I know. We'll have to do the best we can, Camille. Obviously we can't continue to borrow against our retirement funds."

"But if we don't pay the mortgage—"

"I know, but that's the one bill that gives us the most trouble. We can manage to pay everything else on our existing income, can't we?" At her nod he said, "We'll be all right as long as we don't fall too far behind. We won't be in default for another two months. Something will break soon. I can feel it."

As she stood with her face buried in his chest, she shivered. She felt something coming, too.

She didn't care what Reuben said; nothing good could come from not paying their mortgage.

Chapter 42

The Youngs
March 2005

Dawn didn't know what to make of Milo's behavior. But something wasn't right.

Outwardly Milo seemed fine. Yet whenever she said anything to him, he usually responded with, "What?" Maybe he'd developed a hearing problem, but she had a feeling he just wasn't paying attention to what she said.

And then there was their sex life. All of a sudden it had become hotter, more energetic, and much more frequent. He left her breathless. She had no complaints but wondered why the change. He even talked about taking up tennis in the spring. They'd lived in Tobyhanna nearly three years, and the first two summers he'd been too tired to pick up a racket and learn the game. Now he was so anxious to learn.

She repeatedly asked him if anything was wrong, and he always said no. But she didn't feel convinced.

She wished she had someone to talk to. Camille had problems of her own, although she and Reuben seemed to be getting along better these days. They'd begun appearing at get-togethers as a couple again, after months of Camille coming alone. Dawn took it as a good sign that they hadn't sunk into the social withdrawal that had plagued Tanisha and Douglas Cole before they abruptly left the state. Still, Reuben continued to work two part-time jobs, unable to get back into his profession of grocery manager. For that reason Dawn was reluctant to bend Camille's ear with her concerns.

Although Denise King had become a friend through the reading group they formed, Dawn felt she simply didn't know Denise well enough to confide in.

That left Veronica.

"Thanks so much for meeting me," Dawn said as Veronica sat across from her in a booth at Perkin's. Veronica looked great these days, having recently had her hair cut and styled, with side-swept bangs and a little flip. It made her thin hair look fuller.

"It makes for a nice break in an otherwise routine day. I, uh, did get the feeling it was important."

"It's probably silly, but, yes, it's important to me."

"If it's something you can't get off your mind it's not silly. Tell you what—let's get the ordering out of the way so we can talk."

They took a few minutes to peruse the menu and place their orders.

"I need your opinion on something, Veronica," Dawn said when the waitress left. "It's Milo. He's been acting, well, *different* lately."

"Different how?"

Dawn explained his behavior. "He's just more enthusiastic about life than he usually is. I don't know what to make of it. He keeps saying he's fine, but I'm wondering if he's got a girlfriend."

"That doesn't seem feasible, Dawn. After all, didn't you guys just go to New Orleans for your anniversary?"

"That was nine months ago." Dawn didn't want to say that while the trip had been wonderful and they had enjoyed their anniversary, when the bills started coming in they fell back into their old ways, him getting depressed and not wanting to do anything and her trying to coax him into activity. "Veronica, Milo hasn't really adjusted to the commute to the city. He's tired all the time on the weekends. Half the time I can't even get him to mow the lawn." She shrugged. "It's been a source of conflict between us, even though I know he really is tired, and that he's tried."

Veronica nodded. "I used to feel that I'd never adjust myself. I prayed the hospital nearby would hire me quickly. Believe me, I know how Milo feels. I know that Norman goes over to Arlington Acres to play tennis with Reuben and Lemuel and that they've tried to get Milo to join them."

"He's always too tired. It's been almost three years, Veronica. Now all of a sudden he wants to learn how to play? This is why I feel something's wrong."

Veronica thought for a minute. "Dawn, does he leave for work earlier, or come home later?"

"No. We still go in and ride back together."

"That's a good sign, don't you think? He's home with you on weekends. It doesn't sound like he's got *time* to have an affair."

Dawn considered this. Veronica was right. Milo couldn't squeeze an affair into his schedule. He hadn't taken any secret days off from work, either; she called him at the office every day and always reached him. "That makes sense. Besides, he's been awfully frisky lately, if you know what I mean. I don't see how he'd have any energy left."

Veronica reached across the table and patted her forearm. "Has it ever occurred to you that Milo might be doing this for you? My advice is don't worry and don't nag him by asking if something's wrong. Just enjoy it. Get frisky right back with him. And for God's sake, don't shy away from the tennis courts."

"I won't," she said. If Milo's efforts came from a desire to please her, she certainly wouldn't blow it by saying she didn't want to sweat out her hair or anything like that.

Veronica's suggestions explained away all but one of her concerns: why did Milo always seem so distracted?

Chapter 43

"Mama, a man from the bank called," Mitchell said to Camille. "He said it's important that you or Daddy call him back tomorrow."

"Let me see that," Reuben demanded, taking the paper Mitchell held with the name and telephone number. He met Camille's eyes over the table. "Mortgage," he mouthed.

Camille's shoulders immediately went tense. They'd paid only part of the April mortgage, and May would be due soon. They'd filed their tax return on time on April fifteenth, enclosing a check for five hundred dollars toward their five-figure debt. Reuben said that with any luck they wouldn't hear from the IRS until June about setting up an installment agreement. That should give them time to get caught up with the mortgage before they fell behind again.

"Is everything all right?" Mitchell asked. At fourteen, he had excellent instincts. It would be awfully hard to put anything over on him.

"Nothing to worry about," Reuben said airily. "Your mother and I are having a bit of a dispute with the bank. I'd just as soon you not get involved, son. You don't even have to answer the phone if their name comes up on the caller ID, and I'll tell your sister the same thing. Okay?"

"Okay." Mitchell seemed glad to be done with it.

"That was easy," Reuben commented after Mitchell left the kitchen.

"Yeah. I wish the rest of it was as simple."

"I'll take care of calling the bank. Try not to worry, Camille." He kissed her cheek and left the room, phone number in hand.

"Sure," she said to no one. "Don'cha worry 'bout a thing."

Chapter 44

The Youngs
May 2005

Dawn settled on the sofa in the den with a stack of envelopes and the checkbook. "Milo, it's time for us to do the bills." She forced herself to sound cheerful, but she dreaded the end of the month, when they had to face making another mortgage payment and all those credit card payments. She felt as gloomy as the weather outside. Memorial Day was often iffy in the Northeast, and this year the meteorologists had correctly forecast rain.

He ambled out of the kitchen with a beer in hand. "I need to talk to you about something."

"Sure. What's on your mind?"

He remained standing. "I've had it, Dawn. I'm going back to Brooklyn."

Her mouth dropped open. She thought he was about to suggest a new budget or something, not tell her he was leaving. *Leaving?* "What do you mean, you're going back?"

"Donald said I can sleep on the trundle bed in Shawn's room. I'll stay there until I can get a place. Hopefully it won't take long. Donald said that although Carmen consented, she's not happy about it."

"Of course she wouldn't be happy about it. She's my friend. You put her in an awkward position by even asking to stay at their place. No wonder I haven't heard from her this week." She blinked away tears. "I don't understand all this, Milo. Where did it come from? I kept asking if you had something on your mind. You've been acting strangely for months now. But you always said you were fine. Then you drop this bombshell on me, after I start to believe everything really *is* okay."

He sighed. "I'm sorry about that, Dawn. I tried to make the best of it. But it's just not working. I'm miserable here. I want to go back to the city."

She placed her hands on her hips. "Just like that, you want to go back to the city. What about Zach and me? You're going to just leave us here to fend for ourselves?"

"I'll send you as much money as I can. My name's on those credit card bills, too."

"To hell with the credit cards. What about the house? I can't pay this mortgage by myself!"

"Dawn, I'll do the best I can. But I have to get a place to live myself."

"You, you, you!" she shouted, jumping to her feet. Thank God Zach was not home—he'd gone to see that new action movie in Mount Pocono with Mitchell. Milo had dropped them off, and Reuben would pick them up. The boys often sneaked into another theater in the multiplex and saw a second film. She'd hate for them to get caught, but what the hell. It had rained all day, what else were they supposed to do? "You need to think about your son and whether or not he'll have a roof over his head."

He dropped his head. "You don't know how I've agonized over this, Dawn. I stuck it out as long as I did because of Zach. But I just can't do it anymore."

Her hands fell to her sides, all her indignation gone like a ketchup stain in the wash. "You want a divorce? Is that what you're telling me, Milo Young? You want me to go my way and you another?"

He looked up again, walked over to her, and took her hands. "Dawn, we haven't been happy for a long time. All you do is complain about the bills. We don't have fun anymore. I think it's time we called a halt to our suffering. You keep the car, and I'll give you child support for Zach and help you with the bills. At least he likes it here."

"And how am I supposed to pay for this house by myself? We were having trouble paying the household bills with *two* salaries."

He didn't back down. "I'm afraid I can't help you with that. I intend to take my name off the deed."

* * *

Dawn didn't believe Milo really meant to do what he said. If anything, she told herself, his unhappiness with their situation had just gotten the best of him temporarily, but it would pass, maybe as early as tomorrow.

It troubled her when he slept on the couch. Again she told herself that tomorrow he'd be back to normal. But the next morning when she went to rouse him he said he wasn't going in, that he had to pack his things. "I've already talked to Zach," he said.

At that moment she knew he meant to go through with his plans.

"I tried to explain it as best I could, but I think he's still puzzled," he concluded.

"Of course he's puzzled," she snapped. "One minute he has a happy family, and the next his daddy tells him he's leaving."

She managed to keep the turmoil she felt hidden during the ride in and back, telling everyone who asked that Milo had taken the day off. When she returned from work that evening he was gone.

Milo was sharing a room with Carmen and Donald's son back in Brooklyn. Carmen called to apologize, saying Donald had asked her to let him stay but that first Donald had tried to convince Milo to go to his parents. Milo, still smarting over how seldom his parents had driven out to Arlington Acres to visit, felt strongly about not asking them for help. "I didn't want him to be without a place to sleep," she said.

"I understand. It's all right, Carmen. As angry as I am, I don't want him sleeping on a park bench, either. He'd probably do that before he went to his parents. I know how stubborn Milo can be."

"I was so afraid you'd be mad at me."

"No. I'm just disappointed in my husband." She still couldn't believe how easily he'd given up. Anything worth having was supposed to be worth keeping, wasn't it? And didn't he consider her worth having?

Well, she'd show him. Rich and Donna Wellington were talking on the bus about how they'd refinanced their home. She remembered how the Wellingtons had their basement finished last year.

She and Milo hadn't made any significant improvements, other than the sod that now thrived in their raised backyard, holding the soil beneath it in place. But with the rise in real estate prices, that had to be plenty of time for it to have appreciated. She'd just refinance, get twenty or thirty thousand dollars out of the deal, pay off the credit cards, and still have plenty left over. Once Milo saw what she'd done when left to her own devices, he'd apologize to her and plead with her to let him come home again. She'd let him, of course . . . after she took a few days to think it over and let his ass sweat.

"Morning, Dawn," Jeff Willis said as she boarded the bus. He glanced around her, expecting to see Milo, she knew. "Hey, Milo off again?"

"No, Jeff," she said loudly. "He's just not here." She took a seat up front, confident that her cryptic response told her fellow commuters the whole story without her having to put it into words.

Camille immediately moved from her seat in the middle of the bus. "Dawn? I heard what you said. I didn't know. Is there anything I can do?"

Dawn managed a smile. "Thanks, but no. I don't even feel much like talking, if that's okay."

"Whatever you say." Camille took a step back.

"I just need a little space, Camille. Please don't take it personal. We'll walk together when we get to New York like we always do, okay?"

"Sure."

Camille slowly returned to her seat. She made a mental note not to bring up Milo's absence during the daily walk to her and Dawn's office buildings. Her instinct told her the breakup resulted from financial difficulties. Funny. A woman would share the discovery of a philandering husband before she'd admit they couldn't pay their bills.

"I'd like to speak to someone about refinancing my house," Dawn said to the woman who answered the telephone at the mortgage company. In spite of everything she'd been through, she couldn't keep the pride she felt out of her voice. She owned a home.

She was put on hold, and then the recording on the other end of the line asked her to please hold for the next available loan officer. Dawn used the time to paint an enjoyable mental picture of a contrite Milo begging to come home again.

"Good afternoon. This is Kevin Capobianco speaking. May I help you?"

"Hello, Kevin," she began. She introduced herself and explained her reason for calling.

"Wonderful," Kevin exclaimed. "I'd like to ask you a few questions for basic information, and we'll go from there. You said your name was Dawn Young. Do you own the home alone, Ms. Young?"

She decided Milo couldn't possibly have taken his name off the deed in just a few days. "No, my husband is on the mortgage loan as well, but I don't really want to include him on a second mortgage, unless I have to."

"I understand."

You don't understand shit, she thought.

"And, Mrs. Young, where do you live?"

"Here in Tobyhanna. Our house is in Arlington Acres."

The pause that followed made Dawn uncomfortable. "Is there a problem?" she finally asked.

"Well, we find that some of the homes in that particular subdivision have been overvalued. Tell me this, who was your builder?"

She named the construction company.

"Uh-*huh,*" Kevin said, none too reassuringly. "And with whom is your original mortgage?"

Dawn proudly named the major banking institution who made the mortgage loan to she and Milo.

"Was anyone else involved, like—" Kevin named the mortgage lender who had handled the paperwork on behalf of the bank.

"Actually, yes, they were. But the mortgage was secured by the bank. We make our check out to them every month."

"Mrs. Young, that mortgage lending company is owned by the same people who own the construction company that built your house. We've have requests from home owners wishing to refinance, and through those requests we've learned that they engage in unethical practices to qualify borrowers for mortgages who wouldn't otherwise qualify."

"How could they do that?"

"Like paying the rent of home buyers to help them save a down payment, for instance. Banks like to know that the money used to put down came from their clients' savings, not from other loans or arrangements they made with the financier. They also overstate the value of the homes they build by many thousands of dollars."

"Listen, I'm not sure what all this means, but are you saying you won't be able to refinance my house?"

"I'm afraid we won't be able to help you out, Mrs. Young."

Dawn sighed. "Well, lucky for me that you're not the only mortgage bank in town, isn't it? I'll just go to one of your competitors. Thank you." She hung up, none too gently.

Four phone calls later Dawn found a lender who would refinance her house. They arranged for an appraiser to come out on Saturday morning. Elated, she went to bed that night wearing a smile she couldn't reel in. She'd taken the first step. Milo would soon come crawling back and telling her he'd underestimated her.

"Mrs. Young, I'm afraid we won't be able to help you."

Dawn's mouth fell open. Carrie, the loan officer she had worked with, had given her the impression that the refinancing was a done deal, and now she was taking it all back. "I don't understand," she sputtered. "What happened?"

"Our appraiser values your home at $105,000."

"Well, that's ridiculous. We paid $142,000. Why would we pay forty thousand more than the house was worth?"

"Mrs. Young, whoever did the original appraisal on your house inflated its value. I'm hearing that the appraisers were in cahoots with the builder and the lender who preapproved the loans, and got money from the big boys at the bank. I understand the builder is currently under investigation for this. I know I said I was sure we could help you. I'm very sorry."

Dawn, sitting at her desk at work, managed to keep her composure, but she wanted to lay her head down and weep. This was the only way she could think of to get the cash she needed to stay one step ahead of the wolves, and now she couldn't do it. She hated to depend on Milo; she suspected his main concern was renting an apartment for himself. How in heaven's name would she make it?

Chapter 45

The Currys
August 2005

Camille knew that when Reuben closed the door behind them in their bedroom he had bad news. "I talked to the bank today," he began. "They wanted a definite date of when we'll be bringing the mortgage back up-to-date."

"What'd you tell them?"

"That I don't know. That the job market here isn't as plentiful as it is in New York." He paused. "They said they can't wait any longer. They're going to begin foreclosure procedures against us."

Camille felt her heart beating with loud, fast thuds. They would have to leave. But she loved living here, loved seeing wildflowers growing along the side of the road in the summertime. You never saw flowers in New York, unless they were already cut and being sold in bunches by street vendors. She even liked seeing the snow fall in the winter.

Where would they go if they returned to New York? Worse, what would everyone say? Reuben's family would have a field day, making one snide comment after another. But they would have to stay with someone, at least temporarily. They could neither afford to pay their mortgage nor rent an apartment until they had some money saved.

Tears filled her eyes. All she and Reuben had wanted was to live someplace where their children could enjoy the American dream, where riding a bicycle didn't present a logistical nightmare, someplace that would appreciate in value and allow them to have a little something of their own instead of making a landlord richer each month. But due to bad luck and—she couldn't deny—poor planning, they were about to lose it all. They'd only gotten to the very edge of their dream.

Her body went rigid. The people on the *Titanic* who didn't get into lifeboats must have felt this sense of impending doom as the ship descended into the frigid waters of the North Atlantic. But those unfortunate folks all died. She and Reuben wouldn't stop living because they lost their house.

One concern loomed over everything. "Reuben, where will we go?"

"We'll have to figure that out. First we'll have to start packing so we can get our things moved into storage. As far as where we'll stay, I'm sure that Mom will let Mitchell and me stay with her. I thought maybe you and Shayla can stay with Arnelle and Tiffany."

"Arnelle!" Camille felt genuinely horrified by this prospect.

"I know you two have had some rough patches the last couple of years, but Arnelle seemed grateful to us for letting Tiffany come out for the summer. I'm sure she'll want to help us now that we're in a bind."

"I wouldn't be so sure if I were you, Reuben. Tiffany spent the summer here two years ago, just before you got laid off. I'm sure Arnelle's forgotten all about it by now. What she'll remember is that we couldn't accommodate Tiffany last year."

Both Arnelle and Brenda had asked if their daughters could come out for the summer, but Reuben had said no. He explained that at fourteen, Mitchell was old enough to supervise Shayla alone during daytime hours that since he now worked nearby, he could always come home if needed. He also reminded them that with the sharp reduction in their income they couldn't afford another mouth to feed, anyway. Reuben expressed surprise that his sisters didn't show more consideration, to which Camille could only shrug.

"Well, maybe you can stay with your father and stepmother in Inwood," he suggested.

"Oh, I don't want to do that, either. That would put us in a different borough." Camille didn't have to ask why they couldn't all stay together. No one they knew had an extra bedroom. She doubted that anyone even had a sofa bed.

"You'll have to stay someplace, Camille."

"Yes, I know. But we seem to be taking a lot for granted. What if no one wants us to stay with them? It's a lot to ask of a person, Reuben. To have two people descend on you for an unknown length of time. It's a disruption, no matter how hard we'll try not to get in the way. Who knows how long it will be before we can afford a place of our own. You don't even have a job!"

"I know that once I get to New York I'll be working soon. I'll contact the store's human resources department. If anything, they'll hire me. I'm sure there's a department manager job opening somewhere. Once we're living in the city again I won't have any restrictions. I can travel to Westchester or Long Island if I need to. And I won't believe for one minute that there's even a possibility of our families telling us we can't stay with them. They know we have no place else to go."

"I hate the idea of our being separated," she said. She knew she sounded whiny, but she couldn't help it. She hated the thought of her family not living together under the same roof. How had Douglas and Tanisha Cole managed? she wondered. Did they have the same feeling of fear and dread she was experiencing right now? What was it that Mitchell had said? "They didn't even know where they would sleep."

The thought of the Cole family made her remember something. "Reuben, two years ago, when you first lost your job, I promised Mitchell that he would always have a roof over his head, that you and I would take care of him. Douglas and Tanisha had just lost their house, and he was so upset that his friend Alex had to leave Arlington Acres. Now I feel like I've broken a promise to him. I've never done that before."

"You haven't broken your promise. He'll still have a roof over his head, and he'll be taken care of. He won't be going around hungry and sleeping on park benches." She flashed him a "that's horseshit" look, and he went on. "Mitchell isn't a little kid anymore, Camille. He's old enough to know what it means to lose a job. He knows how hard we tried to stay afloat. A few weeks ago he even asked me if he could get a job this summer."

Her lower lip dropped. "You didn't tell me that!"

"I didn't want you to know. I knew his reason for asking. He knew I wasn't making enough money to take care of us. My fourteen-year-old son wanted to get a job and help out. How do you think that made me feel?" Reuben's eyes narrowed, like he was squinting in the sun, but Camille knew he was fighting back tears.

"I'm sorry," she whispered.

"I'm dreading having to tell Mitchell and Shayla that we have to leave here." He bowed his head. "I'm sorry, Camille. I kept hoping that our luck would change. I've even been buying lottery tickets. Don't panic, I only get one ticket per drawing."

"Reuben, someone already died and left us money. I think we've already had our share of luck," she said coldly.

"I know. But I have to hope. Right now it's all I have."

"I don't think we should tell the kids until we have a plan in place about where we'll be staying. It'll be less frightening for them that way than saying 'We don't know' when they ask where we're going. Because you know they'll ask. Besides, they'll be starting school next week, and that's stressful enough by itself."

"Yeah, that's fine." He walked over to the window and went outside on the deck, his hands resting on the railing as he stood in front of it.

She watched him for a minute, then followed him outside. "What's on your mind?"

"It's beautiful, isn't it? Everything I ever dreamed of. A house on the lake. This may sound silly, but I figured we'd be here until we retired. I even imagined Shayla getting married here, provided she didn't invite too many people. I saw it all in my head. I was going to put up a little gazebo for the ceremony, have cloth-covered tables flanking a dance floor . . . It was going to be beautiful." He added a muttered, "Silly, wasn't it?"

"That's not silly, Reuben. I had the same thought."

"I love this house. Before I lost my job I felt like a king in a castle. Even with all the hassle of commuting, it all seemed worth it when you and I got in that tub for a soak and turned on the Jacuzzi jets. I hate like hell to leave it to go sleep on somebody's couch."

"I know." Camille looked out at the scene. One of the home owners was out on the lake in a canoe with his two children wearing life jackets. It seemed almost criminal to think about having to pack up and leave on this beautiful summer day.

Her shoulders twitched at the sound of a sob. She quickly realized it was coming from Reuben. She hastily took his arm and steered him toward the house. This was no place to break down. You never knew who might be lurking around the corner, and the whole neighborhood didn't need to know their problems. Bad enough that they'd all know soon enough. "Come on inside," she coaxed.

"I'm sorry, Camille. I'm so sorry I couldn't pull it off. I guess you hitched your wagon to a loser when you married me."

His words pulled at her heartstrings. She forgot about her resentment and anger, all the feelings of he-should-have-done-this or he-shouldn't-have-done-that she still sometimes harbored, in spite of her efforts to be more supportive of him in recent months. "Reuben, I won't have you thinking that," she said sternly. "It's not true. You're not a loser. You've had bad luck, that's all. Thousands of people lose their jobs every week. A lot of them lose their homes. The insurance companies don't even offer job-loss mortgage-protection insurance anymore because they had to pay out too much money, remember?"

He looked at her sadly. "My God, Camille, I wish there was one good thing that we can say came out of this, but I don't see it. Where the hell is our silver lining?"

She went into his arms. She thought about how annoyed she'd been that she had to rise in the middle of the night while he got to sleep, about all those months when she'd held him personally responsible for their predicament, and she suddenly knew what was most important: Reuben had stuck it out. He hadn't been like Milo Young, walking out on Dawn and Zach. Heaven knows he could have, and he threatened to after that huge fight they had had the first time she and Dawn had touched up each other's hair and she'd made those smart-ass remarks to deliberately embarrass him. She'd been foolish enough not to care, but now she knew she'd be lost without him.

"Maybe it's in the fact that we still love each other," Camille said, "that we're still committed to each other. You and our children are what I live for. I'll do whatever I need to so we can all live together under one roof again."

His voice broke as he said, "I'm sorry, Camille."

She held him tightly, her own tears falling. "Reuben. We won't go hungry. We won't be homeless. It's not your fault. This type of thing happens to people every day. We'll be all right. I'd rather lose the house than lose you or the children."

He buried his face in the nook where her neck met her shoulder. "I love you, Camille."

Chapter 46

The Youngs
September 2005

Dawn happily snatched up the hand-addressed envelope in her mailbox. Milo had been sending her $350 twice a month. She wished he could send more, but at least she was getting by. Zach was old enough to stay at home alone over summer vacation, so she didn't have to pay Destiny King to keep an eye on him. She'd enrolled in consumer credit counseling through the credit union here in Pennsylvania, keeping one credit card for emergencies and cutting up all the rest. She couldn't afford to keep them. Banks and even department stores had started charging thirty to forty dollars if payments were received even one day late, and she couldn't always pay them on time.

She continued to honor her credit-counseling agreement, which made for dramatically lower payments, and kept up with her utility bills. She paid what she could toward the mortgage but usually had caught up within thirty days. Still, she couldn't help wondering how Camille and Reuben managed to hold on to their house all this time.

Once inside the house she opened the envelope from Milo. He usually sent postal money orders so the funds would be available right away. She'd deposit it in her account tomorrow.

She took a deposit slip and began filling it out so it could get in and out of the bank quickly. She glanced at the money order to confirm the amount. Wouldn't it be nice if Milo sent more, like four hundred?

It came as a heart-stopping shock to see that the money order was only for two hundred dollars. She stared at the figure in disbelief. "What the hell . . . ?" Milo hadn't said a word about sending less this time.

She dialed his cell phone. "Milo, what's going on?" she asked without preamble. "You only sent me $200 instead of $350."

"I'm sorry, Dawn. I'm trying to save for a deposit on an apartment. I can't stay here forever, and it's already been four months. It's starting to become really trying for Donald and Carmen to have me underfoot, and I'm sure that even Shawn is wondering how long I'll be sleeping in his room."

"Milo, I was making it with the money you sent. Barely, but I was making it. If you cut me down to $200 a month I can't make it. What am I supposed to do?" she asked, her voice shrill.

"Dawn, I'm doing the best I can. I'm paying Donald and Carmen for their inconvenience, and I've got some bills I take care of, like our cell phones and my Visa."

"I've got the bulk of the cards here, Milo, and you know it!" But even as Dawn said the words she knew he had a point. He couldn't reside with the Triggs family permanently, like an adopted child, and four months was an awfully long visit.

Still, he was the one who had decided to leave. She hadn't thrown him out. She hadn't done anything except try to support him emotionally. Look at how badly Camille Curry treated Reuben as his period of underemployment stretched into years. If anything, she had expected Reuben to be the one to walk out, not her own husband.

Tears filled her eyes. How would she make up for this shortfall? She'd already cut expenses to the bone to come up with extra cash. She turned the water heater off at night, washed the dishes in the kitchen sink instead of running the dishwasher, and did all the wash in cold water.

It was that damn commute, she thought. Since her credit counseling had so greatly reduced her monthly payments, the biggest drain on her salary other than the mortgage was the expense of getting to and from work. If she could only cut down on it . . .

An idea had formed in her head months ago, when Milo first left, but she quickly dismissed it as being a bad idea. Now, with Milo's financial support so diminished, she knew she had no choice.

She spoke to Zach about it when they sat down to dinner. "Zach . . . Your daddy isn't able to help us out as much as he'd like to. He has expenses of his own, living in the city. It's gotten a little uncomfortable for him to continue staying with Miss Carmen and Mr. Donald, and getting an apartment in New York is very expensive."

Zach looked at her with a crushed expression. "Will we have to go back to Brooklyn, too, Mom? I really like it here. When I get to high school I want to go out for the swim team. Besides, I won't be able to keep Stormy if we go back to our old apartment."

She chuckled, in spite of her despair. "That's great about the swim team, Zach. But there's no old apartment in New York to go back to, Zach. Those buildings were built to give middle-income people a decent place to live, but the agreement to charge lower rents is about to expire, which means that anyone moving in will have to pay full market value. An apartment the size of our old one will cost more than this house every month." She hesitated, quickly trying to choose her next words. "I like it here, too, and I'm doing my best to keep the bills paid, but I have to economize even more. There's only one way I can think of to do that, and I'm not sure if it's a good idea."

"What is it, Mom?"

He looked so concerned. When had her baby boy gotten so mature? Regardless of that, Dawn knew he wasn't emotionally ready for what she was about to propose.

"I can save a lot of carfare back and forth if I stay in the city during the week and only come home on the weekends," she finally said. "I have a coworker I can stay with. But it would mean leaving you all alone. Well, other than Stormy," she quickly added.

Zach looked a little insulted. "I'm thirteen. That's old enough to stay by myself. I was here alone all summer."

"Yes, I know, but you're not old enough to stay by yourself overnight. I could get in a lot of trouble if anyone found out. I'd be arrested and taken to jail. It's called child endangerment or something like that."

"I wouldn't tell anybody, Mom. You know I'd never send you to jail."

"I know you wouldn't, Zach. But when you're here by yourself it'll seem different. Our house might suddenly seem very large when you're in it all alone."

"Will you call me?"

He looked a little less confident after her last remark, she noticed.

"Of course I'll call you," she said. "Plus, I'll be available to you day and night, whenever you want to talk to me. I'll carry my cell phone everywhere, even in the bathroom." She laughed in an effort to dissipate his fear. "Listen to me, Zach. If you don't want to stay here alone it's all right. I'm going to leave it up to you." Even as Dawn spoke the words she prayed Zach would go along with the plan. She dreaded having to return to Brooklyn in failure, the object of all her friends' pity.

Instantly she felt a stab of guilt. My God, what kind of mother did that make her—willing to put her own reputation in front of her son's well-being. All this stress had her freaking out big-time. She'd better get hold of herself before she did something really stupid.

"If you come home every night like you do now, what will happen?" Zach asked.

She took a deep breath. "We won't be able to stay here. We'd have to go back to Brooklyn to stay with Grandma and Grandpa, I guess." She shut her eyes briefly, not happy about that thought at all, but where else could she go? Milo had already stretched Carmen and Donald's kindness to the breaking point. "Zach, I really want you to know that I've been trying very, very hard to make it for us. But you have to understand. I'm not just asking you to do this for a week. It'll be on an ongoing basis, until I can get a job here in Pennsylvania, or at least in southern Jersey. Someplace where it won't cost so much to get to work."

"I'll be all right, Mom. Don't worry about me."

Chapter 47

Camille sat as still as a mannequin while Reuben gently explained their plight to Mitchell and Shayla. "So, kids," he concluded, "because my work options are much better in the city, Mommy and I decided to sell this house and move back to New York."

"But I like it here, Daddy," Shayla said. "I don't want to go back to New York."

"I know you like it here, Shayla. Mommy and I did everything we could not to have to disrupt your lives after I lost my job, but it's been two years and I haven't been able to find a job in my field. There comes a time when you have to admit you've been beaten."

"I think you did great, Daddy," Mitchell said. "So are we going back to the Bronx? Are we gonna buy a house there?"

"I'm afraid that first we'll have to get an apartment and see how things go, son."

"An apartment? Will Mitchell and me have our own rooms, like we do now?" Shayla asked.

Camille felt like someone had cut into her chest to tear out her heart. How could they tell their children that their whole world—all the things they were used to—was about to undergo a radical change? No wonder Reuben alluded to the possibility of them buying another house. He couldn't bring himself to tell them they'd never live in a house again, and neither could she. "I'm afraid not,

Shayla. Apartment rents are very high in the city. We'll have to wait a few months before we can get together enough money to rent one."

The child brightened. "That means we'll be able to stay here until we get an apartment."

Reuben took over. "No, Shayla. I made arrangements with the bank that holds the mortgage on our house to vacate right away so they can sell it for us."

"So where will we stay?" Mitchell asked, fear in his newly changed voice.

"We made arrangements with your grandma and Aunt Arnelle," Camille answered. "You and Daddy will stay at Grandma's, Mitchell. Shayla and I will stay with Aunt Arnelle and Tiffany."

"We're not going to live together? Are you and Daddy getting a divorce?" Shayla asked, her eyes dark with suspicion.

"No, dear, not at all," Camille assured her. "It's just that it might be a little while until we can get together enough money to rent an apartment big enough for all of us. And none of the family has enough room to take in all four of us while we save up. That's the only reason why we have to separate. But it's not permanent. I promise."

"Your mother and I are going to do all we can to make sure we're reunited as soon as possible," Reuben added.

Camille looked at Mitchell, who'd been uncharacteristically quiet. "Mitchell? Are you all right?"

"I don't think you're telling the truth," he blurted out. "I think the same thing is happening to you that happened to Alex's parents. The bank might sell our house, but they're not selling it for us. They're taking it from us, aren't they? Otherwise we'd just stay here until someone buys the house from us."

"Shayla, we have to leave," Camille said, grabbing her daughter's hand.

"But Mommy—"

"Right now," she said firmly. Let Reuben and Mitchell have it out in private. She already wished Shayla hadn't heard Mitchell's outburst. She didn't have to know all the family business. Shayla was incapable of keeping a secret. Camille feared she might accidentally blab to one of her friends. Neither Camille nor Reuben wanted their neighbors to know about the pending foreclosure until after they were gone. After that they didn't really care what their neighbors said, but for now they had to live among these people, and they didn't want them in their business.

She hated having to confess the truth to her friends Dawn and Denise, and especially to Veronica, who'd done so well since moving here. They'd played cards at the Lees' last weekend, and Camille couldn't take her eyes off their new kitchen. Norman and Veronica had a house that was as beautiful as it was affordable. For them the dream of home ownership had come true. She doubted Veronica had any problems bigger than forgetting to defrost meat for dinner.

Her world, on the other hand, was falling into tiny pieces at her feet.

Chapter 48

The Youngs and the Lees
October 2005

Dawn, grateful to have another workweek completed and a check earned, carried her groceries to the car. She'd called Zach and told him she was stopping at the store. She'd bought him some of those shortbread cookies with the chocolate drops that he liked so much, along with a few staples.

With a sigh, she turned the key in the ignition.

Nothing happened.

She fought back a rising panic and forced herself to count to twenty before trying again.

Nothing.

Dawn leaned forward, resting her arms on the wheel and putting her head down, careful not to lean on the horn. She was barely managing, but she was hanging on. Why did this have to happen? Didn't she have enough problems without having to cope with a dead battery?

"Dawn? Is that you?"

She raised her head and saw a concerned-looking Veronica standing in the empty space next to her Volvo. "My car won't start," she said tonelessly. "I think it's the battery."

"Do you have an auto club you can call?"

"Not anymore. But I'll deal with it tomorrow. Do you think you can drop me off at home? All I want to do at this point is go home and go to bed." *And see Zach.* But she could hardly tell Veronica she hadn't seen her son since Monday morning.

"Sure, I understand. And maybe Norman can help you then, if it's only a dead battery."

For the first time she began to feel hopeful. "That would be wonderful."

"Come on, lock up the car and get your purse and groceries. I'm parked just a few cars down."

Dawn hesitated. Her suitcase was in the backseat. She feared that leaving it in the car overnight would encourage a break-in and she'd lose a valuable chunk of her wardrobe, but how could she explain it to Veronica if she brought it with her?

She made up her mind in an instant, unlocking the back door and dragging out the bag.

Veronica glanced at it. "You must be bringing some clothes to Milo. That's real nice of you, I must say."

Suddenly all the secrets and deception became too much. Dawn's breath caught in her throat, making a sound of a choking sob. "It isn't Milo's things in this suitcase, Veronica. It's mine. With Milo gone I can't afford to go through a bus pass every fifteen days."

"Oh, Dawn, I'm sorry. Isn't Milo sending you money?"

"Yes, but he's got to live, too, I guess. He just rented an apartment, and he can't send me as much as he did at first."

"What about Zach?"

Dawn hesitated. Even Milo and her parents didn't know Zach was being left alone. She generally called them from her cell phone, anyway, to save long-distance charges. She instructed Zach to tell Milo she was asleep or at the store when he called in the evening. When she called her parents—they never made long-distance calls unless it was an emergency—and they asked to speak with Zach, she conveniently would say he was outside with Stormy, and when she finished talking she would dial him and instruct him to call his grandparents. It was all so complicated, and she felt worn down from all the strain of the charade.

"Dawn?" Veronica pressed. "Is Zach staying home alone all week?"

"Yes," she said, not bothering to try to hold back the tears. "I didn't know what else to do. Nobody knows about it besides Zach and me. If Milo knew I was leaving him alone he'd have me arrested on neglect charges."

"I'm sure he wouldn't do that. And you won't have a problem anymore. From now on Zach will spend weeknights at our house."

Dawn stopped crying out of pure shock, shaking her head. "Veronica, I can't ask you to do that."

"You don't have to ask; I'm offering. It's a perfect solution, Dawn."

Dawn shook her head. "Veronica, I can't put you out like that. It's too much. Zach goes to school here in Tobyhanna, not in Mount Pocono."

"I bring my own kids to school and pick them up. Tobyhanna isn't that far."

"Veronica, I can think of a dozen reasons why you shouldn't do this. Gas prices have gone up, Norman might not like it. . . ."

"Don't you dare worry about either of those." Veronica grasped Dawn's forearm. "We're friends, Dawn, and right now you really need a friend. I know my husband. If someone we know is in trouble, he'd want to do whatever he could to help. Besides, Zach can watch the girls for us for a few hours while we go out to dinner or something. It would be nice to have a little couple time during the week." Veronica realized after she'd spoken that she probably shouldn't have said anything about 'couple time' to a woman whose separation had turned her life upside down. "I'm sorry," she said. "That wasn't very considerate of me, was it?"

"It's all right," Dawn said, wiping her eyes. "I do feel a whole lot better, now that I told somebody."

"I just wish you'd confided in me sooner. It's not easy trying to make it in a new state, miles and miles from anyone we know. We New Yorkers have to stick together."

"That's sweet, Veronica, but I just can't let you commit to watching my son unless you've cleared it with Norman."

"He'll be all for it. You wait and see."

"Why don't you and I talk after you've discussed it with him?" Dawn suggested. "And I won't be upset if he thinks it's too much. I think it's too much myself. But just knowing you want to help means a lot to me. You're a real friend, Veronica. Thank you."

"We'll work this out for you, Dawn. Don't worry. In the meantime let's get you home so you can see Zach."

Norman stared at her incredulously. "You want to *what?*"

"Norman, Dawn is frantic. Milo is gone. Zach is all alone in that big house all week long because she simply can't afford to commute every day. Don't you want to help them?"

"You're telling me that Milo abandoned them?"

"No, but now that he's got an apartment he's not able to send Dawn as much money anymore. She's struggling to pay the mortgage, and she said she can't refinance because the appraiser lied about the worth of her house. It was in that article in last year's paper, about how appraisers were overvaluing homes to mollify the lenders."

"Vee, I feel for Dawn, but I think the most we can do is give Zach our number here at the house and your work number. Between those he'll be able to reach one of us day or night in case of emergency. Obviously, we can get to him a lot quicker than Dawn can from New York. But as for him staying over here and your shuttling him back and forth to school every day, I've got to say no to that. I'd be more willing to help if he lived here in Mount Pocono, but he's in Tobyhanna."

"But Norman—"

"I'm sorry, Veronica. We have to stop all this. We helped your parents make their transition to their condo, and we got involved in Essence's situation with Valerie, and we gave Chucky a nice summer. We let Lucy have her party here, and we let my brothers and their wives spend weekends here. We're not running a social service agency any more than we're running a bed-and-breakfast. Believe me, Dawn will be grateful to us for telling Zach he can call us if he needs anything."

She tried one last tack. "But Norman, you're putting me in an embarrassing position. I practically promised her we could help her." Even though Dawn had given her a way out, she felt embarrassed to take it.

His eyes narrowed. "Since when do you make decisions like that without discussing it with me first? I know you never told me about Essence and I forgot to tell you about Chucky, but at least they're both family."

"Well, it did hinge upon your approval, but I was so sure you'd go for it."

"I'm sorry, but I don't approve. You can only stretch yourself so thin, Vee. Who knows how long this will go on? It's going to get old."

"All right."

* * *

Veronica swallowed with what sounded to her like a crash of a glass bowl hitting the floor. "Dawn, I talked to Milo. We've had some major family issues going on lately, and he really feels that I should take a break. I'm sorry."

"It's all right, Veronica," Dawn replied. "I told you I thought it would be taking on too much."

She sounded upbeat, but Veronica recognized disappointment in her friend's voice. She blamed herself for giving Dawn false hope. She already felt bad for telling Dawn she didn't think Milo had any secret agendas or a girlfriend, but was only trying to please her. Dawn's instinct that something was wrong had obviously been the right one. Milo had left maybe a month after she and Dawn met for lunch at Perkin's.

"But Norman did suggest that you give Zach our number at home and my number at work. In case he has any trouble, we'll be able to get to him a lot quicker than you can from the city. Plus, I'm available even at two or three in the morning; he'd just be calling me at work."

"That's so sweet of you! Yes, I'll do that."

Veronica suddenly had an idea. "Dawn, part of the reason Norman said no is because we live in Mount Pocono, and he felt it would be too much for me to drive back and forth every day to get Zach to and from school. But have you thought about talking to Denise? She lives within walking distance of your house."

"No, Veronica, I don't want anyone else to know. I'm breaking the law, leaving Zach alone all week."

"She and Lemuel might be able to help you. Remember, Denise works for a social service agency."

Dawn remained adamant. "No, Veronica," she repeated firmly. "Forget it."

Chapter 49

The Currys
November 2005

Camille removed the pillows from Arnelle's sofa and spread a sheet over the bottom cushions. She'd already put Shayla to bed in Tiffany's room.

When faced with going either to her father's apartment in Inwood or to Arnelle's in Gun Hill, she chose the latter, simply because it was closer to Reuben's mother's apartment, where Reuben and Mitchell were staying.

As she suspected, Arnelle had hedged when Reuben initially asked if she would take them in. When he'd mentioned they were prepared to give her a hundred dollars a week to compensate her for the inconvenience, Arnelle's excuses of why the arrangement wouldn't work suddenly disappeared. Reuben didn't give his mother a set dollar amount, but he paid for the groceries and gave her fifty dollars here and there.

To Camille's surprise, both their families had expressed sympathy at their plight. "I'm sorry to hear that," Brenda had said when she learned they could no longer afford to keep their house. "It really was a beautiful house."

Saul, recently engaged to his girlfriend, couldn't resist making a cutting remark. After acknowledging what a tough break they'd had, he added, "But I hope you guys aren't expecting your old apartment back," before saying with a casual shrug, "I guess, on behalf of the borough of the Bronx, I should say welcome home."

"Nobody's expecting your family to move out of your apartment," Reuben responded sharply, "so I think you should just shut the fuck up."

Camille listened to the exchange with tight-lipped anger. She could have happily poured some disinfectant into Saul's drink. He didn't have to say that, damn it.

Camille felt relieved that at least she didn't have to hear any remarks along the lines of, 'That's what you get when you get too big for your britches.' She'd gotten Shayla enrolled in school and they saw Reuben and Mitchell a couple of times a week, but she longed for the day when they would have a place of their own again.

She tried to put aside every penny she could, but she worried about their credit. It would take years before the black mark of foreclosure would be removed from their histories. They'd opted to put their belongings in storage in Pennsylvania, where the bill was slightly lower than in New York, but it still cost hundreds of dollars each month to store all their household belongings. Lemuel and Norman had helped with the move. Camille knew that Marianne Willis could probably determine from the resources at her disposal that their house was in preforeclosure status, but she nonetheless told the neighbors that she and Reuben were selling their house and moving to southern New Jersey to accommodate Reuben's new job. No one challenged her story. If they'd heard otherwise from Marianne, they didn't let on.

Reuben did have a new job, and not with his old employer. He was a grocery manager at a twenty-four-hour supermarket in southern Westchester, part of a huge chain that paid him a better salary than he'd earned previously. It was a step in the right direction, but it would still take some time before they would have enough money to rent an apartment and move at least some of their belongings from the storage unit in Pennsylvania.

They still maintained contact with the old neighborhood other than the monthly storage bill they received. Camille met Dawn for lunch occasionally. Dawn usually said things like, "It's not the same without you."

She said this again as they carried their salads and drinks to a table at a Quizno's on Third Avenue.

"Well, you still have Veronica and Denise."

"Yes, but I'm realizing I don't have a whole lot in common with them." Dawn shrugged. "They both seem to be doing so well. Denise and Lemuel just had their basement done."

Camille tried not to feel jealous. "I'll bet it's beautiful."

"It's gorgeous. They've got a pool table down there and a new crescent-shaped sectional sofa opposite a big-screen TV. We played cards with them last weekend, and then we did karaoke. And Veronica and Norman are screening in their patio. You know, Milo and I have been in our house three years, and all we've done is paint."

"That's because you've had to spend money on repairs, for your closet and twice for your backyard," Camille pointed out.

"Yeah, I guess."

Camille sensed that Dawn wasn't telling her everything, but she didn't press.

"How's the apartment hunt going?"

Camille brightened. "Now that Reuben's working, we hope to be in a place of our own within sixty days. Reuben wants to make sure that we can manage the first and last months' rent and the security deposit, plus the cost of transporting our furniture from Pennsylvania to New York."

"Will you get all your furniture?"

"No. We'll have to sell whatever won't fit. Reuben says it doesn't make sense to keep paying to store it. It's expensive, which makes it impractical, since we don't know how long we'll need to keep it there." In her heart Camille suspected they would never again live in a home of their own, but she couldn't bring herself to say the words aloud. It hurt too much to consider just how much she and Reuben had lost. Instead she said, "He's talked to a consignment shop about letting them sell it for us."

"That's too bad, but he's got a point. If you keep your stuff in storage long enough you'll be paying for it all over again."

Camille nodded. Thinking of all her beautiful furniture being sold—her dining room table and matching server, her family room sofa, chairs, and accent tables—made her want to weep. And what about the kids' bedroom furniture? "I can't believe how much rents have gone up," she said. "It'll probably cost us two grand a month just for a two-bedroom apartment. No way can we afford three bed-rooms." She shook her head sadly. "I hate to ask Mitchell to share a room with his little sister again. And which set of furniture do we keep? His bedroom is masculine and Shayla's is all frills."

"I'm sorry, Camille. I wish I could do something to help you guys."

She reached across the table to pat Dawn's hand.

Chapter 50

The Youngs
January 2006

Dawn stared at the notice from the county clerk's office. The bank had won a foreclosure judgment against her. That meant they'd be able to sell her house.

She and Zach would have to leave.

She'd given it her best shot, and she'd lost.

What a piss-poor way to start the year. Damn it, she'd been so certain that with everything she'd done she would at least be able to hold on to the house after Milo left last May. All those cost-cutting measures she'd undertaken, like cutting back to basic cable and staying in New York during the week to save carfare, the latter which she'd always feel guilty about. But in the end, she hadn't lasted seven months. There just wasn't enough money to keep up with the mortgage plus all her other bills. When she did pay the mortgage she couldn't pay her other bills, and the phone rang constantly with what creditors called "courtesy" calls reminding her that her scheduled payment hadn't yet been received. She'd had to instruct Zach not to answer the phone unless he recognized the number in the caller ID. Then her creditors started calling her at work, and she would bring her accounts up to date, in the process falling behind on the mortgage.

In spite of her best efforts she'd fallen several months behind on everything, and now she'd have to vacate.

Milo would be affected by the foreclosure as well. He told her that he'd learned removing his name from the deed wouldn't legally absolve his obligation to pay the note each month, so he left his name intact. But the knowledge that a foreclosure would go on Milo's credit report as well provided cold comfort to Dawn. He'd already gotten his life back on track, having rented a studio in Fort Greene prior to the foreclosure. Would she even be able to rent an apartment with a foreclosure on her credit report, plus all those red flags that she'd paid her credit cards late? And even if someone did rent to her, how would she manage to pay rent if she hadn't been able to pay her mortgage?

The cold, hard truth was that she would be forty-two years old this year, and she had nothing.

Dawn sealed up another box. "Where will we go, Mom?" Zack asked.

"You'll have to stay with your father, now that he has an apartment. I'll continue staying with Lynn. It shouldn't be too long until I can get an apartment, no longer than sixty days at the most."

"Will I be able to live with you then?"

"Yes, that's the plan."

Dawn wondered how successful that arrangement would be. She knew from discussions with Carmen Triggs when Milo was still staying there that he frequently went out on Friday and Saturday nights, and most Sundays as well. Instinctively she knew he wasn't spending that time alone. He was seeing someone, someone he'd probably been thinking of in the months before he actually moved out, like when he never seemed to be paying attention to her, and when he made love to her with such zeal. He was probably fantasizing about some other woman. . . .

"What about Stormy?"

She hesitated. If only Stormy were smaller. "I'll do my best to find an apartment that allows pets. Your father's building does, but I'm not sure how he'll feel about it. Stormy is a large dog, and your daddy only has a one-room apartment."

"I'll ask him."

"And you'd have to walk him every day, even if it's pouring rain."

"I do that now. I don't mind."

Dawn smiled. "I get the feeling you're okay with our having to

move, as long as you get to keep Stormy." Never mind that it probably wouldn't happen. She knew instinctively that Milo would never
consent to having a full-grown bulldog in his tiny apartment. But she
couldn't break Zach's heart again, not so soon after telling him they
had to leave their home. She'd just have to deal with it later.

"Mom, I figured that with Daddy gone you wouldn't be able to
hold on. I knew we were in trouble. I could see it in your eyes."

Zach's words startled Dawn. Here she thought she'd managed to
conceal her fears from him. But her son was growing up. He wasn't
some blissfully unaware kid she could snow with false assurances.
He'd witnessed the tension building between her and Milo before
Milo moved out, and now he'd just lost the last of his innocence.
"I'm sorry things didn't work out, Zach. I know you're going to miss
it out here," she said sadly.

"Will we go back to Brooklyn?"

"At this point I'll go anywhere I can afford that's halfway decent." She didn't want to tell him that because middle income housing
was so expensive, she'd probably only be able to get a one bedroom
apartment. The bedroom would, of course, go to him. Still, she found
it depressing, to be her age without even a bedroom to call her own.

Even when she slept restlessly on her friend Lynn's sofa, worrying
about Zach all alone in Tobyhanna, she at least could take comfort
in the knowledge that she owned a home a hundred miles away.

Now she no longer had even that small consolation.

March 2006

Dawn hoped the combination of oversize sunglasses and tan fedora
hid her identity as she approached her old building in Williamsburg.
She knew that the buildings were in the midst of a transition to private ownership, but she nevertheless hoped that the management
might be able to offer her an apartment. It was probably a futile effort, but it didn't cost anything other than the price of a subway ride.
And she had little else left to lose.

She desperately needed an apartment of her own. Her friend and
coworker Lynn Phillips had been wonderful about allowing her to
camp out on her sofa when Dawn realized she had to save carfare,
but staying there full-time wasn't the same as staying there between

Monday evening and Friday morning. Although Lynn was too polite to say as much, after nearly two months of staying with her friend seven days a week, Dawn sensed she'd overstayed her welcome. Milo must have felt this way after weeks turned into months while he stayed with Donald and Carmen Triggs.

She knew from talking to Milo that he, too, felt a little crowded by having Zach stay with him at his studio. She couldn't blame him—the apartment wasn't meant to house two people—but she suspected that Milo's eagerness to have Zach with her stemmed more from a wish to resume his social life than it did from feeling cramped. He could hardly entertain the female friend Dawn no longer doubted existed in the presence of his teenage son, nor could he spend nights at her place and leave Zach alone.

On Milo's advice, Dawn had enrolled in consumer credit counseling to get the interest rates on her credit cards reduced and to work out manageable monthly payments. They'd turned over most of their furniture to a consignment shop, who sold it for them. It meant having to turn over a hefty part of the proceeds to the shop, but neither of them could bear the thought of standing by as their former neighbors scrutinized their belongings at a garage sale. People would undoubtedly offer insultingly low prices, like $100 for their living room set or $25 for their beautiful patio furniture, and that would only serve to make them fighting mad.

The pieces of their lives were falling into place. All she needed to do now was find an apartment.

She entered the management office, which was accessible from the street, smiling when she recognized the fifty-something woman behind the counter. "Hello, Marie. Do you remember me? Dawn Young. I lived in the other building until about four years ago."

The plump face of the office employee shone with friendly recognition. "Yes, of course I remember. You and your husband bought a house out in Pennsylvania. How are you?"

"Not all that good, to be honest. Things didn't work out with the house, and my husband and I are separated. I came by to see if you had any vacancies here."

"Oh, you've moved back to the city?"

"Yes. I still have my job here."

Marie looked properly solemn at this news. "I'm sorry things didn't work out for you, Dawn. But I'm afraid I can't help you. Even with the change-over to market rates, we've still got a waiting list."

She took the news with a knowing nod. "I thought as much. I wasn't even sure I'd still find you here. I half expected they'd close the office."

"I won't be here much longer. They're going to move us in with the new owner's other offices over on Bedford Avenue. But we feel fortunate that we still have jobs."

"I'm glad for you, Marie." Dawn glanced around the office. She could glimpse a kitchen over to the right, and a partially closed door which she guessed held a bathroom.

The idea, borne of desperation, came to her in a flash. "What will they do with this space?"

Marie looked startled by the urgency in her tone. "I don't really know. Nothing, I suppose. They'll probably just lock it up and let the dust start accumulating. Why?"

"Well, it has a kitchen and a bathroom. It could be an apartment."

Marie chuckled. "This isn't exactly meant for residential use. The bathroom only has a toilet and a sink. No tub."

"Marie, I really need a place to live, even someplace without a bathtub." The important thing was that this office was large enough for her and Zach to be comfortable. The office of the manager could be a bedroom for Zach. Not having a bathtub would present an inconvenience, but she knew life was far from perfect. She'd get an old-fashioned washtub, and they'd have to keep themselves clean that way. Isn't that how the traditional Amish did it? She'd seen that old movie with Harrison Ford. "Would I be able to speak with someone about the possibility?"

"I can speak with Mr. Crawford about it in the morning. He's out of the office this afternoon. I know he remembers you. You and your family were good tenants."

"I'd appreciate it, Marie. My family and I did live here for a long time, and I'm in desperate need for a place to live for my son and me. I don't want to end up on the streets." That last bit was overly dramatic—she could always go to her parents as a last resort and live with the 'I told you so's'—but she had to communicate how frantic she felt. "I know this doesn't meet zoning regulations and all that, but if the buildings are privately owned, can't management do what they want?"

Marie took a moment to absorb this. "I certainly don't want to see you and your son homeless, Dawn, and neither does Mr. Crawford. Why don't you give me your number? I promise I'll call you tomorrow and let you know."

Chapter 51

The Currys
April 2006

"Camille, we have to talk. Right away."

She gripped the telephone receiver tightly as panic started in her belly and spread through her body. She tried to keep her voice down so her coworkers wouldn't hear. "What is it, Reuben? Did anything happen to Mitchell?" Every night she thanked God that they were all healthy, even though they couldn't afford to live together. Hadn't they had enough hard times? Didn't she feel like enough of a failure as a parent?

"Mitchell is fine, but you tell your boss you have a family emergency and you have to leave. Or just tell him you don't feel well. I don't want to tell you this news on the phone, and we have to be alone."

Being alone was practically impossible, with him living at Ginny's and her at Arnelle's. "Reuben, can't you tell me what's going on?"

"No. Come on, Camille," he cajoled. "When's the last time you called in sick—six months ago? You've got some time off due."

She couldn't argue. All of her time off had been arranged in advance. She'd even been able to arrange for her own temporary replacement. George could manage for a half day without her.

"All right. Tell me where you want me to meet you."

Half an hour later she rang the doorbell of her mother-in-law's apartment. At the age of sixty-seven, Ginny still worked as a medical records clerk at Montefiore Medical Center. She often said she couldn't afford to retire.

Reuben promptly opened the door. He smiled at her and took her hands in his as she entered the neat apartment. Reuben slept on the length of the sofa. Propped up against a walnut-toned étagère was the twin-sized air mattress Mitchell slept on, slightly floppy due to loss of air. No bed linens were apparent, and Camille presumed they had been folded and stashed in the linen closet.

"Baby, our troubles are over," he said.

Suddenly, she felt exhausted. "Reuben, will you please stop being so evasive and let me know what's going on?"

He paused dramatically before announcing, "We got five numbers in yesterday's Mega Millions drawing."

"*What?*"

"It's true. Now you know why I needed to see you right away, and without anyone else being around. I mean, I love my family, but if they found out we came into a large sum of money they'll throw out their collective hands so fast it'll set off enough wind to make a tornado."

The air around her suddenly grew thin, like she'd reached the pinnacle of a mountain. "Reuben, we actually won the Mega Millions?" This game, played in about eight states, didn't have jackpots as large as the state Lotto, but paid jackpots in the millions.

"Well, no, not exactly. You win when you have five numbers plus the Mega number. We just had the five numbers."

Camille's euphoria deflated. "Reuben, second prize in Lotto only pays a couple of thousand dollars. You said our troubles are over." She wanted to cry. She'd used precious personal time that she was trying to preserve for when they moved just to hear news of, what— a measly five or ten thousand dollars? The money would help, but it would hardly pay all their debts.

"Mega Millions works differently than Lotto, Camille. I already confirmed the amount we won: $250,000."

She gasped. "Two hundred and fifty . . . Reuben, that's a quarter of a million dollars. Are you sure?" No wonder he didn't want his family to know.

"Yes. They'll probably take out a quarter of it in taxes, and it's not like we can retire or anything, but think of what we *can* do. We can pay off our tax bill. We can pay off everyone we owe and still have plenty to reestablish our savings. It's too late to do anything about the foreclosure, but now we can buy another house."

She looked at him incredulously. "You want to go back to Tobyhanna?"

"No, not there. It's too far from our jobs, now that I'm working in Westchester. Maybe we can find something right here in the Bronx, or even in northern Westchester. It doesn't have to be new construction, as long as it's in good structural condition. The important thing is, we won't make the same mistakes we made the first time."

"Amen," she whispered. "This is wonderful, Reuben, but I have to wonder why this couldn't have happened while we still had our house. I know it wouldn't have been practical to keep living there with your new job in Westchester, but at least we could have sold it instead of being foreclosed on."

He shrugged. "Everything happens for a reason, Camille. But we weren't destined to win until we came back. They don't have Mega Millions in Pennsylvania. We could easily have broken up, you know, like Milo and Dawn. You made no secret of the fact that you were unhappy."

Remorseful, she momentarily averted her eyes.

"I'd even like to see if we can find a house that works for us. Maybe a two- or three-family, with a couple of rental units."

"Sure. Just don't rent to any family members if you expect to receive any rent money," she said with a smile.

"You've got that right. But I would like to do something for Mom. She's just a few years away from being seventy, and she still gets up every day to go to work. She's worried about how she'll get by on her pension and her Social Security. If we're her landlords we can give her a low rent, plus she'll be close by and we can check on her every day." His eyes held a question, and she knew he wanted her consent.

"Yes, I agree," she assured him. "Your mother deserves to be able to enjoy the time she has left without worrying about how she'll eat. And the kids will enjoy having her live with us."

"She can take care of the kids while you and I are on our trip."

"What trip?"

"The trip we have coming to us after all we've been through. You name it. We'll go anywhere in the world you want to go."

"That sounds tempting, but we'll have to be careful not to spend all we have on the frivolous. We still have to rent an apartment while we house hunt, move part of our furniture to it . . . Reuben!"

"What?"

"I just realized the silver lining. We haven't sold our extra furniture yet."

"That's because it's in the back of the storage unit. The guys and I packed it so that we can easily get the things we'd need for an apartment. I wasn't planning on selling it until we had the stuff we're keeping out of there."

"You're not getting what I'm saying, Reuben. Because we haven't sold our dining room and our living room furniture yet, that means we won't have to sell it at all."

"Oh! Yes, that's right. Sure, we'll be able to use patio furniture and a grill and a formal dining room set in our new house."

"And Mitchell and Shayla can keep their bedroom furniture, because they'll each have their own room," Camille said happily. "We can even keep the old living room furniture. If the house we buy doesn't have a family room we'll just put it in the basement."

"Yeah, sure. But back to what you were saying before the furniture fairy bit you on the ass. You're right; we'll have to be careful. I know a quarter mil seems like a lot of money, but after taxes it'll be more like $185,000. That number is gonna start going down pretty damn fast once we take care of Uncle Sam and the rest of our bills, replenish our savings and our retirement accounts, take our vacation, and get an apartment. We'd better plan to make a huge down payment on our new house so we can tell the loan officers to shut up about the foreclosure that's on our record."

"Nothing says 'I mean business' like a hundred grand," she remarked.

"That's right. So while you and I can probably stand to replace our car, if your father and brother come to you and ask if you plan to bring them along to the car dealership to pick out new vehicles, the answer is no. The same for my relatives, of course," he added quickly. "Once we get settled life will go on as usual."

"Not as usual, Reuben. The way we always dreamed of."

And this time it wouldn't be merely the edge of a dream, but the real thing.

Chapter 52

The Currys and the Lees
April 2007

"It'll be good to see Norman and Veronica again," Camille said as she poured Splenda-sweetened lemonade over ice. She'd dropped thirty pounds during the most stressful time of her life, but she worked hard to keep it off. The Lees were coming in to the city to visit their family's newest member. The daughter of Norman's brother Eddie had just given birth to a baby boy.

"Yes, it will be." He shook his head. "But if Shayla has a baby before she's married I'll kill her."

"That part isn't our business, Reuben. Veronica said Norman's niece is twenty years old. Even her father can't tell her what to do." Nevertheless, Camille superstitiously knocked on the wood of the kitchen drawer.

An hour later, Camille squealed as she opened the front door. "Norman, Veronica, it's so good to see you!" She drew in her breath. "Lorinda, Simone, look at you two. I know you probably hate it when people tell you how much you've grown, but you really have! And you're both beautiful."

The girls, now both teenagers, grinned self-consciously.

Reuben came downstairs and greeted the Lee family with genuine gusto, patting Norman's newly shaved head. "Yeah, my hairline had receded as far back as my ears, so I decided to shave it all off," Norman said good-naturedly.

"Camille, I've never seen you look better," Veronica marveled.

"Thanks. It's my newfound security combined with my weight loss," she said frankly. "In the days before we lost the house I was so worried I could barely keep anything down. When Shayla and I moved in with Reuben's sister I still couldn't eat. The pounds just melted off. By the time Reuben's Mega Millions numbers hit, I'd learned to eat less fatty foods. Plus I walked a lot. It helped with the stress."

"My wife's beautiful, isn't she?" Reuben asked proudly. "She looks better now than she did when I met her fifteen years ago."

"She looks great," Norman agreed before saying, "Tell me, how'd your families react to your win?"

"Everybody wanted something, and none of them got a cent from us," Reuben stated matter-of-factly.

"We couldn't afford it," Camille said. "By the time we took care of all our obligations, we barely had enough to put down on the house. We had to make a huge down payment because of what happened in Tobyhanna."

Veronica nodded. "I can understand that."

"But my brother and sisters were happy that we invited my mother to live with us," Reuben said. "I think we all had concerns about her continuing to work at her age, but none of us were in a position to help her. But it all worked out well. Since we bought right here in the Bronx, Mom's not too far from her friends."

They'd seen a house they liked in Northern Westchester County, but decided against it. The quiet tree-lined street had great appeal and reminded them of Tobyhanna, but the house, a typical suburban ranch style, had only three bedrooms and two baths, making it suitable for just the four of them and no one else. The house they ended up buying—just eight blocks north of their old apartment—had four bedrooms and two baths on the three upper floors, plus an efficiency apartment in the basement. Mitchell and Ginny had rooms on the second floor, with Shayla's room on the third floor, next to Camille and Reuben.

Camille felt they'd made the right decision. Sure, she worried about Mitchell and Shayla whenever they left the house. She'd warned Shayla not to take her eyes off her bicycle for a minute. This was, after all, Morrisania, not Tobyhanna. But she could get to work with one swipe of her MetroCard, not an expensive Metro-North pass. Ginny surely would have balked if they moved forty miles up the

Hudson, and Camille couldn't blame her. All her friends were in the city. She wouldn't want to leave the familiar to move to a town she'd never heard of at that stage of her life either.

Ginny paid them five hundred dollars a month, and they rented the efficiency for nine hundred dollars. That income helped them meet their mortgage and helped them build a financial cushion that could make the difference between success and failure if times ever got hard again.

"I'm real glad to hear that. And this house is real nice, guys," Veronica said, looking around at the spacious room, which was furnished with the pastel-colored furniture that had decorated their living room in Tobyhanna.

Reuben shrugged. "It's a lot older than the house we had in Tobyhanna, but it's comfortable."

Veronica chuckled. "Well, as you know, I'm partial to older houses."

"This one's over a hundred years old," Camille said.

Norman whistled. "It's obviously been remodeled. It looks real modern to me."

Their conversation was briefly interrupted by the appearance of Mitchell and Shayla, who greeted Norman and Veronica before inviting Lorinda and Simone to see their rooms.

"I'm real glad you two landed on your feet," Norman remarked after the teens noisily ascended the stairs.

Reuben nodded. "Yeah, we were lucky, all right. And that's all it was. Pure luck."

"This time everything will work out," Camille stated confidently.

"How's it going with your tenant?" Veronica asked.

"Oh, it's working out beautifully. No loud music, no rowdy guests, just nice, quiet people."

"Is it a couple?"

"Well, it's two people, but they're not a couple." Camille stood up. "Come on, I want to give you a tour of the house. We'll start with the apartment downstairs."

Veronica's eyebrows dipped. "The rental apartment? You can't just bring company down there to look at your tenant's apartment, can you? Isn't that an invasion of privacy?"

"Oh, our tenant is very understanding," Camille said as she headed for the kitchen, gesturing with her head for them to follow.

With an uncertain shrug, Veronica followed Camille through the kitchen and down the basement stairs. Norman and Reuben brought up the rear.

One corner of the basement was walled off as a laundry room. A few pieces of extra furniture, accent tables, and other odds and ends that Camille couldn't bring herself to part with, despite not having room for them, were stacked in another corner. The bulk of the basement was taken up by a walled-off area with a door in one corner. Camille knocked on the door. "Open up, it's your landlord," she barked. She turned to the Lees in time to see them exchange incredulous looks.

The door opened, and the tenant stepped out.

Veronica gasped.

Norman chuckled. "Well, I'll be."

Dawn held out a hand toward the inside of the apartment. "Hi, guys. Welcome to my cozy abode."

"Y'all rented to Dawn!" Veronica exclaimed.

"Why not? They had to rent to somebody," Dawn said good-naturedly. "Come on in and sit down. I've got some Miller Genuine Draft on ice."

Chapter 53

The Youngs
May 2007

Dawn entered the bank, eager to deposit the check Milo had sent her for Zach's care.

It still hurt to think that her marriage had come to an end, like a cross-country highway. She'd held on to the hope that she and Milo would reconcile once she, too, admitted defeat and left Tobyhanna. Instead he'd merely asked where she and Zach planned to stay. He hadn't been too thrilled to learn that her plan called for Zach to stay with him. "Why don't you go to your folks?" he'd asked.

"For the same reason you didn't go to *yours*," had been her salty reply.

Milo could do nothing but agree to take Zach in. As Dawn expected, Zach had been brokenhearted to learn that he had to give up Stormy, but they'd found a good home for him with Lorinda and Simone Lee. Norman and Veronica's daughters had always enjoyed playing with the dog.

Zach seemed happy living with his father in the studio Milo claimed had a higher rent than their old two-bedroom, but Dawn had a feeling it had been a happy day for Milo when she took Zach to live with her.

She'd been thrilled when Mr. Crawford consented to rent the former renting office to her, with the caveat that if the housing board found out that the commercial space was being used for residential purposes, she would have to vacate. When she told Milo about the arrangements she'd made, she'd asked if she and Zach would be able to come by his place on the weekends to take showers. Milo consented, but whenever they went over to Fort Greene, she got the uneasy feeling that he didn't want them to linger.

Finally, one day while Zach was showering she came out and asked him. "So, Milo, what do you see happening with us?"

"I've asked myself that same question, Dawn. I do care about you, and because of that I want to be honest. I don't see us getting back together. These past couple of years have worn me out. We had some good times after we bought that house, but they were mostly bad. Even seeing you now, I'm reminded of all the bad stuff."

She absorbed this and slowly nodded, hoping he couldn't see her pain. "Just tell me one thing, Milo. Did you meet her before or after you moved out?"

He opened his mouth, then closed it. "How did you know?"

She guessed he'd been about to deny the existence of another woman in his life, but thought better of it.

"I met her before. But I swear to you, Dawn, all I did was take her to lunch. I didn't begin dating her until after I moved in with Donald and Carmen."

She stared at him wordlessly. *Yeah, and I've got a bridge for sale.* "And she gave you something you weren't getting from me?" She fought back tears.

He hung his head, like he was talking to the floor. "I met her at work. I wasn't looking for someone else, Dawn. It's just that I felt trapped and miserable. She represented a different side of life. She's unencumbered, fun . . ."

"And I'm sure she's got a good credit rating that you can't wait to share."

"That's not it, Dawn," he said sharply. "Nobody carries me. Nobody ever has. I'm my own man."

"Milo, you know that this is going to follow us around for years. I wonder if I'll ever be able to get a decent apartment. I know you say you're giving me as much as you can to help with Zach—"

"I say that because it's true. Don't start insinuating there's something else going on, Dawn. We both agreed that we have to pay off our credit card bills before we can really move on."

She had to agree, but she still wondered how much money he'd spent pursuing his girlfriend.

"I don't even have a car anymore," he pointed out. "I left it with you, remember?"

"All right, all right. But you have to admit, it might get a little awkward, me coming to your place to shower after you move in with your new girlfriend."

Milo's reply died in his throat when Zach emerged from the bathroom. "We'll talk later," he said crisply.

They had, when they were alone, but there'd been surprisingly little to say. Their marriage was, at least in Milo's opinion, irreparably broken, and knowing he felt that way made it a little easier for her. She had no wish to hold on to someone who didn't want her.

Dawn often felt that she had precious little to look forward to, but at least she and Zach had a decent place to live, thanks to Camille and Reuben.

She'd been so happy for them when they won such a substantial Mega Millions jackpot. She couldn't help thinking that it might have been her and Milo. She knew the Curry marriage was on shaky ground, even more so than hers and Milo's was, but nevertheless they weathered the devastating loss of their house, plus months of living apart. If anything, their ordeal had strengthened their bond. Dawn felt Reuben's selecting five of six winning lottery numbers was a reward from above for sticking out the hard times.

She felt a wave of depression coming at her like a sudden downpour. Maybe when she finished making her deposit she'd stop at McDonald's and get an ice-cream cone.

That made her smile. If anyone had told her five years ago that she'd buy a $1.25 ice-cream cone to cheer herself up instead of buying a new outfit or getting a facial, she'd have laughed in their face. But she couldn't afford to indulge herself any more than that, not with thousands of dollars of credit card debt. Milo was right—they had to pay those off before they could do anything else . . . like file for divorce.

She wished she could get something for her date Saturday night. The senior auditor on assignment at her employer had little to do with payroll, which was traditionally worked on by guys and gals just out of college. He had noticed her and struck up a casual conversation one day while they were both waiting for an elevator. After that they exchanged a few words here and there, but when they found themselves alone a second time he told her they would soon be wrapping up their assignment and asked if she would have dinner with him.

At least she had a babysitter, she thought happily as she filled out the deposit slip. Camille told her that she could always send Zach upstairs so he wouldn't have to see her date pick her up. Camille seemed more excited about her date than she was. Dawn didn't anticipate anything coming out of this date, but Erwin was a nice enough guy, if maybe a little on the dull side. And she had few opportunities to date eligible—Erwin was divorced—and successful men in their forties. Milo had moved on. It was time for her to do the same. How nice to know that a full-figured sister could still catch the eye of the opposite sex.

Maybe her future wasn't so bleak after all.

"Hi, Teresa," she said to the teller, a black woman in her late twenties who often handled her financial transactions. "What's new?"

"I'm glad you asked. I'm so excited, Ms. Young. My husband and I are buying a house in Tobyhanna, Pennsylvania."

Dawn carefully concealed her surprise. "Really. Isn't that a little far?"

"About a hundred miles from Manhattan. My husband will commute to work. They say that the train service will probably begin next year. Our plan is for me to get a job at a bank over there so I won't have to commute because it's so expensive. Hopefully, I won't be working for long. We're hoping to start a family soon."

"Well, congratulations to both of you, Teresa. I'm sure you'll be very happy."

"Thanks, Ms. Young. I can't wait. We just found out this morning that our loan's been approved."

"Is it a new house?"

"Not brand-new, but it's only five years old. It was built in 2002. Three bedrooms, two bathrooms, full basement, deck, and a great backyard. And it's on a lake. Isn't it wonderful? We'll be able to watch the sun come up over the lake in the mornings, at least the mornings that we don't have to go to work. We got a good deal on the house; it was a foreclosure."

Dawn's ears started to ring, like an alarm only she could hear. Through the ringing sound she could dimly hear Eric Nylund's voice giving her and Milo his sales pitch. "And it was in good condition?"

"Perfect. The people who got foreclosed on didn't do much in the way of decorating, but they planted beautiful grass in the backyard. I can't wait to get in there and plant a garden." Teresa's voice grew quiet, almost like she was filling Dawn in on a secret. "But the former owners painted the bedrooms weird colors, like blue with a green ceiling and cranberry with an orange ceiling."

Dawn's eyebrows shot up. *My God; this teller bought my old house.* "Um . . . That sounds unique."

Teresa made a face. "I think it looks awful. We'll paint over it eventually, probably make it a nice neutral color like tan. But there's really no rush. We'll be there the rest of our lives."

"I'm happy for you." Dawn saw a little of herself five years ago in Teresa's excited face. She wisely kept quiet about what she knew about the house, certain that the teller wouldn't appreciate the irony. Maybe one day she would write her and tell her the truth.

After all, she already knew the address of Teresa's new house.

"Thanks, Ms. Young." The teller had held Dawn's receipt in her hand as she shared her news. "Here you go. Have a great weekend."

"You do the same, dear." Dawn smiled as she tucked the receipt into her wallet.

She continued to smile as she walked down the street into McDonald's. Life in Tobyhanna seemed like a million years ago. So much had changed in a few short years. She and Milo had gone to a Luther Vandross concert before driving out to Arlington Acres for the first time. Luther was gone now. In the midst of their troubles they had flown to New Orleans to celebrate their fifteenth anniversary. Hurricane Katrina had since devastated New Orleans and the Mississippi Gulf Coast.

Other things had remained the same. Terrorism was still a concern. Hardly a week went by without news of people being detained after being found to have false passports, or trying to smuggle some suspicious item aboard a plane. The world was changing around her. She couldn't stay the same.

And she wouldn't.

She emerged from the restaurant, ice-cream cone in hand. Soon she blended into the anonymous cityscape of the thousands of people who came to midtown Manhattan every day to make a living, and perhaps even to make their dreams come true.

IF THESE WALLS COULD TALK

BETTYE GRIFFIN

ABOUT THIS GUIDE

The questions and discussion topics that
follow are intended to enhance
your group's reading of this book.

ENJOY!

DISCUSSION QUESTIONS

1. Milo and Dawn lived the high life in Brooklyn, extravagant with cars, clothing, and evenings out because they felt they would never be able to afford a home. Do you think people in areas of high-priced real estate should try to save for a home nonetheless, or concentrate strictly on enjoying their lives?

2. Why do you think Zach acted the way he did upon hearing of the murder of their neighbor and friend, Hazel?

3. Veronica told Norman he was making too much of the issue when he expressed repeated concerns about the racial mix of their potential new neighborhood. Do you agree? Why or why not?

4. Camille and Reuben sent their children to the library after school, where they stayed until their parents returned from work. How do you feel about parents utilizing libraries as free day care centers? Would you feel the same if you were a librarian?

5. Would you be willing to engage in a daily commute of two hours each way if it was the only way you could own a home?

6. How do you feel about Camille's attitude toward Reuben after he lost his job?

7. Do you feel that Dawn should have tried to hold on to her house after Milo left, or cut her losses?

8. What do you think Milo would have done if he knew that Dawn was leaving Zach alone on weeknights while she slept in New York?

9. Norman vetoed Veronica's plan to care for Zach in Dawn's absence. What is your opinion on his reasoning? Do you agree with his solution?

10. Do you think that the Currys would have made a go of it in Pennsylvania had Reuben not lost his job?

11. What is your overall opinion of this book?

DISCARDED
Appomattox Regional Library System
Hopewell, Virginia 23860
07/07

CAR